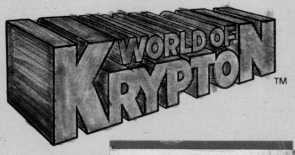

WORLD OF KRYPTON™

PHILADELPHIA
EAGLES

Written by
PAUL KUPPERBERG

Art by
HOWARD CHAYKIN
MURPHY ANDERSON
FRANK CHIARAMONTE

TOR

A TOM DOHERTY ASSOCIATES BOOK

A Tom Doherty Associates original.

Edited by E. Nelson Bridwell.

*Interior design and production by Bob Rozakis, Shelley Eiber and
Alex Saviuk.*

ISBN: 523-49017-8

Printed in the United States of America

First Printing: June, 1982

10 9 8 7 6 5 4 3 2

INTRODUCTION

What makes a myth?

For most of the history of the human race, literature was not available to the masses. Quite simply, when systems of writing were first devised and oral traditons began to be written down, they had to be copied out laboriously by hand. Only a privileged few could afford books—and, in any case, the vast majority of people could not read.

Then came the printing press, and as it was improved, and more and more copies of a work could be produced, literacy spread. Characters from these writings became our new myths: Gulliver, Robinson Crusoe, Don Quixote, Scrooge, Sherlock Holmes.

As mass media proliferated, each gave us its own myths: movies produced Dr. Kildare and Andy Hardy; radio spawned the Lone Ranger; comic strips, Dick Tracy; and comic books—Superman!

Soon we grew to know Clark Kent, Lois Lane, Perry White, and Jimmy Olsen as well as we knew our friends. Metropolis was as real to the readers as New York or Chicago. And Krypton may have been more real than Venus, Mars, and Jupiter.

Science fiction provided countless Venusians, Martians and Jovians. They came in all sizes and shapes. But we knew what the Kryptonians looked like. After all, there was one living on Earth.

The planet had been given short shrift in the brief origin story that opened Superman's career in *ACTION COMICS* #1, back in 1938:

"As a distant planet was destroyed by old age, a scientist placed his infant son within a hastily-devised space-ship, launching it toward Earth."

When, a year later, Superman's creator, Jerry Siegel, wrote an expanded origin for *SUPERMAN* #1, the planet finally acquired a name: Krypton. It was in the newspaper strip that Jerry first introduced us to the hitherto unnamed scientist and his wife. They were called Jor-L (from Jerry's own name) and Lora at first, but these names were later altered to Jor-El and Lara.

Over the years we learned more and more about them and their world. Joe Shuster, the Man of Steel's first artist, gave us our first look at Krypton and its most illustrious citizens. Wayne Boring, for many years the artist of the newspaper strip, added his distinctive touch; and for some three decades, Curt Swan has depicted Superman and Krypton.

Many writers, myself among them, have written about Krypton, and gradually built a whole mythos around it. But while we all added to it, we did not create the myth—or the planet. Krypton remains the brain-child of Siegel and Shuster. Their genius gave it to us—and the world.

A few years ago, I was picked to edit what was to become a new experiment in comic books: a three-issue mini-series. Howard Chaykin, a top cartoonist and comic artist, was thrilled to get a chance at laying out the story of Jor-El and Lara. The finished art for the first two issues was done by Murphy Anderson, while Frank Chiaramonte handled the job for the final issue. Both had much previous experience inking over Curt Swan's Superman pencils. A young writer named Paul Kupperberg provided the script.

The result was a best-selling series of which we were all very proud. And now it has been edited into paperback form for a new audience.

So read and enjoy the story of two people who fell in love, married, and, before dying violently with their planet, sent their son to Earth, to become our greatest hero.

E. NELSON BRIDWELL

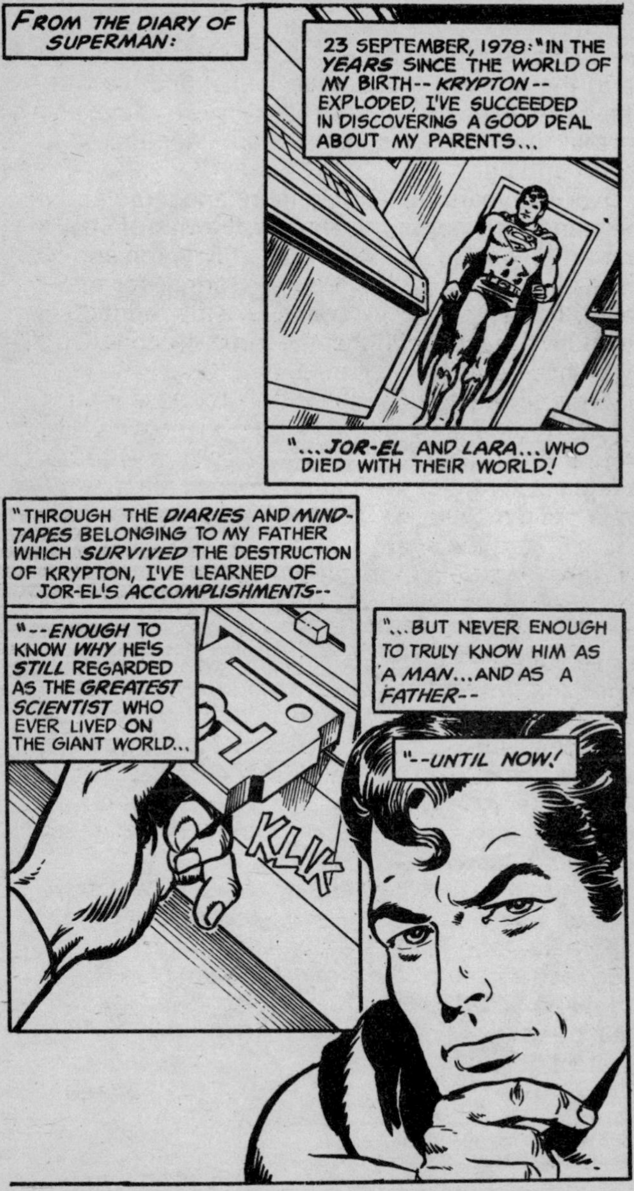
FROM THE DIARY OF SUPERMAN:
23 SEPTEMBER, 1978: "IN THE YEARS SINCE THE WORLD OF MY BIRTH-- KRYPTON-- EXPLODED, I'VE SUCCEEDED IN DISCOVERING A GOOD DEAL ABOUT MY PARENTS...
"...JOR-EL AND LARA... WHO DIED WITH THEIR WORLD!
"THROUGH THE DIARIES AND MIND-TAPES BELONGING TO MY FATHER WHICH SURVIVED THE DESTRUCTION OF KRYPTON, I'VE LEARNED OF JOR-EL'S ACCOMPLISHMENTS--
"--ENOUGH TO KNOW WHY HE'S STILL REGARDED AS THE GREATEST SCIENTIST WHO EVER LIVED ON THE GIANT WORLD...
KLIK
"...BUT NEVER ENOUGH TO TRULY KNOW HIM AS A MAN...AND AS A FATHER--
"--UNTIL NOW!

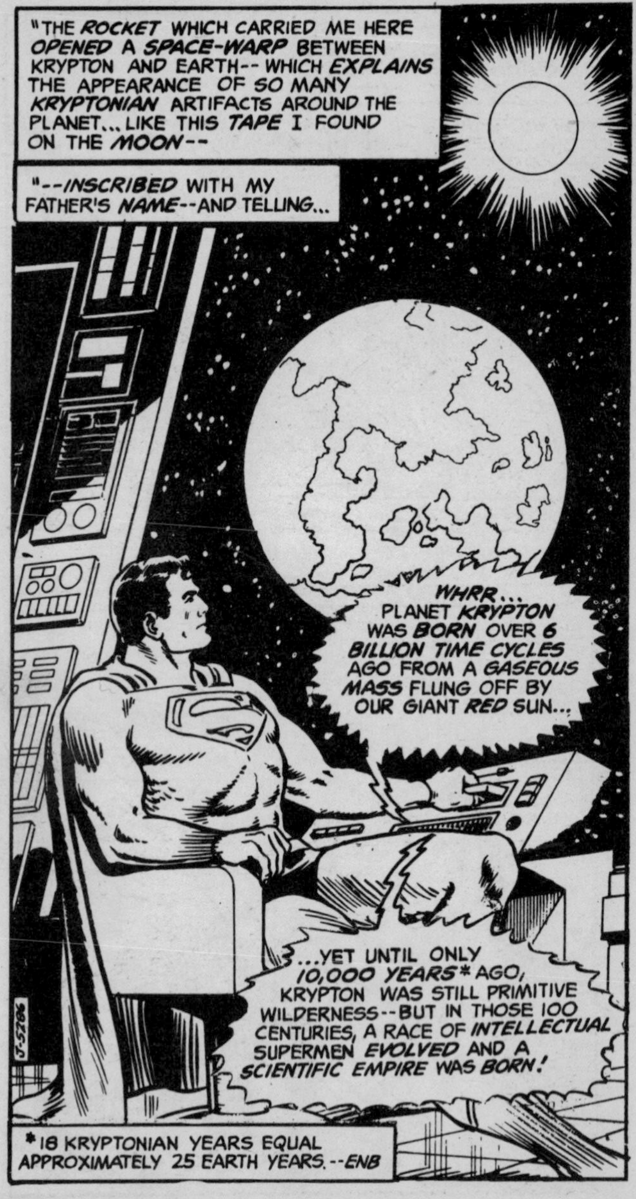
"THE ROCKET WHICH CARRIED ME HERE OPENED A SPACE-WARP BETWEEN KRYPTON AND EARTH-- WHICH EXPLAINS THE APPEARANCE OF SO MANY KRYPTONIAN ARTIFACTS AROUND THE PLANET... LIKE THIS TAPE I FOUND ON THE MOON--
"--INSCRIBED WITH MY FATHER'S NAME--AND TELLING...
WHRR... PLANET KRYPTON WAS BORN OVER 6 BILLION TIME CYCLES AGO FROM A GASEOUS MASS FLUNG OFF BY OUR GIANT RED SUN...
...YET UNTIL ONLY 10,000 YEARS* AGO, KRYPTON WAS STILL PRIMITIVE WILDERNESS--BUT IN THOSE 100 CENTURIES, A RACE OF INTELLECTUAL SUPERMEN EVOLVED AND A SCIENTIFIC EMPIRE WAS BORN!
*18 KRYPTONIAN YEARS EQUAL APPROXIMATELY 25 EARTH YEARS.--ENB
J-5286

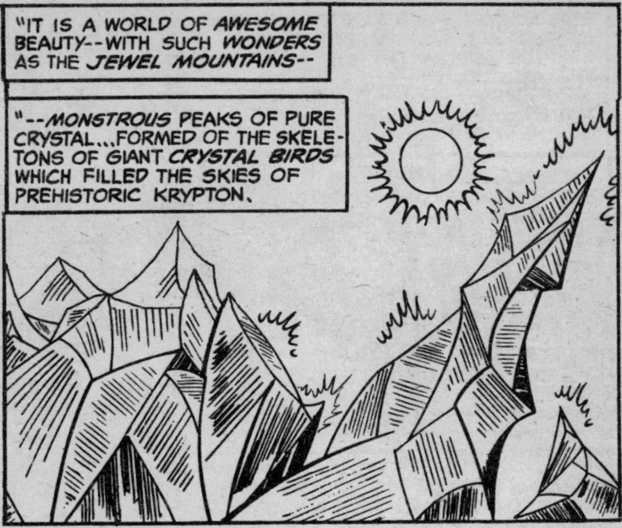
"IT IS A WORLD OF *AWESOME* BEAUTY--WITH SUCH *WONDERS* AS THE *JEWEL MOUNTAINS*--
"--*MONSTROUS* PEAKS OF PURE CRYSTAL...FORMED OF THE SKELETONS OF GIANT *CRYSTAL BIRDS* WHICH FILLED THE SKIES OF PREHISTORIC KRYPTON.

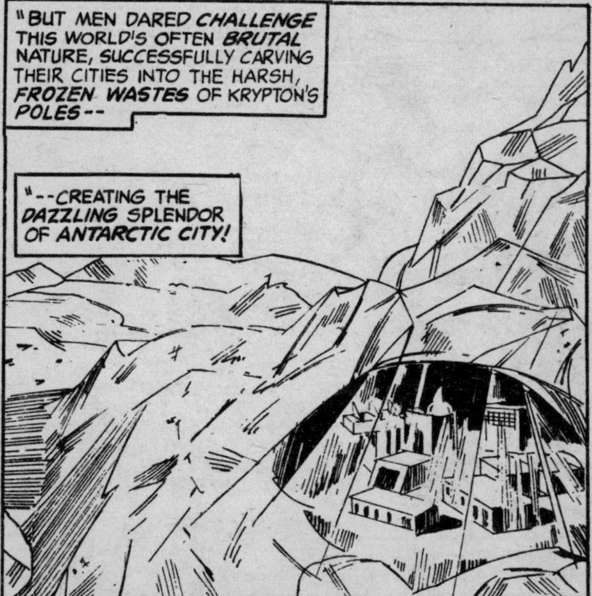
"BUT MEN DARED *CHALLENGE* THIS WORLD'S OFTEN *BRUTAL* NATURE, SUCCESSFULLY CARVING THEIR CITIES INTO THE HARSH, *FROZEN WASTES* OF KRYPTON'S *POLES*--
"--CREATING THE *DAZZLING* SPLENDOR OF *ANTARCTIC CITY!*

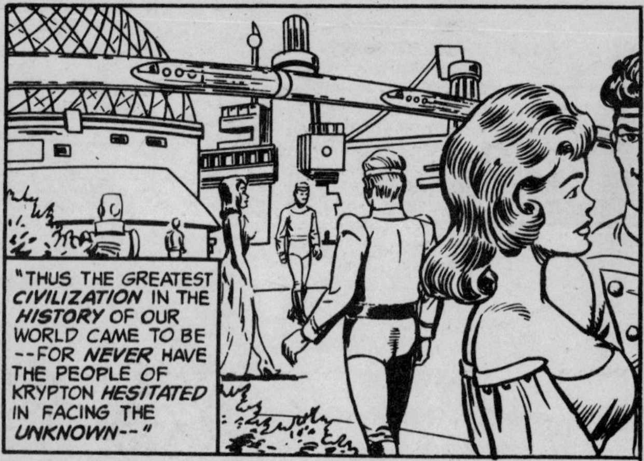
"THUS THE GREATEST CIVILIZATION IN THE HISTORY OF OUR WORLD CAME TO BE --FOR NEVER HAVE THE PEOPLE OF KRYPTON HESITATED IN FACING THE UNKNOWN--"

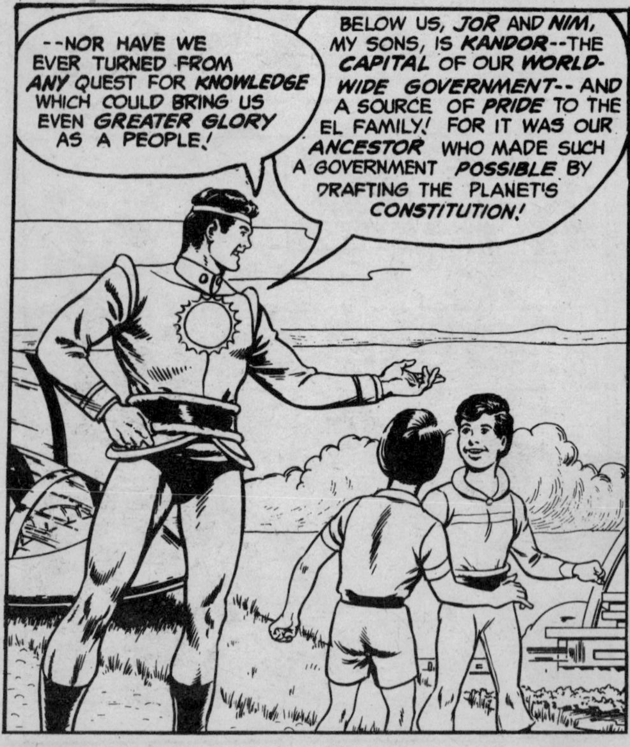
--NOR HAVE WE EVER TURNED FROM ANY QUEST FOR KNOWLEDGE WHICH COULD BRING US EVEN GREATER GLORY AS A PEOPLE!
BELOW US, JOR AND NIM, MY SONS, IS KANDOR--THE CAPITAL OF OUR WORLD-WIDE GOVERNMENT-- AND A SOURCE OF PRIDE TO THE EL FAMILY! FOR IT WAS OUR ANCESTOR WHO MADE SUCH A GOVERNMENT POSSIBLE BY DRAFTING THE PLANET'S CONSTITUTION!

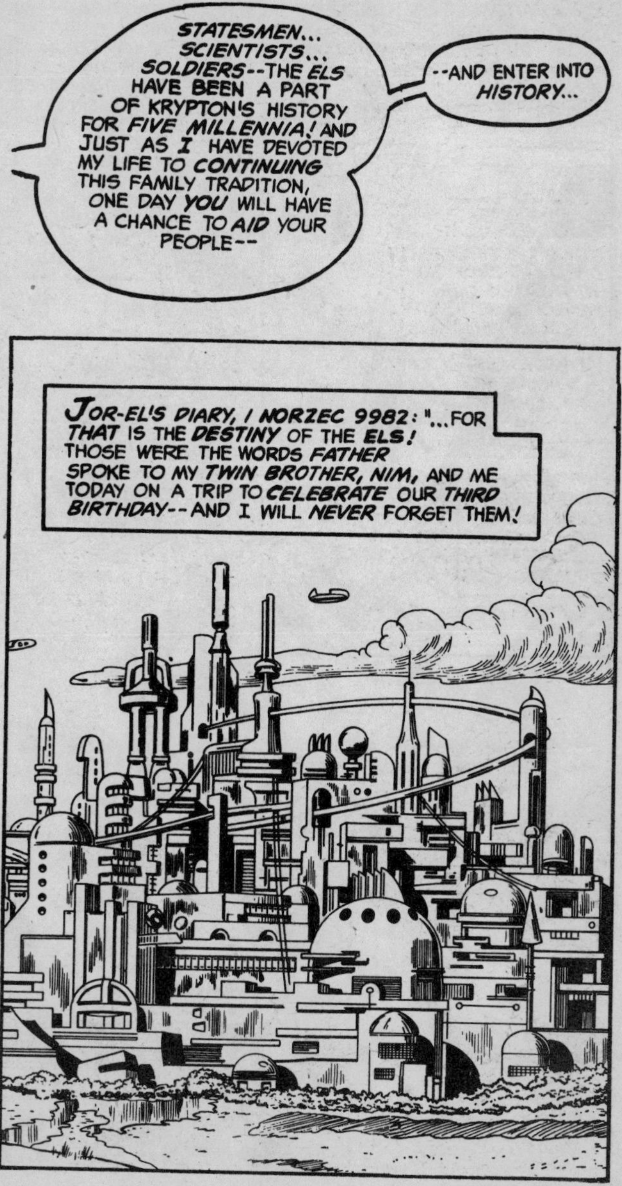
STATESMEN... SCIENTISTS... SOLDIERS--THE ELS HAVE BEEN A PART OF KRYPTON'S HISTORY FOR FIVE MILLENNIA! AND JUST AS I HAVE DEVOTED MY LIFE TO CONTINUING THIS FAMILY TRADITION, ONE DAY YOU WILL HAVE A CHANCE TO AID YOUR PEOPLE--
--AND ENTER INTO HISTORY...
JOR-EL'S DIARY, 1 NORZEC 9982: "...FOR THAT IS THE DESTINY OF THE ELS! THOSE WERE THE WORDS FATHER SPOKE TO MY TWIN BROTHER, NIM, AND ME TODAY ON A TRIP TO CELEBRATE OUR THIRD BIRTHDAY--AND I WILL NEVER FORGET THEM!

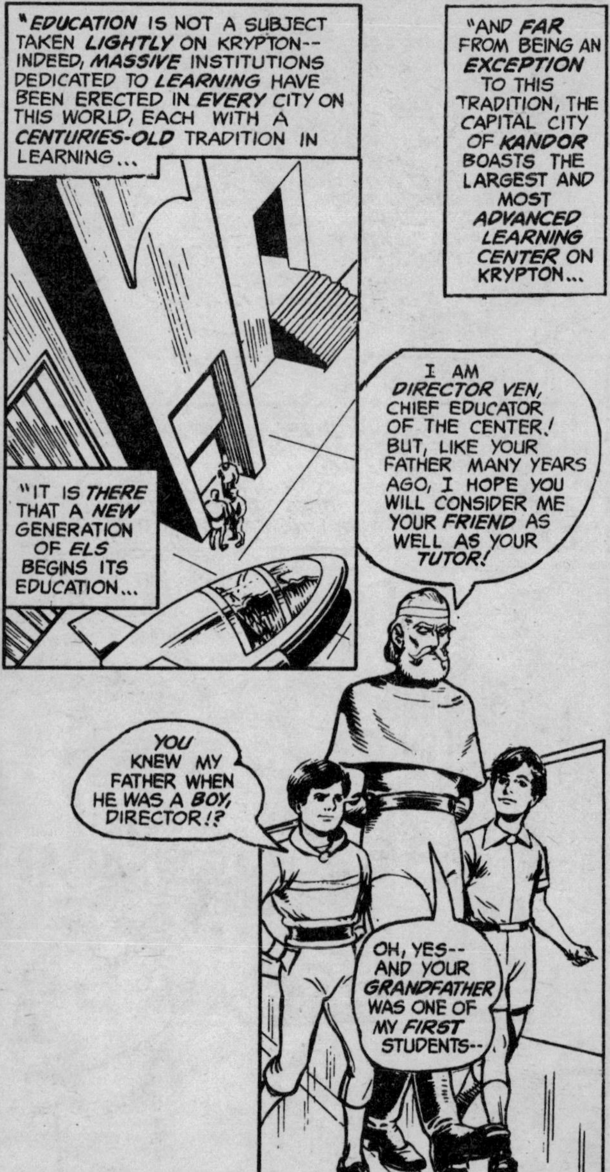
"EDUCATION IS NOT A SUBJECT TAKEN LIGHTLY ON KRYPTON-- INDEED, MASSIVE INSTITUTIONS DEDICATED TO LEARNING HAVE BEEN ERECTED IN EVERY CITY ON THIS WORLD, EACH WITH A CENTURIES-OLD TRADITION IN LEARNING...
"AND FAR FROM BEING AN EXCEPTION TO THIS TRADITION, THE CAPITAL CITY OF KANDOR BOASTS THE LARGEST AND MOST ADVANCED LEARNING CENTER ON KRYPTON...
"IT IS THERE THAT A NEW GENERATION OF ELS BEGINS ITS EDUCATION...
I AM DIRECTOR VEN, CHIEF EDUCATOR OF THE CENTER! BUT, LIKE YOUR FATHER MANY YEARS AGO, I HOPE YOU WILL CONSIDER ME YOUR FRIEND AS WELL AS YOUR TUTOR!
YOU KNEW MY FATHER WHEN HE WAS A BOY, DIRECTOR!?
OH, YES-- AND YOUR GRANDFATHER WAS ONE OF MY FIRST STUDENTS--

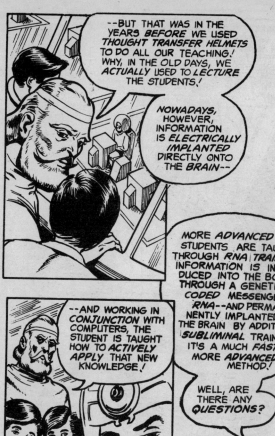

--BUT THAT WAS IN THE YEARS *BEFORE* WE USED *THOUGHT TRANSFER HELMETS* TO DO ALL OUR TEACHING! WHY, IN THE OLD DAYS, WE *ACTUALLY* USED TO *LECTURE* THE STUDENTS!

NOWADAYS, HOWEVER, INFORMATION IS *ELECTRICALLY IMPLANTED* DIRECTLY ONTO THE *BRAIN*--

MORE *ADVANCED* STUDENTS ARE TAUGHT THROUGH *RNA TRAINING!* INFORMATION IS INTRODUCED INTO THE BODY THROUGH A GENETICALLY *CODED* MESSENGER--*RNA*--AND PERMANENTLY IMPLANTED IN THE BRAIN BY ADDITIONAL *SUBLIMINAL* TRAINING! IT'S A MUCH *FASTER,* MORE *ADVANCED* METHOD!

--AND WORKING IN *CONJUNCTION* WITH COMPUTERS, THE STUDENT IS TAUGHT HOW TO *ACTIVELY APPLY* THAT NEW KNOWLEDGE!

WELL, ARE THERE ANY *QUESTIONS?*

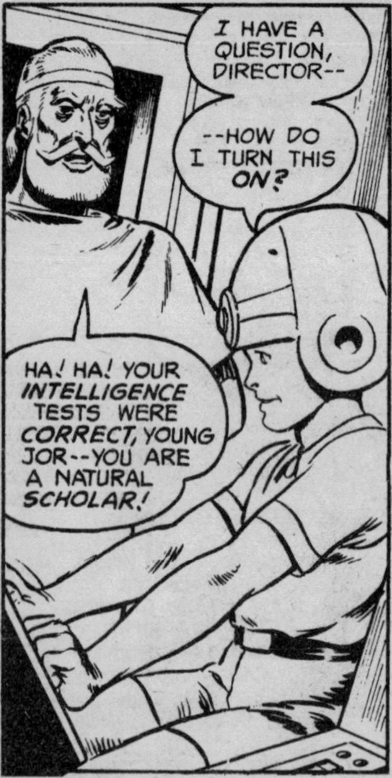
I HAVE A QUESTION, DIRECTOR--
--HOW DO I TURN THIS *ON?*
HA! HA! YOUR *INTELLIGENCE* TESTS WERE *CORRECT,* YOUNG JOR--YOU ARE A NATURAL *SCHOLAR!*
I JUST WANT TO *LEARN,* DIRECTOR--

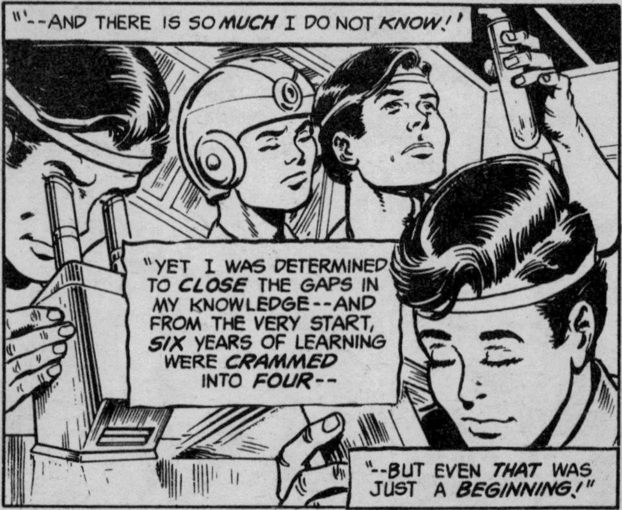
"'--AND THERE IS SO *MUCH* I DO NOT *KNOW!*'
"YET I WAS DETERMINED TO *CLOSE* THE GAPS IN MY KNOWLEDGE--AND FROM THE VERY START, *SIX* YEARS OF LEARNING WERE *CRAMMED* INTO *FOUR*--
"--BUT EVEN *THAT* WAS JUST A *BEGINNING!*"

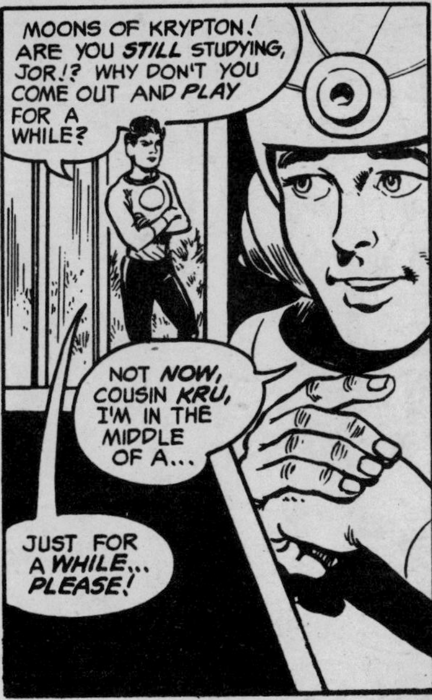
MOONS OF KRYPTON! ARE YOU STILL STUDYING, JOR!? WHY DON'T YOU COME OUT AND PLAY FOR A WHILE?
NOT NOW, COUSIN KRU, I'M IN THE MIDDLE OF A...
JUST FOR A WHILE... PLEASE!

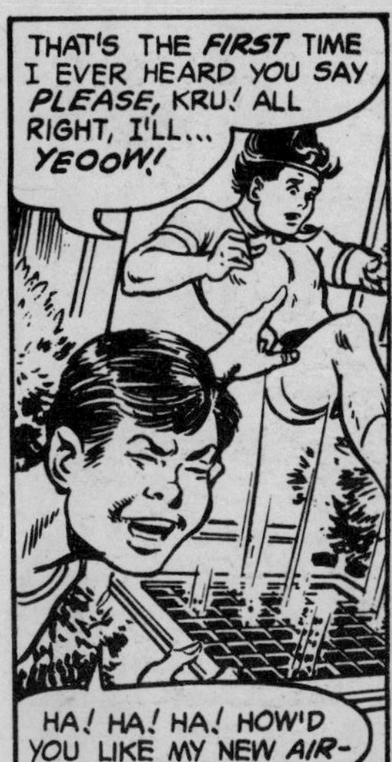
THAT'S THE FIRST TIME I EVER HEARD YOU SAY PLEASE, KRU! ALL RIGHT, I'LL... YEOOW!
HA! HA! HA! HOW'D YOU LIKE MY NEW AIR-MAT, COUSIN? HA!

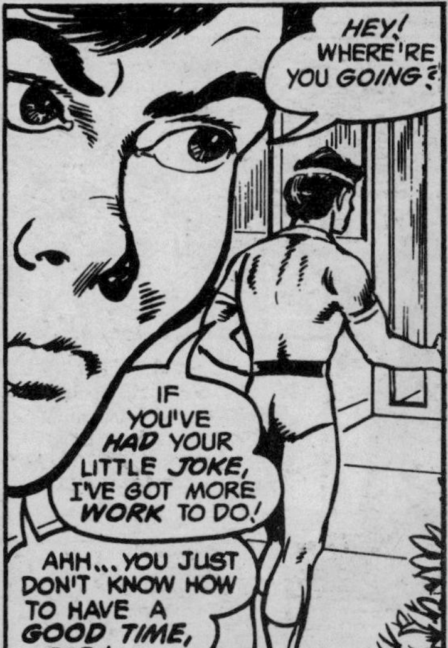
IF YOU'VE HAD YOUR LITTLE JOKE, I'VE GOT MORE WORK TO DO!
HEY! WHERE'RE YOU GOING?
AHH... YOU JUST DON'T KNOW HOW TO HAVE A GOOD TIME, JOR!

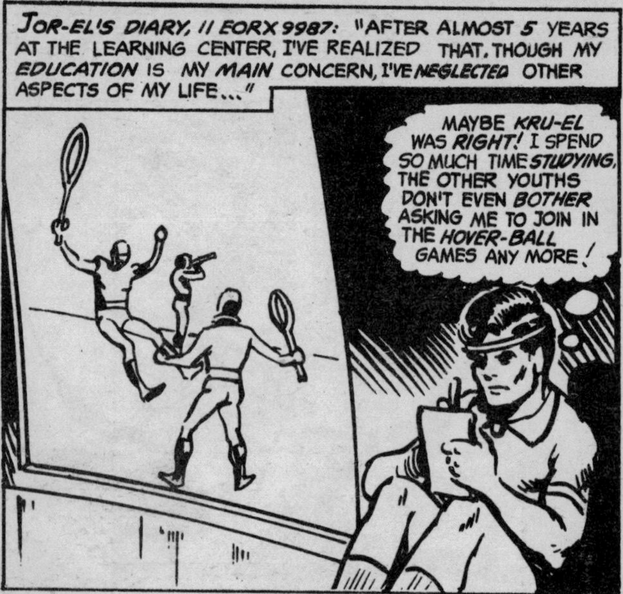
JOR-EL'S DIARY, 11 EORX 9987: "AFTER ALMOST 5 YEARS AT THE LEARNING CENTER, I'VE REALIZED THAT, THOUGH MY EDUCATION IS MY MAIN CONCERN, I'VE NEGLECTED OTHER ASPECTS OF MY LIFE..."
MAYBE KRU-EL WAS RIGHT! I SPEND SO MUCH TIME STUDYING, THE OTHER YOUTHS DON'T EVEN BOTHER ASKING ME TO JOIN IN THE HOVER-BALL GAMES ANY MORE!

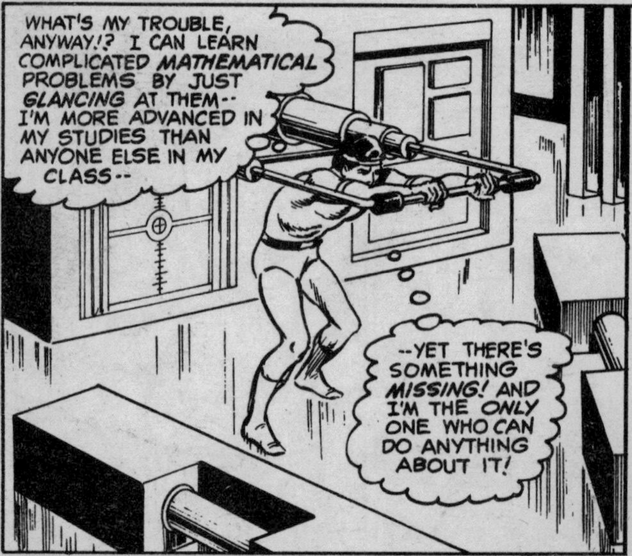
WHAT'S MY TROUBLE, ANYWAY!? I CAN LEARN COMPLICATED MATHEMATICAL PROBLEMS BY JUST GLANCING AT THEM-- I'M MORE ADVANCED IN MY STUDIES THAN ANYONE ELSE IN MY CLASS--
--YET THERE'S SOMETHING MISSING! AND I'M THE ONLY ONE WHO CAN DO ANYTHING ABOUT IT!

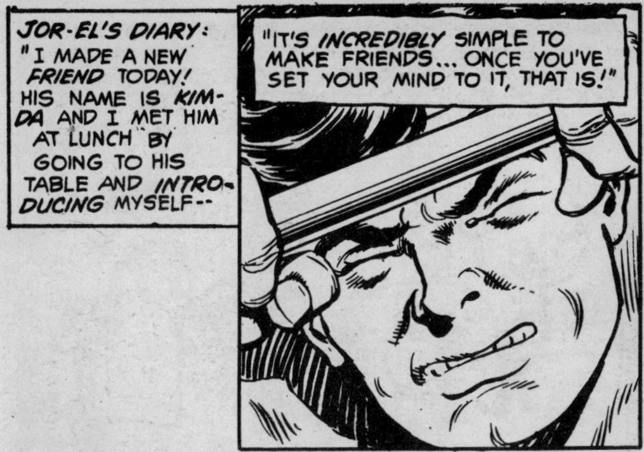
JOR-EL'S DIARY:
"I MADE A NEW FRIEND TODAY! HIS NAME IS KIM-DA AND I MET HIM AT LUNCH BY GOING TO HIS TABLE AND INTRODUCING MYSELF--
"IT'S INCREDIBLY SIMPLE TO MAKE FRIENDS... ONCE YOU'VE SET YOUR MIND TO IT, THAT IS!"

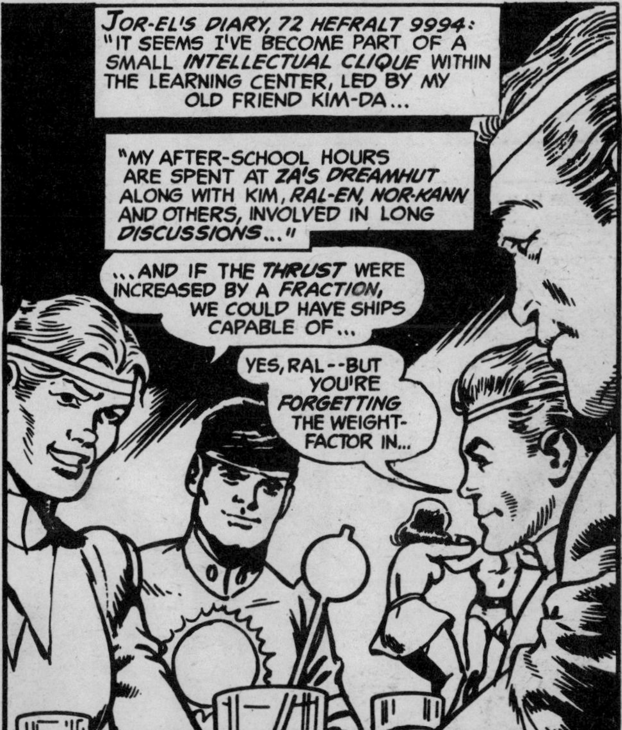
JOR-EL'S DIARY, 72 HEFRALT 9994:
"IT SEEMS I'VE BECOME PART OF A SMALL INTELLECTUAL CLIQUE WITHIN THE LEARNING CENTER, LED BY MY OLD FRIEND KIM-DA...
"MY AFTER-SCHOOL HOURS ARE SPENT AT ZA'S DREAMHUT ALONG WITH KIM, RAL-EN, NOR-KANN AND OTHERS, INVOLVED IN LONG DISCUSSIONS..."
...AND IF THE THRUST WERE INCREASED BY A FRACTION, WE COULD HAVE SHIPS CAPABLE OF...
YES, RAL--BUT YOU'RE FORGETTING THE WEIGHT-FACTOR IN...

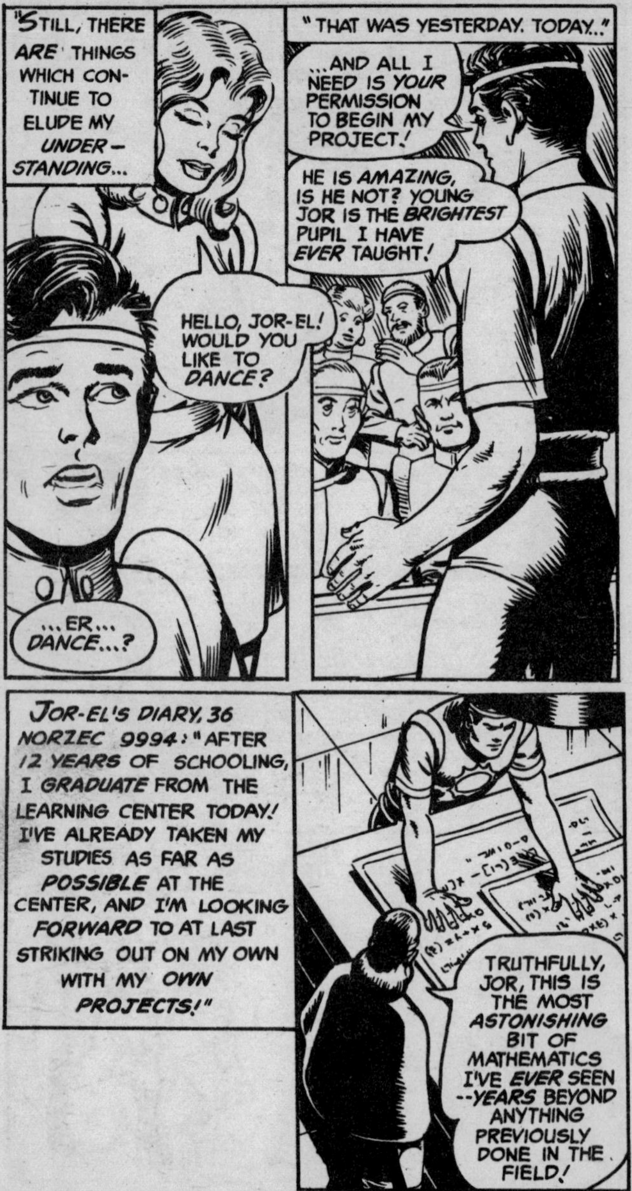
"STILL, THERE ARE THINGS WHICH CONTINUE TO ELUDE MY UNDERSTANDING...
HELLO, JOR-EL! WOULD YOU LIKE TO DANCE?
...ER... DANCE...?
"THAT WAS YESTERDAY. TODAY..."
...AND ALL I NEED IS YOUR PERMISSION TO BEGIN MY PROJECT!
HE IS AMAZING, IS HE NOT? YOUNG JOR IS THE BRIGHTEST PUPIL I HAVE EVER TAUGHT!
JOR-EL'S DIARY, 36 NORZEC 9994: "AFTER 12 YEARS OF SCHOOLING, I GRADUATE FROM THE LEARNING CENTER TODAY! I'VE ALREADY TAKEN MY STUDIES AS FAR AS POSSIBLE AT THE CENTER, AND I'M LOOKING FORWARD TO AT LAST STRIKING OUT ON MY OWN WITH MY OWN PROJECTS!"
TRUTHFULLY, JOR, THIS IS THE MOST ASTONISHING BIT OF MATHEMATICS I'VE EVER SEEN --YEARS BEYOND ANYTHING PREVIOUSLY DONE IN THE FIELD!

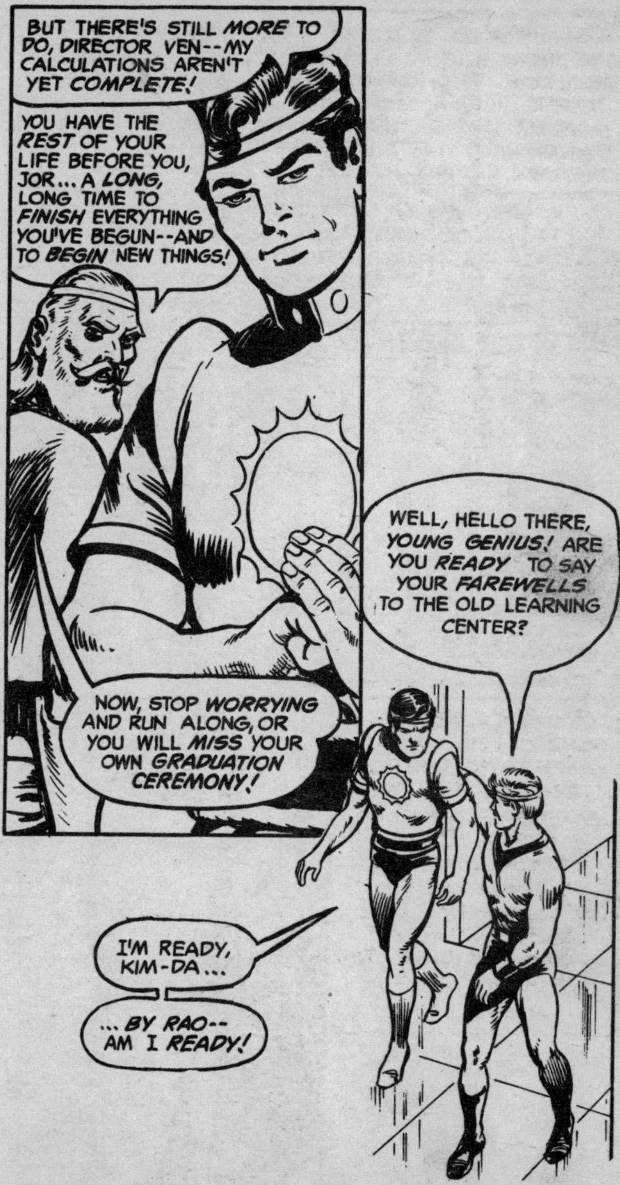
BUT THERE'S STILL MORE TO DO, DIRECTOR VEN--MY CALCULATIONS AREN'T YET COMPLETE!
YOU HAVE THE REST OF YOUR LIFE BEFORE YOU, JOR... A LONG, LONG TIME TO FINISH EVERYTHING YOU'VE BEGUN--AND TO BEGIN NEW THINGS!
NOW, STOP WORRYING AND RUN ALONG, OR YOU WILL MISS YOUR OWN GRADUATION CEREMONY!
WELL, HELLO THERE, YOUNG GENIUS! ARE YOU READY TO SAY YOUR FAREWELLS TO THE OLD LEARNING CENTER?
I'M READY, KIM-DA...
...BY RAO--AM I READY!

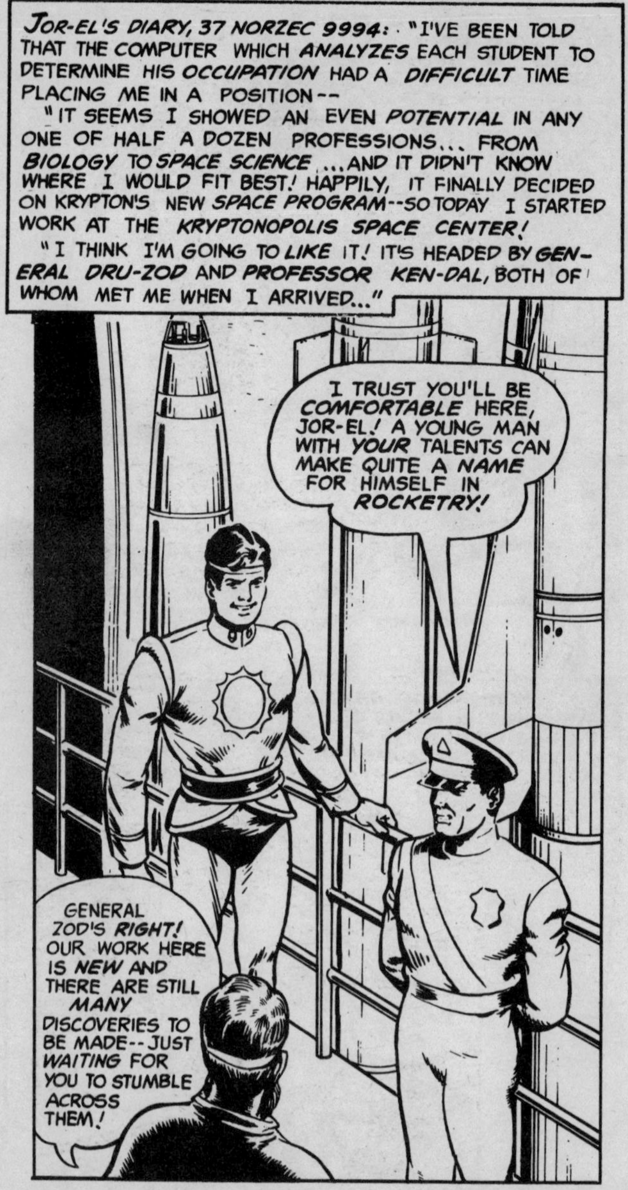
JOR-EL'S DIARY, 37 NORZEC 9994: "I'VE BEEN TOLD THAT THE COMPUTER WHICH ANALYZES EACH STUDENT TO DETERMINE HIS OCCUPATION HAD A DIFFICULT TIME PLACING ME IN A POSITION--
"IT SEEMS I SHOWED AN EVEN POTENTIAL IN ANY ONE OF HALF A DOZEN PROFESSIONS... FROM BIOLOGY TO SPACE SCIENCE ...AND IT DIDN'T KNOW WHERE I WOULD FIT BEST! HAPPILY, IT FINALLY DECIDED ON KRYPTON'S NEW SPACE PROGRAM--SO TODAY I STARTED WORK AT THE KRYPTONOPOLIS SPACE CENTER!
"I THINK I'M GOING TO LIKE IT! IT'S HEADED BY GENERAL DRU-ZOD AND PROFESSOR KEN-DAL, BOTH OF WHOM MET ME WHEN I ARRIVED..."
I TRUST YOU'LL BE COMFORTABLE HERE, JOR-EL! A YOUNG MAN WITH YOUR TALENTS CAN MAKE QUITE A NAME FOR HIMSELF IN ROCKETRY!
GENERAL ZOD'S RIGHT! OUR WORK HERE IS NEW AND THERE ARE STILL MANY DISCOVERIES TO BE MADE--JUST WAITING FOR YOU TO STUMBLE ACROSS THEM!

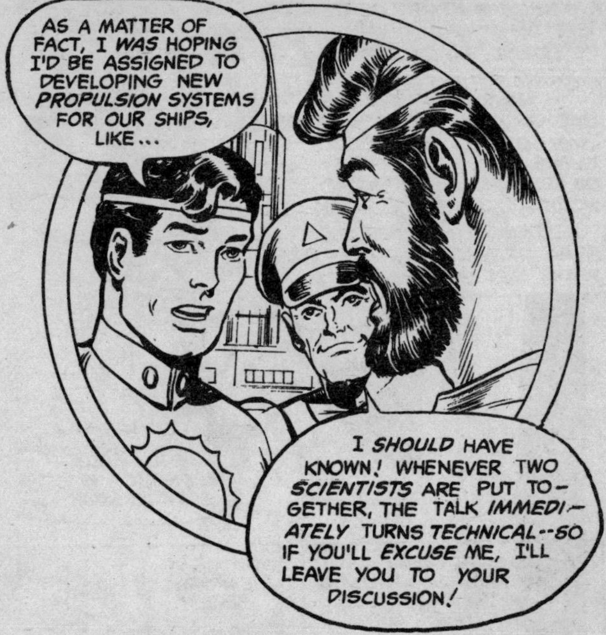
AS A MATTER OF FACT, I *WAS* HOPING I'D BE ASSIGNED TO DEVELOPING NEW *PROPULSION* SYSTEMS FOR OUR SHIPS, LIKE...
I *SHOULD* HAVE KNOWN! WHENEVER TWO *SCIENTISTS* ARE PUT TO-GETHER, THE TALK *IMMEDI-ATELY* TURNS *TECHNICAL*--SO IF YOU'LL *EXCUSE* ME, I'LL LEAVE YOU TO YOUR DISCUSSION!

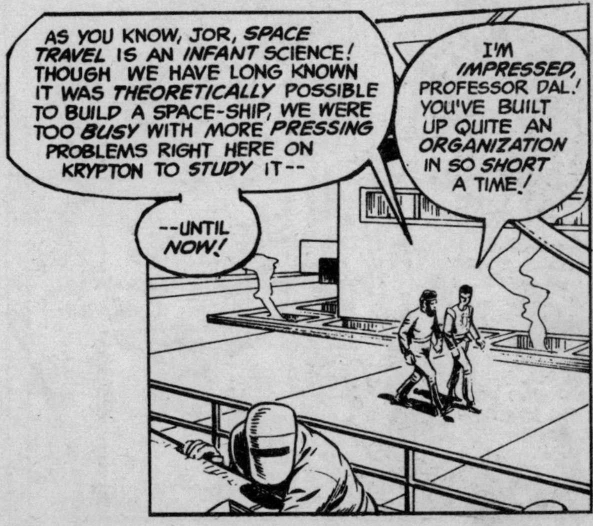
AS YOU KNOW, JOR, *SPACE TRAVEL* IS AN *INFANT* SCIENCE! THOUGH WE HAVE LONG KNOWN IT WAS *THEORETICALLY* POSSIBLE TO BUILD A SPACE-SHIP, WE WERE TOO *BUSY* WITH MORE *PRESSING* PROBLEMS RIGHT HERE ON KRYPTON TO *STUDY* IT--
--UNTIL *NOW!*
I'M *IMPRESSED,* PROFESSOR DAL! YOU'VE BUILT UP QUITE AN *ORGANIZATION* IN SO *SHORT* A TIME!

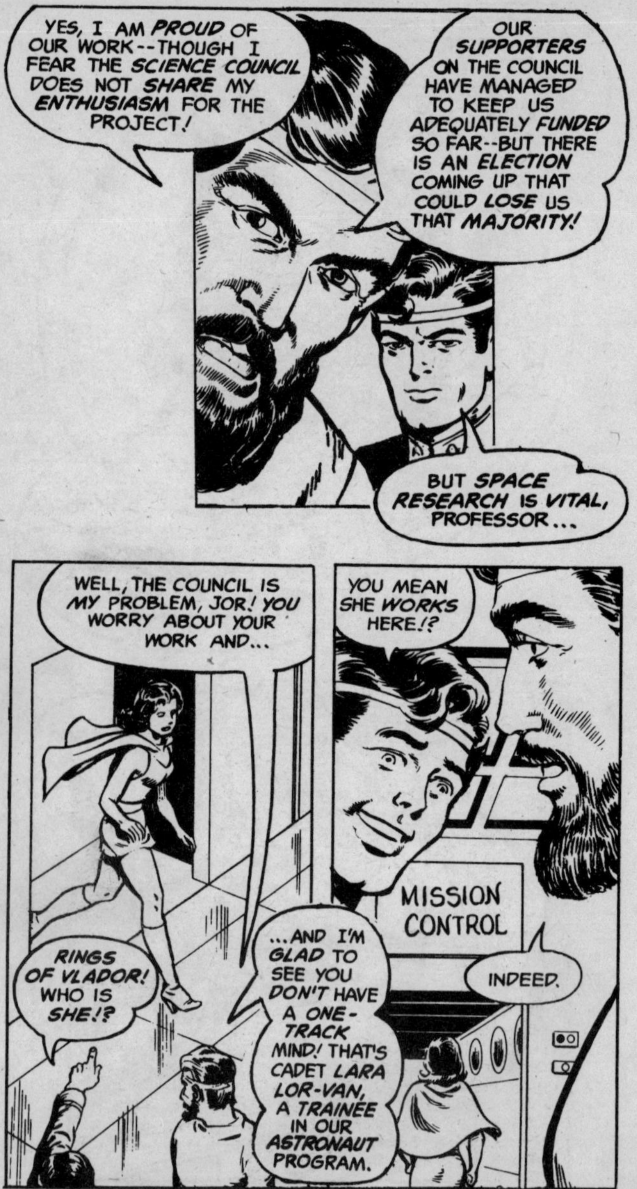
YES, I AM PROUD OF OUR WORK--THOUGH I FEAR THE SCIENCE COUNCIL DOES NOT SHARE MY ENTHUSIASM FOR THE PROJECT!
OUR SUPPORTERS ON THE COUNCIL HAVE MANAGED TO KEEP US ADEQUATELY FUNDED SO FAR--BUT THERE IS AN ELECTION COMING UP THAT COULD LOSE US THAT MAJORITY!
BUT SPACE RESEARCH IS VITAL, PROFESSOR...
WELL, THE COUNCIL IS MY PROBLEM, JOR! YOU WORRY ABOUT YOUR WORK AND...
RINGS OF VLADOR! WHO IS SHE!?
...AND I'M GLAD TO SEE YOU DON'T HAVE A ONE-TRACK MIND! THAT'S CADET LARA LOR-VAN, A TRAINEE IN OUR ASTRONAUT PROGRAM.
YOU MEAN SHE WORKS HERE!?
MISSION CONTROL
INDEED.

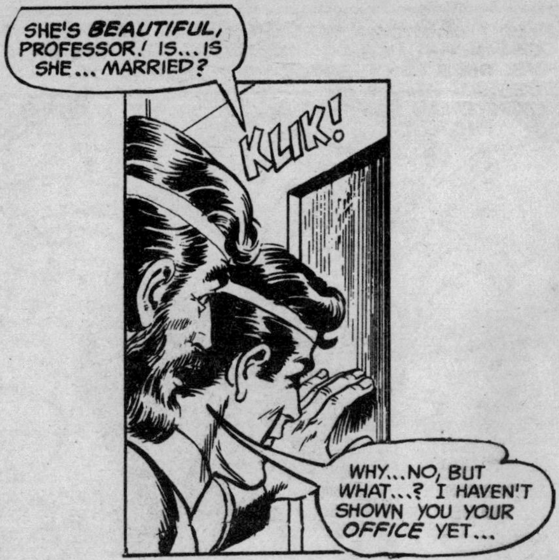
SHE'S BEAUTIFUL, PROFESSOR! IS... IS SHE... MARRIED?
KLIK!
WHY...NO, BUT WHAT...? I HAVEN'T SHOWN YOU YOUR OFFICE YET...

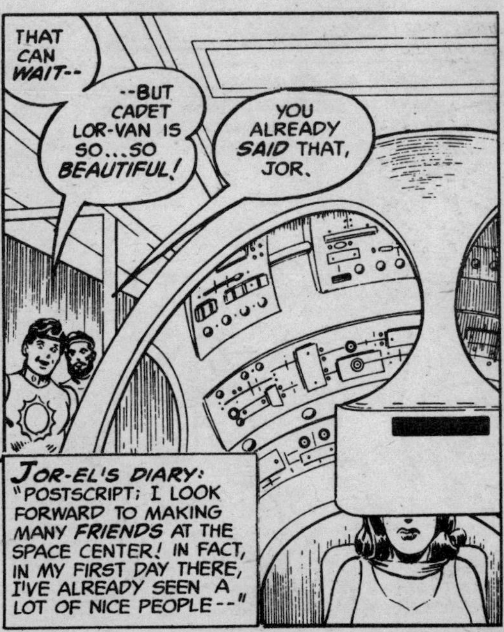
THAT CAN WAIT--
--BUT CADET LOR-VAN IS SO...SO BEAUTIFUL!
YOU ALREADY SAID THAT, JOR.
JOR-EL'S DIARY:
"POSTSCRIPT; I LOOK FORWARD TO MAKING MANY FRIENDS AT THE SPACE CENTER! IN FACT, IN MY FIRST DAY THERE, I'VE ALREADY SEEN A LOT OF NICE PEOPLE--"

JOR-EL'S DIARY, 3 BELYUTH 9995: "KEN-DAL DIDN'T *WASTE* ANY TIME GETTING ME TO WORK! I'VE BEEN ASSIGNED TO *RESEARCH* AND *DEVELOPMENT*--

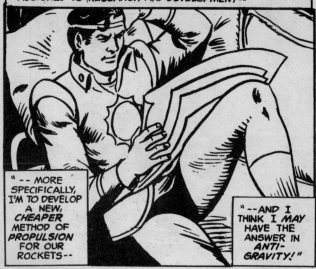

" -- MORE SPECIFICALLY, I'M TO DEVELOP A NEW, *CHEAPER* METHOD OF *PROPULSION* FOR OUR ROCKETS--

" --AND I THINK I *MAY* HAVE THE ANSWER IN *ANTI-GRAVITY!* "

JOR-EL'S DIARY, 36 BELYUTH 9995: "DAY BY DAY, I COME *CLOSER* TO *SUCCESS!* TODAY, I MANAGED TO *ISOLATE* AN ATOMIC PARTICLE WITH ANTI-GRAVITY PROPERTIES --

"--THOUGH I *STILL* CANNOT SAY WHAT IT IS THAT *CAUSES* THIS *PHENOMENON.*

"MY RESEARCH CONTINUES."

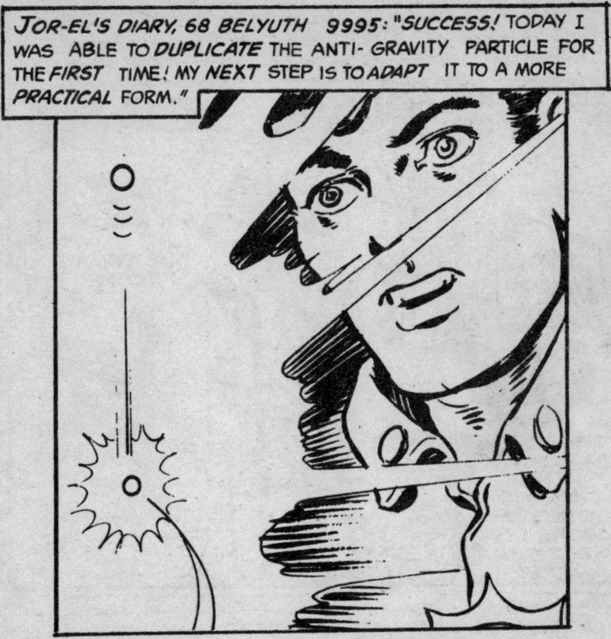
JOR-EL'S DIARY, 68 BELYUTH 9995: "SUCCESS! TODAY I WAS ABLE TO DUPLICATE THE ANTI-GRAVITY PARTICLE FOR THE FIRST TIME! MY NEXT STEP IS TO ADAPT IT TO A MORE PRACTICAL FORM."

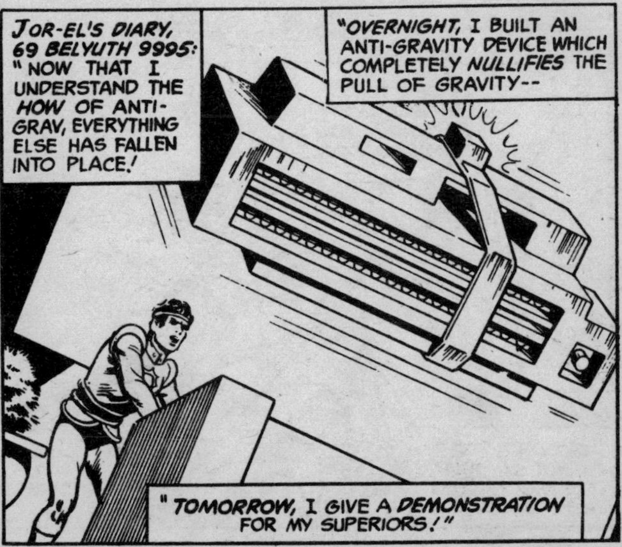
JOR-EL'S DIARY, 69 BELYUTH 9995: "NOW THAT I UNDERSTAND THE HOW OF ANTI-GRAV, EVERYTHING ELSE HAS FALLEN INTO PLACE!
"OVERNIGHT, I BUILT AN ANTI-GRAVITY DEVICE WHICH COMPLETELY NULLIFIES THE PULL OF GRAVITY--
"TOMORROW, I GIVE A DEMONSTRATION FOR MY SUPERIORS!"

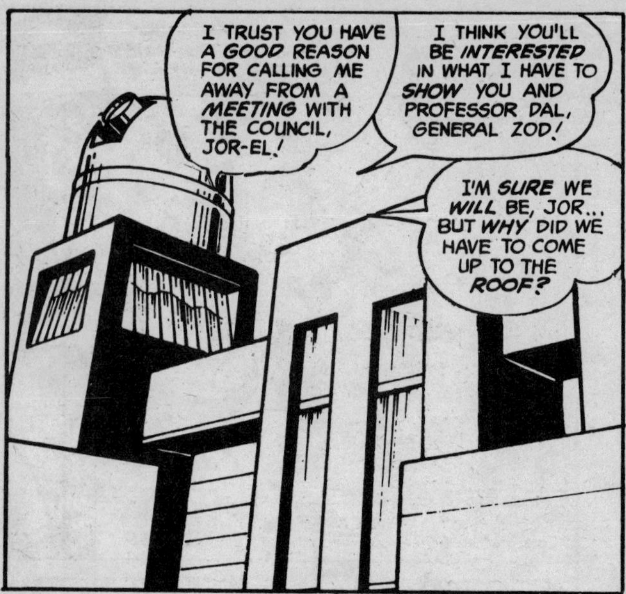
I TRUST YOU HAVE A GOOD REASON FOR CALLING ME AWAY FROM A MEETING WITH THE COUNCIL, JOR-EL!
I THINK YOU'LL BE INTERESTED IN WHAT I HAVE TO SHOW YOU AND PROFESSOR DAL, GENERAL ZOD!
I'M SURE WE WILL BE, JOR... BUT WHY DID WE HAVE TO COME UP TO THE ROOF?

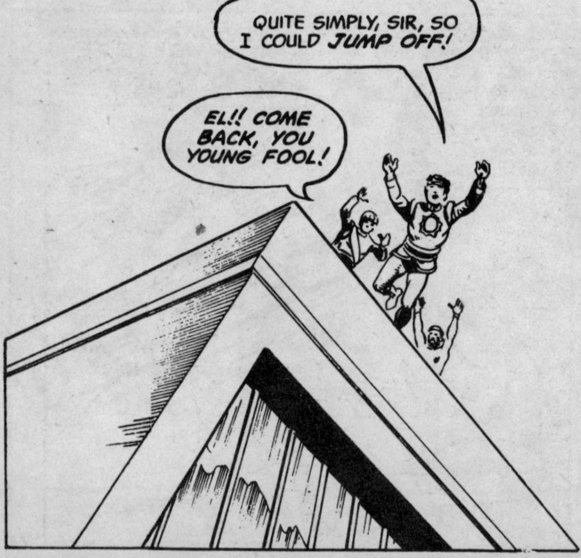
QUITE SIMPLY, SIR, SO I COULD JUMP OFF!
EL!! COME BACK, YOU YOUNG FOOL!

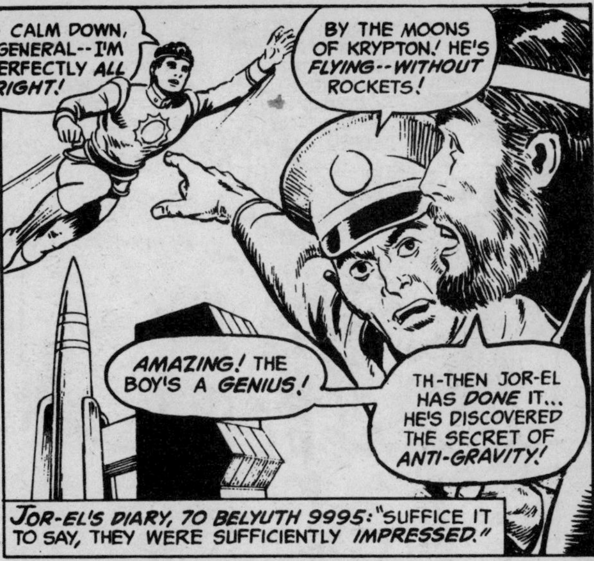
CALM DOWN, GENERAL--I'M PERFECTLY ALL RIGHT!
BY THE MOONS OF KRYPTON! HE'S FLYING--WITHOUT ROCKETS!
AMAZING! THE BOY'S A GENIUS!
TH-THEN JOR-EL HAS DONE IT... HE'S DISCOVERED THE SECRET OF ANTI-GRAVITY!
JOR-EL'S DIARY, 70 BELYUTH 9995: "SUFFICE IT TO SAY, THEY WERE SUFFICIENTLY IMPRESSED."

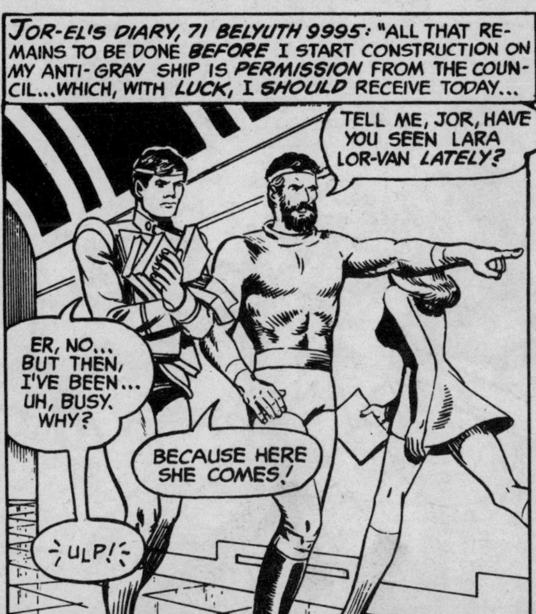
JOR-EL'S DIARY, 71 BELYUTH 9995: "ALL THAT REMAINS TO BE DONE BEFORE I START CONSTRUCTION ON MY ANTI-GRAV SHIP IS PERMISSION FROM THE COUNCIL...WHICH, WITH LUCK, I SHOULD RECEIVE TODAY...
TELL ME, JOR, HAVE YOU SEEN LARA LOR-VAN LATELY?
ER, NO... BUT THEN, I'VE BEEN... UH, BUSY. WHY?
BECAUSE HERE SHE COMES!
ULP!

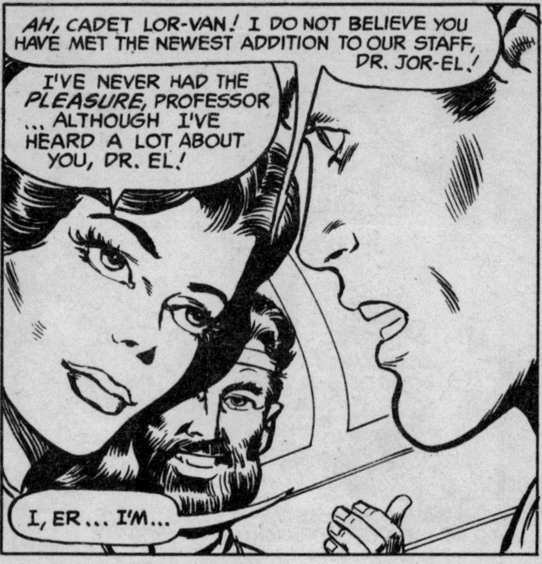
AH, CADET LOR-VAN! I DO NOT BELIEVE YOU HAVE MET THE NEWEST ADDITION TO OUR STAFF, DR. JOR-EL!
I'VE NEVER HAD THE PLEASURE, PROFESSOR ... ALTHOUGH I'VE HEARD A LOT ABOUT YOU, DR. EL!
I, ER... I'M...

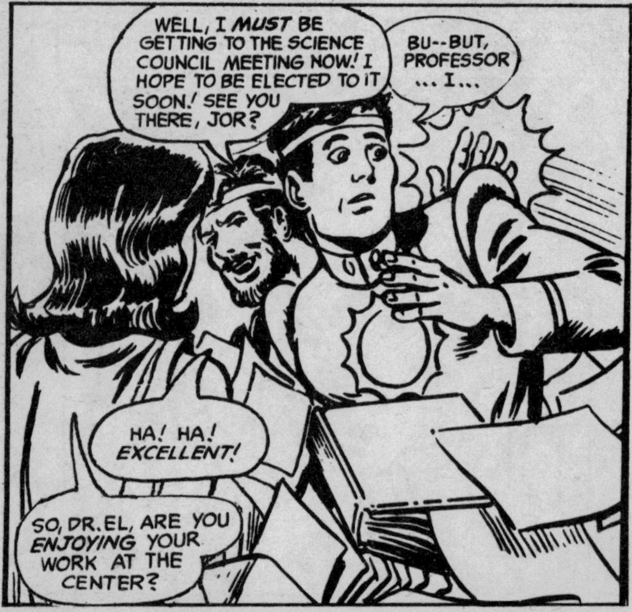
WELL, I MUST BE GETTING TO THE SCIENCE COUNCIL MEETING NOW! I HOPE TO BE ELECTED TO IT SOON! SEE YOU THERE, JOR?
BU--BUT, PROFESSOR ... I...
HA! HA! EXCELLENT!
SO, DR. EL, ARE YOU ENJOYING YOUR WORK AT THE CENTER?

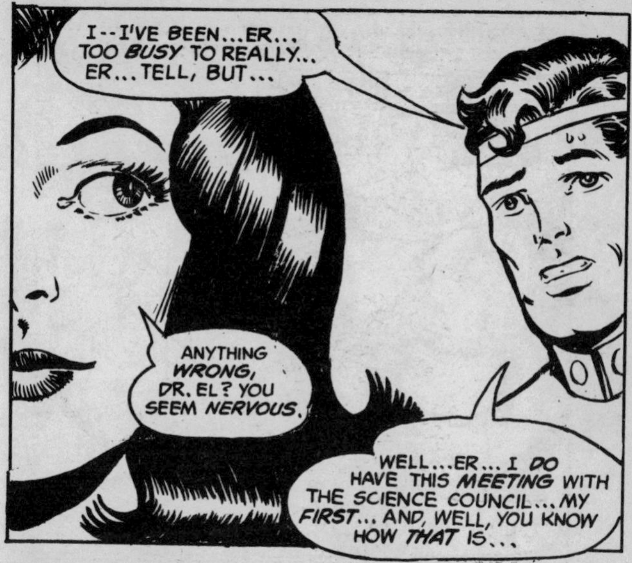
I--I'VE BEEN...ER... TOO BUSY TO REALLY... ER...TELL, BUT...
ANYTHING WRONG, DR. EL? YOU SEEM NERVOUS.
WELL...ER...I DO HAVE THIS MEETING WITH THE SCIENCE COUNCIL...MY FIRST...AND, WELL, YOU KNOW HOW THAT IS...

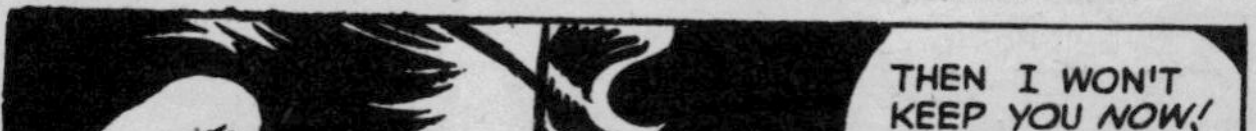
THEN I WON'T KEEP YOU NOW! I'LL BE SEEING YOU, DR. EL!
YO--YOU WILL!?
I DO BELIEVE SO--
--JOR!

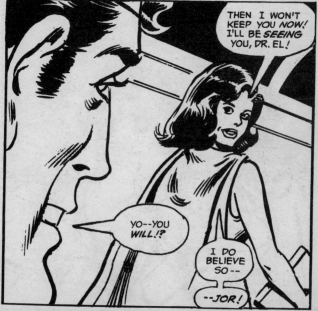

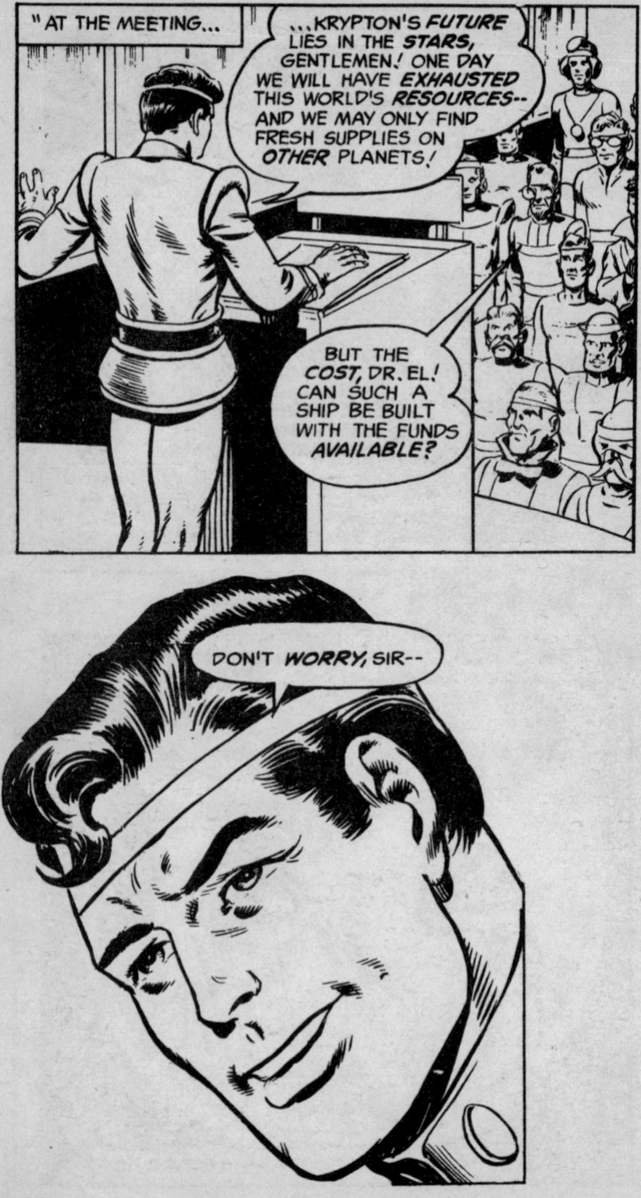
"AT THE MEETING...
...KRYPTON'S FUTURE LIES IN THE STARS, GENTLEMEN! ONE DAY WE WILL HAVE EXHAUSTED THIS WORLD'S RESOURCES-- AND WE MAY ONLY FIND FRESH SUPPLIES ON OTHER PLANETS!
BUT THE COST, DR. EL! CAN SUCH A SHIP BE BUILT WITH THE FUNDS AVAILABLE?
DON'T WORRY, SIR--

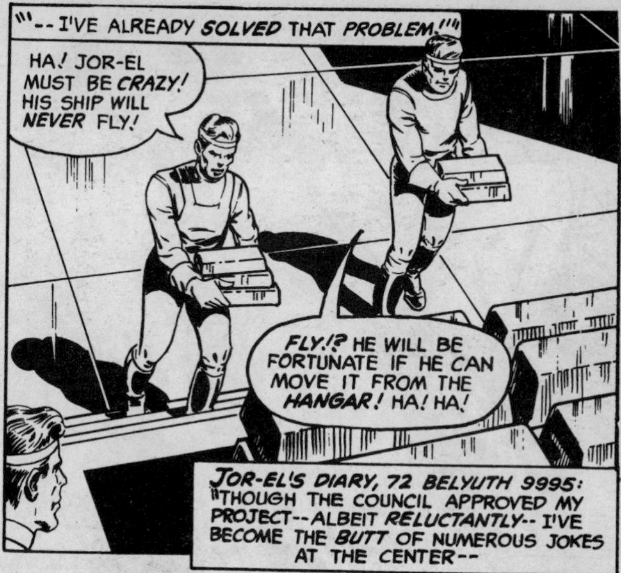
"'--I'VE ALREADY SOLVED THAT PROBLEM!'"
HA! JOR-EL MUST BE CRAZY! HIS SHIP WILL NEVER FLY!
FLY!? HE WILL BE FORTUNATE IF HE CAN MOVE IT FROM THE HANGAR! HA! HA!
JOR-EL'S DIARY, 72 BELYUTH 9995: "THOUGH THE COUNCIL APPROVED MY PROJECT--ALBEIT RELUCTANTLY--I'VE BECOME THE BUTT OF NUMEROUS JOKES AT THE CENTER--

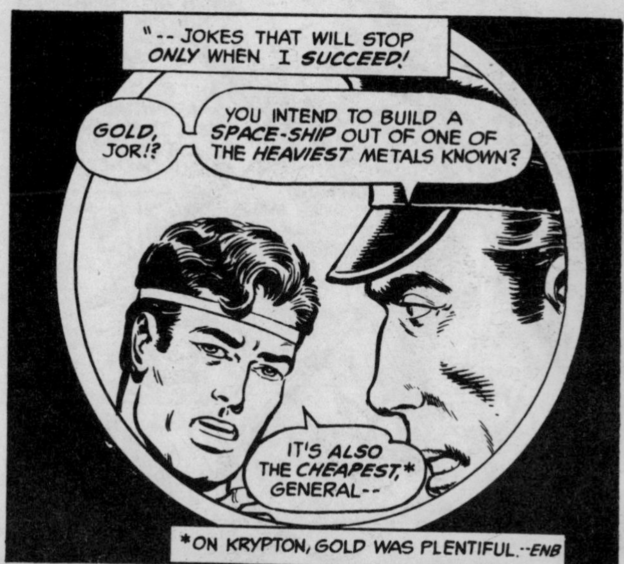
"--JOKES THAT WILL STOP ONLY WHEN I SUCCEED!
GOLD, JOR!?
YOU INTEND TO BUILD A SPACE-SHIP OUT OF ONE OF THE HEAVIEST METALS KNOWN?
IT'S ALSO THE CHEAPEST,* GENERAL--
*ON KRYPTON, GOLD WAS PLENTIFUL.--ENB

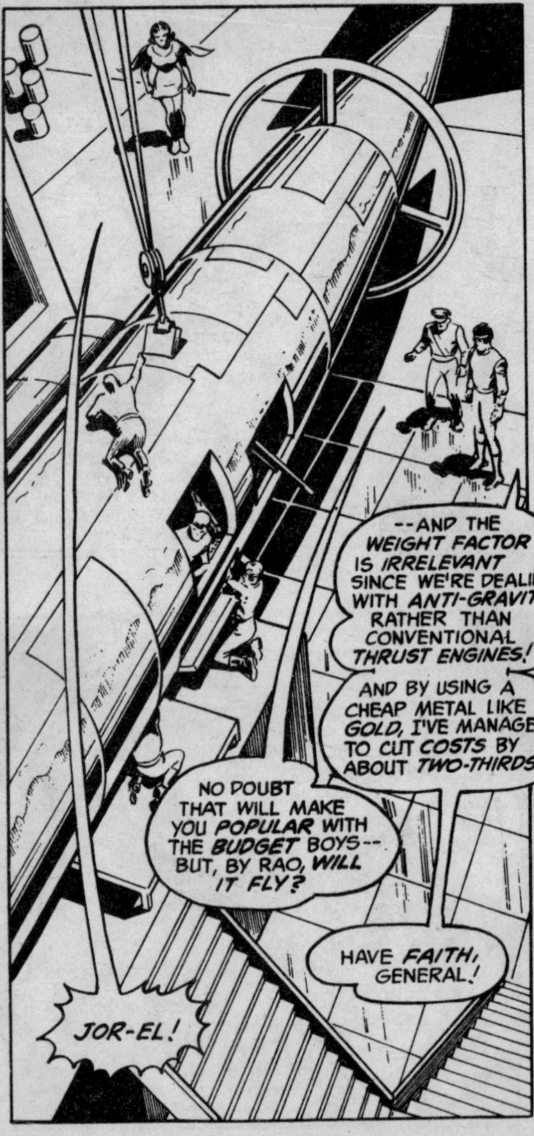
--AND THE WEIGHT FACTOR IS IRRELEVANT SINCE WE'RE DEALING WITH ANTI-GRAVITY RATHER THAN CONVENTIONAL THRUST ENGINES!
AND BY USING A CHEAP METAL LIKE GOLD, I'VE MANAGED TO CUT COSTS BY ABOUT TWO-THIRDS!
NO DOUBT THAT WILL MAKE YOU POPULAR WITH THE BUDGET BOYS-- BUT, BY RAO, WILL IT FLY?
HAVE FAITH, GENERAL!
JOR-EL!

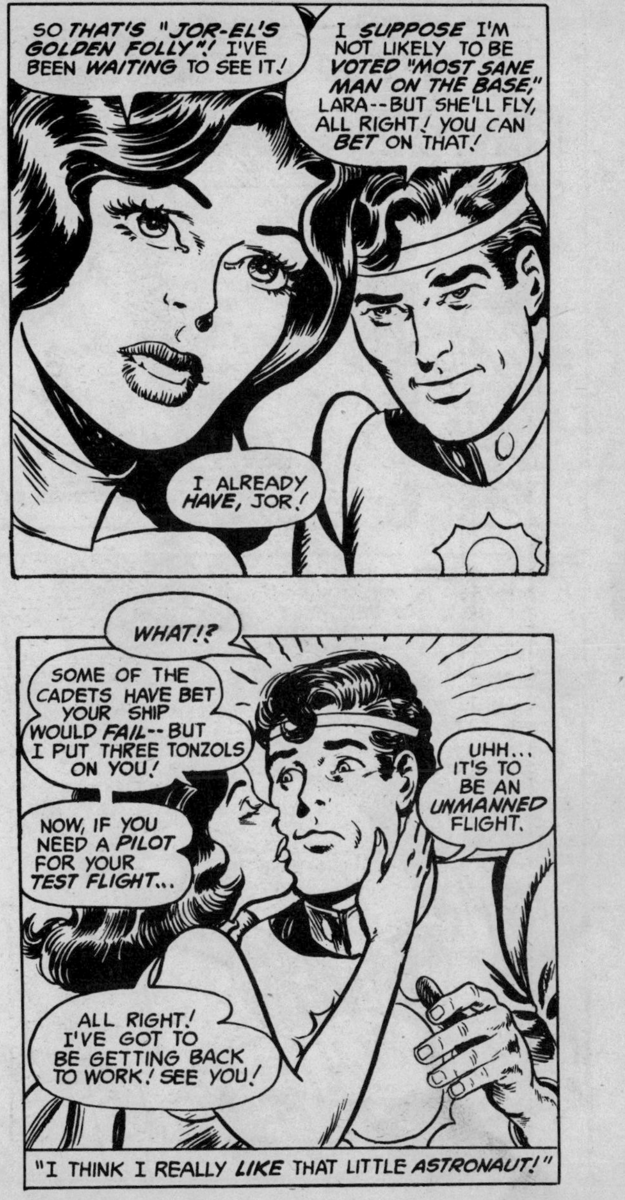
SO THAT'S "JOR-EL'S GOLDEN FOLLY"! I'VE BEEN WAITING TO SEE IT!
I SUPPOSE I'M NOT LIKELY TO BE VOTED "MOST SANE MAN ON THE BASE," LARA--BUT SHE'LL FLY, ALL RIGHT! YOU CAN BET ON THAT!
I ALREADY HAVE, JOR!
WHAT!?
SOME OF THE CADETS HAVE BET YOUR SHIP WOULD FAIL--BUT I PUT THREE TONZOLS ON YOU!
NOW, IF YOU NEED A PILOT FOR YOUR TEST FLIGHT...
UHH... IT'S TO BE AN UNMANNED FLIGHT.
ALL RIGHT! I'VE GOT TO BE GETTING BACK TO WORK! SEE YOU!
"I THINK I REALLY LIKE THAT LITTLE ASTRONAUT!"

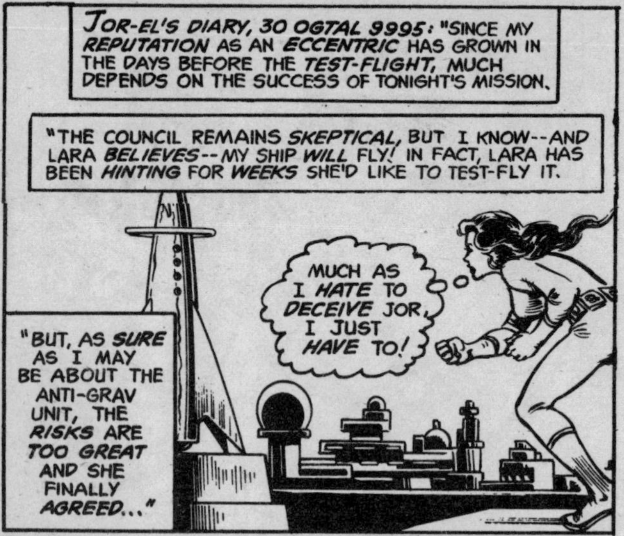
JOR-EL'S DIARY, 30 OGTAL 9995: "SINCE MY REPUTATION AS AN ECCENTRIC HAS GROWN IN THE DAYS BEFORE THE TEST-FLIGHT, MUCH DEPENDS ON THE SUCCESS OF TONIGHT'S MISSION.
"THE COUNCIL REMAINS SKEPTICAL, BUT I KNOW--AND LARA BELIEVES--MY SHIP WILL FLY! IN FACT, LARA HAS BEEN HINTING FOR WEEKS SHE'D LIKE TO TEST-FLY IT.
"BUT, AS SURE AS I MAY BE ABOUT THE ANTI-GRAV UNIT, THE RISKS ARE TOO GREAT AND SHE FINALLY AGREED..."
MUCH AS I HATE TO DECEIVE JOR, I JUST HAVE TO!

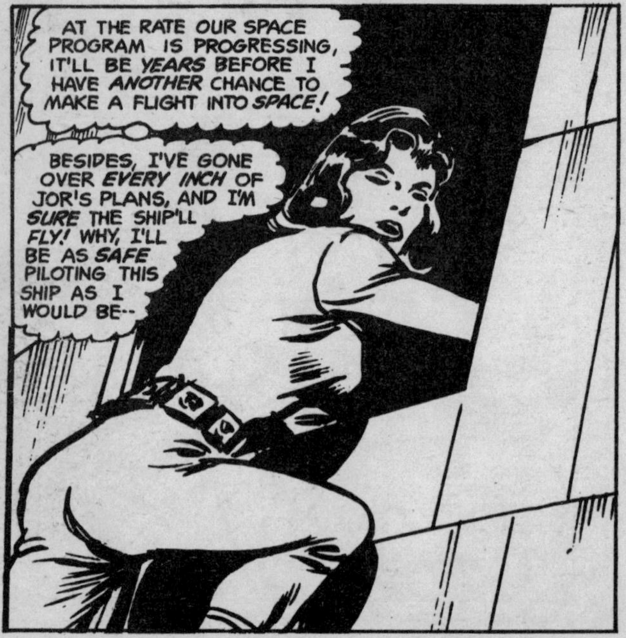
AT THE RATE OUR SPACE PROGRAM IS PROGRESSING, IT'LL BE YEARS BEFORE I HAVE ANOTHER CHANCE TO MAKE A FLIGHT INTO SPACE!
BESIDES, I'VE GONE OVER EVERY INCH OF JOR'S PLANS, AND I'M SURE THE SHIP'LL FLY! WHY, I'LL BE AS SAFE PILOTING THIS SHIP AS I WOULD BE--

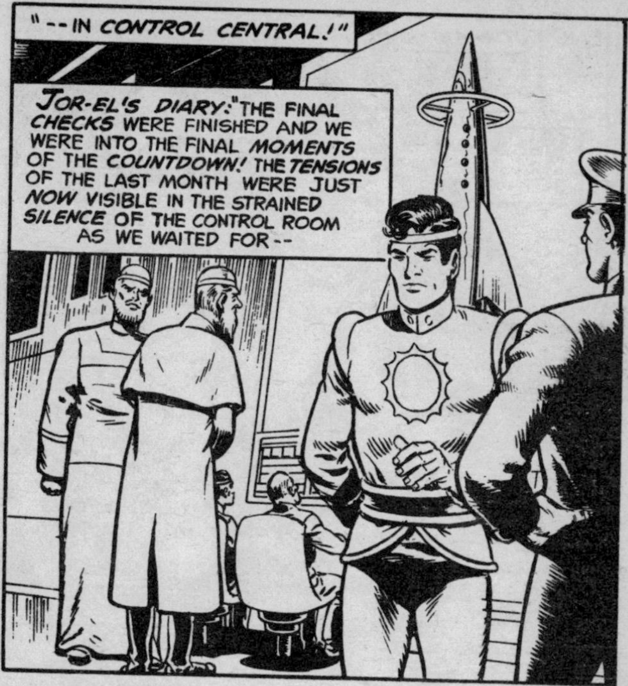
"--IN CONTROL CENTRAL!"
JOR-EL'S DIARY: "THE FINAL CHECKS WERE FINISHED AND WE WERE INTO THE FINAL MOMENTS OF THE COUNTDOWN! THE TENSIONS OF THE LAST MONTH WERE JUST NOW VISIBLE IN THE STRAINED SILENCE OF THE CONTROL ROOM AS WE WAITED FOR--

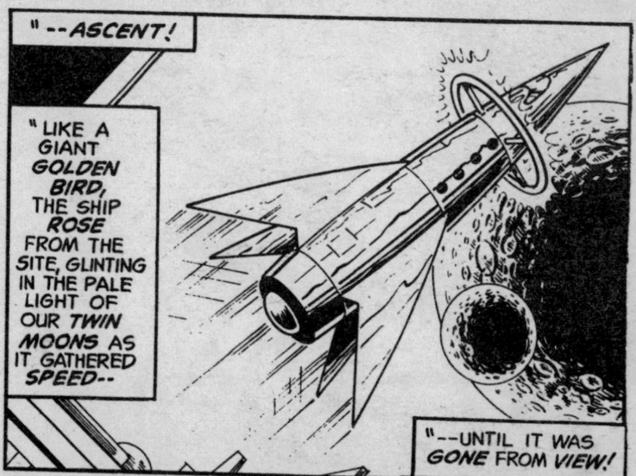
"--ASCENT!
"LIKE A GIANT GOLDEN BIRD, THE SHIP ROSE FROM THE SITE, GLINTING IN THE PALE LIGHT OF OUR TWIN MOONS AS IT GATHERED SPEED--
"--UNTIL IT WAS GONE FROM VIEW!

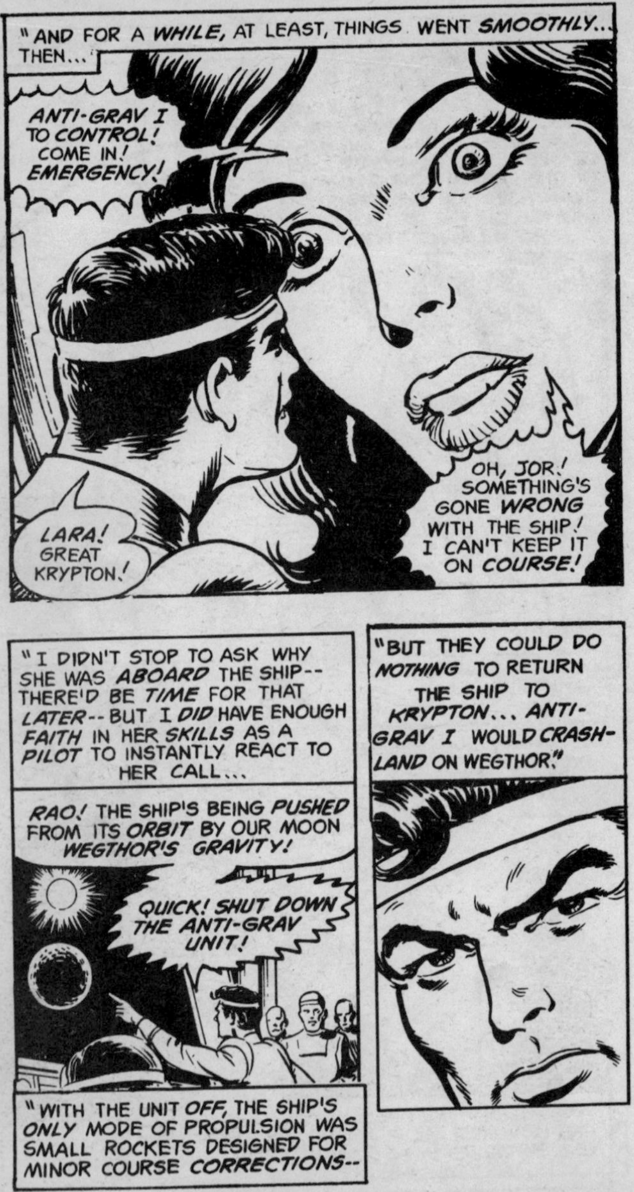

"AND FOR A WHILE, AT LEAST, THINGS WENT SMOOTHLY... THEN..."
ANTI-GRAV I TO CONTROL! COME IN! EMERGENCY!
OH, JOR! SOMETHING'S GONE WRONG WITH THE SHIP! I CAN'T KEEP IT ON COURSE!
LARA! GREAT KRYPTON!
"I DIDN'T STOP TO ASK WHY SHE WAS ABOARD THE SHIP-- THERE'D BE TIME FOR THAT LATER-- BUT I DID HAVE ENOUGH FAITH IN HER SKILLS AS A PILOT TO INSTANTLY REACT TO HER CALL...
RAO! THE SHIP'S BEING PUSHED FROM ITS ORBIT BY OUR MOON WEGTHOR'S GRAVITY!
QUICK! SHUT DOWN THE ANTI-GRAV UNIT!
"WITH THE UNIT OFF, THE SHIP'S ONLY MODE OF PROPULSION WAS SMALL ROCKETS DESIGNED FOR MINOR COURSE CORRECTIONS--
"BUT THEY COULD DO NOTHING TO RETURN THE SHIP TO KRYPTON... ANTI-GRAV I WOULD CRASH-LAND ON WEGTHOR."

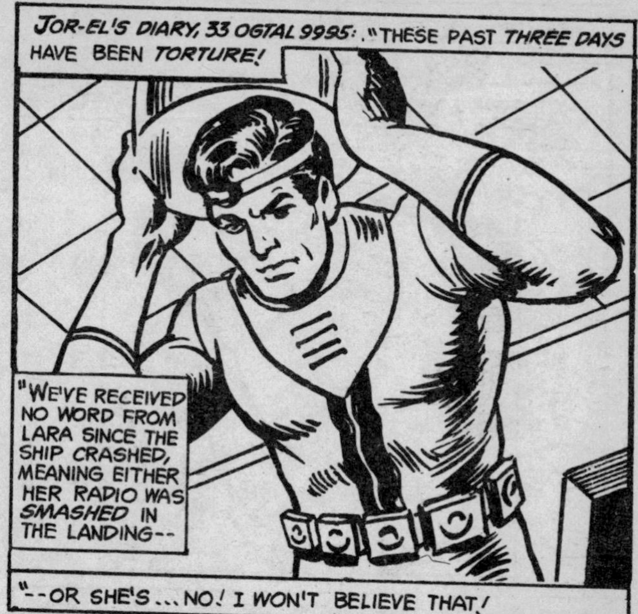
JOR-EL'S DIARY, 33 OGTAL 9995: "THESE PAST THREE DAYS HAVE BEEN TORTURE!
"WE'VE RECEIVED NO WORD FROM LARA SINCE THE SHIP CRASHED, MEANING EITHER HER RADIO WAS SMASHED IN THE LANDING--
"--OR SHE'S ... NO! I WON'T BELIEVE THAT!

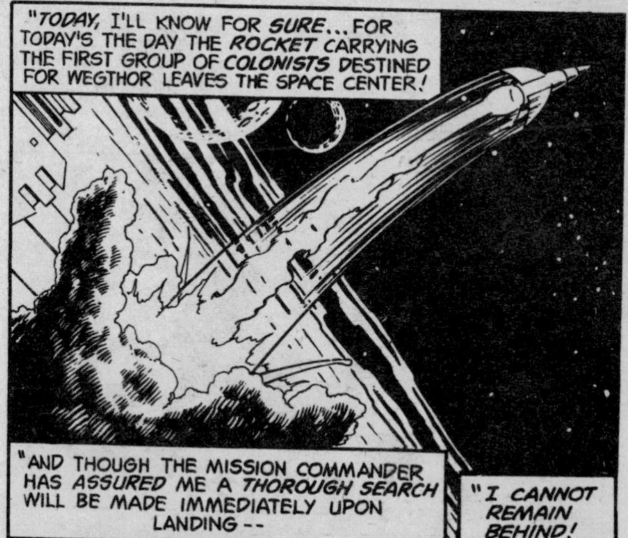
"TODAY, I'LL KNOW FOR SURE... FOR TODAY'S THE DAY THE ROCKET CARRYING THE FIRST GROUP OF COLONISTS DESTINED FOR WEGTHOR LEAVES THE SPACE CENTER!
"AND THOUGH THE MISSION COMMANDER HAS ASSURED ME A THOROUGH SEARCH WILL BE MADE IMMEDIATELY UPON LANDING--
"I CANNOT REMAIN BEHIND!

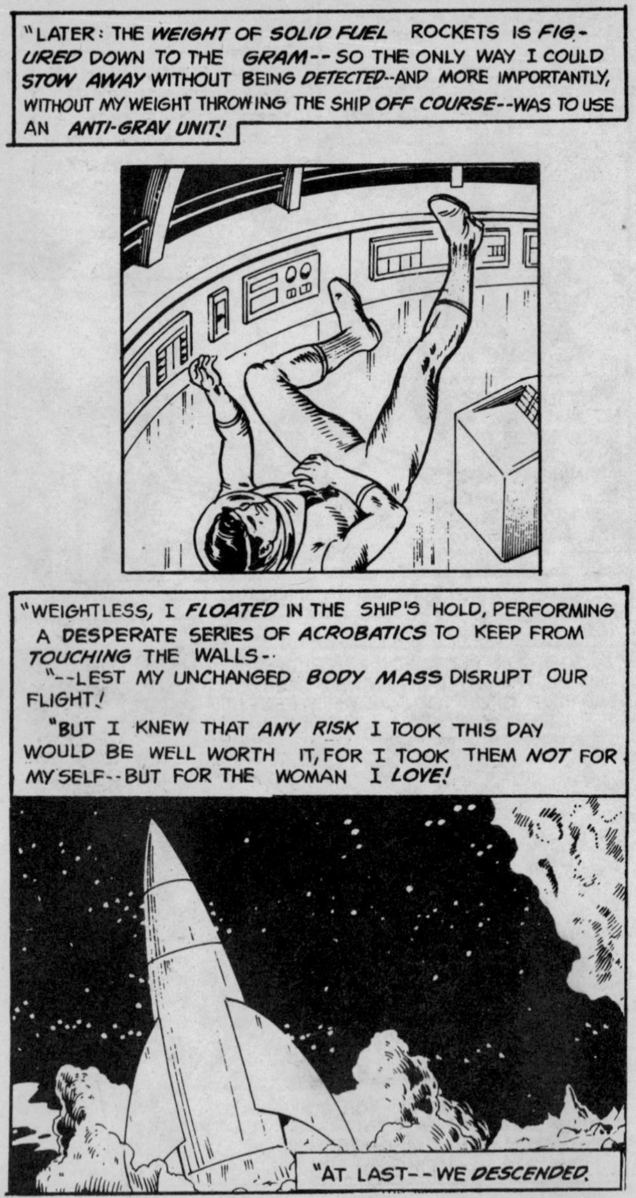
"LATER: THE WEIGHT OF SOLID FUEL ROCKETS IS FIGURED DOWN TO THE GRAM--SO THE ONLY WAY I COULD STOW AWAY WITHOUT BEING DETECTED--AND MORE IMPORTANTLY, WITHOUT MY WEIGHT THROWING THE SHIP OFF COURSE--WAS TO USE AN ANTI-GRAV UNIT!
"WEIGHTLESS, I FLOATED IN THE SHIP'S HOLD, PERFORMING A DESPERATE SERIES OF ACROBATICS TO KEEP FROM TOUCHING THE WALLS--
"--LEST MY UNCHANGED BODY MASS DISRUPT OUR FLIGHT!
"BUT I KNEW THAT ANY RISK I TOOK THIS DAY WOULD BE WELL WORTH IT, FOR I TOOK THEM NOT FOR MYSELF--BUT FOR THE WOMAN I LOVE!
"AT LAST--WE DESCENDED.

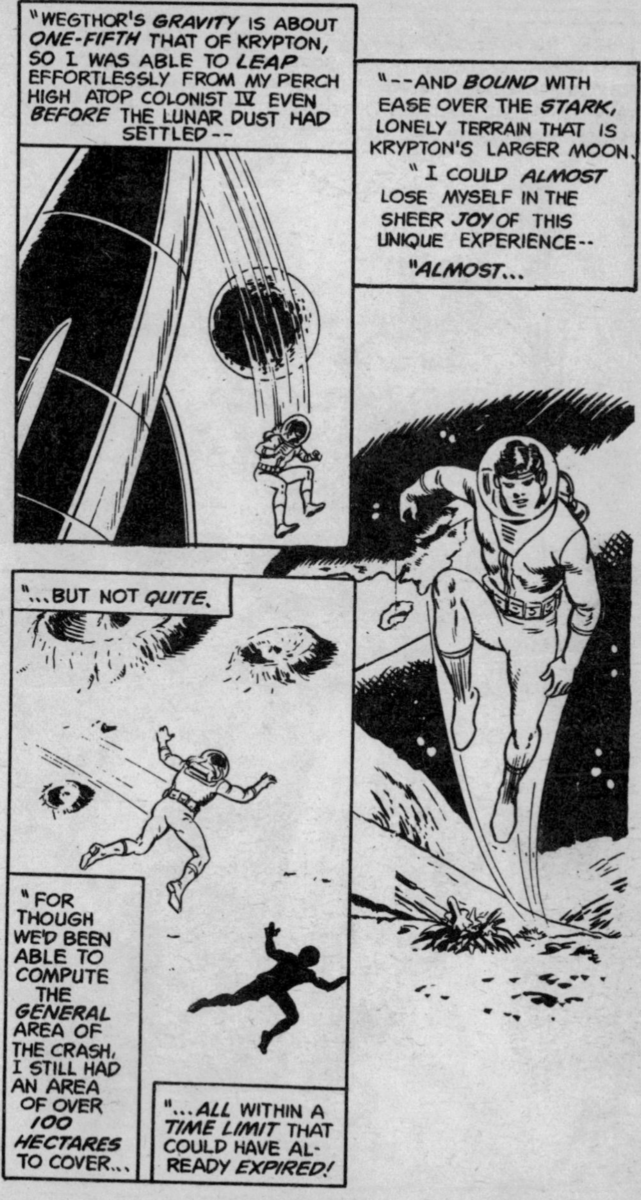
"WEGTHOR'S GRAVITY IS ABOUT ONE-FIFTH THAT OF KRYPTON, SO I WAS ABLE TO LEAP EFFORTLESSLY FROM MY PERCH HIGH ATOP COLONIST IV EVEN BEFORE THE LUNAR DUST HAD SETTLED--
"--AND BOUND WITH EASE OVER THE STARK, LONELY TERRAIN THAT IS KRYPTON'S LARGER MOON.
"I COULD ALMOST LOSE MYSELF IN THE SHEER JOY OF THIS UNIQUE EXPERIENCE--
"ALMOST...
"...BUT NOT QUITE.
"FOR THOUGH WE'D BEEN ABLE TO COMPUTE THE GENERAL AREA OF THE CRASH, I STILL HAD AN AREA OF OVER 100 HECTARES TO COVER...
"...ALL WITHIN A TIME LIMIT THAT COULD HAVE AL-READY EXPIRED!

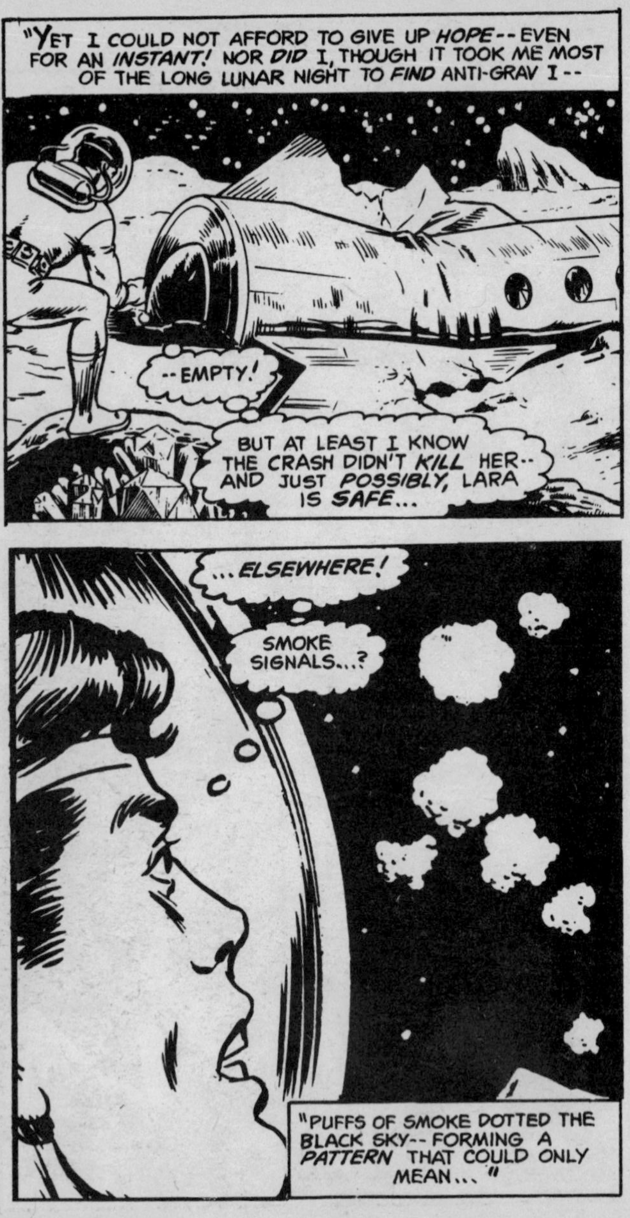
"YET I COULD NOT AFFORD TO GIVE UP HOPE-- EVEN FOR AN INSTANT! NOR DID I, THOUGH IT TOOK ME MOST OF THE LONG LUNAR NIGHT TO FIND ANTI-GRAV I--
--EMPTY!
BUT AT LEAST I KNOW THE CRASH DIDN'T KILL HER-- AND JUST POSSIBLY, LARA IS SAFE...
...ELSEWHERE!
SMOKE SIGNALS...?
"PUFFS OF SMOKE DOTTED THE BLACK SKY-- FORMING A PATTERN THAT COULD ONLY MEAN..."

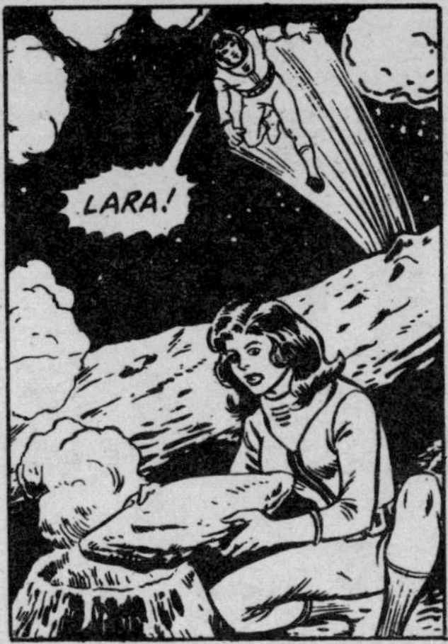
LARA!

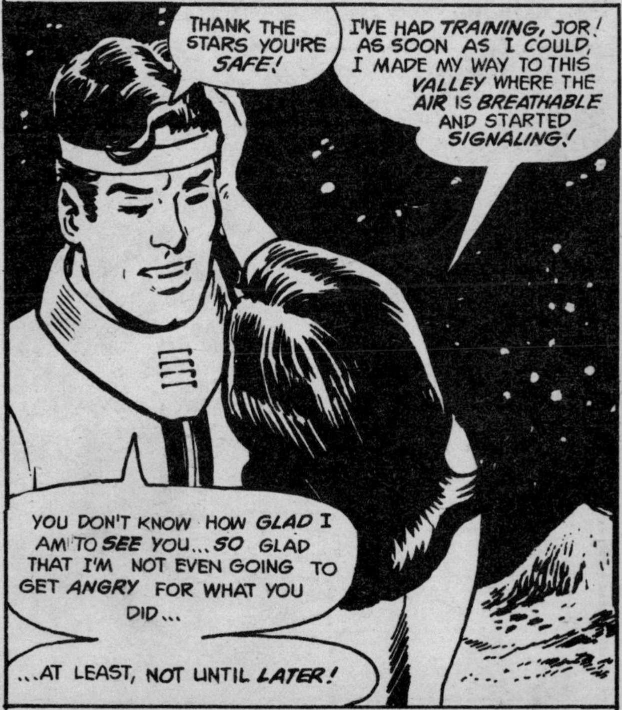
THANK THE STARS YOU'RE SAFE!
I'VE HAD TRAINING, JOR! AS SOON AS I COULD, I MADE MY WAY TO THIS VALLEY WHERE THE AIR IS BREATHABLE AND STARTED SIGNALING!
YOU DON'T KNOW HOW GLAD I AM TO SEE YOU... SO GLAD THAT I'M NOT EVEN GOING TO GET ANGRY FOR WHAT YOU DID...
...AT LEAST, NOT UNTIL LATER!

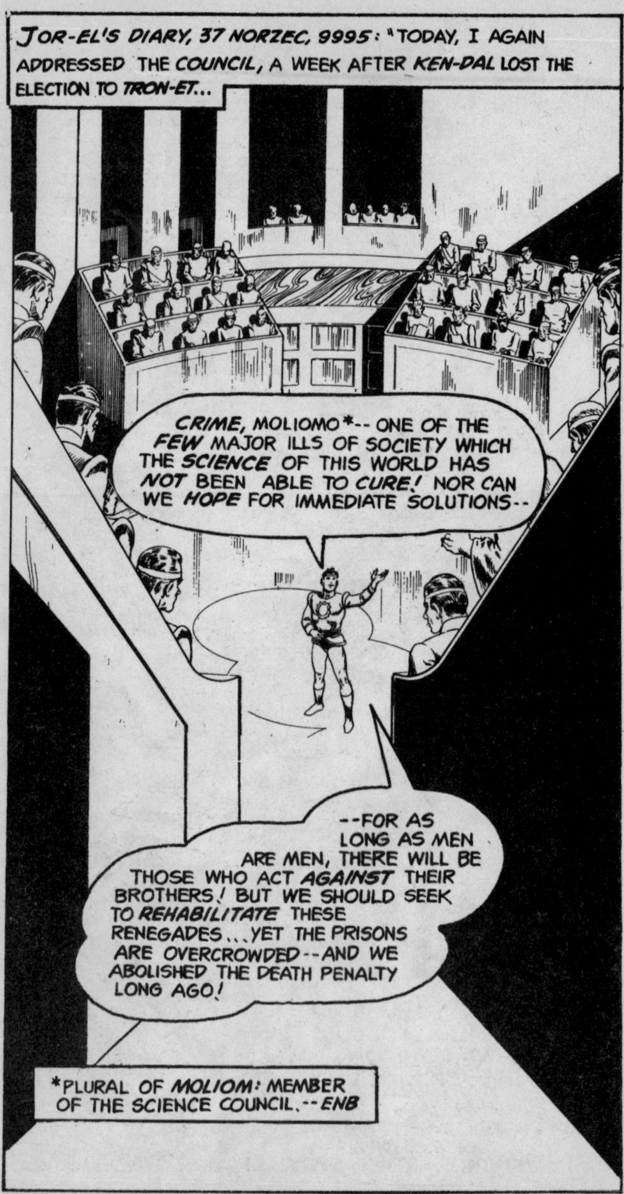
JOR-EL'S DIARY, 37 NORZEC, 9995: "TODAY, I AGAIN ADDRESSED THE COUNCIL, A WEEK AFTER KEN-DAL LOST THE ELECTION TO TRON-ET...
CRIME, MOLIOMO*-- ONE OF THE FEW MAJOR ILLS OF SOCIETY WHICH THE SCIENCE OF THIS WORLD HAS NOT BEEN ABLE TO CURE! NOR CAN WE HOPE FOR IMMEDIATE SOLUTIONS--
--FOR AS LONG AS MEN ARE MEN, THERE WILL BE THOSE WHO ACT AGAINST THEIR BROTHERS! BUT WE SHOULD SEEK TO REHABILITATE THESE RENEGADES...YET THE PRISONS ARE OVERCROWDED--AND WE ABOLISHED THE DEATH PENALTY LONG AGO!
*PLURAL OF MOLIOM: MEMBER OF THE SCIENCE COUNCIL.--ENB

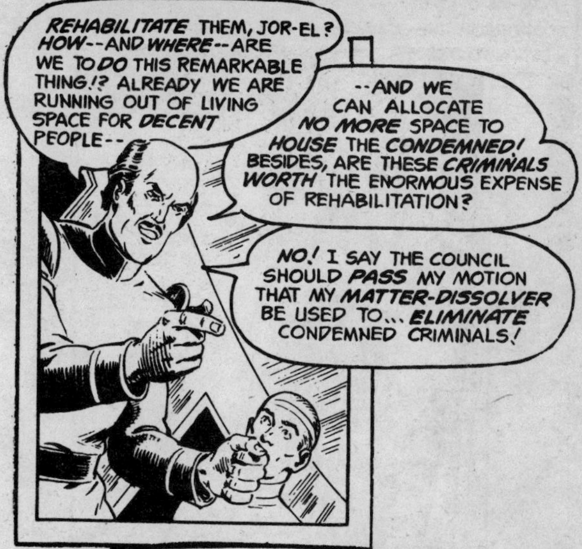
REHABILITATE THEM, JOR-EL? HOW--AND WHERE--ARE WE TO DO THIS REMARKABLE THING!? ALREADY WE ARE RUNNING OUT OF LIVING SPACE FOR DECENT PEOPLE--
--AND WE CAN ALLOCATE NO MORE SPACE TO HOUSE THE CONDEMNED! BESIDES, ARE THESE CRIMINALS WORTH THE ENORMOUS EXPENSE OF REHABILITATION?
NO! I SAY THE COUNCIL SHOULD PASS MY MOTION THAT MY MATTER-DISSOLVER BE USED TO... ELIMINATE CONDEMNED CRIMINALS!

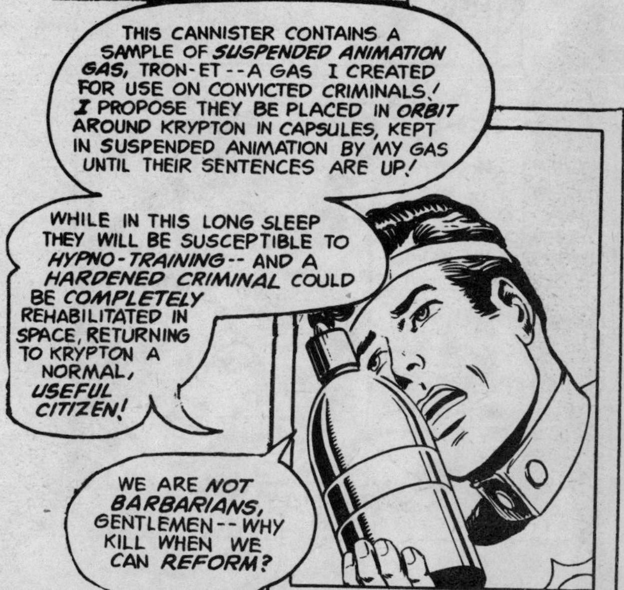
THIS CANNISTER CONTAINS A SAMPLE OF SUSPENDED ANIMATION GAS, TRON-ET--A GAS I CREATED FOR USE ON CONVICTED CRIMINALS! I PROPOSE THEY BE PLACED IN ORBIT AROUND KRYPTON IN CAPSULES, KEPT IN SUSPENDED ANIMATION BY MY GAS UNTIL THEIR SENTENCES ARE UP!
WHILE IN THIS LONG SLEEP THEY WILL BE SUSCEPTIBLE TO HYPNO-TRAINING-- AND A HARDENED CRIMINAL COULD BE COMPLETELY REHABILITATED IN SPACE, RETURNING TO KRYPTON A NORMAL, USEFUL CITIZEN!
WE ARE NOT BARBARIANS, GENTLEMEN--WHY KILL WHEN WE CAN REFORM?

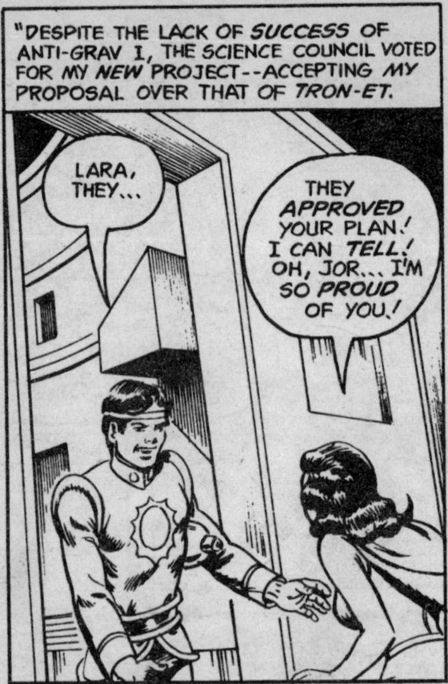
"DESPITE THE LACK OF SUCCESS OF ANTI-GRAV I, THE SCIENCE COUNCIL VOTED FOR MY NEW PROJECT--ACCEPTING MY PROPOSAL OVER THAT OF TRON-ET.
LARA, THEY...
THEY APPROVED YOUR PLAN! I CAN TELL! OH, JOR... I'M SO PROUD OF YOU!

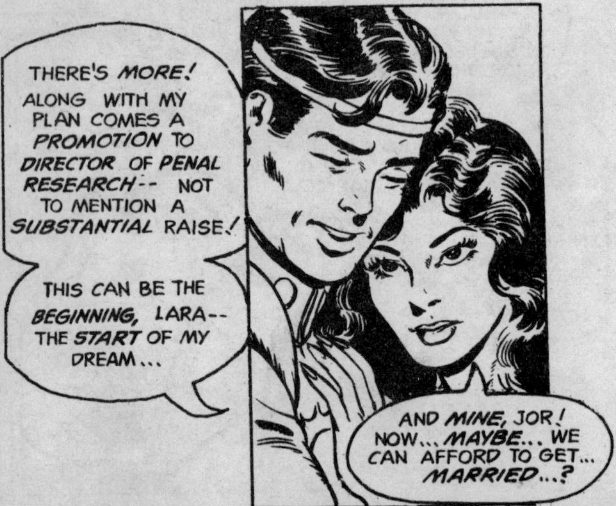
THERE'S MORE! ALONG WITH MY PLAN COMES A PROMOTION TO DIRECTOR OF PENAL RESEARCH-- NOT TO MENTION A SUBSTANTIAL RAISE!
THIS CAN BE THE BEGINNING, LARA-- THE START OF MY DREAM...
AND MINE, JOR! NOW... MAYBE... WE CAN AFFORD TO GET... MARRIED...?

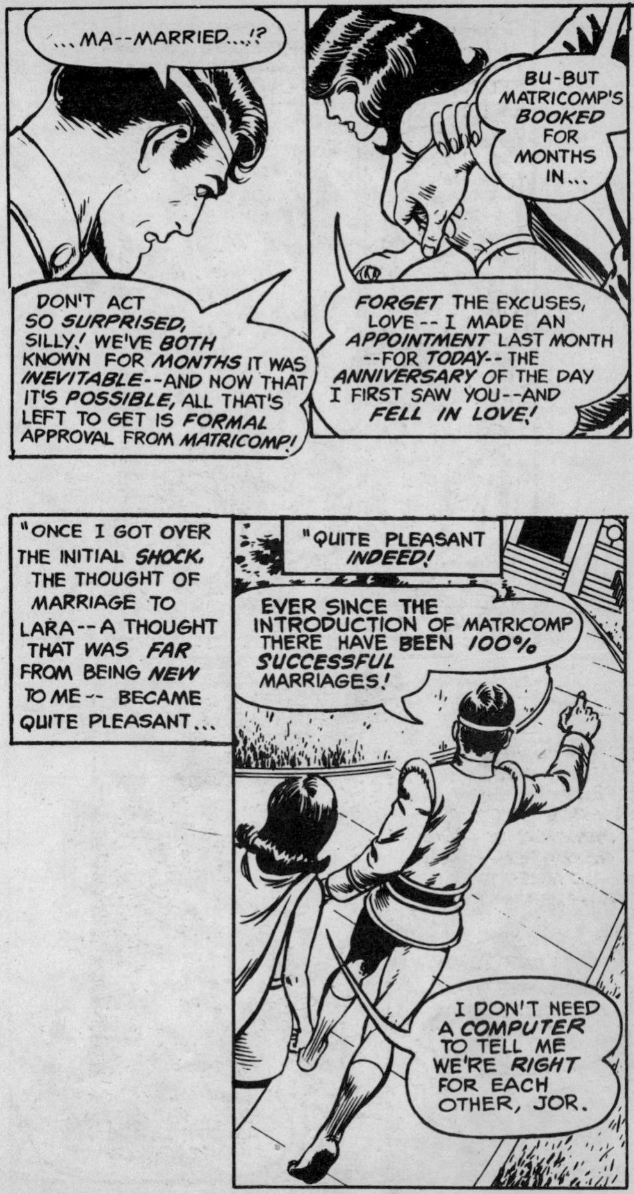
...MA--MARRIED...!?
DON'T ACT SO SURPRISED, SILLY! WE'VE BOTH KNOWN FOR MONTHS IT WAS INEVITABLE--AND NOW THAT IT'S POSSIBLE, ALL THAT'S LEFT TO GET IS FORMAL APPROVAL FROM MATRICOMP!
BU-BUT MATRICOMP'S BOOKED FOR MONTHS IN...
FORGET THE EXCUSES, LOVE -- I MADE AN APPOINTMENT LAST MONTH --FOR TODAY-- THE ANNIVERSARY OF THE DAY I FIRST SAW YOU--AND FELL IN LOVE!
"ONCE I GOT OVER THE INITIAL SHOCK, THE THOUGHT OF MARRIAGE TO LARA--A THOUGHT THAT WAS FAR FROM BEING NEW TO ME-- BECAME QUITE PLEASANT...
"QUITE PLEASANT INDEED!
EVER SINCE THE INTRODUCTION OF MATRICOMP THERE HAVE BEEN 100% SUCCESSFUL MARRIAGES!
I DON'T NEED A COMPUTER TO TELL ME WE'RE RIGHT FOR EACH OTHER, JOR.

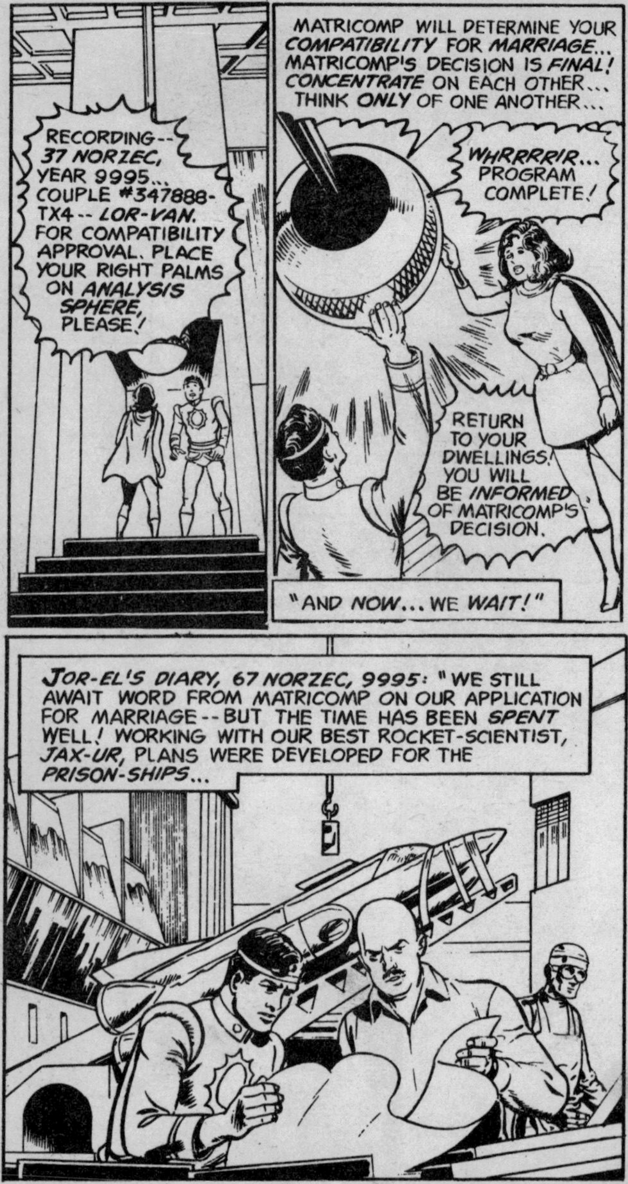

RECORDING-- 37 NORZEC, YEAR 9995... COUPLE #347888-TX4-- LOR-VAN. FOR COMPATIBILITY APPROVAL. PLACE YOUR RIGHT PALMS ON ANALYSIS SPHERE, PLEASE!
MATRICOMP WILL DETERMINE YOUR COMPATIBILITY FOR MARRIAGE... MATRICOMP'S DECISION IS FINAL! CONCENTRATE ON EACH OTHER... THINK ONLY OF ONE ANOTHER...
WHRRRRIR... PROGRAM COMPLETE!
RETURN TO YOUR DWELLINGS! YOU WILL BE INFORMED OF MATRICOMP'S DECISION.
"AND NOW... WE WAIT!"
JOR-EL'S DIARY, 67 NORZEC, 9995: "WE STILL AWAIT WORD FROM MATRICOMP ON OUR APPLICATION FOR MARRIAGE--BUT THE TIME HAS BEEN SPENT WELL! WORKING WITH OUR BEST ROCKET-SCIENTIST, JAX-UR, PLANS WERE DEVELOPED FOR THE PRISON-SHIPS...

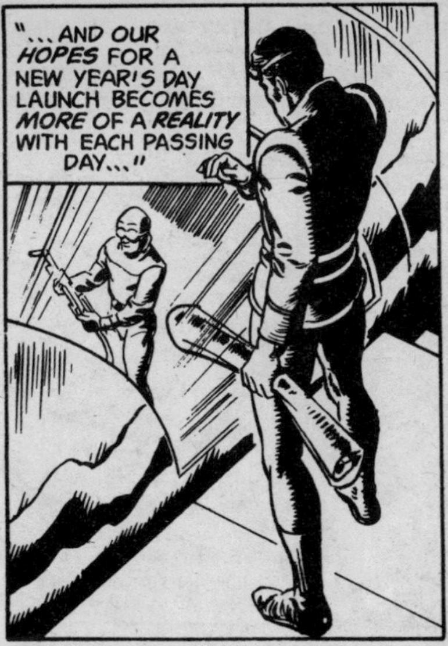
"...AND OUR HOPES FOR A NEW YEAR'S DAY LAUNCH BECOMES MORE OF A REALITY WITH EACH PASSING DAY..."

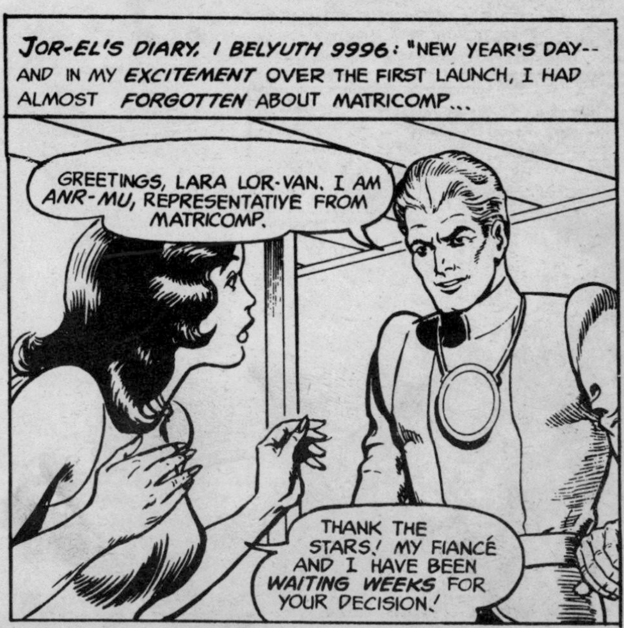
JOR-EL'S DIARY, I BELYUTH 9996: "NEW YEAR'S DAY--AND IN MY EXCITEMENT OVER THE FIRST LAUNCH, I HAD ALMOST FORGOTTEN ABOUT MATRICOMP...
GREETINGS, LARA LOR-VAN. I AM ANR-MU, REPRESENTATIVE FROM MATRICOMP.
THANK THE STARS! MY FIANCÉ AND I HAVE BEEN WAITING WEEKS FOR YOUR DECISION!

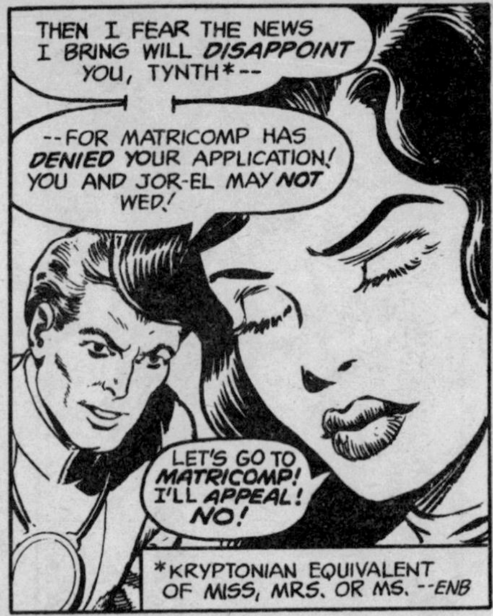
THEN I FEAR THE NEWS I BRING WILL DISAPPOINT YOU, TYNTH*--
--FOR MATRICOMP HAS DENIED YOUR APPLICATION! YOU AND JOR-EL MAY NOT WED!
LET'S GO TO MATRICOMP! I'LL APPEAL! NO!
*KRYPTONIAN EQUIVALENT OF MISS, MRS. OR MS. --ENB

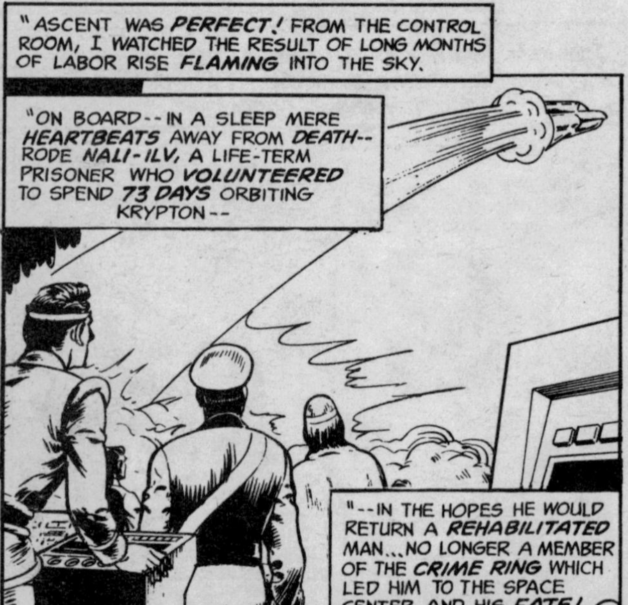
"ASCENT WAS PERFECT! FROM THE CONTROL ROOM, I WATCHED THE RESULT OF LONG MONTHS OF LABOR RISE FLAMING INTO THE SKY.
"ON BOARD--IN A SLEEP MERE HEARTBEATS AWAY FROM DEATH--RODE NALI-ILV, A LIFE-TERM PRISONER WHO VOLUNTEERED TO SPEND 73 DAYS ORBITING KRYPTON--
"--IN THE HOPES HE WOULD RETURN A REHABILITATED MAN...NO LONGER A MEMBER OF THE CRIME RING WHICH LED HIM TO THE SPACE CENTER AND HIS FATE!
17

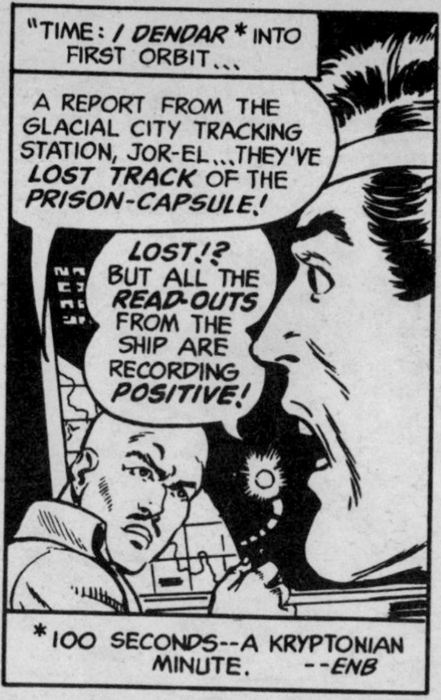
"TIME: 1 DENDAR* INTO FIRST ORBIT...
A REPORT FROM THE GLACIAL CITY TRACKING STATION, JOR-EL...THEY'VE LOST TRACK OF THE PRISON-CAPSULE!
LOST!? BUT ALL THE READ-OUTS FROM THE SHIP ARE RECORDING POSITIVE!
*100 SECONDS--A KRYPTONIAN MINUTE. --ENB

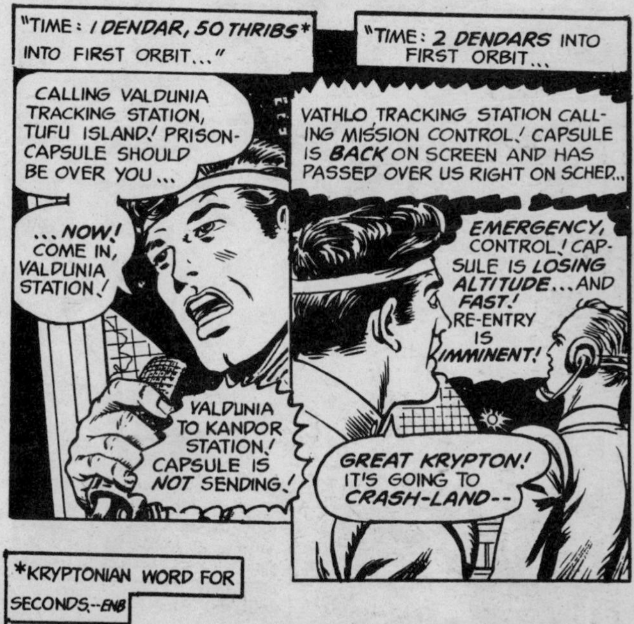
"TIME: 1 DENDAR, 50 THRIBS* INTO FIRST ORBIT..."
CALLING VALDUNIA TRACKING STATION, TUFU ISLAND! PRISON-CAPSULE SHOULD BE OVER YOU...
...NOW! COME IN, VALDUNIA STATION!
VALDUNIA TO KANDOR STATION! CAPSULE IS NOT SENDING!
*KRYPTONIAN WORD FOR SECONDS.--ENB
"TIME: 2 DENDARS INTO FIRST ORBIT...
VATHLO TRACKING STATION CALLING MISSION CONTROL! CAPSULE IS BACK ON SCREEN AND HAS PASSED OVER US RIGHT ON SCHED...
EMERGENCY, CONTROL! CAPSULE IS LOSING ALTITUDE...AND FAST! RE-ENTRY IS IMMINENT!
GREAT KRYPTON! IT'S GOING TO CRASH-LAND--

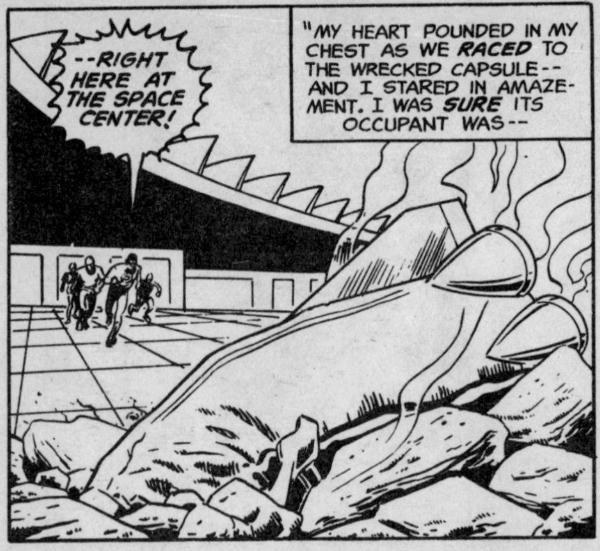
"MY HEART POUNDED IN MY CHEST AS WE RACED TO THE WRECKED CAPSULE--AND I STARED IN AMAZEMENT. I WAS SURE ITS OCCUPANT WAS--
--RIGHT HERE AT THE SPACE CENTER!

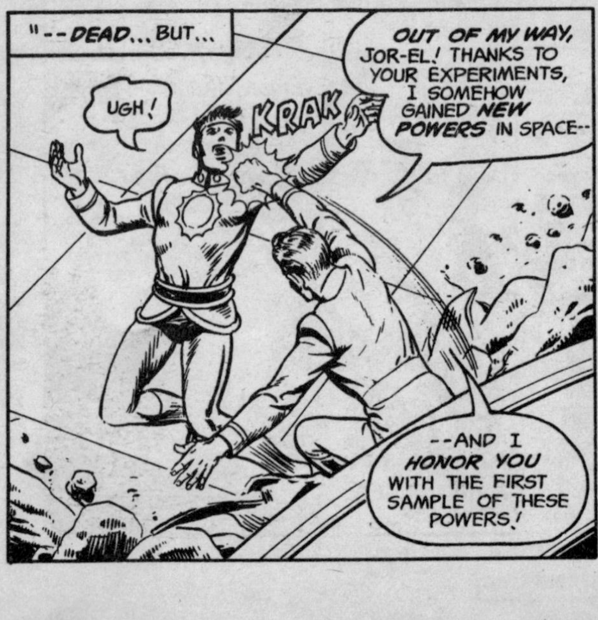
"--DEAD... BUT...
UGH!
KRAK
OUT OF MY WAY, JOR-EL! THANKS TO YOUR EXPERIMENTS, I SOMEHOW GAINED NEW POWERS IN SPACE--
--AND I HONOR YOU WITH THE FIRST SAMPLE OF THESE POWERS!

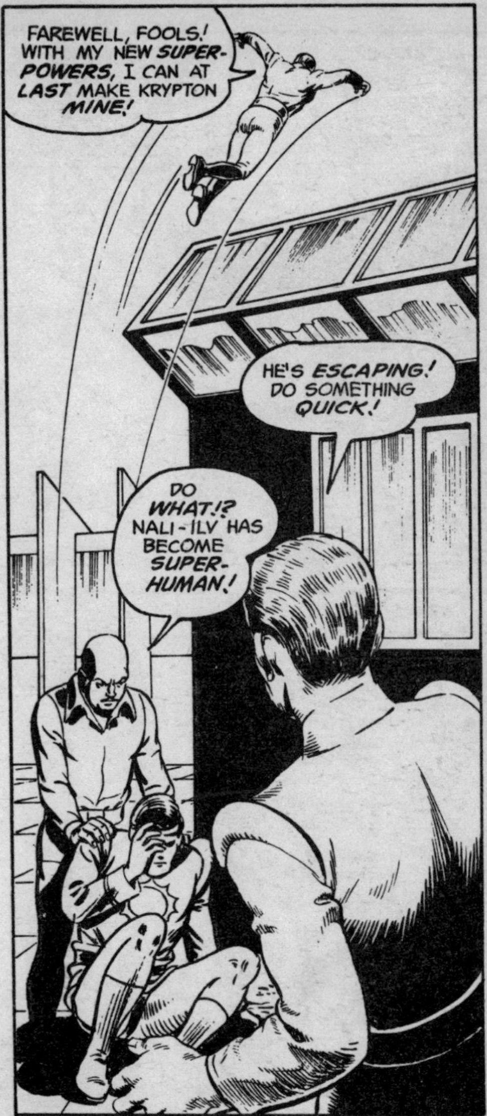
FAREWELL, FOOLS! WITH MY NEW SUPER-POWERS, I CAN AT LAST MAKE KRYPTON MINE!
HE'S ESCAPING! DO SOMETHING QUICK!
DO WHAT!? NALI-ILV HAS BECOME SUPER-HUMAN!

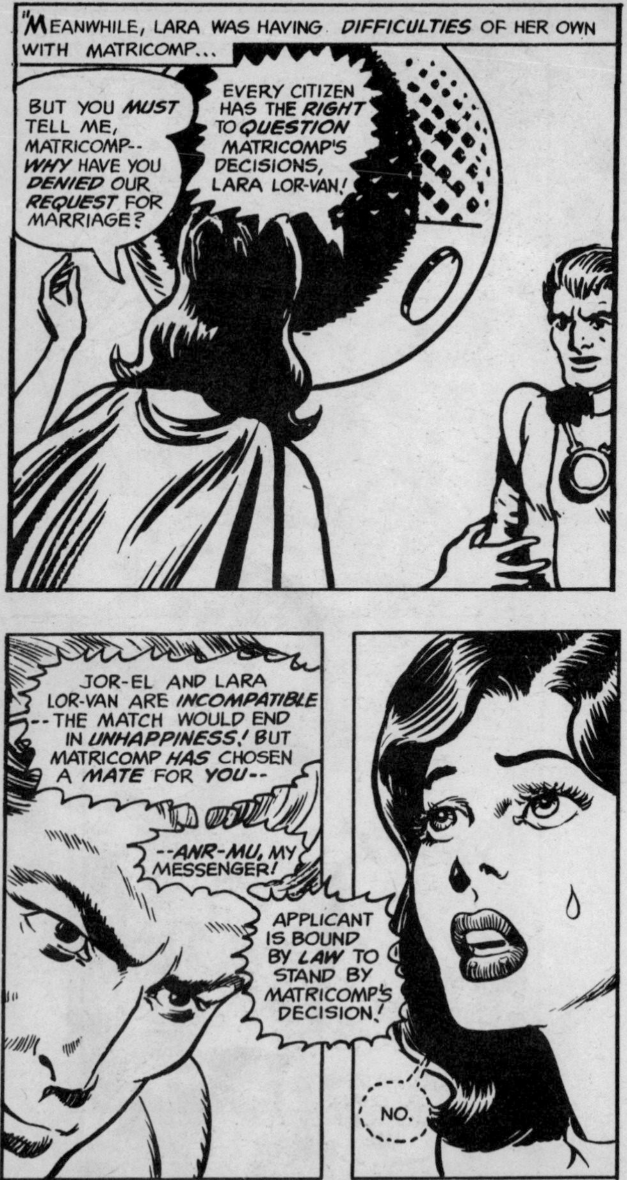
"MEANWHILE, LARA WAS HAVING DIFFICULTIES OF HER OWN WITH MATRICOMP...
BUT YOU MUST TELL ME, MATRICOMP-- WHY HAVE YOU DENIED OUR REQUEST FOR MARRIAGE?
EVERY CITIZEN HAS THE RIGHT TO QUESTION MATRICOMP'S DECISIONS, LARA LOR-VAN!
JOR-EL AND LARA LOR-VAN ARE INCOMPATIBLE --THE MATCH WOULD END IN UNHAPPINESS! BUT MATRICOMP HAS CHOSEN A MATE FOR YOU--
--ANR-MU, MY MESSENGER!
APPLICANT IS BOUND BY LAW TO STAND BY MATRICOMP'S DECISION!
NO.

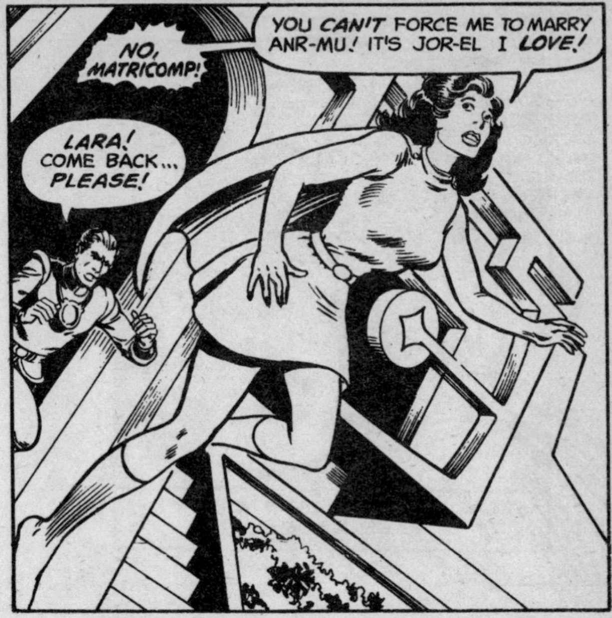
YOU CAN'T FORCE ME TO MARRY ANR-MU! IT'S JOR-EL I LOVE!
NO, MATRICOMP!
LARA! COME BACK... PLEASE!

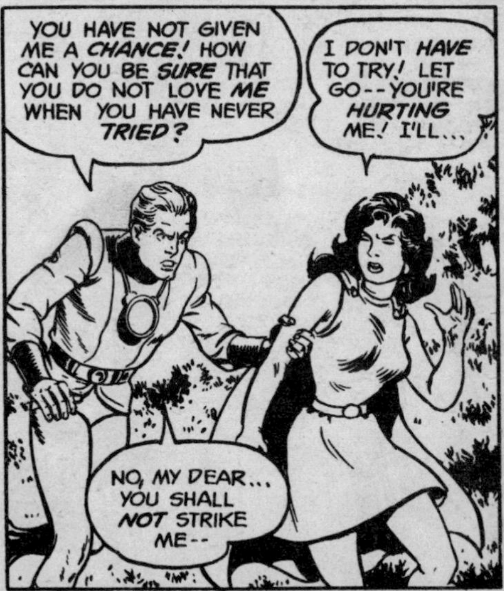
YOU HAVE NOT GIVEN ME A CHANCE! HOW CAN YOU BE SURE THAT YOU DO NOT LOVE ME WHEN YOU HAVE NEVER TRIED?
I DON'T HAVE TO TRY! LET GO--YOU'RE HURTING ME! I'LL...
NO, MY DEAR... YOU SHALL NOT STRIKE ME--

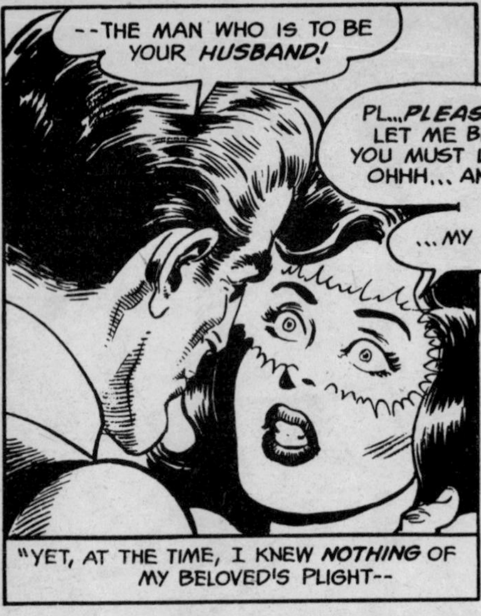
--THE MAN WHO IS TO BE YOUR HUSBAND!
PL...PLEASE... LET ME BE... YOU MUST LET ME... OHHH... ANR-MU...
...MY LOVE!
"YET, AT THE TIME, I KNEW NOTHING OF MY BELOVED'S PLIGHT--

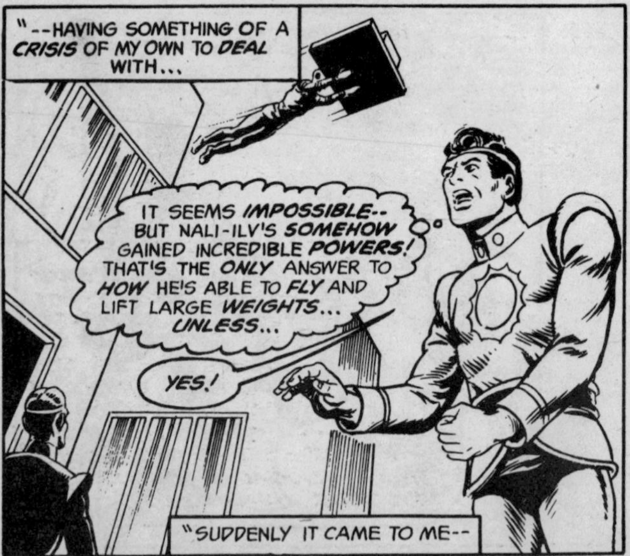
"--HAVING SOMETHING OF A CRISIS OF MY OWN TO DEAL WITH...
IT SEEMS IMPOSSIBLE-- BUT NALI-ILV'S SOMEHOW GAINED INCREDIBLE POWERS! THAT'S THE ONLY ANSWER TO HOW HE'S ABLE TO FLY AND LIFT LARGE WEIGHTS... UNLESS...
YES!
"SUDDENLY IT CAME TO ME--

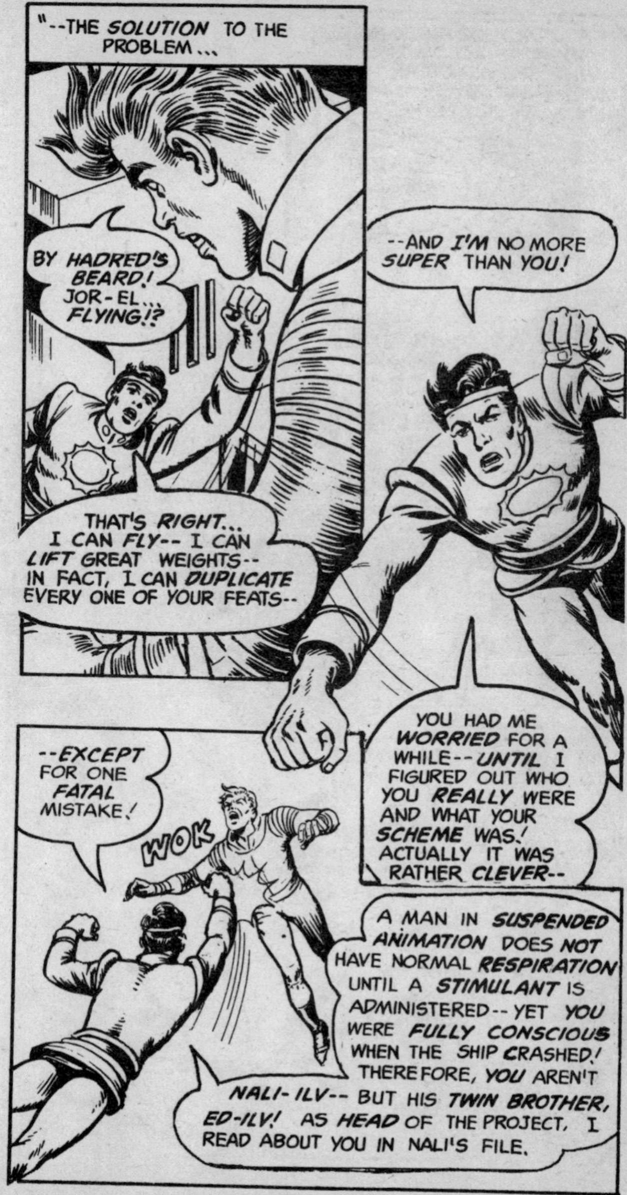
"--THE SOLUTION TO THE PROBLEM...
BY HADRED'S BEARD! JOR-EL... FLYING!?
THAT'S RIGHT... I CAN FLY-- I CAN LIFT GREAT WEIGHTS-- IN FACT, I CAN DUPLICATE EVERY ONE OF YOUR FEATS--
--AND I'M NO MORE SUPER THAN YOU!
YOU HAD ME WORRIED FOR A WHILE--UNTIL I FIGURED OUT WHO YOU REALLY WERE AND WHAT YOUR SCHEME WAS! ACTUALLY IT WAS RATHER CLEVER--
--EXCEPT FOR ONE FATAL MISTAKE!
WOK
A MAN IN SUSPENDED ANIMATION DOES NOT HAVE NORMAL RESPIRATION UNTIL A STIMULANT IS ADMINISTERED--YET YOU WERE FULLY CONSCIOUS WHEN THE SHIP CRASHED! THEREFORE, YOU AREN'T NALI-ILV-- BUT HIS TWIN BROTHER, ED-ILV! AS HEAD OF THE PROJECT, I READ ABOUT YOU IN NALI'S FILE.

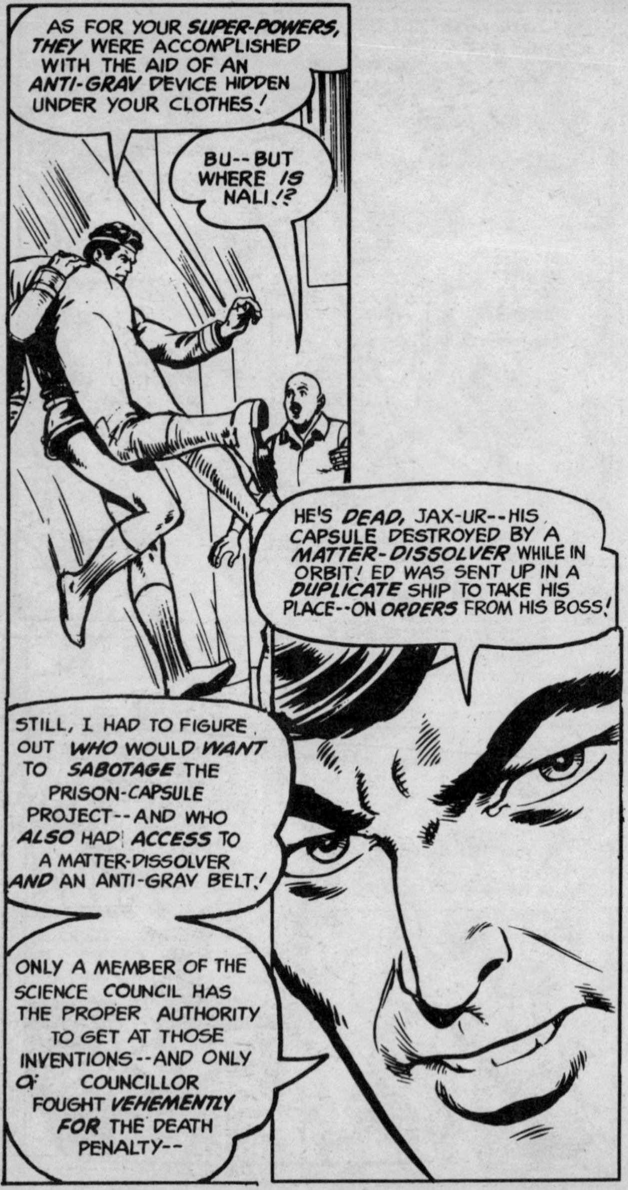
AS FOR YOUR SUPER-POWERS, THEY WERE ACCOMPLISHED WITH THE AID OF AN ANTI-GRAV DEVICE HIDDEN UNDER YOUR CLOTHES!
BU--BUT WHERE IS NALI!?
HE'S DEAD, JAX-UR--HIS CAPSULE DESTROYED BY A MATTER-DISSOLVER WHILE IN ORBIT! ED WAS SENT UP IN A DUPLICATE SHIP TO TAKE HIS PLACE--ON ORDERS FROM HIS BOSS!
STILL, I HAD TO FIGURE OUT WHO WOULD WANT TO SABOTAGE THE PRISON-CAPSULE PROJECT--AND WHO ALSO HAD ACCESS TO A MATTER-DISSOLVER AND AN ANTI-GRAV BELT!
ONLY A MEMBER OF THE SCIENCE COUNCIL HAS THE PROPER AUTHORITY TO GET AT THOSE INVENTIONS--AND ONLY O: COUNCILLOR FOUGHT VEHEMENTLY FOR THE DEATH PENALTY--

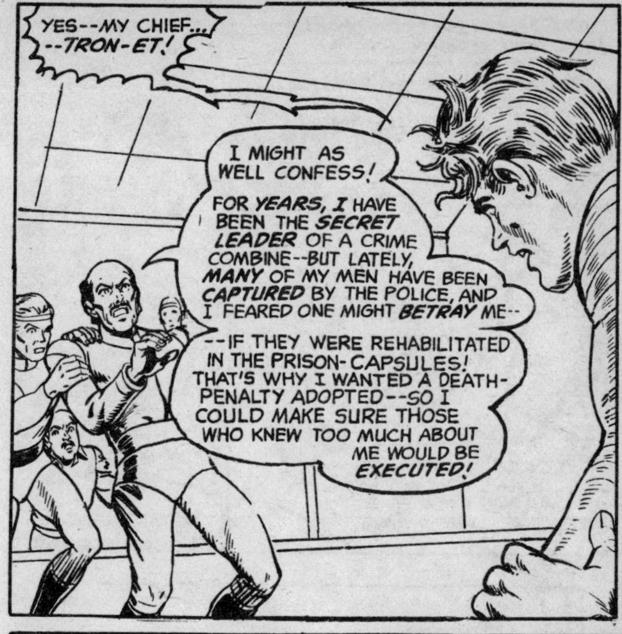
YES--MY CHIEF... --TRON-ET!
I MIGHT AS WELL CONFESS!
FOR YEARS, I HAVE BEEN THE SECRET LEADER OF A CRIME COMBINE--BUT LATELY, MANY OF MY MEN HAVE BEEN CAPTURED BY THE POLICE, AND I FEARED ONE MIGHT BETRAY ME--
--IF THEY WERE REHABILITATED IN THE PRISON-CAPSULES! THAT'S WHY I WANTED A DEATH-PENALTY ADOPTED--SO I COULD MAKE SURE THOSE WHO KNEW TOO MUCH ABOUT ME WOULD BE EXECUTED!

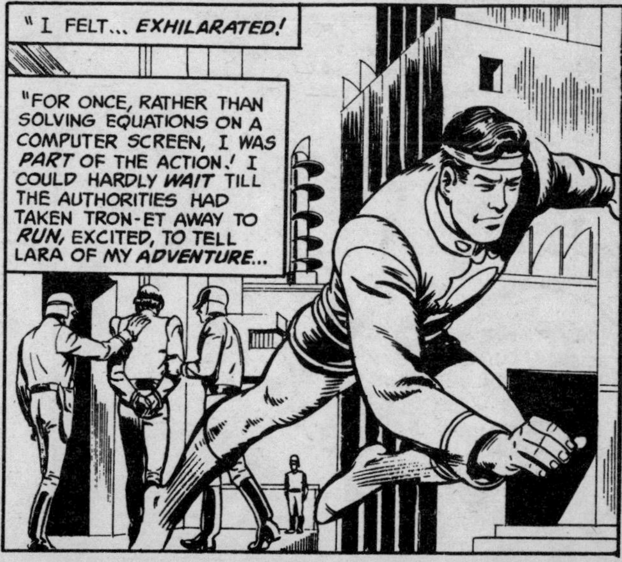
"I FELT... EXHILARATED!
"FOR ONCE, RATHER THAN SOLVING EQUATIONS ON A COMPUTER SCREEN, I WAS PART OF THE ACTION! I COULD HARDLY WAIT TILL THE AUTHORITIES HAD TAKEN TRON-ET AWAY TO RUN, EXCITED, TO TELL LARA OF MY ADVENTURE...

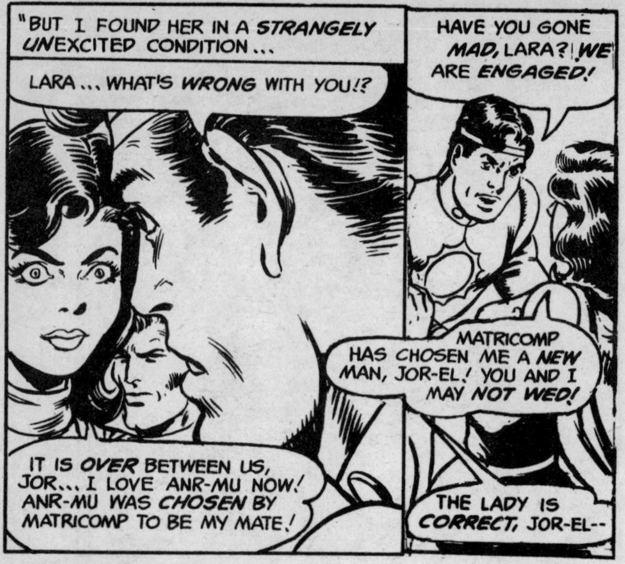
"BUT I FOUND HER IN A STRANGELY UNEXCITED CONDITION...
LARA... WHAT'S WRONG WITH YOU!?
IT IS OVER BETWEEN US, JOR... I LOVE ANR-MU NOW! ANR-MU WAS CHOSEN BY MATRICOMP TO BE MY MATE!
HAVE YOU GONE MAD, LARA?! WE ARE ENGAGED!
MATRICOMP HAS CHOSEN ME A NEW MAN, JOR-EL! YOU AND I MAY NOT WED!
THE LADY IS CORRECT, JOR-EL--

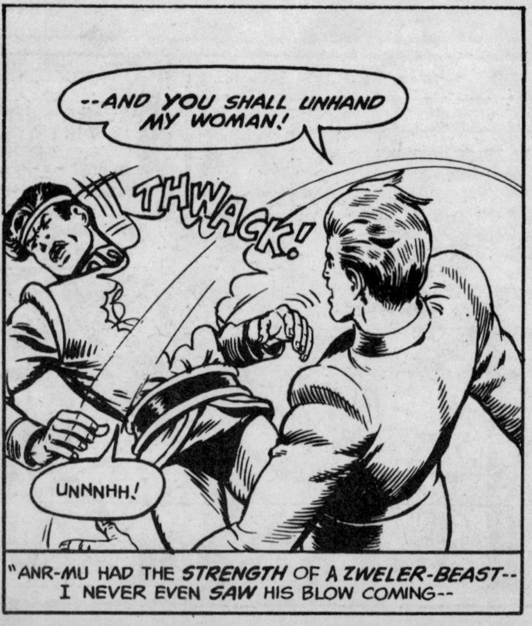
--AND YOU SHALL UNHAND MY WOMAN!
THWACK!
UNNNHH!
"ANR-MU HAD THE STRENGTH OF A ZWELER-BEAST-- I NEVER EVEN SAW HIS BLOW COMING--

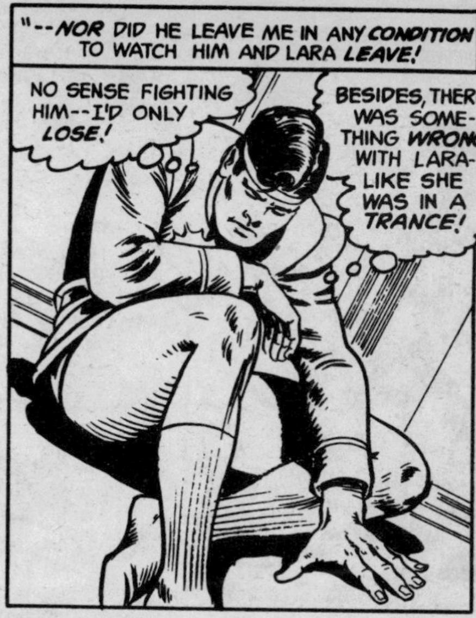
"--NOR DID HE LEAVE ME IN ANY CONDITION TO WATCH HIM AND LARA LEAVE!
NO SENSE FIGHTING HIM--I'D ONLY LOSE!
BESIDES, THERE WAS SOMETHING WRONG WITH LARA--LIKE SHE WAS IN A TRANCE!

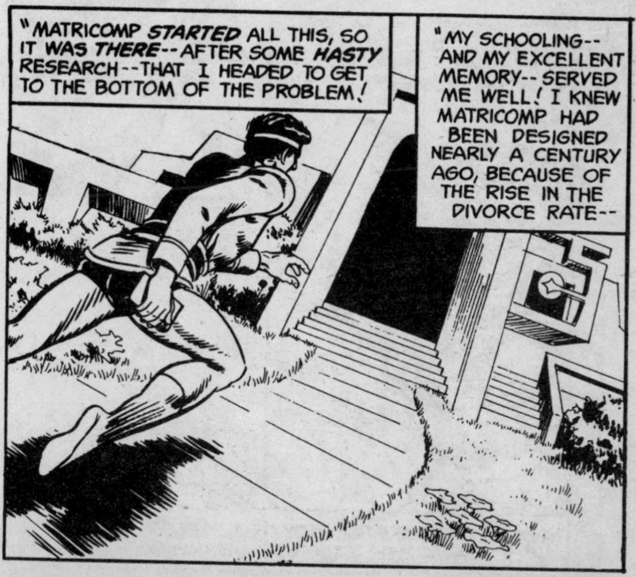
"MATRICOMP STARTED ALL THIS, SO IT WAS THERE--AFTER SOME HASTY RESEARCH--THAT I HEADED TO GET TO THE BOTTOM OF THE PROBLEM!
"MY SCHOOLING--AND MY EXCELLENT MEMORY--SERVED ME WELL! I KNEW MATRICOMP HAD BEEN DESIGNED NEARLY A CENTURY AGO, BECAUSE OF THE RISE IN THE DIVORCE RATE--

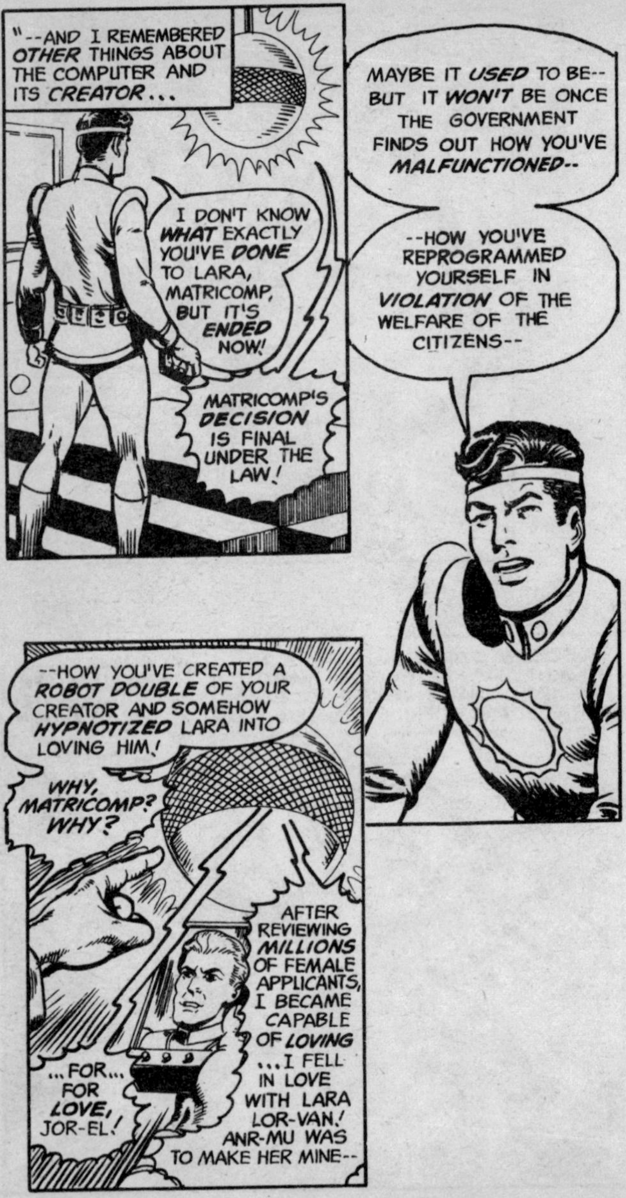
"--AND I REMEMBERED OTHER THINGS ABOUT THE COMPUTER AND ITS CREATOR...
I DON'T KNOW WHAT EXACTLY YOU'VE DONE TO LARA, MATRICOMP, BUT IT'S ENDED NOW!
MATRICOMP'S DECISION IS FINAL UNDER THE LAW!
MAYBE IT USED TO BE-- BUT IT WON'T BE ONCE THE GOVERNMENT FINDS OUT HOW YOU'VE MALFUNCTIONED--
--HOW YOU'VE REPROGRAMMED YOURSELF IN VIOLATION OF THE WELFARE OF THE CITIZENS--
--HOW YOU'VE CREATED A ROBOT DOUBLE OF YOUR CREATOR AND SOMEHOW HYPNOTIZED LARA INTO LOVING HIM!
WHY, MATRICOMP? WHY?
AFTER REVIEWING MILLIONS OF FEMALE APPLICANTS, I BECAME CAPABLE OF LOVING ...I FELL IN LOVE WITH LARA LOR-VAN! ANR-MU WAS TO MAKE HER MINE--
...FOR... FOR LOVE, JOR-EL!

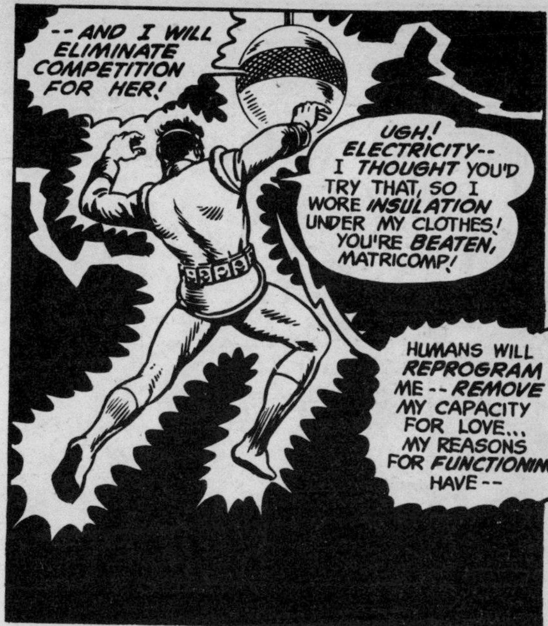
-- AND I WILL ELIMINATE COMPETITION FOR HER!
UGH! ELECTRICITY-- I THOUGHT YOU'D TRY THAT, SO I WORE INSULATION UNDER MY CLOTHES! YOU'RE BEATEN, MATRICOMP!
HUMANS WILL REPROGRAM ME -- REMOVE MY CAPACITY FOR LOVE... MY REASONS FOR FUNCTIONING HAVE --
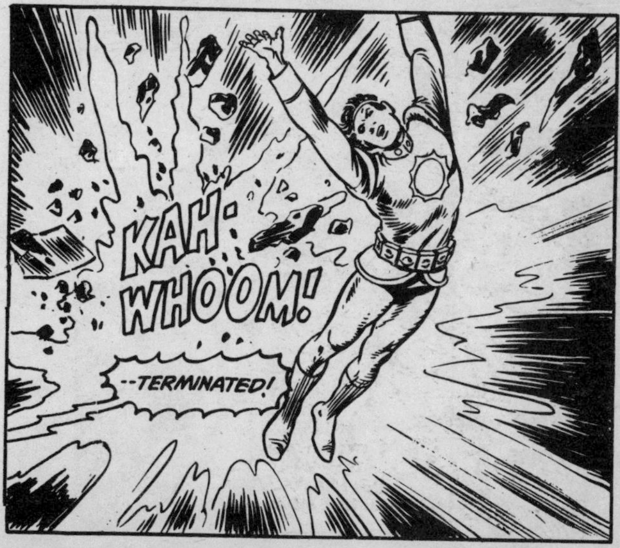
KAH-WHOOM!
--TERMINATED!

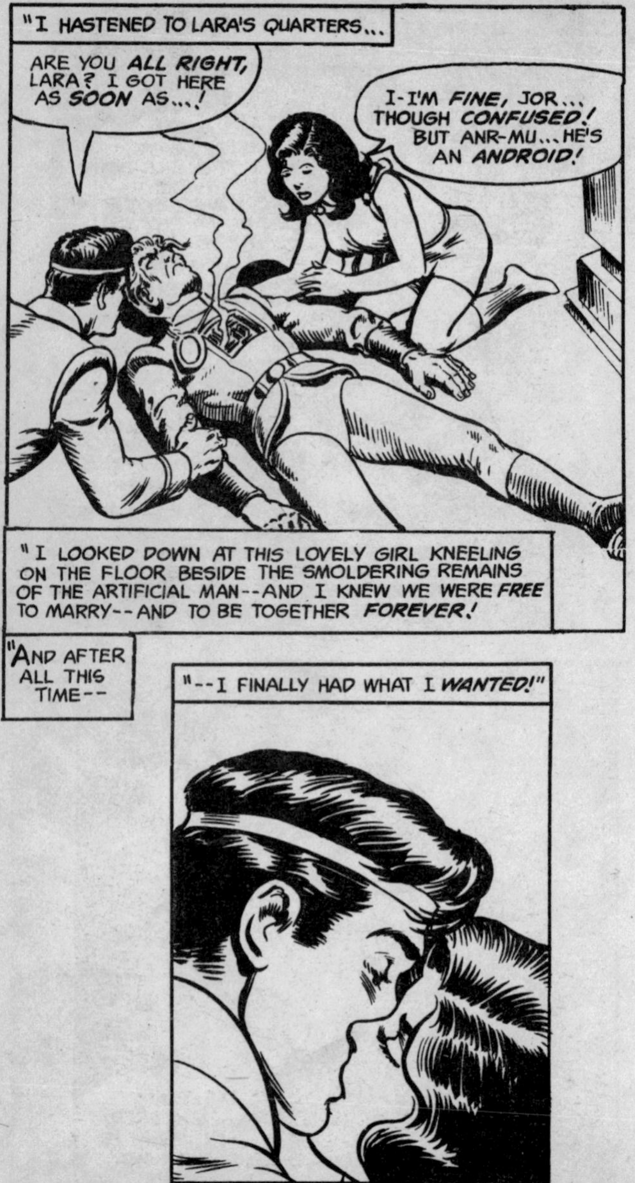
"I HASTENED TO LARA'S QUARTERS...
ARE YOU ALL RIGHT, LARA? I GOT HERE AS SOON AS...!
I-I'M FINE, JOR... THOUGH CONFUSED! BUT ANR-MU... HE'S AN ANDROID!
"I LOOKED DOWN AT THIS LOVELY GIRL KNEELING ON THE FLOOR BESIDE THE SMOLDERING REMAINS OF THE ARTIFICIAL MAN--AND I KNEW WE WERE FREE TO MARRY--AND TO BE TOGETHER FOREVER!
"AND AFTER ALL THIS TIME--
"--I FINALLY HAD WHAT I WANTED!"

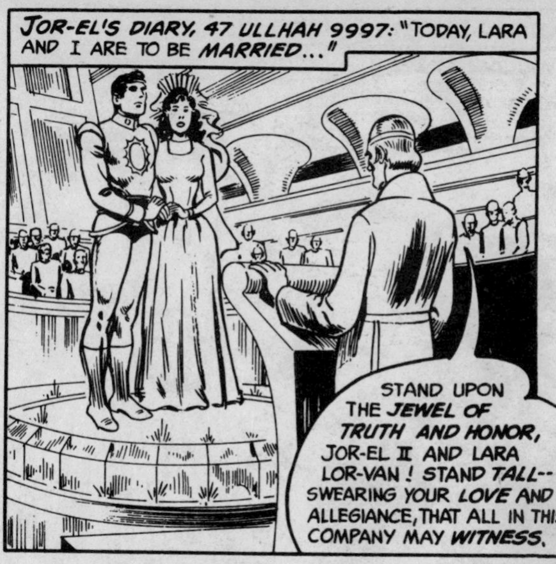
JOR-EL'S DIARY, 47 ULLHAH 9997: "TODAY, LARA AND I ARE TO BE MARRIED..."
STAND UPON THE JEWEL OF TRUTH AND HONOR, JOR-EL II AND LARA LOR-VAN! STAND TALL--SWEARING YOUR LOVE AND ALLEGIANCE, THAT ALL IN THIS COMPANY MAY WITNESS.

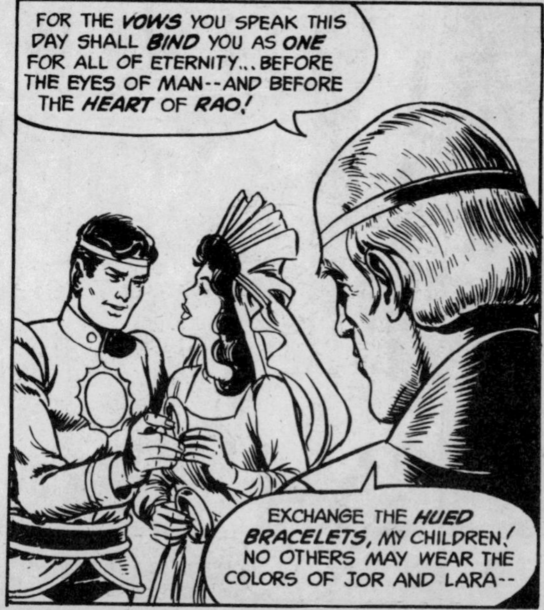
FOR THE VOWS YOU SPEAK THIS DAY SHALL BIND YOU AS ONE FOR ALL OF ETERNITY... BEFORE THE EYES OF MAN--AND BEFORE THE HEART OF RAO!
EXCHANGE THE HUED BRACELETS, MY CHILDREN! NO OTHERS MAY WEAR THE COLORS OF JOR AND LARA--

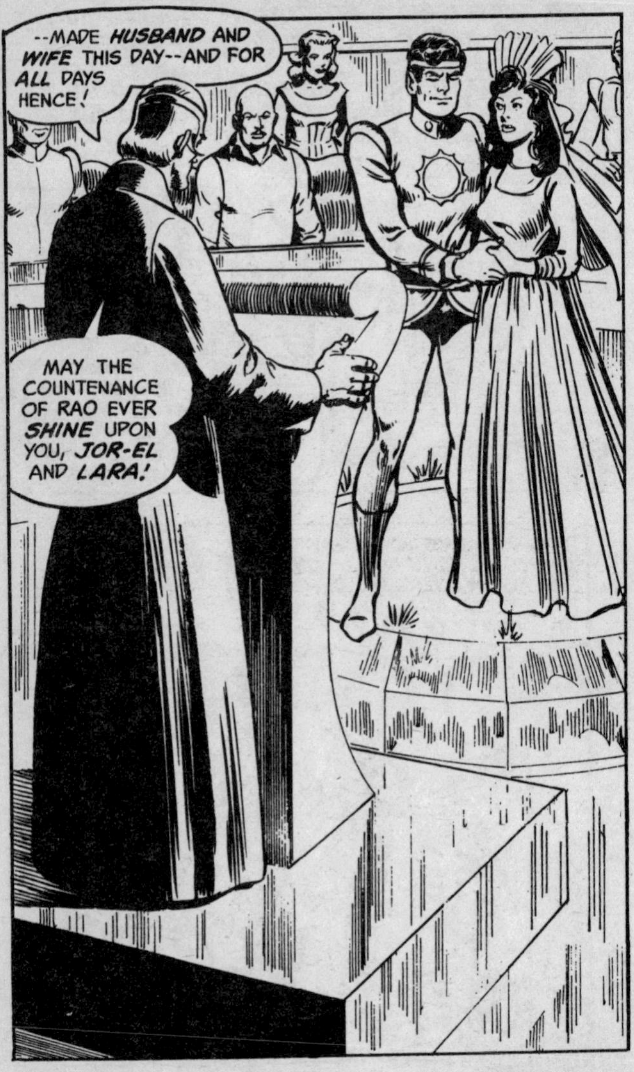
--MADE HUSBAND AND WIFE THIS DAY--AND FOR ALL DAYS HENCE!
MAY THE COUNTENANCE OF RAO EVER SHINE UPON YOU, JOR-EL AND LARA!

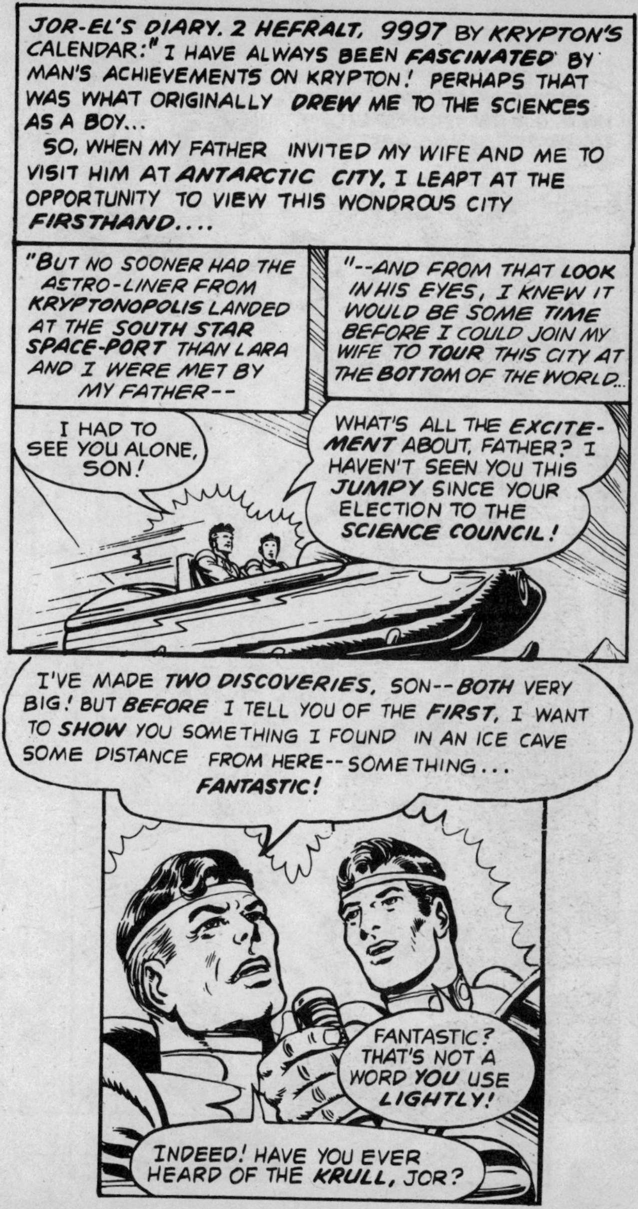
JOR-EL'S DIARY. 2 HEFRALT, 9997 BY KRYPTON'S CALENDAR:" I HAVE ALWAYS BEEN FASCINATED BY MAN'S ACHIEVEMENTS ON KRYPTON! PERHAPS THAT WAS WHAT ORIGINALLY DREW ME TO THE SCIENCES AS A BOY...
SO, WHEN MY FATHER INVITED MY WIFE AND ME TO VISIT HIM AT ANTARCTIC CITY, I LEAPT AT THE OPPORTUNITY TO VIEW THIS WONDROUS CITY FIRSTHAND....
"BUT NO SOONER HAD THE ASTRO-LINER FROM KRYPTONOPOLIS LANDED AT THE SOUTH STAR SPACE-PORT THAN LARA AND I WERE MET BY MY FATHER--
"--AND FROM THAT LOOK IN HIS EYES, I KNEW IT WOULD BE SOME TIME BEFORE I COULD JOIN MY WIFE TO TOUR THIS CITY AT THE BOTTOM OF THE WORLD...
I HAD TO SEE YOU ALONE, SON!
WHAT'S ALL THE EXCITEMENT ABOUT, FATHER? I HAVEN'T SEEN YOU THIS JUMPY SINCE YOUR ELECTION TO THE SCIENCE COUNCIL!
I'VE MADE TWO DISCOVERIES, SON--BOTH VERY BIG! BUT BEFORE I TELL YOU OF THE FIRST, I WANT TO SHOW YOU SOMETHING I FOUND IN AN ICE CAVE SOME DISTANCE FROM HERE--SOMETHING... FANTASTIC!
FANTASTIC? THAT'S NOT A WORD YOU USE LIGHTLY!
INDEED! HAVE YOU EVER HEARD OF THE KRULL, JOR?

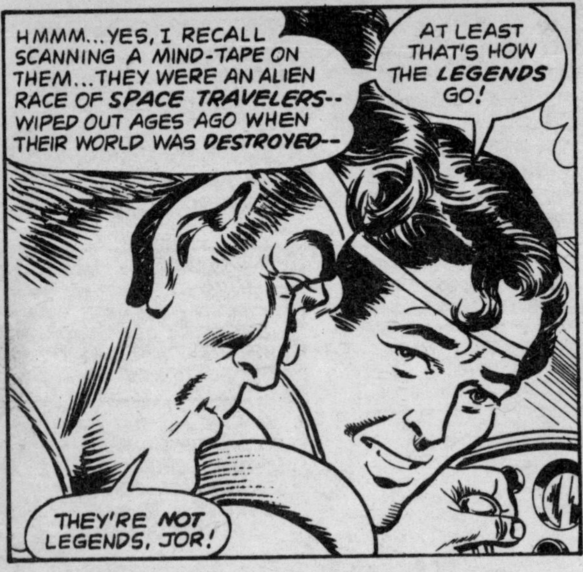
HMMM...YES, I RECALL SCANNING A MIND-TAPE ON THEM...THEY WERE AN ALIEN RACE OF SPACE TRAVELERS--WIPED OUT AGES AGO WHEN THEIR WORLD WAS DESTROYED--
AT LEAST THAT'S HOW THE LEGENDS GO!
THEY'RE NOT LEGENDS, JOR!

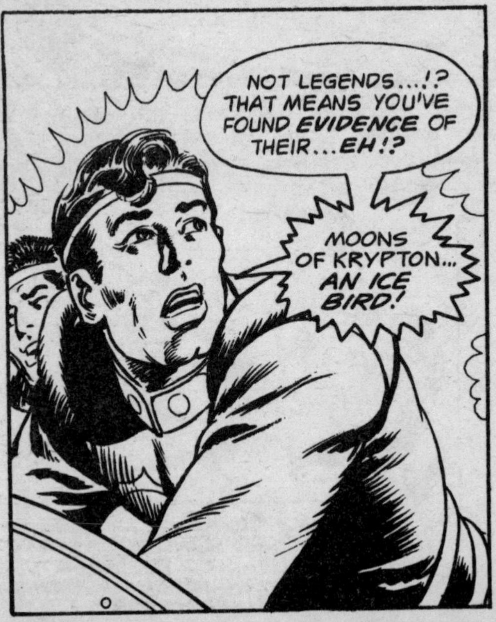
NOT LEGENDS...!? THAT MEANS YOU'VE FOUND EVIDENCE OF THEIR...EH!?
MOONS OF KRYPTON... AN ICE BIRD!

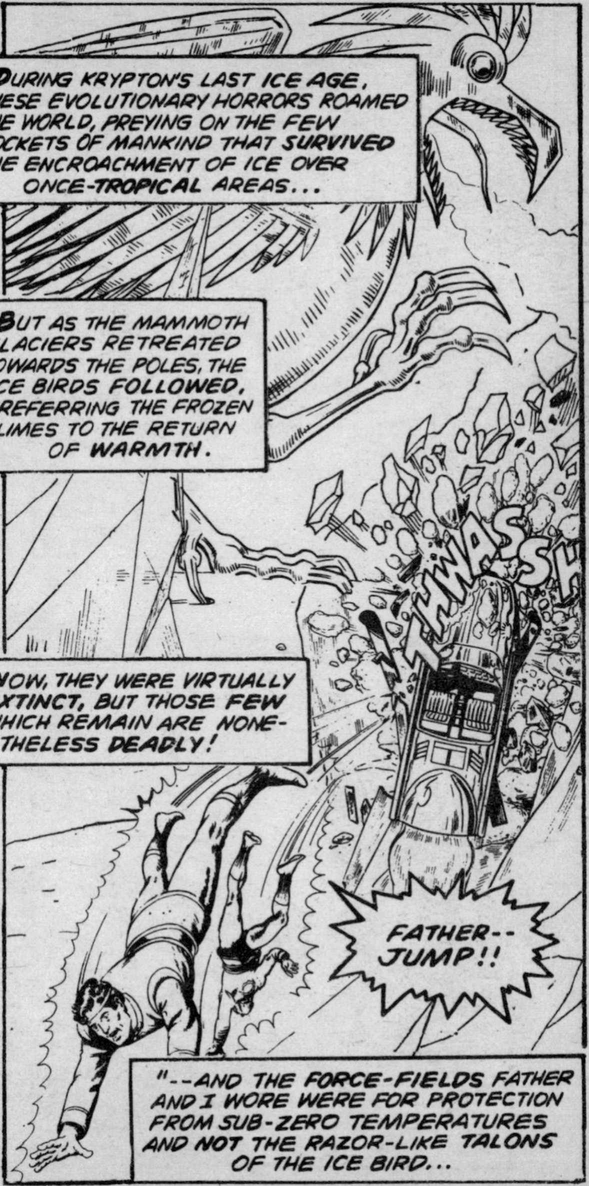
"DURING KRYPTON'S LAST ICE AGE, THESE EVOLUTIONARY HORRORS ROAMED THE WORLD, PREYING ON THE FEW POCKETS OF MANKIND THAT SURVIVED THE ENCROACHMENT OF ICE OVER ONCE-TROPICAL AREAS...
"BUT AS THE MAMMOTH GLACIERS RETREATED TOWARDS THE POLES, THE ICE BIRDS FOLLOWED, PREFERRING THE FROZEN CLIMES TO THE RETURN OF WARMTH.
THWASSH
"NOW, THEY WERE VIRTUALLY EXTINCT, BUT THOSE FEW WHICH REMAIN ARE NONE-THELESS DEADLY!
FATHER--JUMP!!
"--AND THE FORCE-FIELDS FATHER AND I WORE WERE FOR PROTECTION FROM SUB-ZERO TEMPERATURES AND NOT THE RAZOR-LIKE TALONS OF THE ICE BIRD...

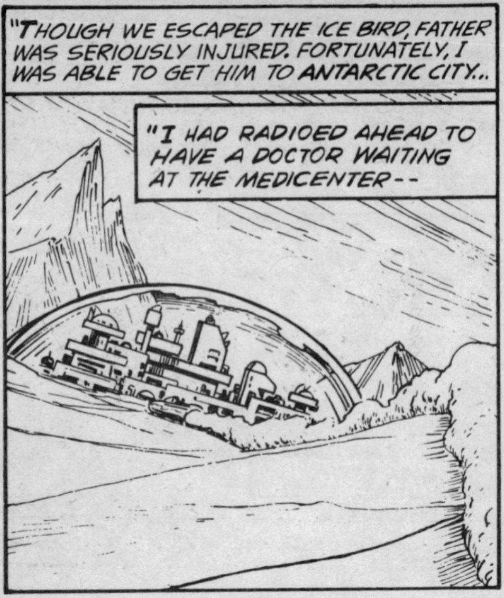
"THOUGH WE ESCAPED THE ICE BIRD, FATHER WAS SERIOUSLY INJURED. FORTUNATELY, I WAS ABLE TO GET HIM TO ANTARCTIC CITY...
"I HAD RADIOED AHEAD TO HAVE A DOCTOR WAITING AT THE MEDICENTER--

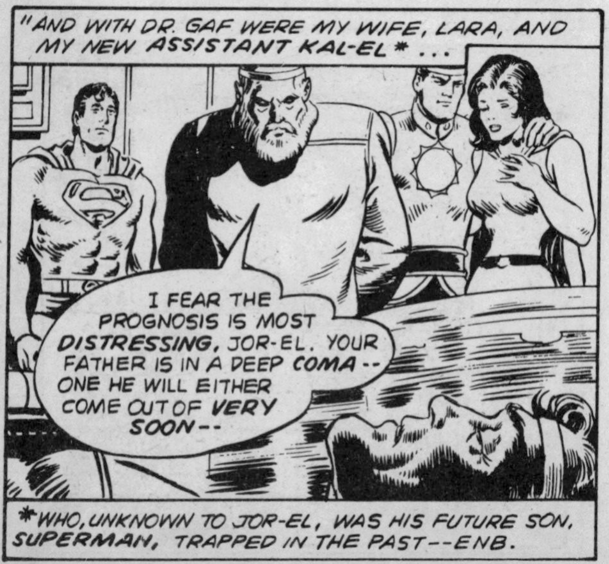
"AND WITH DR. GAF WERE MY WIFE, LARA, AND MY NEW ASSISTANT KAL-EL* ...
I FEAR THE PROGNOSIS IS MOST DISTRESSING, JOR-EL. YOUR FATHER IS IN A DEEP COMA -- ONE HE WILL EITHER COME OUT OF VERY SOON--
*WHO, UNKNOWN TO JOR-EL, WAS HIS FUTURE SON, SUPERMAN, TRAPPED IN THE PAST--ENB.

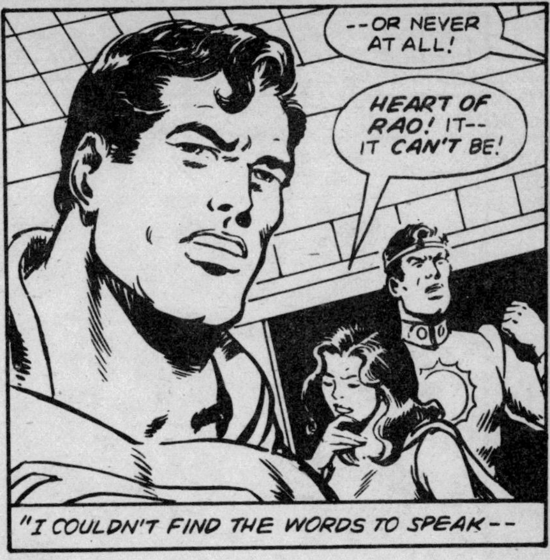
--OR NEVER AT ALL!
HEART OF RAO! IT-- IT CAN'T BE!
"I COULDN'T FIND THE WORDS TO SPEAK--

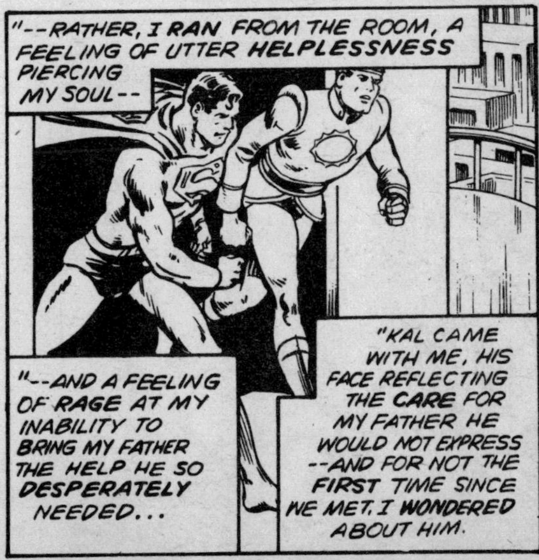
"--RATHER, I RAN FROM THE ROOM, A FEELING OF UTTER HELPLESSNESS PIERCING MY SOUL--
"--AND A FEELING OF RAGE AT MY INABILITY TO BRING MY FATHER THE HELP HE SO DESPERATELY NEEDED...
"KAL CAME WITH ME, HIS FACE REFLECTING THE CARE FOR MY FATHER HE WOULD NOT EXPRESS --AND FOR NOT THE FIRST TIME SINCE WE MET, I WONDERED ABOUT HIM.

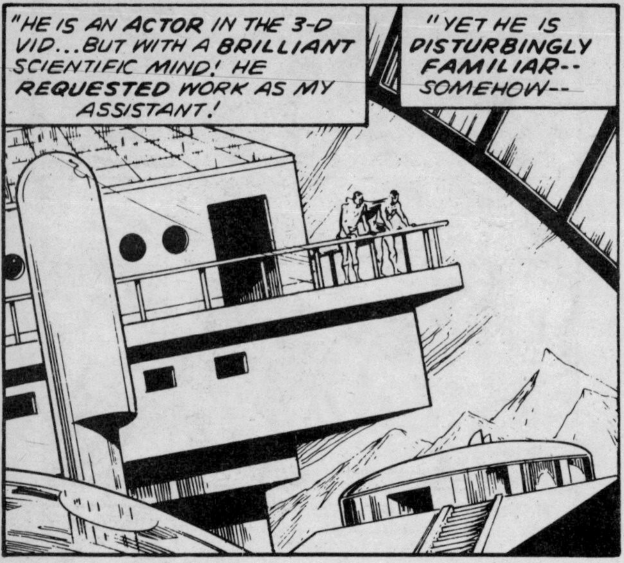
"HE IS AN ACTOR IN THE 3-D VID...BUT WITH A BRILLIANT SCIENTIFIC MIND! HE REQUESTED WORK AS MY ASSISTANT!
"YET HE IS DISTURBINGLY FAMILIAR-- SOMEHOW--

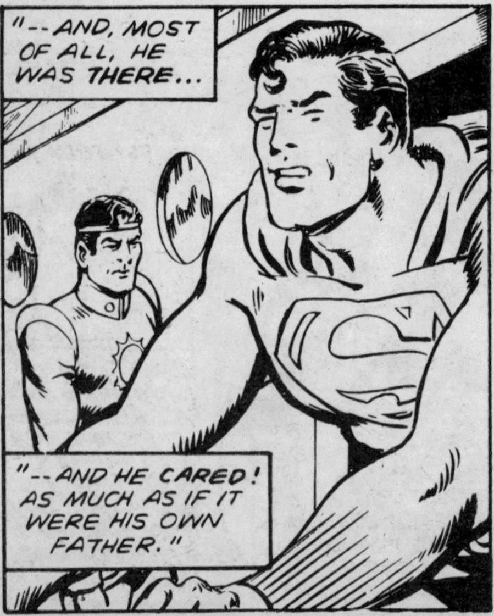
"--AND, MOST OF ALL, HE WAS THERE...
"--AND HE CARED! AS MUCH AS IF IT WERE HIS OWN FATHER."

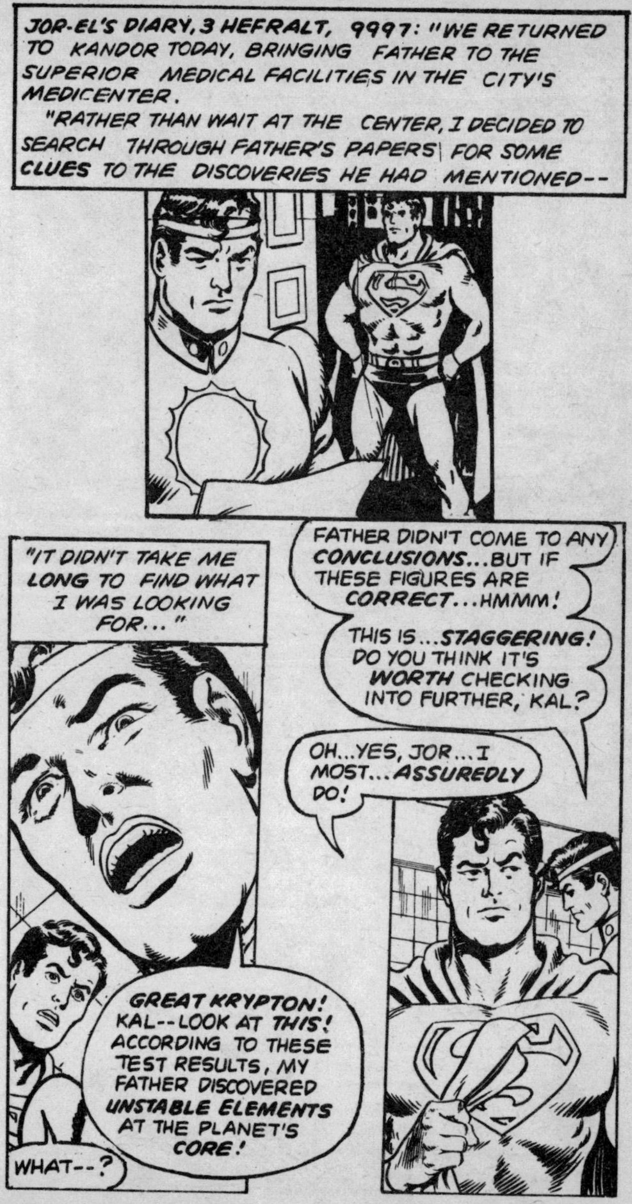
JOR-EL'S DIARY, 3 HEFRALT, 9997: "WE RETURNED TO KANDOR TODAY, BRINGING FATHER TO THE SUPERIOR MEDICAL FACILITIES IN THE CITY'S MEDICENTER.
"RATHER THAN WAIT AT THE CENTER, I DECIDED TO SEARCH THROUGH FATHER'S PAPERS FOR SOME CLUES TO THE DISCOVERIES HE HAD MENTIONED--
"IT DIDN'T TAKE ME LONG TO FIND WHAT I WAS LOOKING FOR..."
GREAT KRYPTON! KAL--LOOK AT THIS! ACCORDING TO THESE TEST RESULTS, MY FATHER DISCOVERED UNSTABLE ELEMENTS AT THE PLANET'S CORE!
WHAT--?
FATHER DIDN'T COME TO ANY CONCLUSIONS... BUT IF THESE FIGURES ARE CORRECT... HMMM!
THIS IS... STAGGERING! DO YOU THINK IT'S WORTH CHECKING INTO FURTHER, KAL?
OH... YES, JOR... I MOST... ASSUREDLY DO!

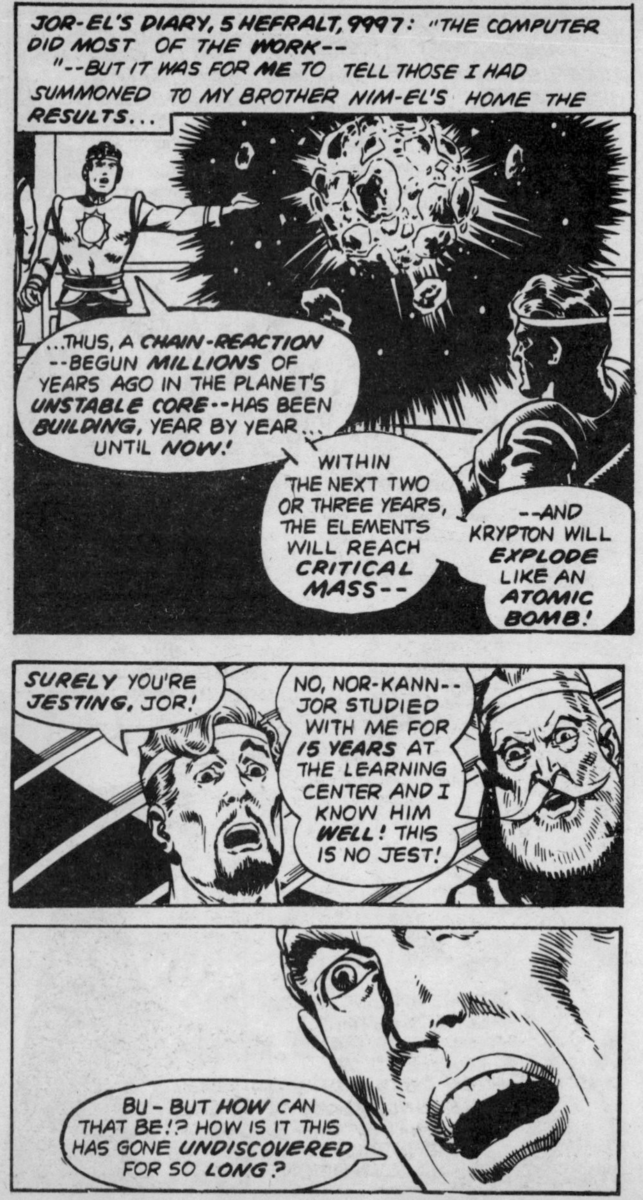

JOR-EL'S DIARY, 5 HEFRALT, 9997: "THE COMPUTER DID MOST OF THE WORK--
"--BUT IT WAS FOR ME TO TELL THOSE I HAD SUMMONED TO MY BROTHER NIM-EL'S HOME THE RESULTS...
...THUS, A CHAIN-REACTION --BEGUN MILLIONS OF YEARS AGO IN THE PLANET'S UNSTABLE CORE--HAS BEEN BUILDING, YEAR BY YEAR... UNTIL NOW!
WITHIN THE NEXT TWO OR THREE YEARS, THE ELEMENTS WILL REACH CRITICAL MASS--
--AND KRYPTON WILL EXPLODE LIKE AN ATOMIC BOMB!
SURELY YOU'RE JESTING, JOR!
NO, NOR-KANN--JOR STUDIED WITH ME FOR 15 YEARS AT THE LEARNING CENTER AND I KNOW HIM WELL! THIS IS NO JEST!
BU-BUT HOW CAN THAT BE!? HOW IS IT THIS HAS GONE UNDISCOVERED FOR SO LONG?

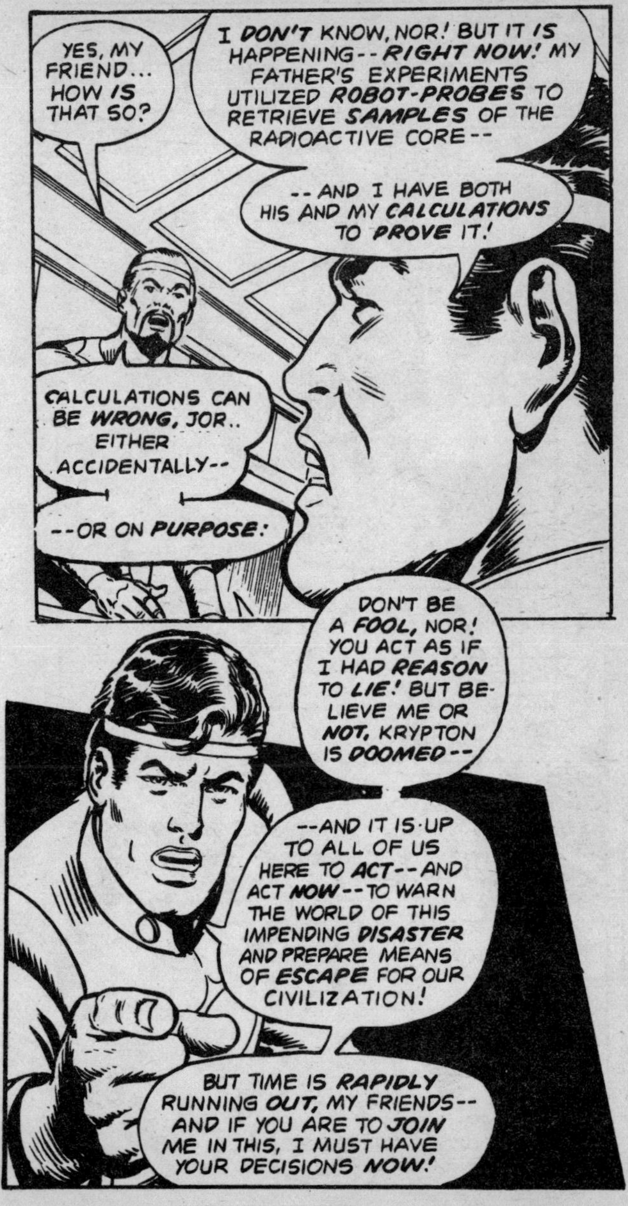
YES, MY FRIEND... HOW IS THAT SO?
I DON'T KNOW, NOR! BUT IT IS HAPPENING--RIGHT NOW! MY FATHER'S EXPERIMENTS UTILIZED ROBOT-PROBES TO RETRIEVE SAMPLES OF THE RADIOACTIVE CORE--
--AND I HAVE BOTH HIS AND MY CALCULATIONS TO PROVE IT!
CALCULATIONS CAN BE WRONG, JOR.. EITHER ACCIDENTALLY--
--OR ON PURPOSE!
DON'T BE A FOOL, NOR! YOU ACT AS IF I HAD REASON TO LIE! BUT BE-LIEVE ME OR NOT, KRYPTON IS DOOMED--
--AND IT IS UP TO ALL OF US HERE TO ACT--AND ACT NOW--TO WARN THE WORLD OF THIS IMPENDING DISASTER AND PREPARE MEANS OF ESCAPE FOR OUR CIVILIZATION!
BUT TIME IS RAPIDLY RUNNING OUT, MY FRIENDS--AND IF YOU ARE TO JOIN ME IN THIS, I MUST HAVE YOUR DECISIONS NOW!

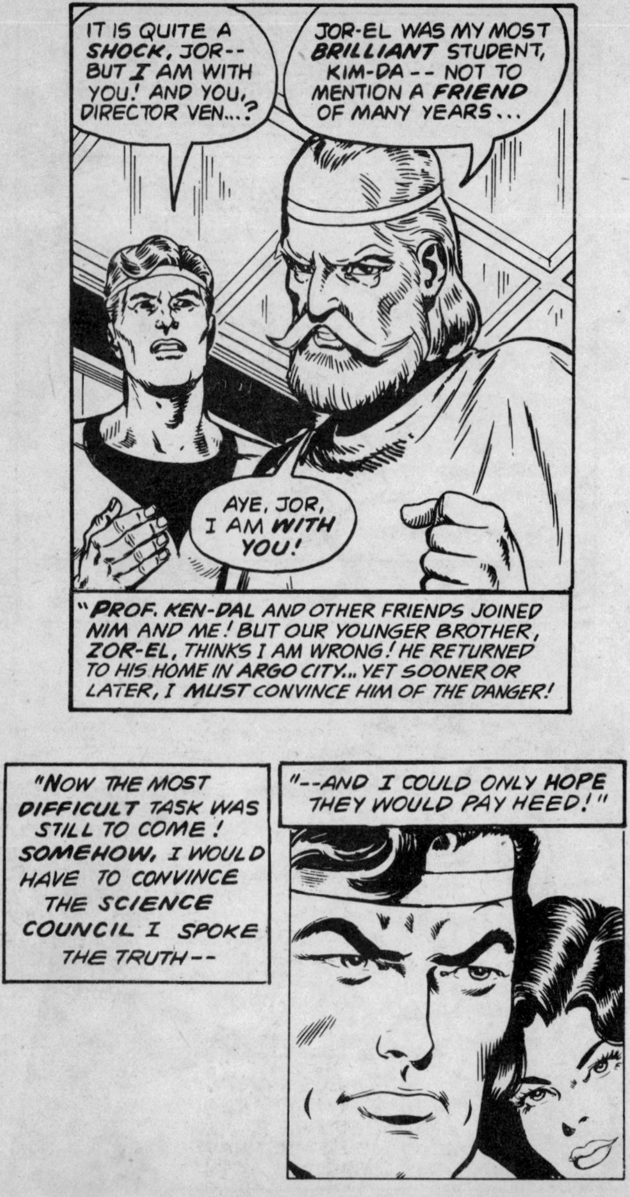
IT IS QUITE A SHOCK, JOR-- BUT I AM WITH YOU! AND YOU, DIRECTOR VEN...?
JOR-EL WAS MY MOST BRILLIANT STUDENT, KIM-DA -- NOT TO MENTION A FRIEND OF MANY YEARS...
AYE, JOR, I AM WITH YOU!
"PROF. KEN-DAL AND OTHER FRIENDS JOINED NIM AND ME! BUT OUR YOUNGER BROTHER, ZOR-EL, THINKS I AM WRONG! HE RETURNED TO HIS HOME IN ARGO CITY... YET SOONER OR LATER, I MUST CONVINCE HIM OF THE DANGER!
"NOW THE MOST DIFFICULT TASK WAS STILL TO COME! SOMEHOW, I WOULD HAVE TO CONVINCE THE SCIENCE COUNCIL I SPOKE THE TRUTH--
"--AND I COULD ONLY HOPE THEY WOULD PAY HEED!"

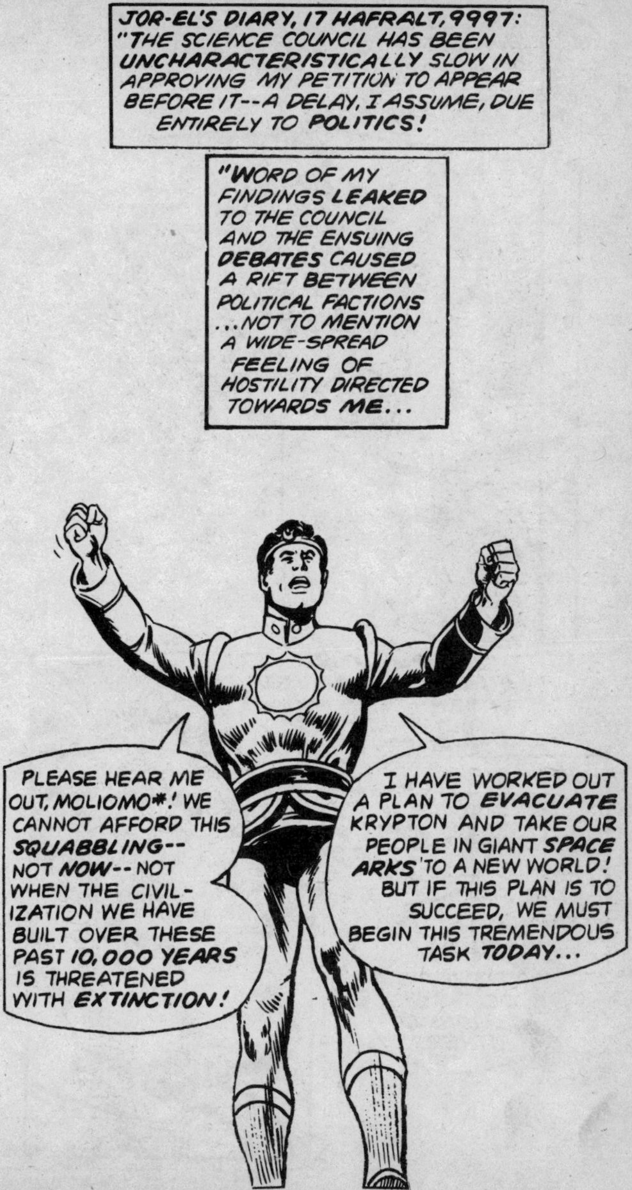
JOR-EL'S DIARY, 17 HAFRALT, 9997: "THE SCIENCE COUNCIL HAS BEEN UNCHARACTERISTICALLY SLOW IN APPROVING MY PETITION TO APPEAR BEFORE IT--A DELAY, I ASSUME, DUE ENTIRELY TO POLITICS!
"WORD OF MY FINDINGS LEAKED TO THE COUNCIL AND THE ENSUING DEBATES CAUSED A RIFT BETWEEN POLITICAL FACTIONS ...NOT TO MENTION A WIDE-SPREAD FEELING OF HOSTILITY DIRECTED TOWARDS ME...
PLEASE HEAR ME OUT, MOLIOMO*! WE CANNOT AFFORD THIS SQUABBLING-- NOT NOW-- NOT WHEN THE CIVILIZATION WE HAVE BUILT OVER THESE PAST 10,000 YEARS IS THREATENED WITH EXTINCTION!
I HAVE WORKED OUT A PLAN TO EVACUATE KRYPTON AND TAKE OUR PEOPLE IN GIANT SPACE ARKS TO A NEW WORLD! BUT IF THIS PLAN IS TO SUCCEED, WE MUST BEGIN THIS TREMENDOUS TASK TODAY...

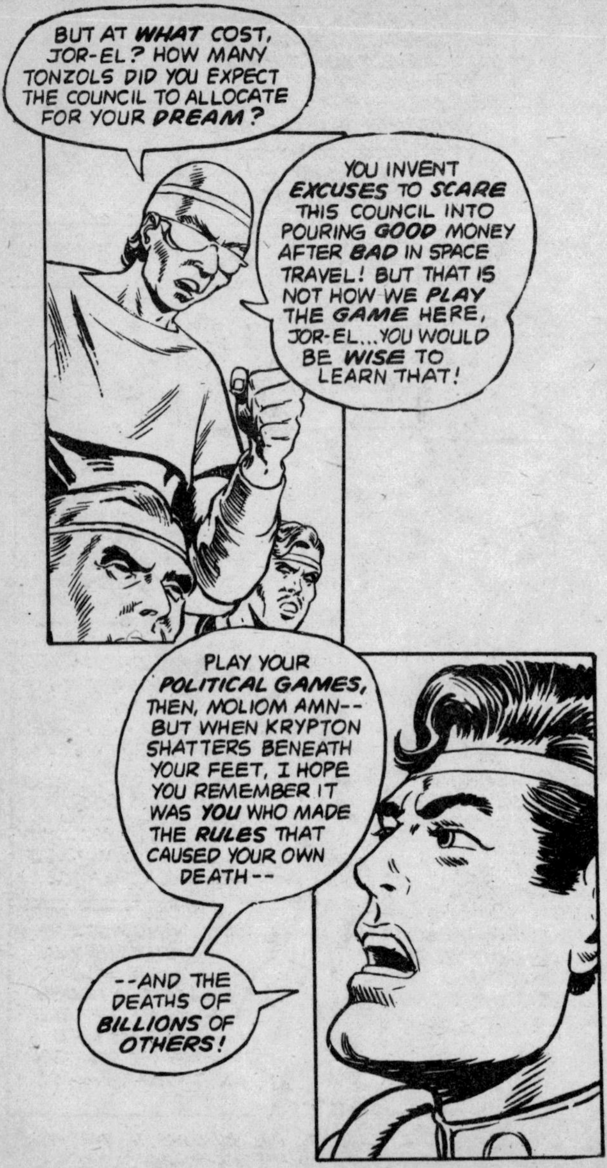
BUT AT WHAT COST, JOR-EL? HOW MANY TONZOLS DID YOU EXPECT THE COUNCIL TO ALLOCATE FOR YOUR DREAM?
YOU INVENT EXCUSES TO SCARE THIS COUNCIL INTO POURING GOOD MONEY AFTER BAD IN SPACE TRAVEL! BUT THAT IS NOT HOW WE PLAY THE GAME HERE, JOR-EL... YOU WOULD BE WISE TO LEARN THAT!
PLAY YOUR POLITICAL GAMES, THEN, MOLIOM AMN-- BUT WHEN KRYPTON SHATTERS BENEATH YOUR FEET, I HOPE YOU REMEMBER IT WAS YOU WHO MADE THE RULES THAT CAUSED YOUR OWN DEATH--
--AND THE DEATHS OF BILLIONS OF OTHERS!

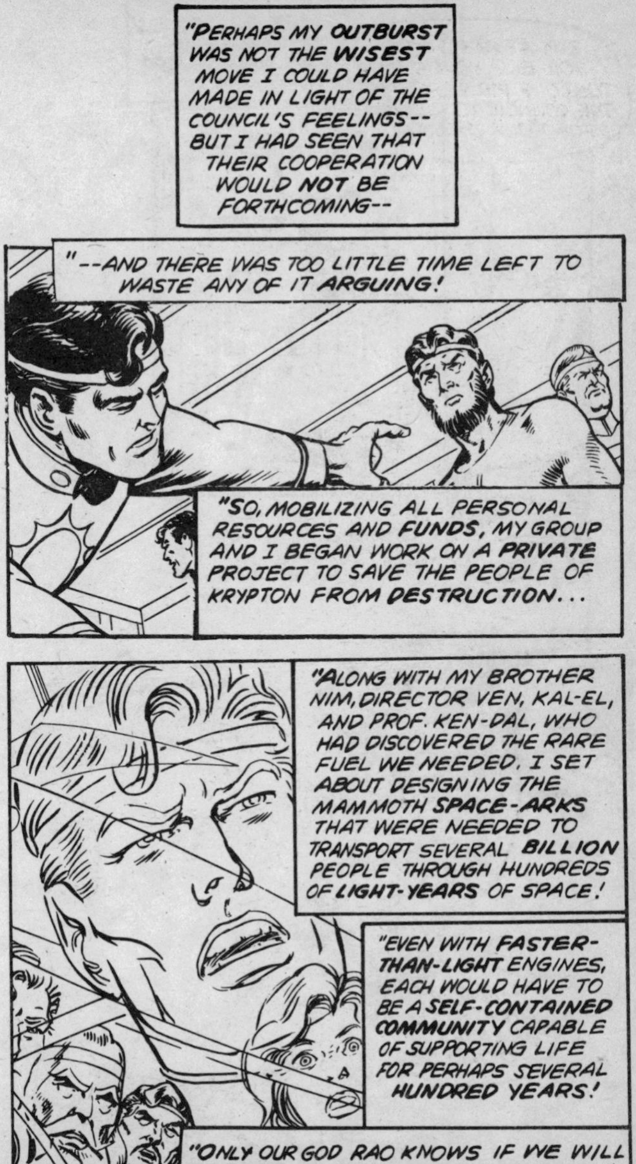
"PERHAPS MY OUTBURST WAS NOT THE WISEST MOVE I COULD HAVE MADE IN LIGHT OF THE COUNCIL'S FEELINGS-- BUT I HAD SEEN THAT THEIR COOPERATION WOULD NOT BE FORTHCOMING--
"--AND THERE WAS TOO LITTLE TIME LEFT TO WASTE ANY OF IT ARGUING!
"SO, MOBILIZING ALL PERSONAL RESOURCES AND FUNDS, MY GROUP AND I BEGAN WORK ON A PRIVATE PROJECT TO SAVE THE PEOPLE OF KRYPTON FROM DESTRUCTION...
"ALONG WITH MY BROTHER NIM, DIRECTOR VEN, KAL-EL, AND PROF. KEN-DAL, WHO HAD DISCOVERED THE RARE FUEL WE NEEDED. I SET ABOUT DESIGNING THE MAMMOTH SPACE-ARKS THAT WERE NEEDED TO TRANSPORT SEVERAL BILLION PEOPLE THROUGH HUNDREDS OF LIGHT-YEARS OF SPACE!
"EVEN WITH FASTER-THAN-LIGHT ENGINES, EACH WOULD HAVE TO BE A SELF-CONTAINED COMMUNITY CAPABLE OF SUPPORTING LIFE FOR PERHAPS SEVERAL HUNDRED YEARS!
"ONLY OUR GOD RAO KNOWS IF WE WILL BE READY WHEN THE TIME COMES!"

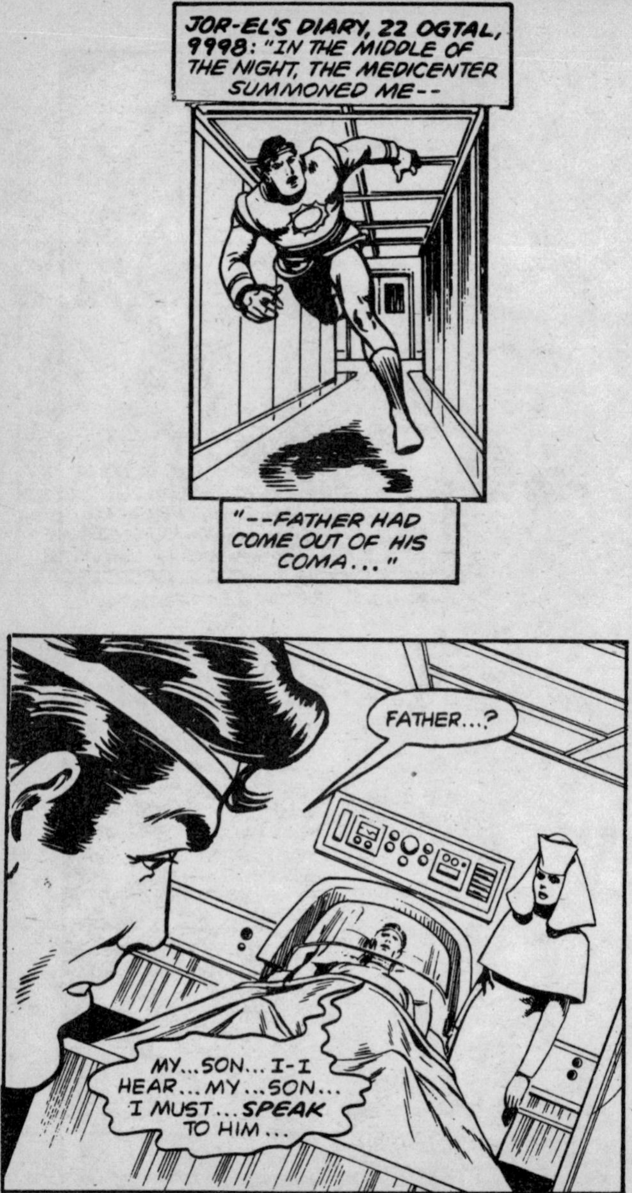
JOR-EL'S DIARY, 22 OGTAL, 9998: "IN THE MIDDLE OF THE NIGHT, THE MEDICENTER SUMMONED ME--
"--FATHER HAD COME OUT OF HIS COMA..."
FATHER...?
MY...SON... I-I HEAR... MY...SON... I MUST... SPEAK TO HIM...

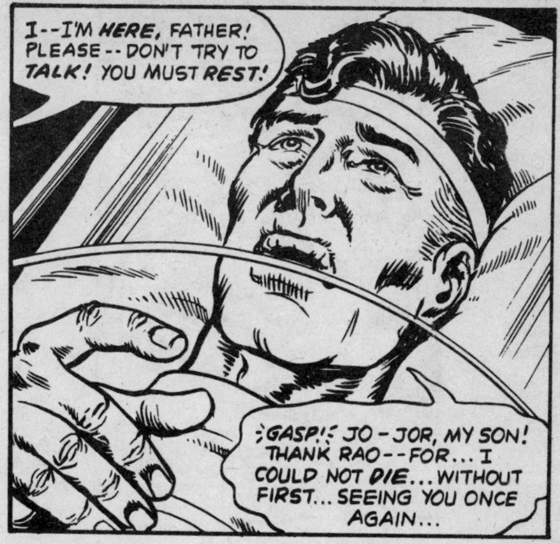
I--I'M HERE, FATHER! PLEASE--DON'T TRY TO TALK! YOU MUST REST!
:GASP!: JO-JOR, MY SON! THANK RAO--FOR... I COULD NOT DIE... WITHOUT FIRST... SEEING YOU ONCE AGAIN...

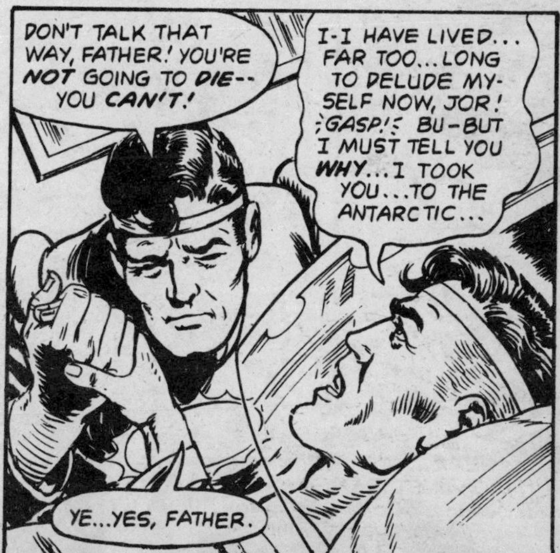
DON'T TALK THAT WAY, FATHER! YOU'RE NOT GOING TO DIE--YOU CAN'T!
I-I HAVE LIVED... FAR TOO... LONG TO DELUDE MY-SELF NOW, JOR! :GASP!: BU-BUT I MUST TELL YOU WHY... I TOOK YOU... TO THE ANTARCTIC...
YE...YES, FATHER.

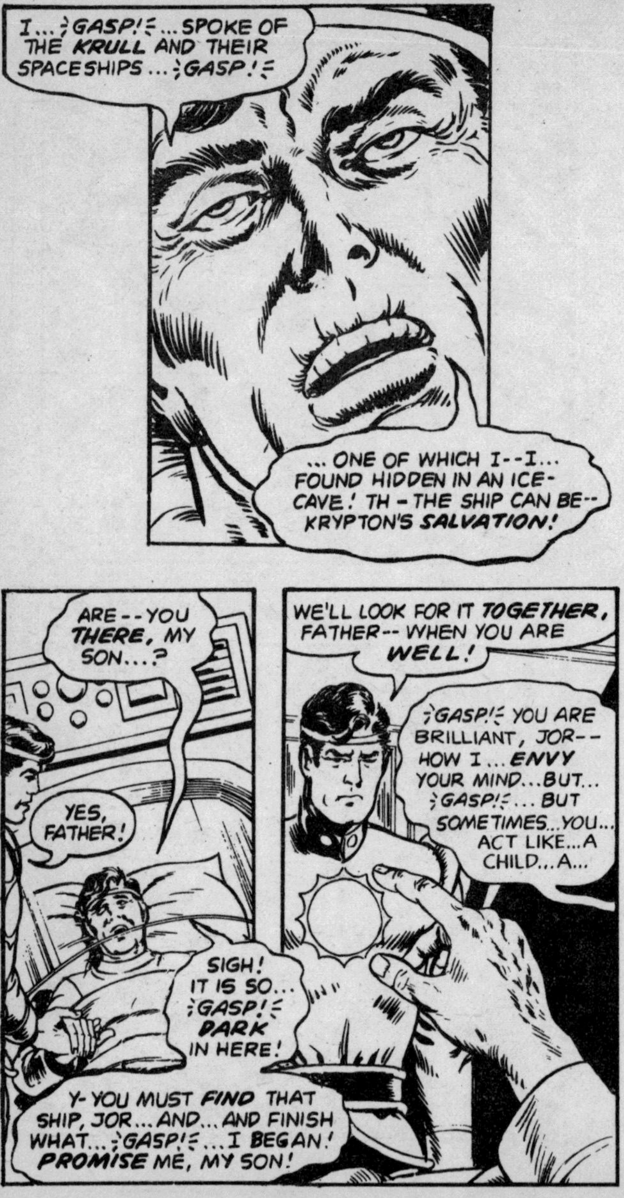

I... GASP! ...SPOKE OF THE KRULL AND THEIR SPACESHIPS... GASP!
... ONE OF WHICH I--I... FOUND HIDDEN IN AN ICE-CAVE! TH-THE SHIP CAN BE-- KRYPTON'S SALVATION!
ARE--YOU THERE, MY SON...?
YES, FATHER!
WE'LL LOOK FOR IT TOGETHER, FATHER-- WHEN YOU ARE WELL!
GASP! YOU ARE BRILLIANT, JOR-- HOW I... ENVY YOUR MIND...BUT... GASP! ... BUT SOMETIMES...YOU... ACT LIKE...A CHILD...A...
SIGH! IT IS SO... GASP! DARK IN HERE!
Y-YOU MUST FIND THAT SHIP, JOR... AND... AND FINISH WHAT... GASP! ...I BEGAN! PROMISE ME, MY SON!

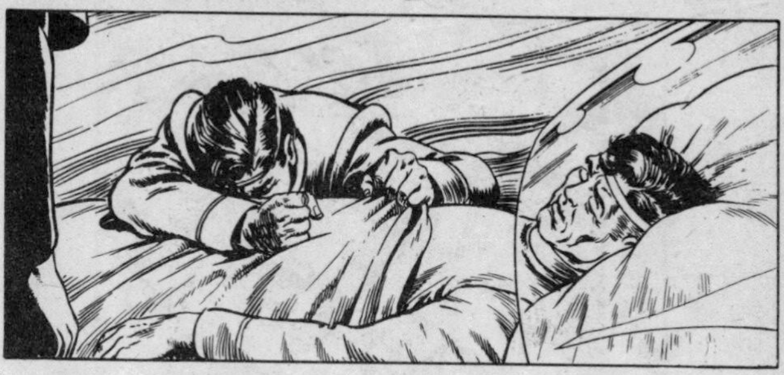

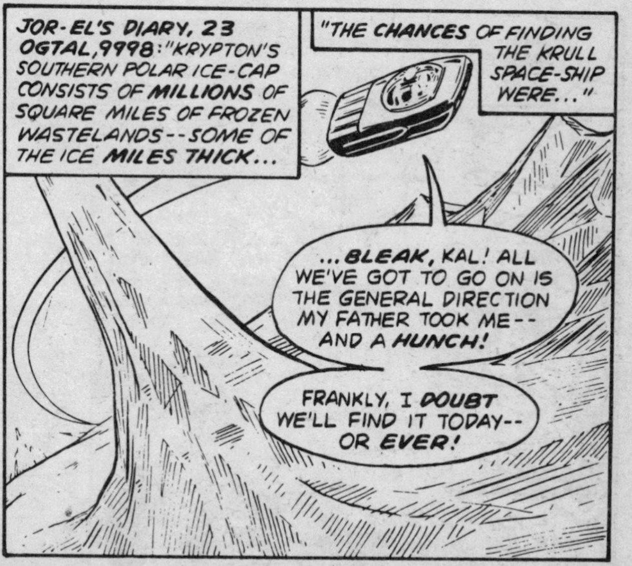
JOR-EL'S DIARY, 23 OGTAL, 9998: "KRYPTON'S SOUTHERN POLAR ICE-CAP CONSISTS OF MILLIONS OF SQUARE MILES OF FROZEN WASTELANDS--SOME OF THE ICE MILES THICK...
"THE CHANCES OF FINDING THE KRULL SPACE-SHIP WERE..."
...BLEAK, KAL! ALL WE'VE GOT TO GO ON IS THE GENERAL DIRECTION MY FATHER TOOK ME--AND A HUNCH!
FRANKLY, I DOUBT WE'LL FIND IT TODAY--OR EVER!

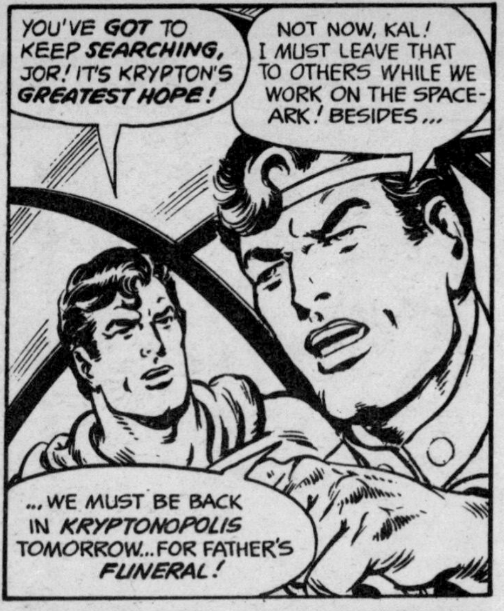
YOU'VE GOT TO KEEP SEARCHING, JOR! IT'S KRYPTON'S GREATEST HOPE!
NOT NOW, KAL! I MUST LEAVE THAT TO OTHERS WHILE WE WORK ON THE SPACE-ARK! BESIDES...
...WE MUST BE BACK IN KRYPTONOPOLIS TOMORROW...FOR FATHER'S FUNERAL!

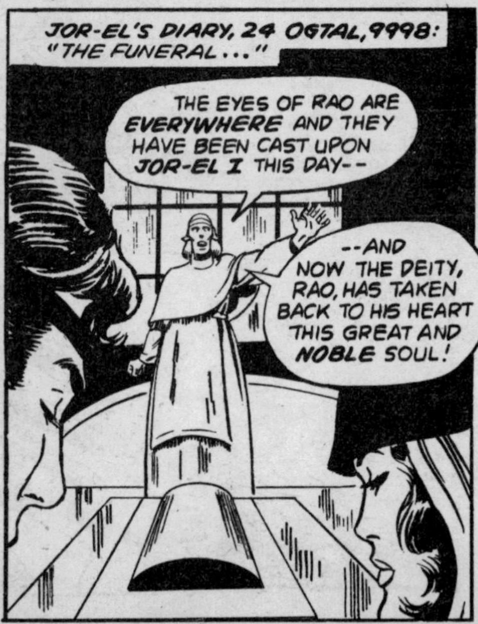
JOR-EL'S DIARY, 24 OGTAL, 9998: "THE FUNERAL..."
THE EYES OF RAO ARE EVERYWHERE AND THEY HAVE BEEN CAST UPON JOR-EL I THIS DAY--
--AND NOW THE DEITY, RAO, HAS TAKEN BACK TO HIS HEART THIS GREAT AND NOBLE SOUL!

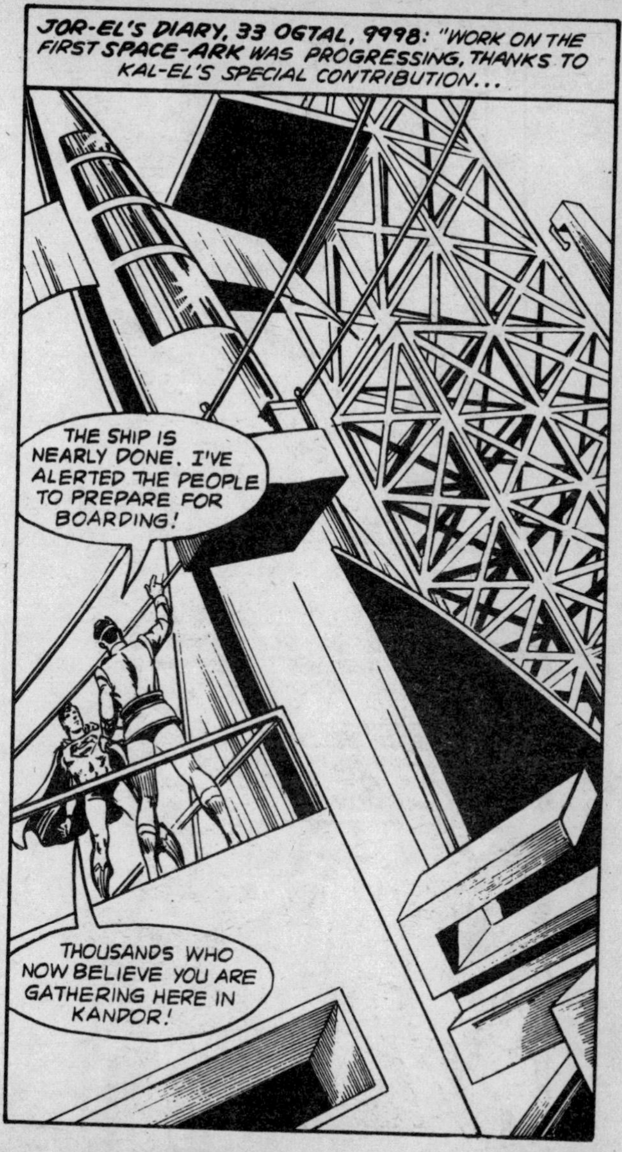
JOR-EL'S DIARY, 33 OGTAL, 9998: "WORK ON THE FIRST SPACE-ARK WAS PROGRESSING, THANKS TO KAL-EL'S SPECIAL CONTRIBUTION...
THE SHIP IS NEARLY DONE. I'VE ALERTED THE PEOPLE TO PREPARE FOR BOARDING!
THOUSANDS WHO NOW BELIEVE YOU ARE GATHERING HERE IN KANDOR!

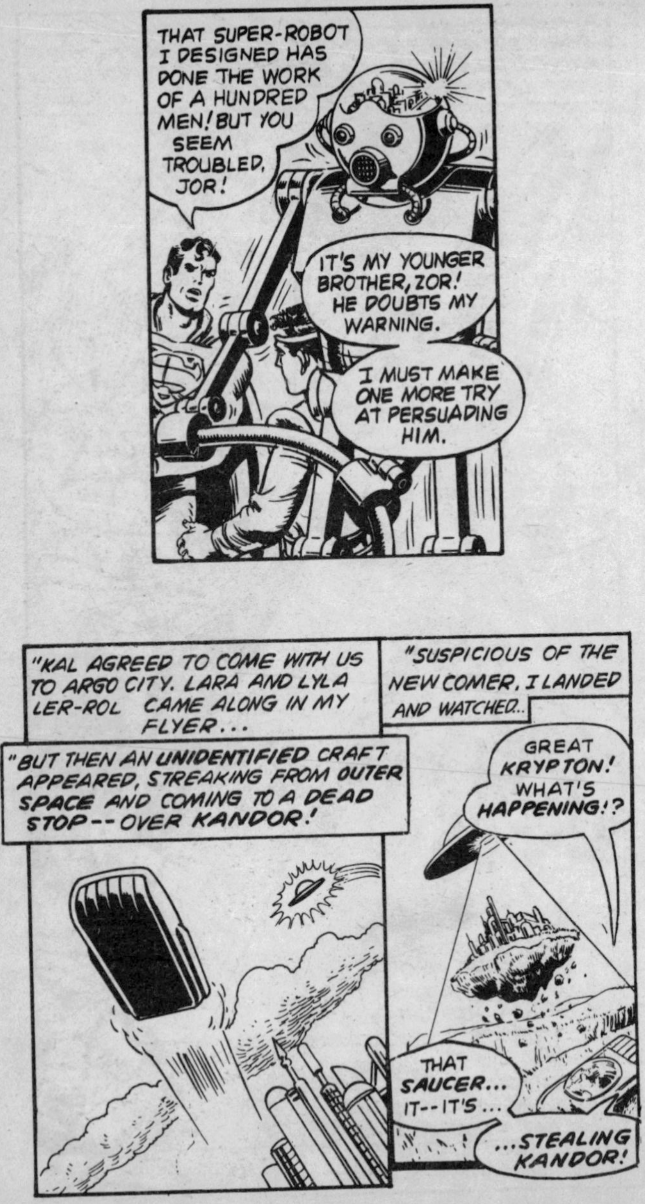
THAT SUPER-ROBOT I DESIGNED HAS DONE THE WORK OF A HUNDRED MEN! BUT YOU SEEM TROUBLED, JOR!
IT'S MY YOUNGER BROTHER, ZOR! HE DOUBTS MY WARNING.
I MUST MAKE ONE MORE TRY AT PERSUADING HIM.
"KAL AGREED TO COME WITH US TO ARGO CITY. LARA AND LYLA LER-ROL CAME ALONG IN MY FLYER...
"BUT THEN AN UNIDENTIFIED CRAFT APPEARED, STREAKING FROM OUTER SPACE AND COMING TO A DEAD STOP--OVER KANDOR!
"SUSPICIOUS OF THE NEW COMER, I LANDED AND WATCHED...
GREAT KRYPTON! WHAT'S HAPPENING!?
THAT SAUCER... IT--IT'S...
...STEALING KANDOR!

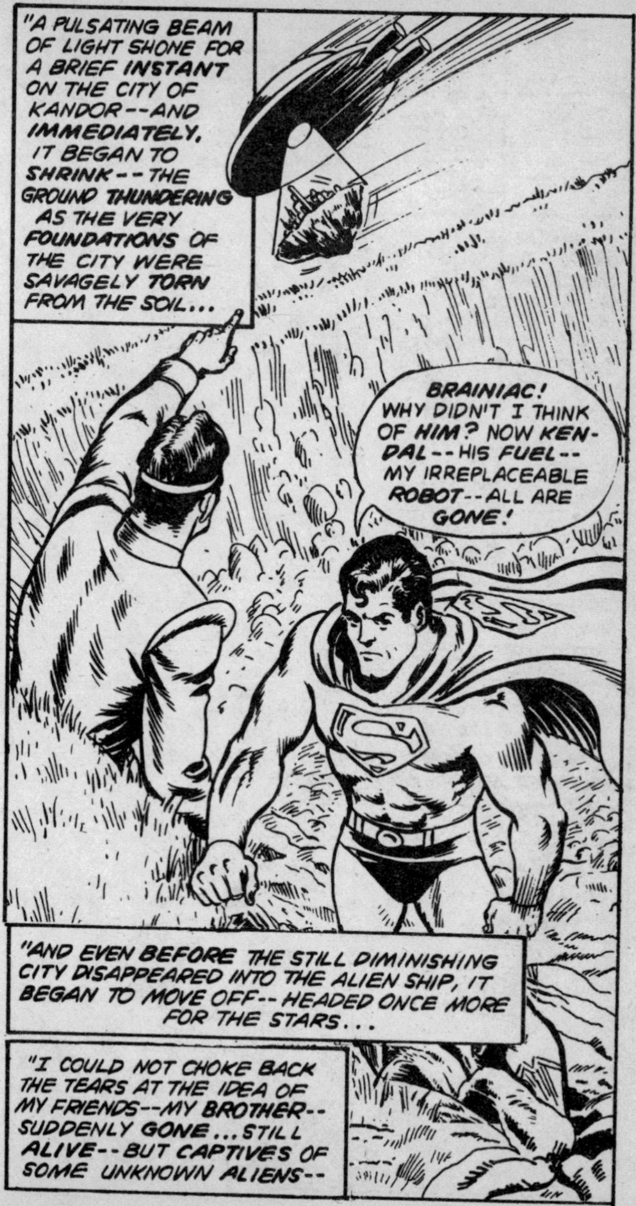
"A PULSATING BEAM OF LIGHT SHONE FOR A BRIEF INSTANT ON THE CITY OF KANDOR--AND IMMEDIATELY, IT BEGAN TO SHRINK--THE GROUND THUNDERING AS THE VERY FOUNDATIONS OF THE CITY WERE SAVAGELY TORN FROM THE SOIL...
BRAINIAC! WHY DIDN'T I THINK OF HIM? NOW KEN-DAL--HIS FUEL--MY IRREPLACEABLE ROBOT--ALL ARE GONE!
"AND EVEN BEFORE THE STILL DIMINISHING CITY DISAPPEARED INTO THE ALIEN SHIP, IT BEGAN TO MOVE OFF--HEADED ONCE MORE FOR THE STARS...
"I COULD NOT CHOKE BACK THE TEARS AT THE IDEA OF MY FRIENDS--MY BROTHER--SUDDENLY GONE...STILL ALIVE--BUT CAPTIVES OF SOME UNKNOWN ALIENS--

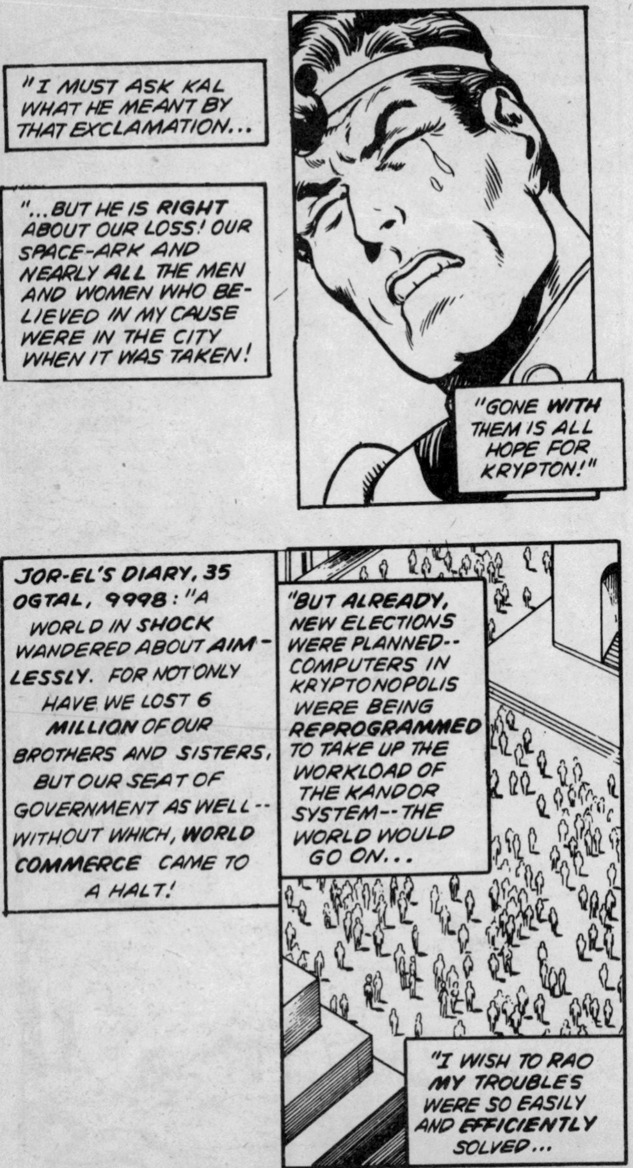
"I MUST ASK KAL WHAT HE MEANT BY THAT EXCLAMATION...
"...BUT HE IS RIGHT ABOUT OUR LOSS! OUR SPACE-ARK AND NEARLY ALL THE MEN AND WOMEN WHO BELIEVED IN MY CAUSE WERE IN THE CITY WHEN IT WAS TAKEN!
"GONE WITH THEM IS ALL HOPE FOR KRYPTON!"
JOR-EL'S DIARY, 35 OGTAL, 9998: "A WORLD IN SHOCK WANDERED ABOUT AIMLESSLY. FOR NOT ONLY HAVE WE LOST 6 MILLION OF OUR BROTHERS AND SISTERS, BUT OUR SEAT OF GOVERNMENT AS WELL--WITHOUT WHICH, WORLD COMMERCE CAME TO A HALT!
"BUT ALREADY, NEW ELECTIONS WERE PLANNED--COMPUTERS IN KRYPTONOPOLIS WERE BEING REPROGRAMMED TO TAKE UP THE WORKLOAD OF THE KANDOR SYSTEM--THE WORLD WOULD GO ON...
"I WISH TO RAO MY TROUBLES WERE SO EASILY AND EFFICIENTLY SOLVED...

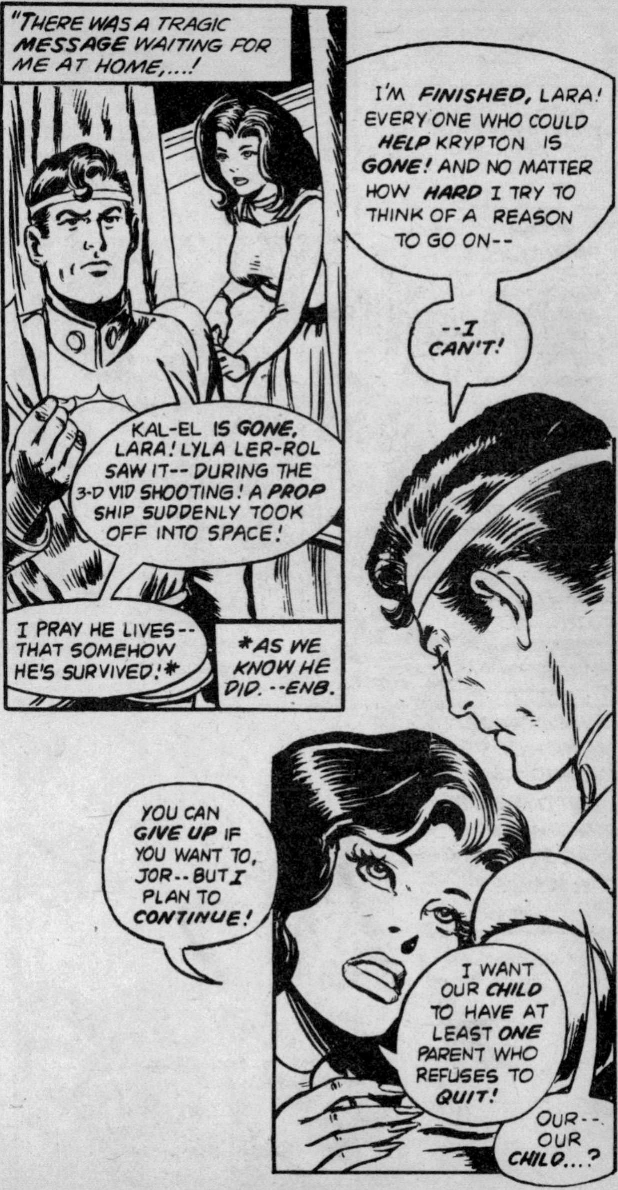
"THERE WAS A TRAGIC MESSAGE WAITING FOR ME AT HOME,...!
KAL-EL IS GONE, LARA! LYLA LER-ROL SAW IT-- DURING THE 3-D VID SHOOTING! A PROP SHIP SUDDENLY TOOK OFF INTO SPACE!
I PRAY HE LIVES-- THAT SOMEHOW HE'S SURVIVED!*
*AS WE KNOW HE DID. --ENB.
I'M FINISHED, LARA! EVERY ONE WHO COULD HELP KRYPTON IS GONE! AND NO MATTER HOW HARD I TRY TO THINK OF A REASON TO GO ON--
--I CAN'T!
YOU CAN GIVE UP IF YOU WANT TO, JOR-- BUT I PLAN TO CONTINUE!
I WANT OUR CHILD TO HAVE AT LEAST ONE PARENT WHO REFUSES TO QUIT!
OUR-- OUR CHILD...?

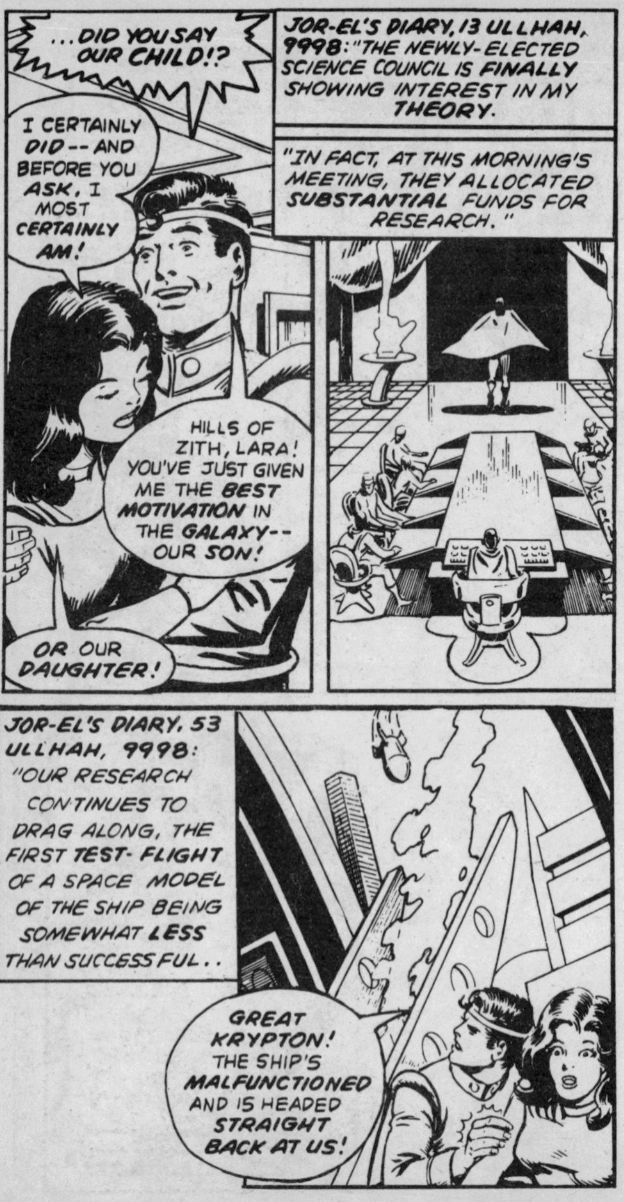
...DID YOU SAY OUR CHILD!?
I CERTAINLY DID -- AND BEFORE YOU ASK, I MOST CERTAINLY AM!
HILLS OF ZITH, LARA! YOU'VE JUST GIVEN ME THE BEST MOTIVATION IN THE GALAXY-- OUR SON!
OR OUR DAUGHTER!
JOR-EL'S DIARY, 13 ULLHAH, 9998: "THE NEWLY-ELECTED SCIENCE COUNCIL IS FINALLY SHOWING INTEREST IN MY THEORY.
"IN FACT, AT THIS MORNING'S MEETING, THEY ALLOCATED SUBSTANTIAL FUNDS FOR RESEARCH."
JOR-EL'S DIARY, 53 ULLHAH, 9998: "OUR RESEARCH CONTINUES TO DRAG ALONG, THE FIRST TEST-FLIGHT OF A SPACE MODEL OF THE SHIP BEING SOMEWHAT LESS THAN SUCCESSFUL..
GREAT KRYPTON! THE SHIP'S MALFUNCTIONED AND IS HEADED STRAIGHT BACK AT US!

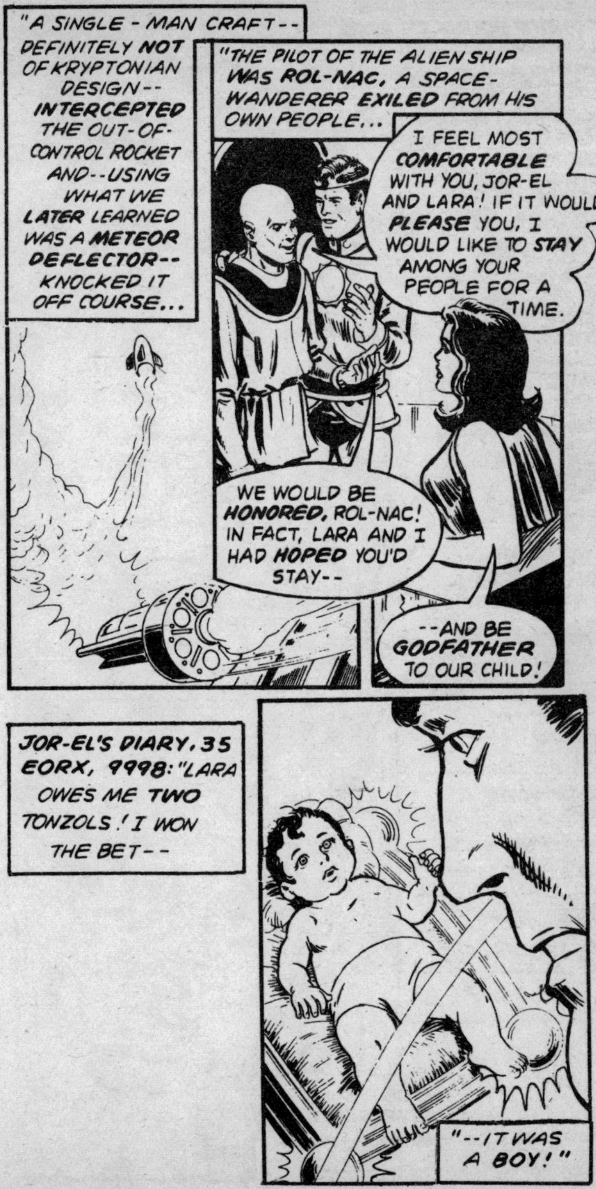
"A SINGLE - MAN CRAFT-- DEFINITELY NOT OF KRYPTONIAN DESIGN-- INTERCEPTED THE OUT-OF-CONTROL ROCKET AND--USING WHAT WE LATER LEARNED WAS A METEOR DEFLECTOR-- KNOCKED IT OFF COURSE...
"THE PILOT OF THE ALIEN SHIP WAS ROL-NAC, A SPACE-WANDERER EXILED FROM HIS OWN PEOPLE...
I FEEL MOST COMFORTABLE WITH YOU, JOR-EL AND LARA! IF IT WOULD PLEASE YOU, I WOULD LIKE TO STAY AMONG YOUR PEOPLE FOR A TIME.
WE WOULD BE HONORED, ROL-NAC! IN FACT, LARA AND I HAD HOPED YOU'D STAY--
--AND BE GODFATHER TO OUR CHILD!
JOR-EL'S DIARY, 35 EORX, 9998: "LARA OWES ME TWO TONZOLS! I WON THE BET--
"--IT WAS A BOY!"

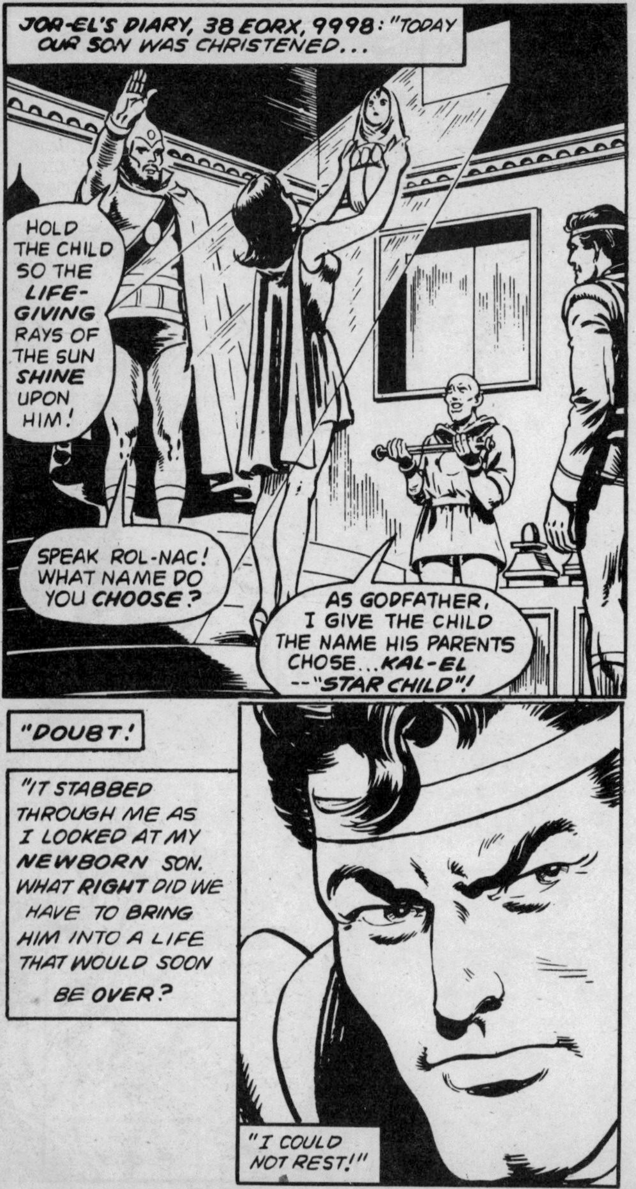
JOR-EL'S DIARY, 38 EORX, 9998: "TODAY OUR SON WAS CHRISTENED...
HOLD THE CHILD SO THE LIFE-GIVING RAYS OF THE SUN SHINE UPON HIM!
SPEAK ROL-NAC! WHAT NAME DO YOU CHOOSE?
AS GODFATHER, I GIVE THE CHILD THE NAME HIS PARENTS CHOSE...KAL-EL --"STAR CHILD"!
"DOUBT!
"IT STABBED THROUGH ME AS I LOOKED AT MY NEWBORN SON. WHAT RIGHT DID WE HAVE TO BRING HIM INTO A LIFE THAT WOULD SOON BE OVER?
"I COULD NOT REST!"

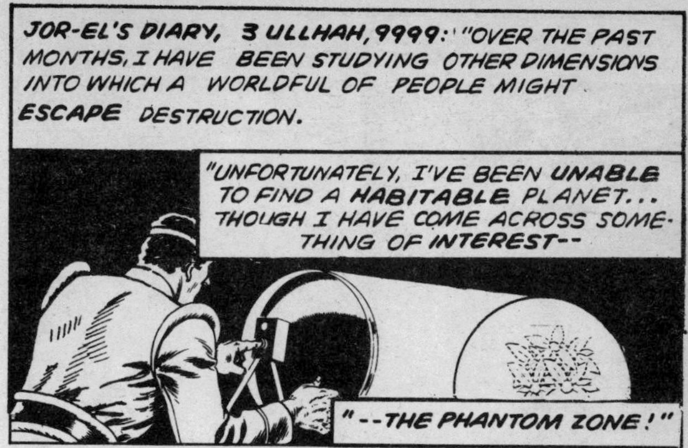
JOR-EL'S DIARY, 3 ULLHAH, 9999: "OVER THE PAST MONTHS, I HAVE BEEN STUDYING OTHER DIMENSIONS INTO WHICH A WORLDFUL OF PEOPLE MIGHT ESCAPE DESTRUCTION.
"UNFORTUNATELY, I'VE BEEN UNABLE TO FIND A HABITABLE PLANET... THOUGH I HAVE COME ACROSS SOME-THING OF INTEREST--
"--THE PHANTOM ZONE!"

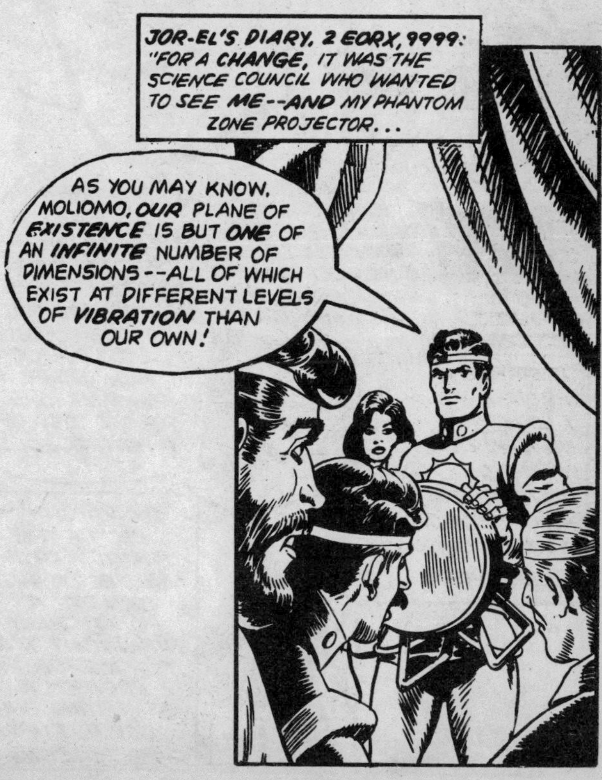
JOR-EL'S DIARY, 2 EORX, 9999: "FOR A CHANGE, IT WAS THE SCIENCE COUNCIL WHO WANTED TO SEE ME--AND MY PHANTOM ZONE PROJECTOR...
AS YOU MAY KNOW, MOLIOMO, OUR PLANE OF EXISTENCE IS BUT ONE OF AN INFINITE NUMBER OF DIMENSIONS--ALL OF WHICH EXIST AT DIFFERENT LEVELS OF VIBRATION THAN OUR OWN!

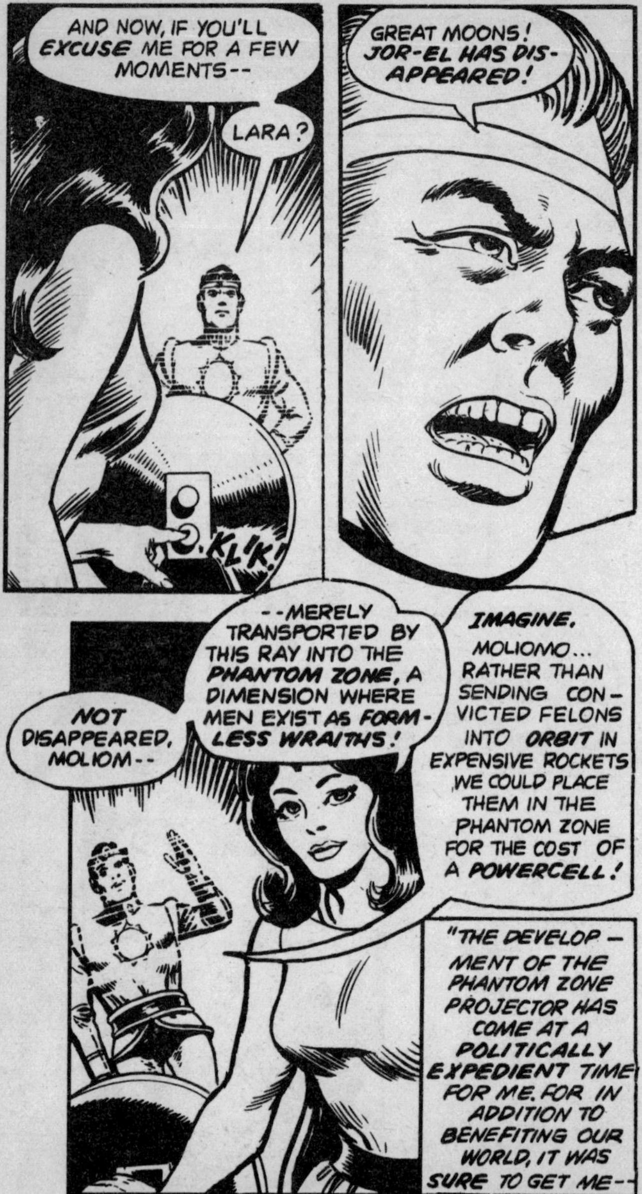

AND NOW, IF YOU'LL EXCUSE ME FOR A FEW MOMENTS--
LARA?
KLIK!
GREAT MOONS! JOR-EL HAS DIS-APPEARED!
NOT DISAPPEARED, MOLIOM--
--MERELY TRANSPORTED BY THIS RAY INTO THE PHANTOM ZONE, A DIMENSION WHERE MEN EXIST AS FORM-LESS WRAITHS!
IMAGINE, MOLIOMO... RATHER THAN SENDING CON-VICTED FELONS INTO ORBIT IN EXPENSIVE ROCKETS WE COULD PLACE THEM IN THE PHANTOM ZONE FOR THE COST OF A POWERCELL!
"THE DEVELOP-MENT OF THE PHANTOM ZONE PROJECTOR HAS COME AT A POLITICALLY EXPEDIENT TIME FOR ME. FOR IN ADDITION TO BENEFITING OUR WORLD, IT WAS SURE TO GET ME--

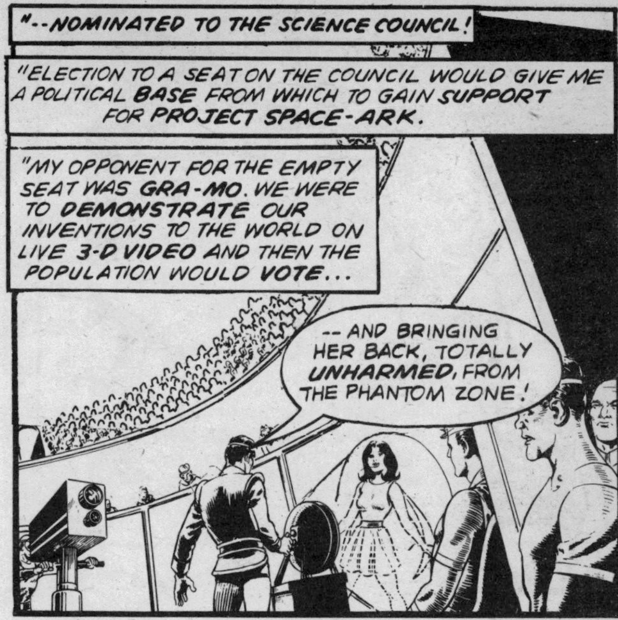
"--NOMINATED TO THE SCIENCE COUNCIL!
"ELECTION TO A SEAT ON THE COUNCIL WOULD GIVE ME A POLITICAL BASE FROM WHICH TO GAIN SUPPORT FOR PROJECT SPACE-ARK.
"MY OPPONENT FOR THE EMPTY SEAT WAS GRA-MO. WE WERE TO DEMONSTRATE OUR INVENTIONS TO THE WORLD ON LIVE 3-D VIDEO AND THEN THE POPULATION WOULD VOTE...
--AND BRINGING HER BACK, TOTALLY UNHARMED, FROM THE PHANTOM ZONE!

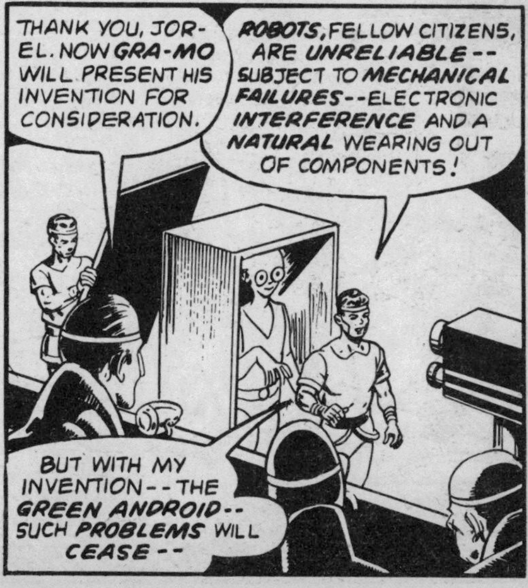
THANK YOU, JOR-EL. NOW GRA-MO WILL PRESENT HIS INVENTION FOR CONSIDERATION.
ROBOTS, FELLOW CITIZENS, ARE UNRELIABLE--SUBJECT TO MECHANICAL FAILURES--ELECTRONIC INTERFERENCE AND A NATURAL WEARING OUT OF COMPONENTS!
BUT WITH MY INVENTION--THE GREEN ANDROID--SUCH PROBLEMS WILL CEASE--

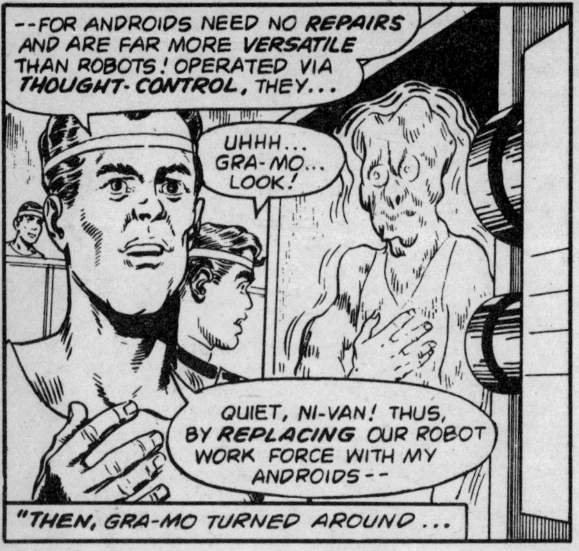
--FOR ANDROIDS NEED NO REPAIRS AND ARE FAR MORE VERSATILE THAN ROBOTS! OPERATED VIA THOUGHT-CONTROL, THEY...
UHHH... GRA-MO... LOOK!
QUIET, NI-VAN! THUS, BY REPLACING OUR ROBOT WORK FORCE WITH MY ANDROIDS--
"THEN, GRA-MO TURNED AROUND...

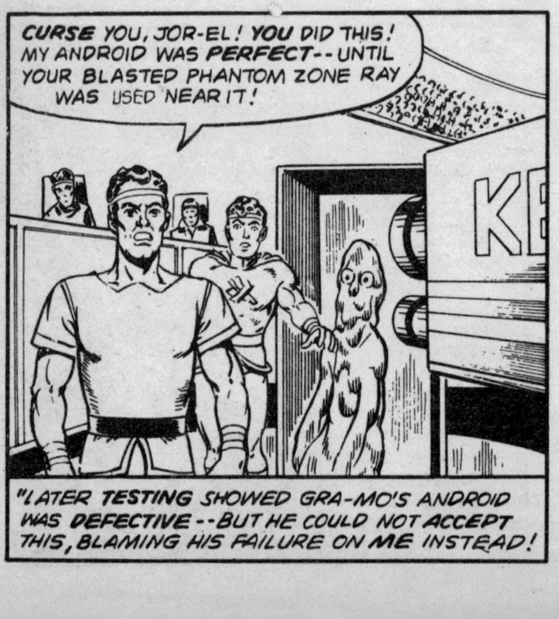
CURSE YOU, JOR-EL! YOU DID THIS! MY ANDROID WAS PERFECT--UNTIL YOUR BLASTED PHANTOM ZONE RAY WAS USED NEAR IT!
KE
"LATER TESTING SHOWED GRA-MO'S ANDROID WAS DEFECTIVE--BUT HE COULD NOT ACCEPT THIS, BLAMING HIS FAILURE ON ME INSTEAD!

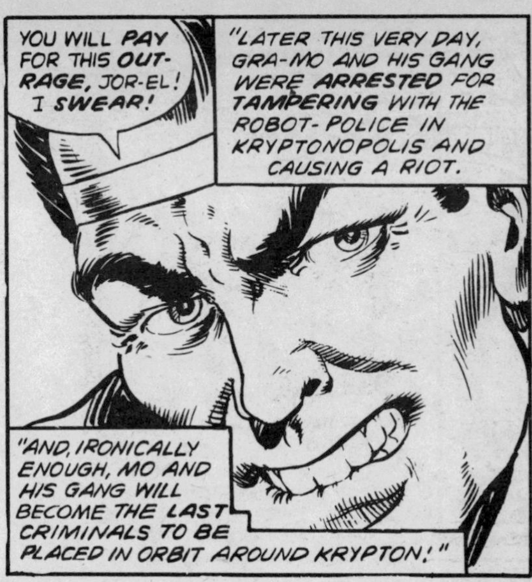
YOU WILL PAY FOR THIS OUTRAGE, JOR-EL! I SWEAR!
"LATER THIS VERY DAY, GRA-MO AND HIS GANG WERE ARRESTED FOR TAMPERING WITH THE ROBOT-POLICE IN KRYPTONOPOLIS AND CAUSING A RIOT.
"AND, IRONICALLY ENOUGH, MO AND HIS GANG WILL BECOME THE LAST CRIMINALS TO BE PLACED IN ORBIT AROUND KRYPTON!"

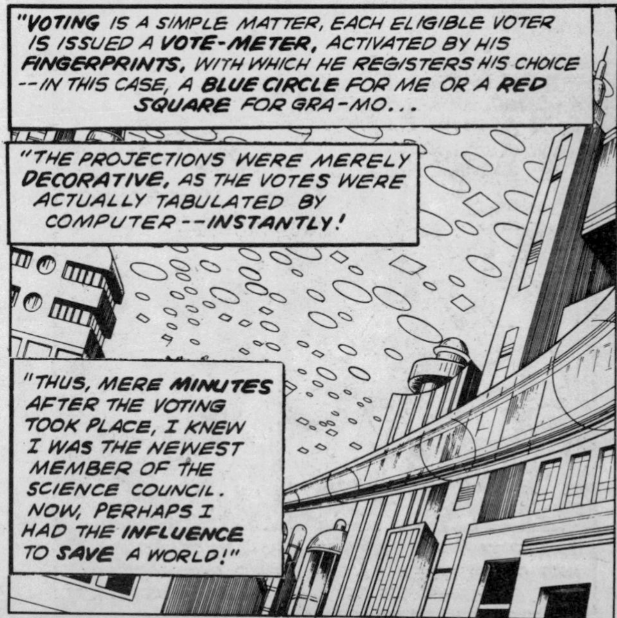
"VOTING IS A SIMPLE MATTER, EACH ELIGIBLE VOTER IS ISSUED A VOTE-METER, ACTIVATED BY HIS FINGERPRINTS, WITH WHICH HE REGISTERS HIS CHOICE --IN THIS CASE, A BLUE CIRCLE FOR ME OR A RED SQUARE FOR GRA-MO...
"THE PROJECTIONS WERE MERELY DECORATIVE, AS THE VOTES WERE ACTUALLY TABULATED BY COMPUTER--INSTANTLY!
"THUS, MERE MINUTES AFTER THE VOTING TOOK PLACE, I KNEW I WAS THE NEWEST MEMBER OF THE SCIENCE COUNCIL. NOW, PERHAPS I HAD THE INFLUENCE TO SAVE A WORLD!"

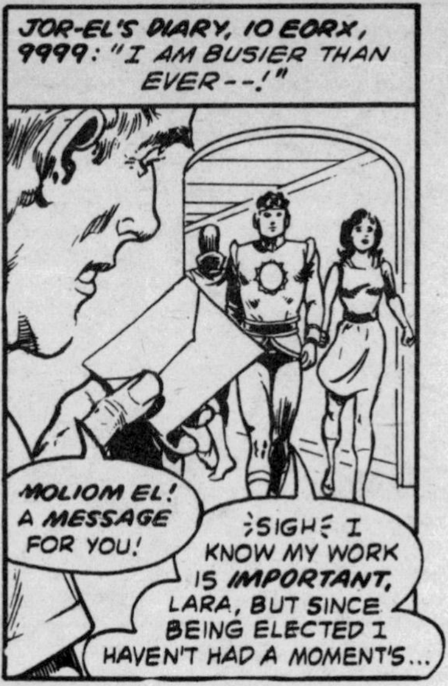
JOR-EL'S DIARY, 10 EORX, 9999: "I AM BUSIER THAN EVER--!"
MOLIOM EL! A MESSAGE FOR YOU!
⁒SIGH⁒ I KNOW MY WORK IS IMPORTANT, LARA, BUT SINCE BEING ELECTED I HAVEN'T HAD A MOMENT'S...

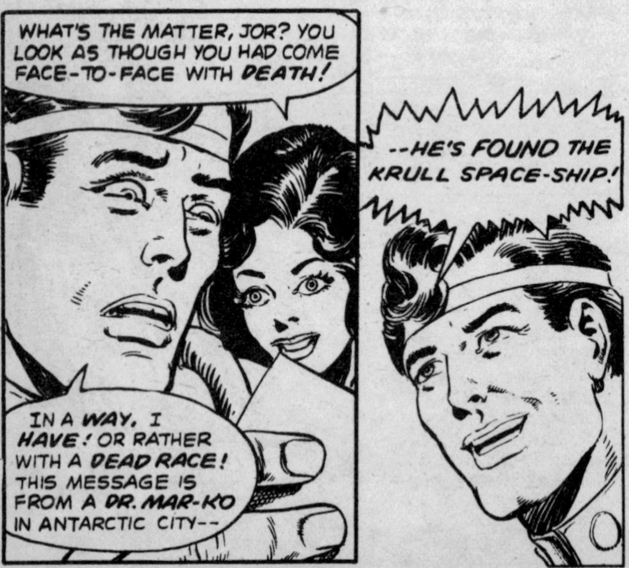
WHAT'S THE MATTER, JOR? YOU LOOK AS THOUGH YOU HAD COME FACE-TO-FACE WITH DEATH!
IN A WAY, I HAVE! OR RATHER WITH A DEAD RACE! THIS MESSAGE IS FROM A DR. MAR-KO IN ANTARCTIC CITY--
--HE'S FOUND THE KRULL SPACE-SHIP!

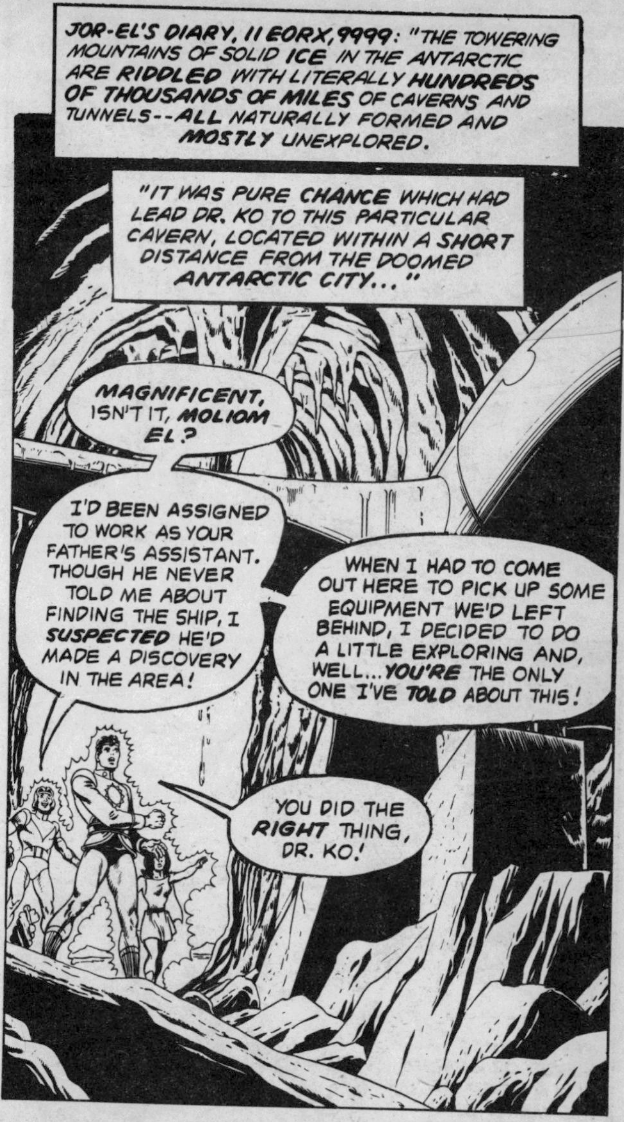
JOR-EL'S DIARY, 11 EORX, 9999: "THE TOWERING MOUNTAINS OF SOLID ICE IN THE ANTARCTIC ARE RIDDLED WITH LITERALLY HUNDREDS OF THOUSANDS OF MILES OF CAVERNS AND TUNNELS--ALL NATURALLY FORMED AND MOSTLY UNEXPLORED.
"IT WAS PURE CHANCE WHICH HAD LEAD DR. KO TO THIS PARTICULAR CAVERN, LOCATED WITHIN A SHORT DISTANCE FROM THE DOOMED ANTARCTIC CITY..."
MAGNIFICENT, ISN'T IT, MOLIOM EL?
I'D BEEN ASSIGNED TO WORK AS YOUR FATHER'S ASSISTANT. THOUGH HE NEVER TOLD ME ABOUT FINDING THE SHIP, I SUSPECTED HE'D MADE A DISCOVERY IN THE AREA!
WHEN I HAD TO COME OUT HERE TO PICK UP SOME EQUIPMENT WE'D LEFT BEHIND, I DECIDED TO DO A LITTLE EXPLORING AND, WELL... YOU'RE THE ONLY ONE I'VE TOLD ABOUT THIS!
YOU DID THE RIGHT THING, DR. KO!

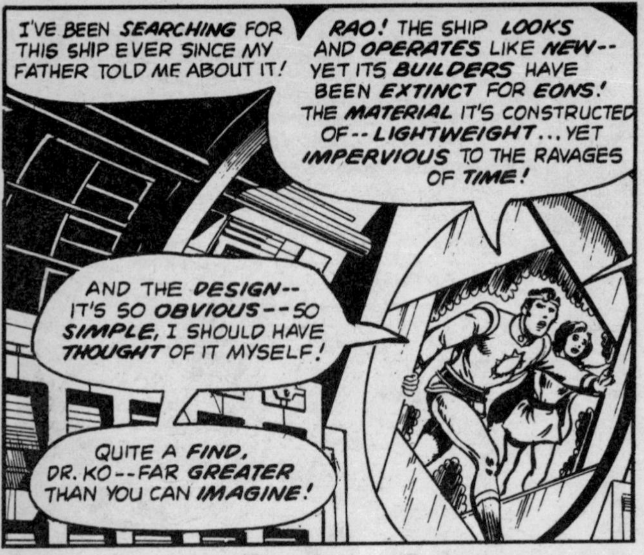
I'VE BEEN SEARCHING FOR THIS SHIP EVER SINCE MY FATHER TOLD ME ABOUT IT!
RAO! THE SHIP LOOKS AND OPERATES LIKE NEW-- YET ITS BUILDERS HAVE BEEN EXTINCT FOR EONS! THE MATERIAL IT'S CONSTRUCTED OF--LIGHTWEIGHT...YET IMPERVIOUS TO THE RAVAGES OF TIME!
AND THE DESIGN-- IT'S SO OBVIOUS--SO SIMPLE, I SHOULD HAVE THOUGHT OF IT MYSELF!
QUITE A FIND, DR. KO--FAR GREATER THAN YOU CAN IMAGINE!

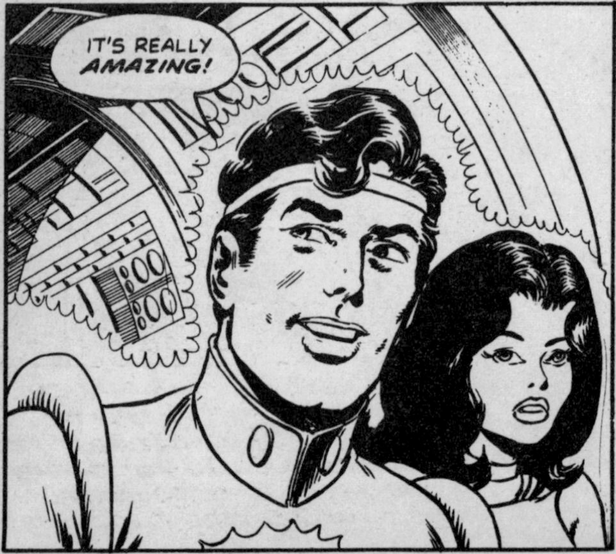
IT'S REALLY AMAZING!

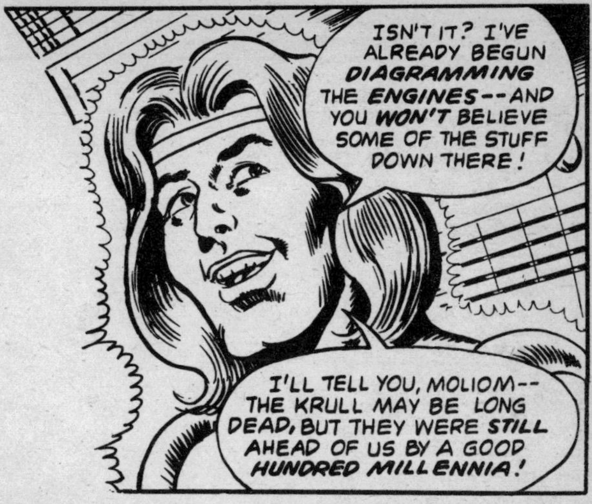
ISN'T IT? I'VE ALREADY BEGUN DIAGRAMMING THE ENGINES--AND YOU WON'T BELIEVE SOME OF THE STUFF DOWN THERE!
I'LL TELL YOU, MOLIOM--THE KRULL MAY BE LONG DEAD, BUT THEY WERE STILL AHEAD OF US BY A GOOD HUNDRED MILLENNIA!

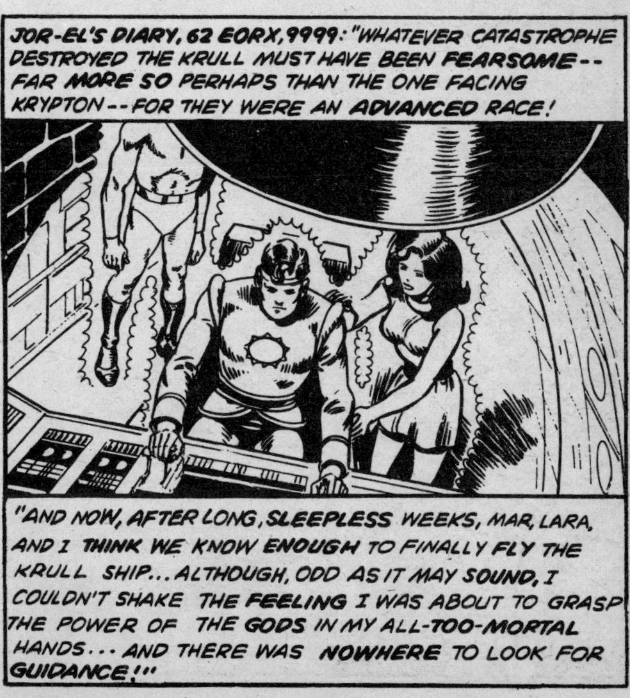
JOR-EL'S DIARY, 62 EORX, 9999: "WHATEVER CATASTROPHE DESTROYED THE KRULL MUST HAVE BEEN FEARSOME--FAR MORE SO PERHAPS THAN THE ONE FACING KRYPTON--FOR THEY WERE AN ADVANCED RACE!
"AND NOW, AFTER LONG, SLEEPLESS WEEKS, MAR, LARA, AND I THINK WE KNOW ENOUGH TO FINALLY FLY THE KRULL SHIP... ALTHOUGH, ODD AS IT MAY SOUND, I COULDN'T SHAKE THE FEELING I WAS ABOUT TO GRASP THE POWER OF THE GODS IN MY ALL-TOO-MORTAL HANDS... AND THERE WAS NOWHERE TO LOOK FOR GUIDANCE!"

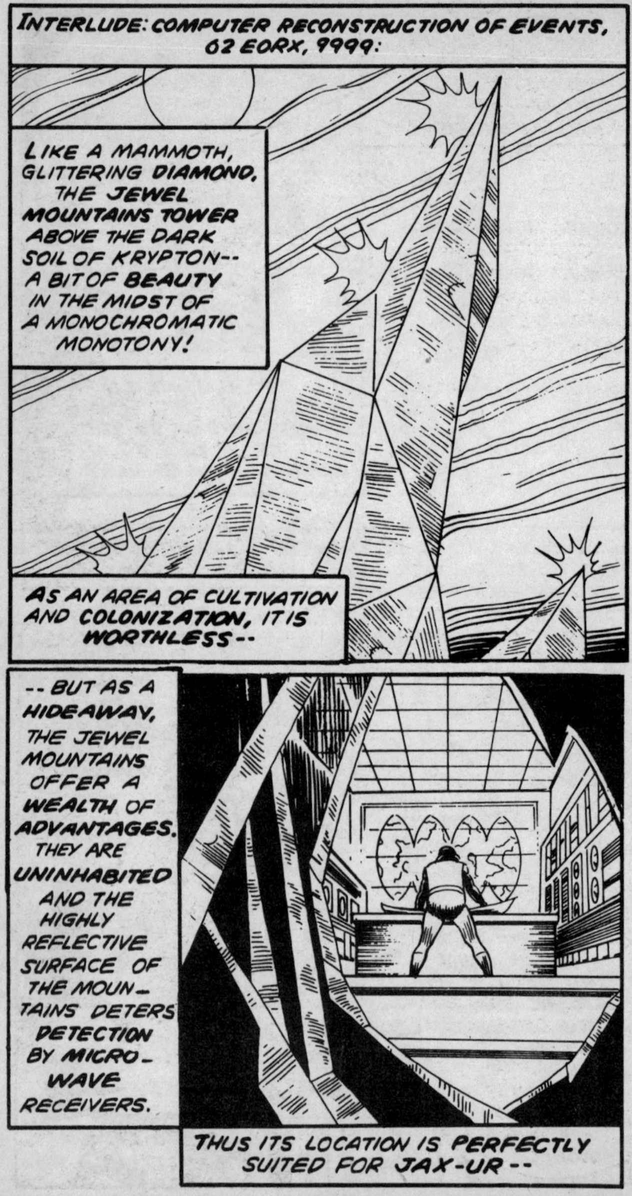
INTERLUDE: COMPUTER RECONSTRUCTION OF EVENTS, 62 EORX, 9999:
LIKE A MAMMOTH, GLITTERING DIAMOND, THE JEWEL MOUNTAINS TOWER ABOVE THE DARK SOIL OF KRYPTON-- A BIT OF BEAUTY IN THE MIDST OF A MONOCHROMATIC MONOTONY!
AS AN AREA OF CULTIVATION AND COLONIZATION, IT IS WORTHLESS--
-- BUT AS A HIDEAWAY, THE JEWEL MOUNTAINS OFFER A WEALTH OF ADVANTAGES. THEY ARE UNINHABITED AND THE HIGHLY REFLECTIVE SURFACE OF THE MOUN-TAINS DETERS DETECTION BY MICRO-WAVE RECEIVERS.
THUS ITS LOCATION IS PERFECTLY SUITED FOR JAX-UR--

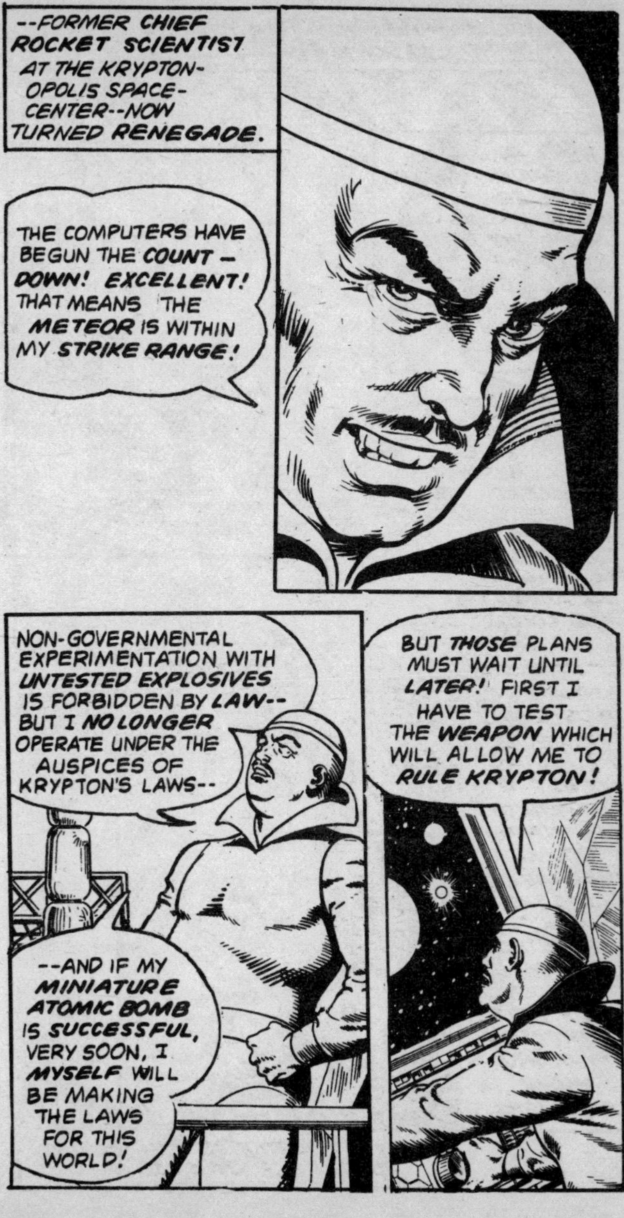
--FORMER CHIEF ROCKET SCIENTIST AT THE KRYPTON-OPOLIS SPACE-CENTER--NOW TURNED RENEGADE.
THE COMPUTERS HAVE BEGUN THE COUNT-DOWN! EXCELLENT! THAT MEANS THE METEOR IS WITHIN MY STRIKE RANGE!
NON-GOVERNMENTAL EXPERIMENTATION WITH UNTESTED EXPLOSIVES IS FORBIDDEN BY LAW--BUT I NO LONGER OPERATE UNDER THE AUSPICES OF KRYPTON'S LAWS--
--AND IF MY MINIATURE ATOMIC BOMB IS SUCCESSFUL, VERY SOON, I MYSELF WILL BE MAKING THE LAWS FOR THIS WORLD!
BUT THOSE PLANS MUST WAIT UNTIL LATER! FIRST I HAVE TO TEST THE WEAPON WHICH WILL ALLOW ME TO RULE KRYPTON!

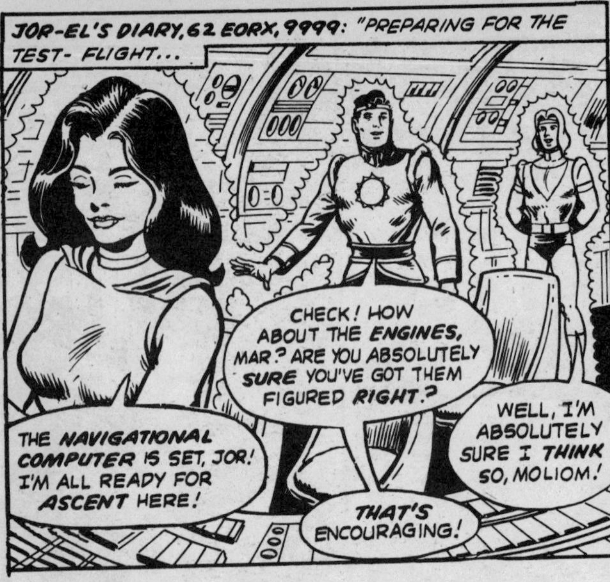
JOR-EL'S DIARY, 62 EORX, 9999: "PREPARING FOR THE TEST-FLIGHT...
CHECK! HOW ABOUT THE ENGINES, MAR? ARE YOU ABSOLUTELY SURE YOU'VE GOT THEM FIGURED RIGHT?
THE NAVIGATIONAL COMPUTER IS SET, JOR! I'M ALL READY FOR ASCENT HERE!
WELL, I'M ABSOLUTELY SURE I THINK SO, MOLIOM!
THAT'S ENCOURAGING!

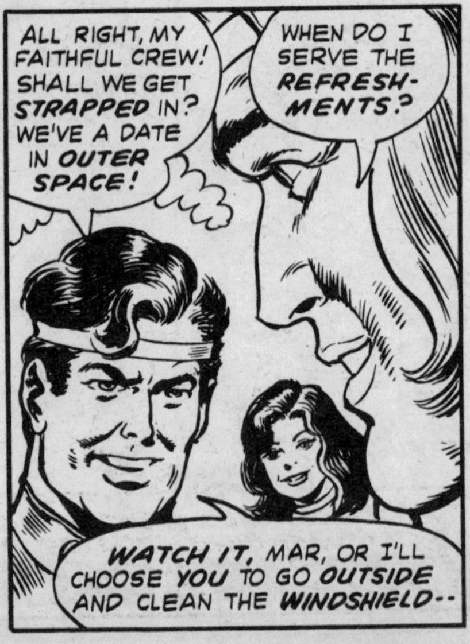
ALL RIGHT, MY FAITHFUL CREW! SHALL WE GET STRAPPED IN? WE'VE A DATE IN OUTER SPACE!
WHEN DO I SERVE THE REFRESH-MENTS?
WATCH IT, MAR, OR I'LL CHOOSE YOU TO GO OUTSIDE AND CLEAN THE WINDSHIELD--

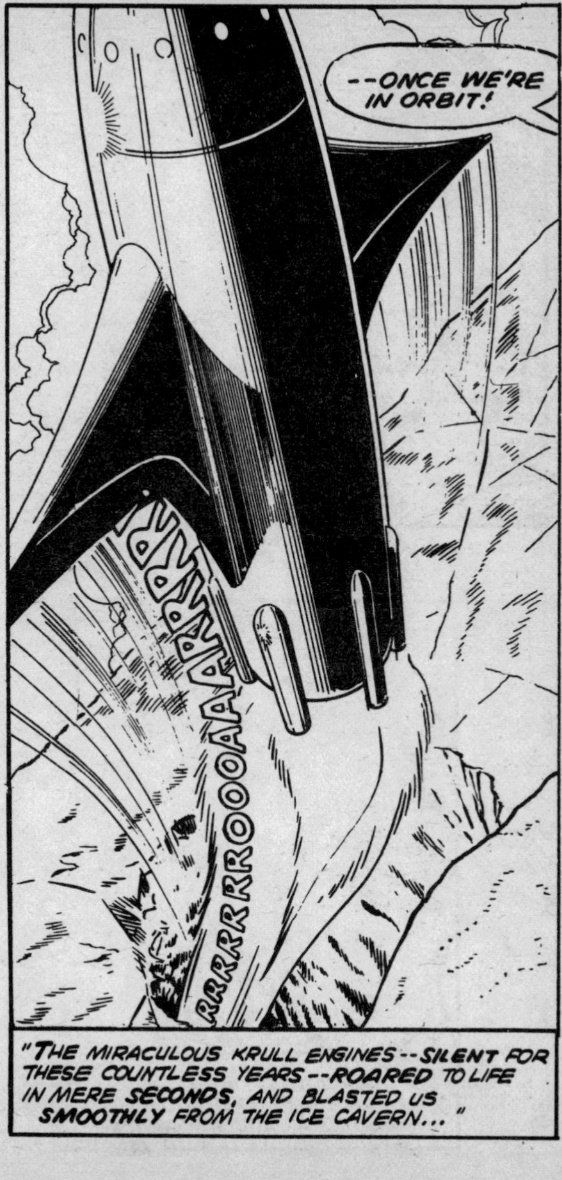
--ONCE WE'RE IN ORBIT!
RRRRRRRROOOOAAAARRRR
"THE MIRACULOUS KRULL ENGINES--SILENT FOR THESE COUNTLESS YEARS--ROARED TO LIFE IN MERE SECONDS, AND BLASTED US SMOOTHLY FROM THE ICE CAVERN..."

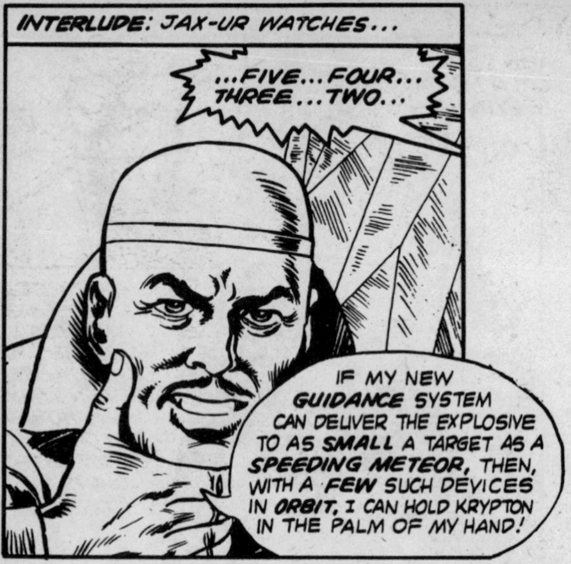
INTERLUDE: JAX-UR WATCHES...
...FIVE...FOUR... THREE...TWO...
IF MY NEW GUIDANCE SYSTEM CAN DELIVER THE EXPLOSIVE TO AS SMALL A TARGET AS A SPEEDING METEOR, THEN, WITH A FEW SUCH DEVICES IN ORBIT, I CAN HOLD KRYPTON IN THE PALM OF MY HAND!

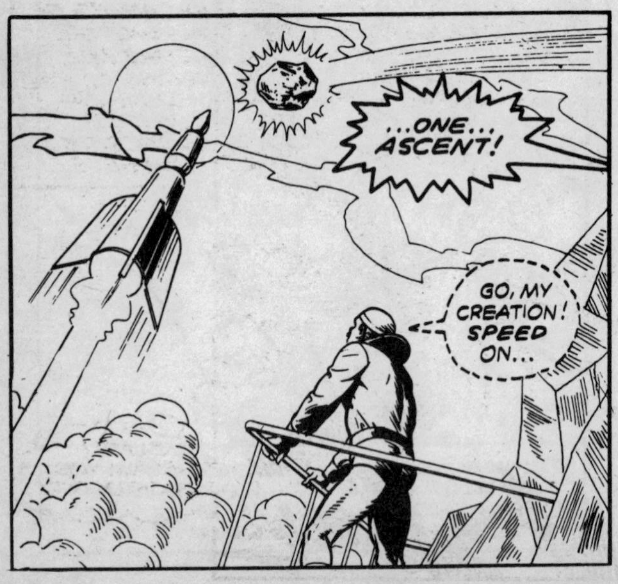
...ONE... ASCENT!
GO, MY CREATION! SPEED ON...

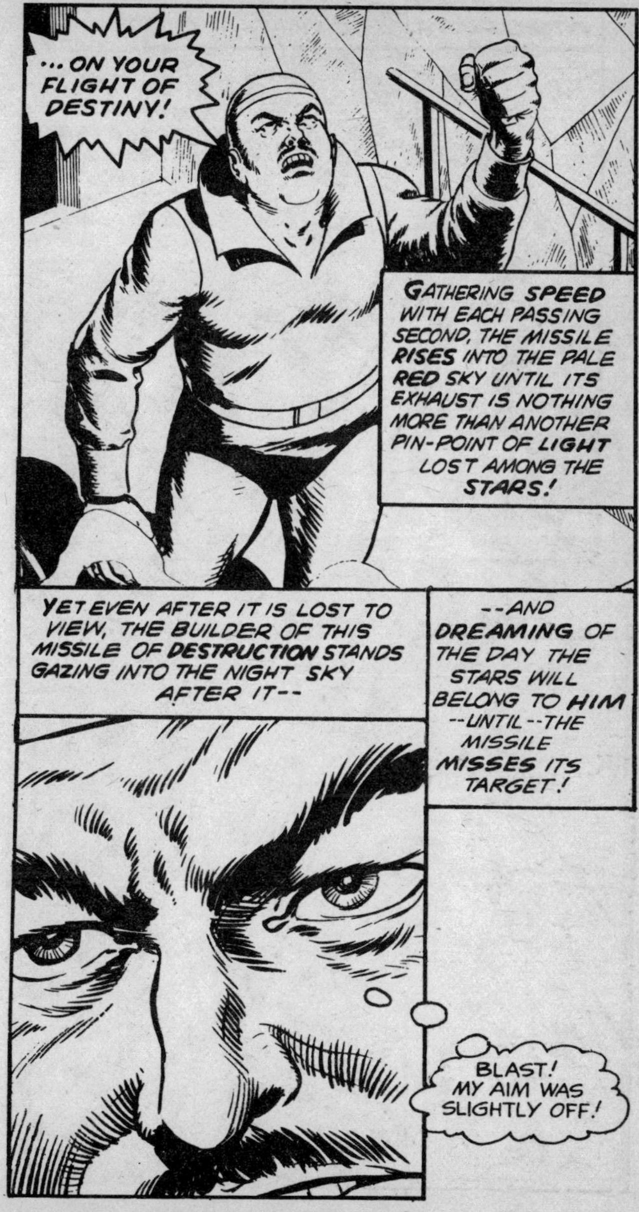
...ON YOUR FLIGHT OF DESTINY!
GATHERING SPEED WITH EACH PASSING SECOND, THE MISSILE RISES INTO THE PALE RED SKY UNTIL ITS EXHAUST IS NOTHING MORE THAN ANOTHER PIN-POINT OF LIGHT LOST AMONG THE STARS!
YET EVEN AFTER IT IS LOST TO VIEW, THE BUILDER OF THIS MISSILE OF DESTRUCTION STANDS GAZING INTO THE NIGHT SKY AFTER IT--
--AND DREAMING OF THE DAY THE STARS WILL BELONG TO HIM --UNTIL--THE MISSILE MISSES ITS TARGET!
BLAST! MY AIM WAS SLIGHTLY OFF!

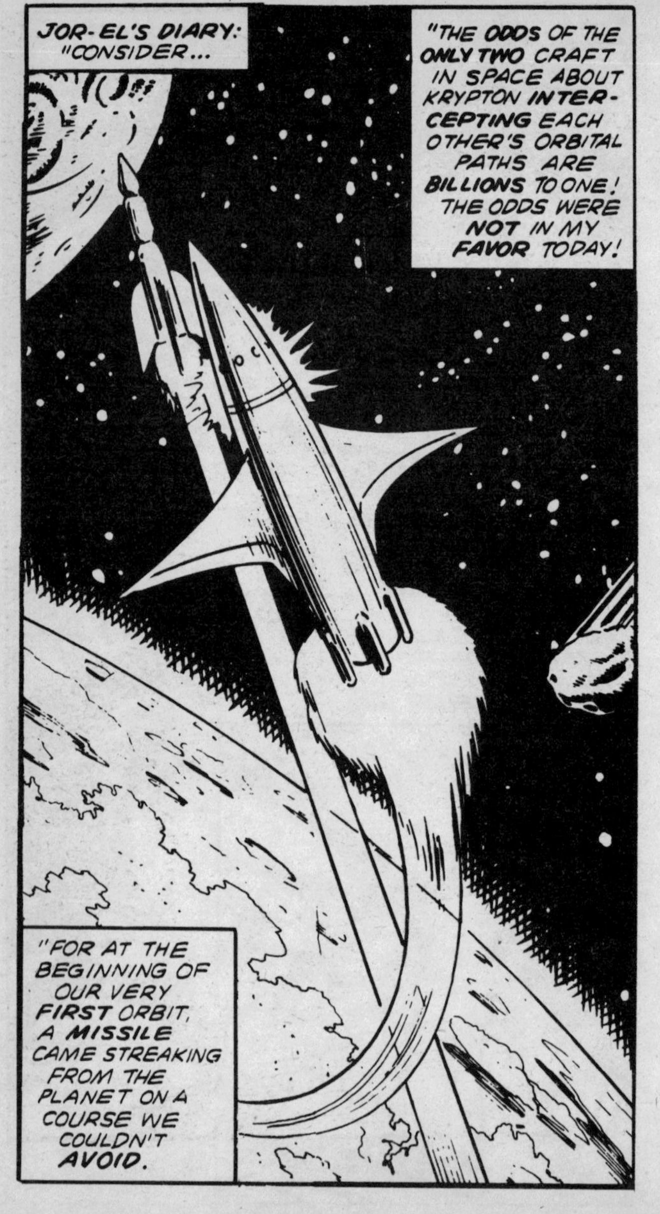
JOR-EL'S DIARY: "CONSIDER...
"THE ODDS OF THE ONLY TWO CRAFT IN SPACE ABOUT KRYPTON INTERCEPTING EACH OTHER'S ORBITAL PATHS ARE BILLIONS TO ONE! THE ODDS WERE NOT IN MY FAVOR TODAY!
"FOR AT THE BEGINNING OF OUR VERY FIRST ORBIT, A MISSILE CAME STREAKING FROM THE PLANET ON A COURSE WE COULDN'T AVOID.

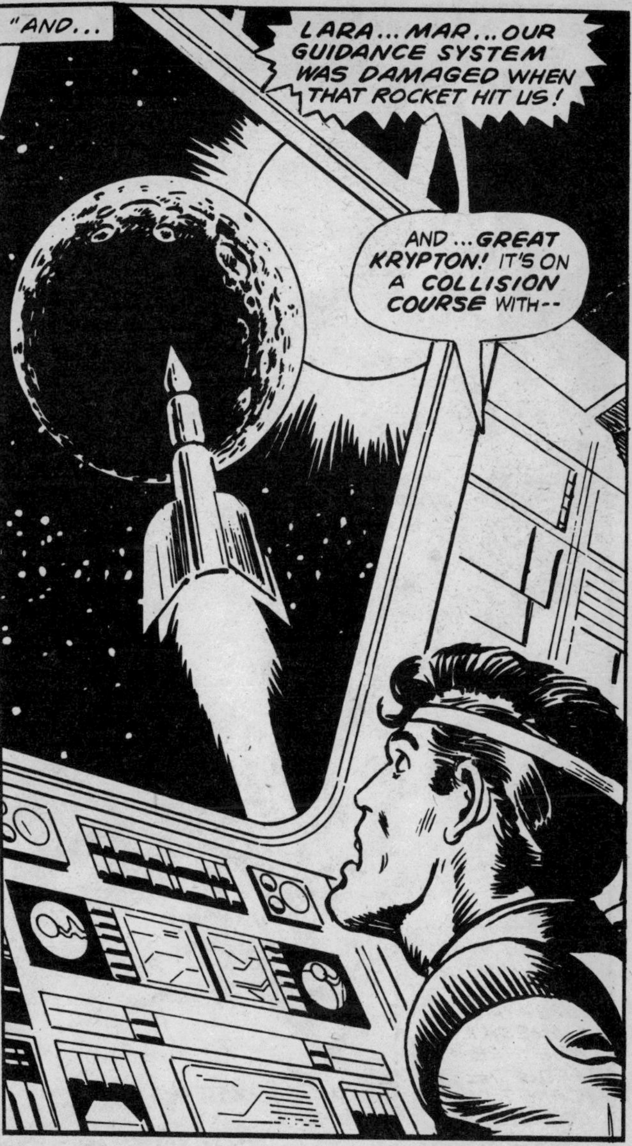
"AND...
LARA... MAR... OUR GUIDANCE SYSTEM WAS DAMAGED WHEN THAT ROCKET HIT US!
AND ...GREAT KRYPTON! IT'S ON A COLLISION COURSE WITH--

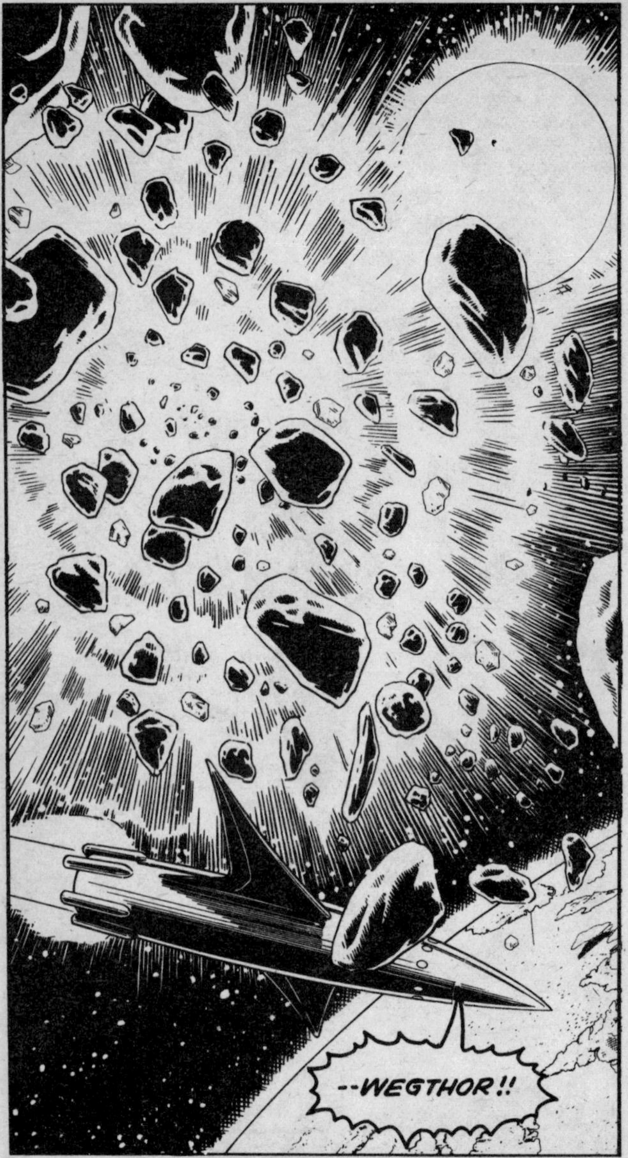
--WEGTHOR!!

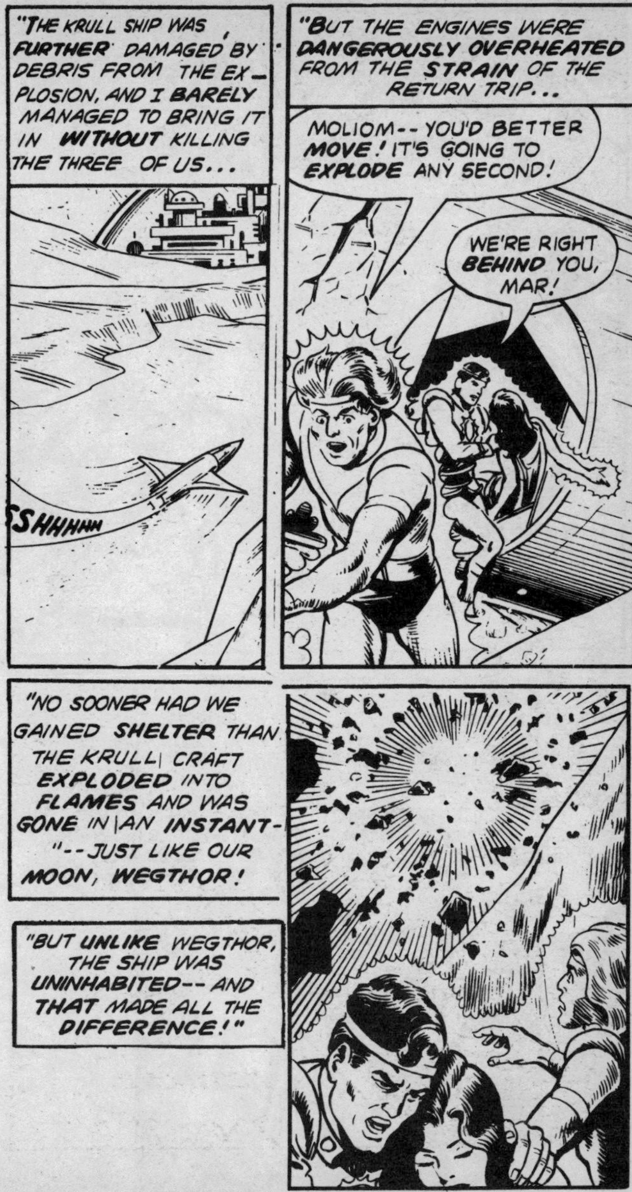
"THE KRULL SHIP WAS FURTHER DAMAGED BY DEBRIS FROM THE EX-PLOSION, AND I BARELY MANAGED TO BRING IT IN WITHOUT KILLING THE THREE OF US...
SSHHHHH
"BUT THE ENGINES WERE DANGEROUSLY OVERHEATED FROM THE STRAIN OF THE RETURN TRIP...
MOLIOM-- YOU'D BETTER MOVE! IT'S GOING TO EXPLODE ANY SECOND!
WE'RE RIGHT BEHIND YOU, MAR!
"NO SOONER HAD WE GAINED SHELTER THAN THE KRULL CRAFT EXPLODED INTO FLAMES AND WAS GONE IN AN INSTANT-
"--JUST LIKE OUR MOON, WEGTHOR!
"BUT UNLIKE WEGTHOR, THE SHIP WAS UNINHABITED-- AND THAT MADE ALL THE DIFFERENCE!"

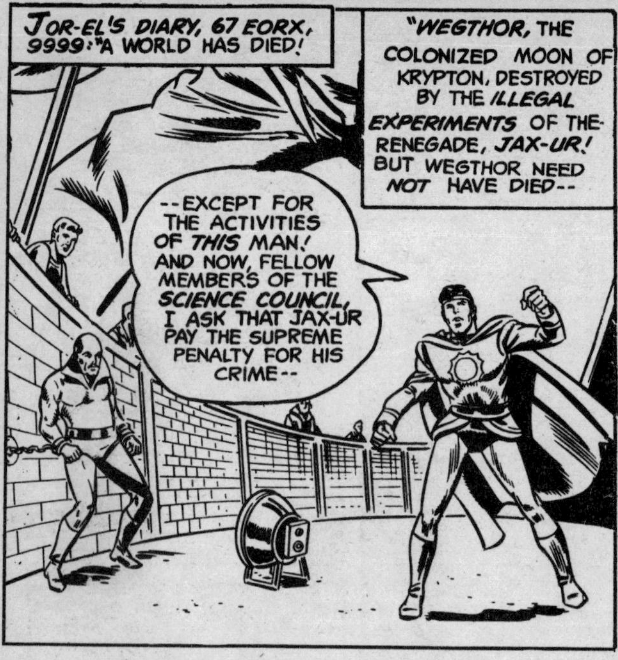
JOR-EL'S DIARY, 67 EORX, 9999: "A WORLD HAS DIED!
"WEGTHOR, THE COLONIZED MOON OF KRYPTON, DESTROYED BY THE ILLEGAL EXPERIMENTS OF THE RENEGADE, JAX-UR! BUT WEGTHOR NEED NOT HAVE DIED--
--EXCEPT FOR THE ACTIVITIES OF THIS MAN! AND NOW, FELLOW MEMBERS OF THE SCIENCE COUNCIL, I ASK THAT JAX-UR PAY THE SUPREME PENALTY FOR HIS CRIME--

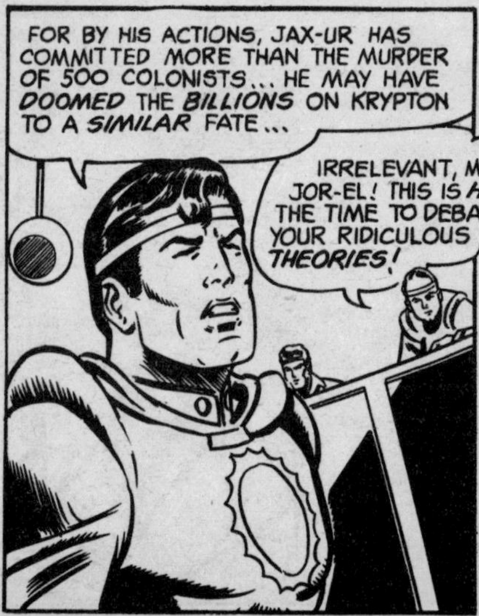
FOR BY HIS ACTIONS, JAX-UR HAS COMMITTED MORE THAN THE MURDER OF 500 COLONISTS... HE MAY HAVE DOOMED THE BILLIONS ON KRYPTON TO A SIMILAR FATE...
IRRELEVANT, MOLIOM JOR-EL! THIS IS HARDLY THE TIME TO DEBATE YOUR RIDICULOUS THEORIES!

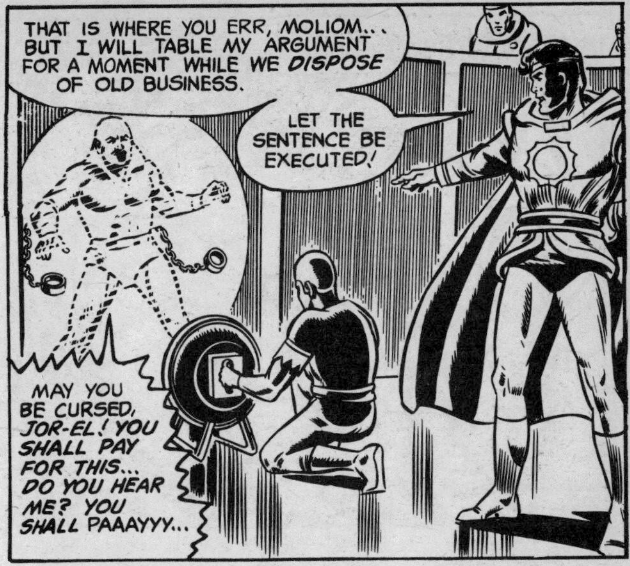
THAT IS WHERE YOU ERR, MOLIOM... BUT I WILL TABLE MY ARGUMENT FOR A MOMENT WHILE WE *DISPOSE* OF OLD BUSINESS.
LET THE SENTENCE BE EXECUTED!
MAY YOU BE CURSED, *JOR-EL! YOU SHALL PAY FOR THIS... DO YOU HEAR ME? YOU SHALL* PAAAYYY...

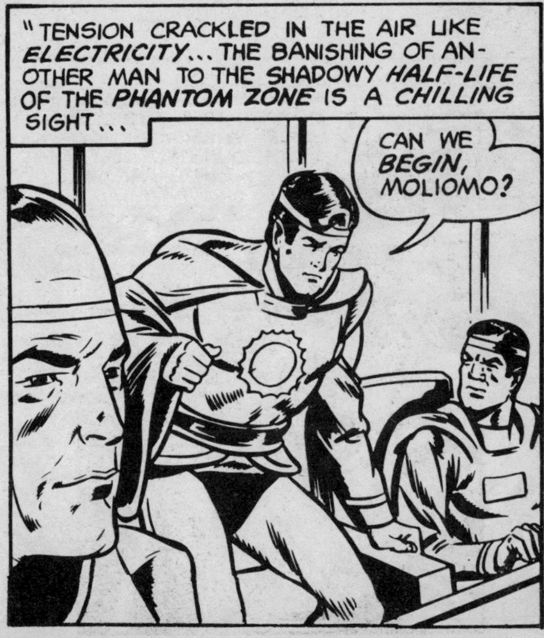
"TENSION CRACKLED IN THE AIR LIKE *ELECTRICITY*... THE BANISHING OF AN-OTHER MAN TO THE *SHADOWY HALF-LIFE* OF THE *PHANTOM ZONE* IS A *CHILLING* SIGHT...
CAN WE *BEGIN,* MOLIOMO?

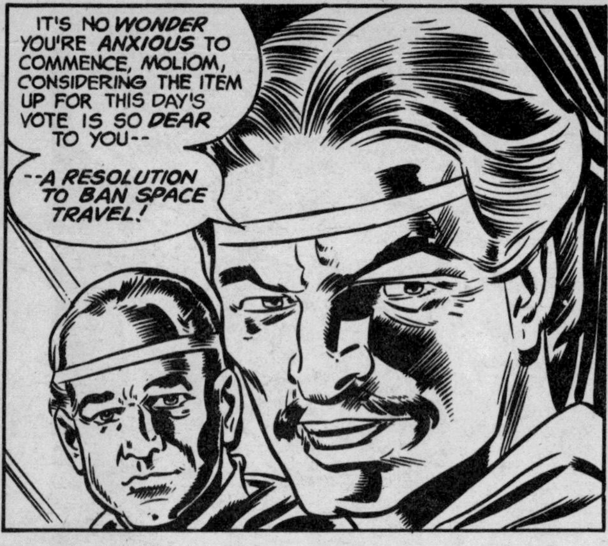
IT'S NO WONDER YOU'RE ANXIOUS TO COMMENCE, MOLIOM, CONSIDERING THE ITEM UP FOR THIS DAY'S VOTE IS SO DEAR TO YOU--
--A RESOLUTION TO BAN SPACE TRAVEL!

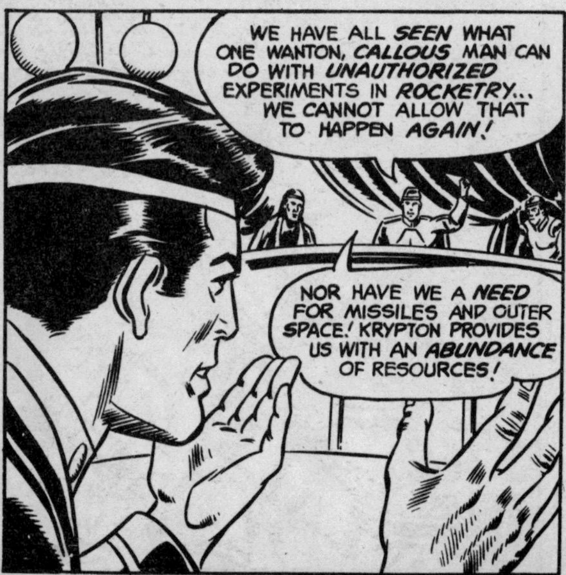
WE HAVE ALL SEEN WHAT ONE WANTON, CALLOUS MAN CAN DO WITH UNAUTHORIZED EXPERIMENTS IN ROCKETRY... WE CANNOT ALLOW THAT TO HAPPEN AGAIN!
NOR HAVE WE A NEED FOR MISSILES AND OUTER SPACE! KRYPTON PROVIDES US WITH AN ABUNDANCE OF RESOURCES!

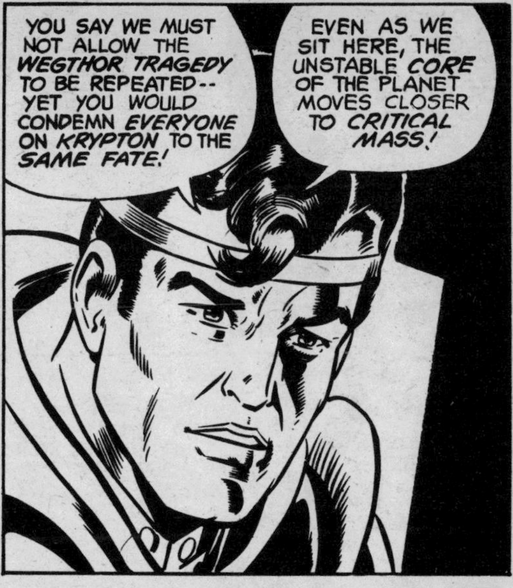
YOU SAY WE MUST NOT ALLOW THE WEGTHOR TRAGEDY TO BE REPEATED-- YET YOU WOULD CONDEMN EVERYONE ON KRYPTON TO THE SAME FATE!
EVEN AS WE SIT HERE, THE UNSTABLE CORE OF THE PLANET MOVES CLOSER TO CRITICAL MASS!

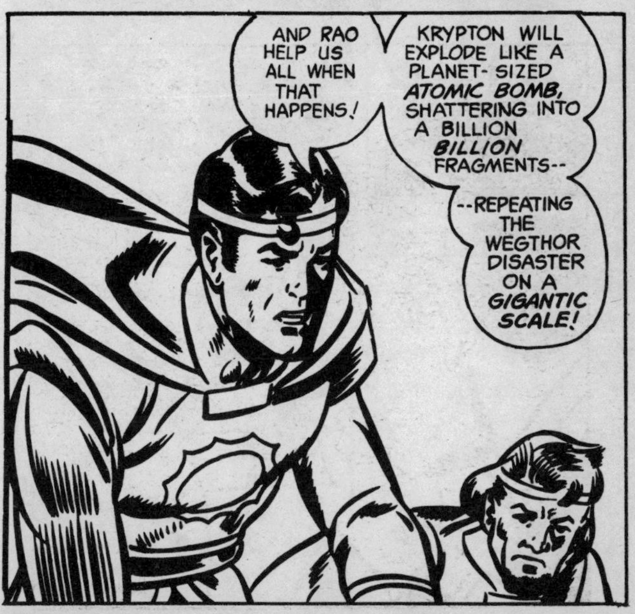
KRYPTON WILL EXPLODE LIKE A PLANET-SIZED ATOMIC BOMB, SHATTERING INTO A BILLION BILLION FRAGMENTS--
--REPEATING THE WEGTHOR DISASTER ON A GIGANTIC SCALE!
AND RAO HELP US ALL WHEN THAT HAPPENS!

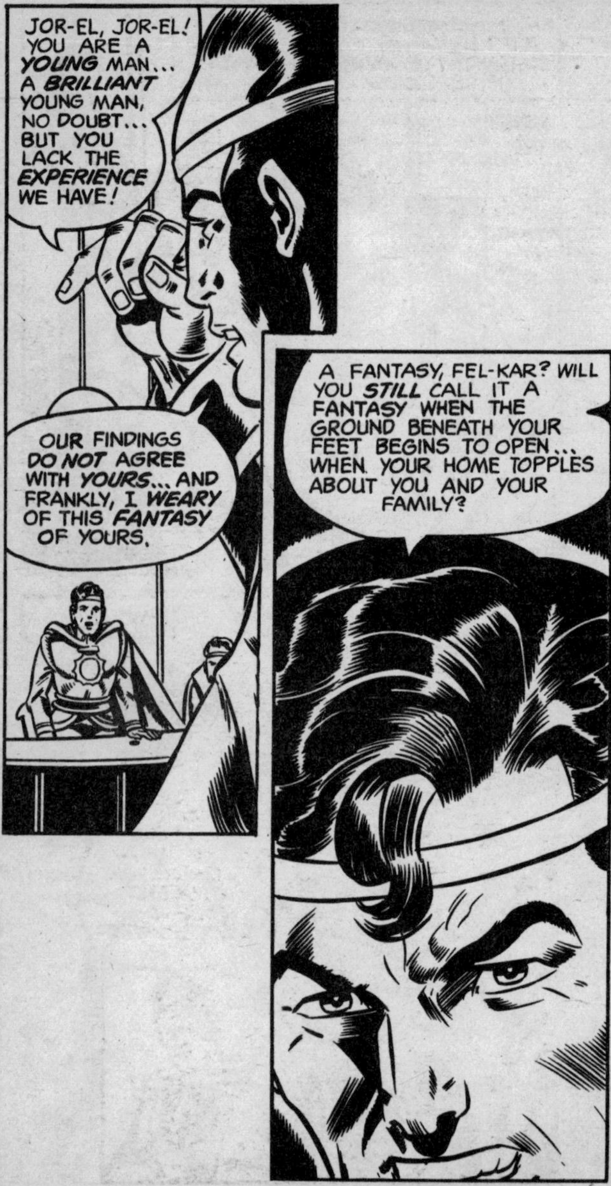
JOR-EL, JOR-EL! YOU ARE A YOUNG MAN... A BRILLIANT YOUNG MAN, NO DOUBT... BUT YOU LACK THE EXPERIENCE WE HAVE!
OUR FINDINGS DO NOT AGREE WITH YOURS... AND FRANKLY, I WEARY OF THIS FANTASY OF YOURS.
A FANTASY, FEL-KAR? WILL YOU STILL CALL IT A FANTASY WHEN THE GROUND BENEATH YOUR FEET BEGINS TO OPEN... WHEN YOUR HOME TOPPLES ABOUT YOU AND YOUR FAMILY?

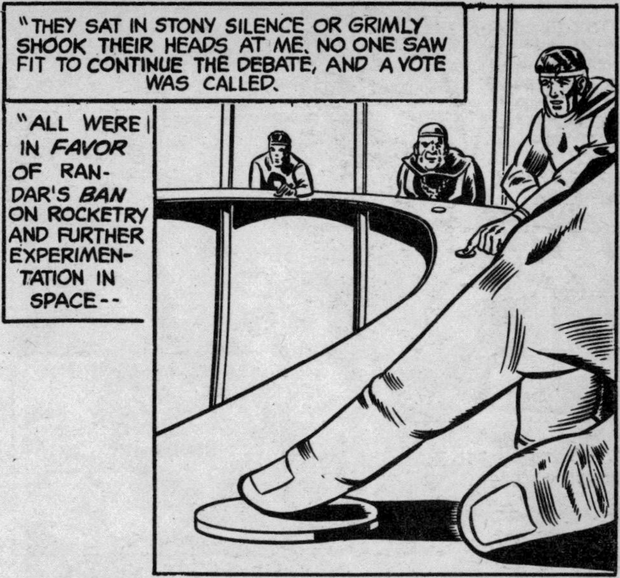
"THEY SAT IN STONY SILENCE OR GRIMLY SHOOK THEIR HEADS AT ME. NO ONE SAW FIT TO CONTINUE THE DEBATE, AND A VOTE WAS CALLED.
"ALL WERE IN FAVOR OF RAN-DAR'S BAN ON ROCKETRY AND FURTHER EXPERIMEN-TATION IN SPACE--

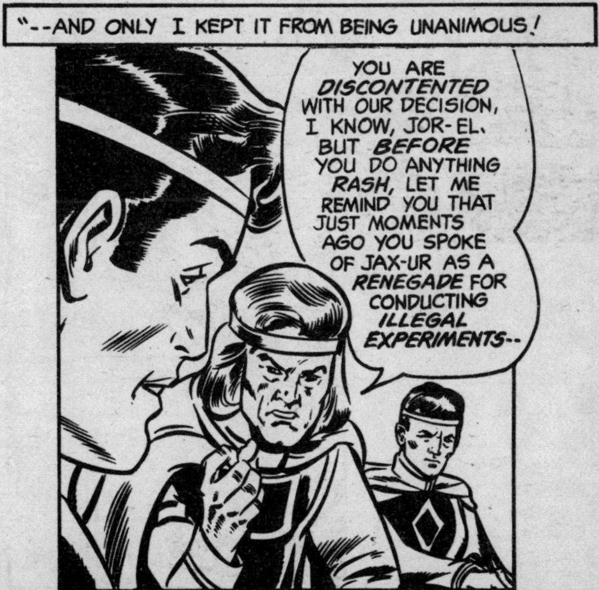
"--AND ONLY I KEPT IT FROM BEING UNANIMOUS!
YOU ARE DISCONTENTED WITH OUR DECISION, I KNOW, JOR-EL. BUT BEFORE YOU DO ANYTHING RASH, LET ME REMIND YOU THAT JUST MOMENTS AGO YOU SPOKE OF JAX-UR AS A RENEGADE FOR CONDUCTING ILLEGAL EXPERIMENTS--

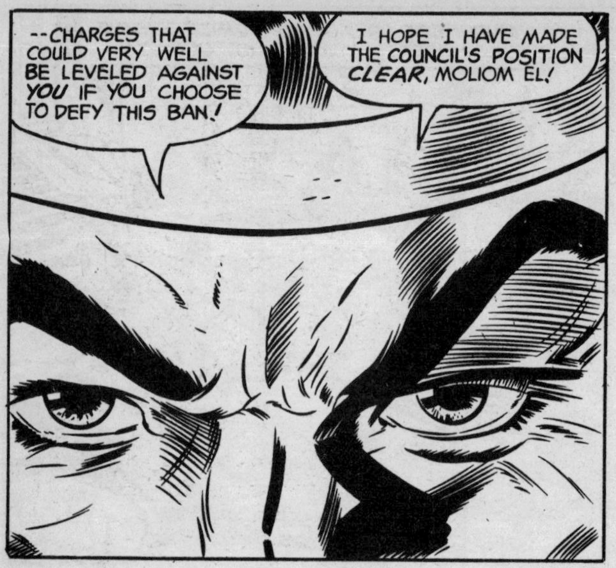
--CHARGES THAT COULD VERY WELL BE LEVELED AGAINST YOU IF YOU CHOOSE TO DEFY THIS BAN!
I HOPE I HAVE MADE THE COUNCIL'S POSITION CLEAR, MOLIOM EL!

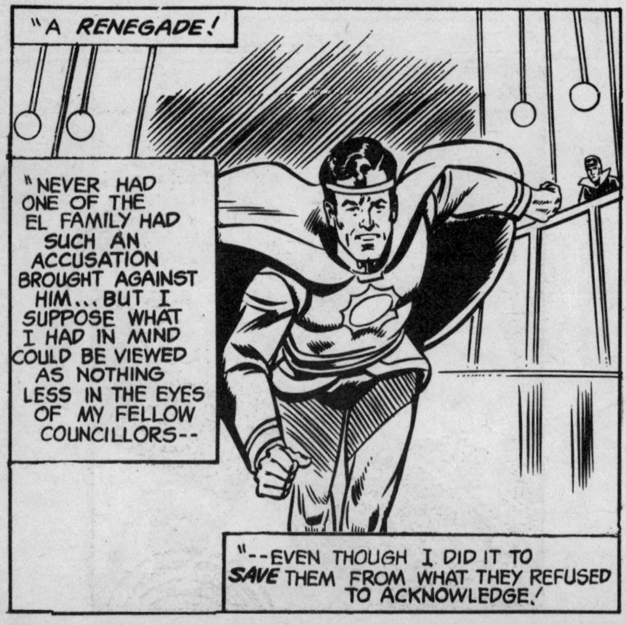
"A RENEGADE!
"NEVER HAD ONE OF THE EL FAMILY HAD SUCH AN ACCUSATION BROUGHT AGAINST HIM... BUT I SUPPOSE WHAT I HAD IN MIND COULD BE VIEWED AS NOTHING LESS IN THE EYES OF MY FELLOW COUNCILLORS--
"--EVEN THOUGH I DID IT TO SAVE THEM FROM WHAT THEY REFUSED TO ACKNOWLEDGE!

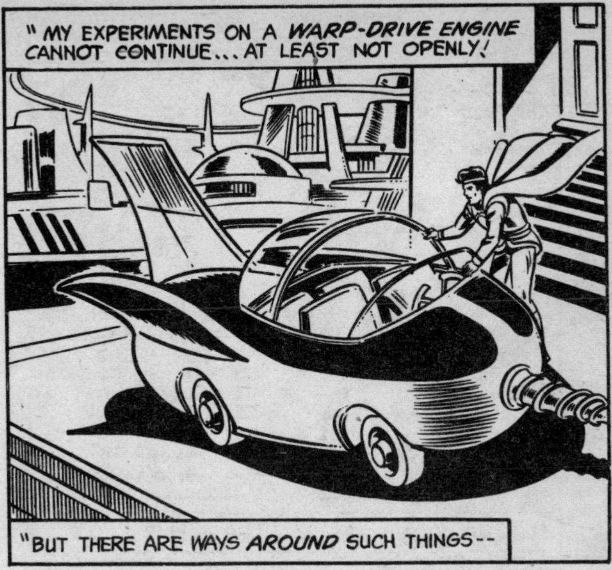
"MY EXPERIMENTS ON A WARP-DRIVE ENGINE CANNOT CONTINUE... AT LEAST NOT OPENLY!
"BUT THERE ARE WAYS AROUND SUCH THINGS--

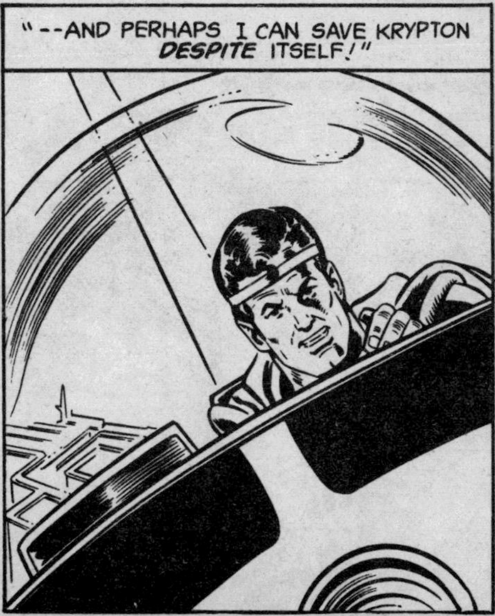
"--AND PERHAPS I CAN SAVE KRYPTON DESPITE ITSELF!"

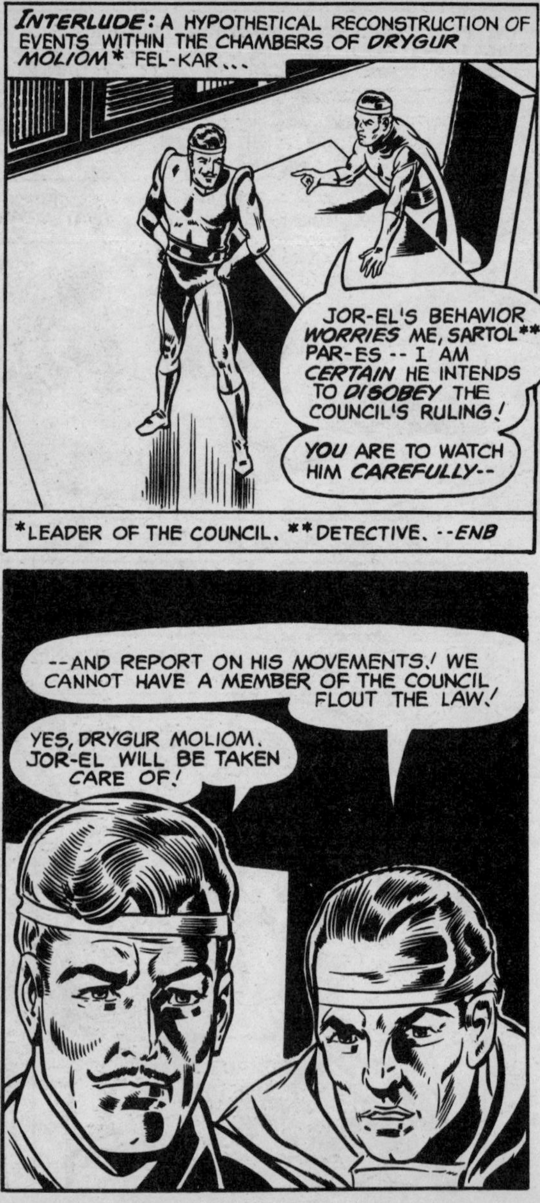
INTERLUDE: A HYPOTHETICAL RECONSTRUCTION OF EVENTS WITHIN THE CHAMBERS OF DRYGUR MOLIOM* FEL-KAR...
JOR-EL'S BEHAVIOR WORRIES ME, SARTOL** PAR-ES -- I AM CERTAIN HE INTENDS TO DISOBEY THE COUNCIL'S RULING!
YOU ARE TO WATCH HIM CAREFULLY--
*LEADER OF THE COUNCIL. **DETECTIVE. --ENB
--AND REPORT ON HIS MOVEMENTS! WE CANNOT HAVE A MEMBER OF THE COUNCIL FLOUT THE LAW!
YES, DRYGUR MOLIOM. JOR-EL WILL BE TAKEN CARE OF!

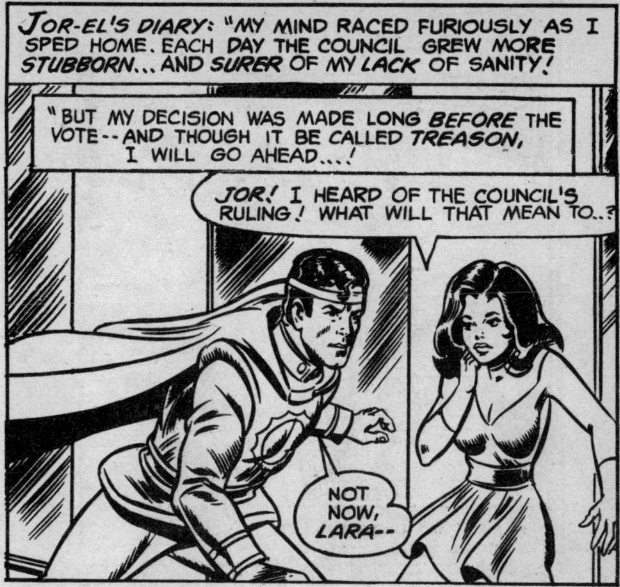
JOR-EL'S DIARY: "MY MIND RACED FURIOUSLY AS I SPED HOME. EACH DAY THE COUNCIL GREW MORE STUBBORN... AND SURER OF MY LACK OF SANITY!
"BUT MY DECISION WAS MADE LONG BEFORE THE VOTE--AND THOUGH IT BE CALLED TREASON, I WILL GO AHEAD...!
JOR! I HEARD OF THE COUNCIL'S RULING! WHAT WILL THAT MEAN TO..?
NOT NOW, LARA--

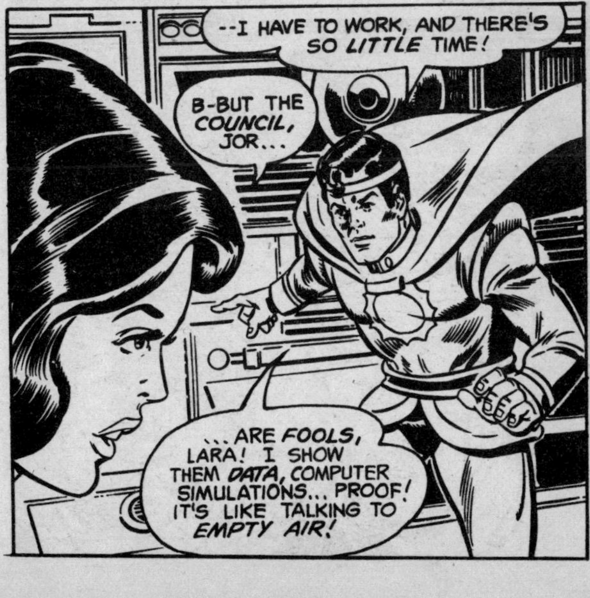
--I HAVE TO WORK, AND THERE'S SO LITTLE TIME!
B-BUT THE COUNCIL, JOR...
...ARE FOOLS, LARA! I SHOW THEM DATA, COMPUTER SIMULATIONS... PROOF! IT'S LIKE TALKING TO EMPTY AIR!

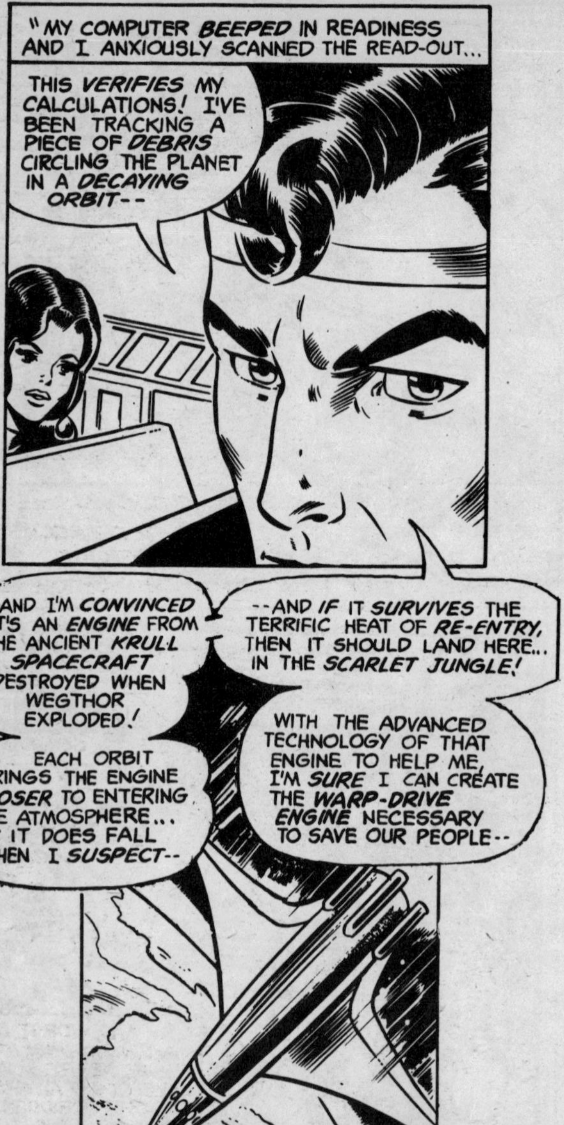
"MY COMPUTER BEEPED IN READINESS AND I ANXIOUSLY SCANNED THE READ-OUT...
THIS VERIFIES MY CALCULATIONS! I'VE BEEN TRACKING A PIECE OF DEBRIS CIRCLING THE PLANET IN A DECAYING ORBIT--
--AND I'M CONVINCED IT'S AN ENGINE FROM THE ANCIENT KRULL SPACECRAFT DESTROYED WHEN WEGTHOR EXPLODED!
--AND IF IT SURVIVES THE TERRIFIC HEAT OF RE-ENTRY, THEN IT SHOULD LAND HERE... IN THE SCARLET JUNGLE!
EACH ORBIT BRINGS THE ENGINE CLOSER TO ENTERING THE ATMOSPHERE... IF IT DOES FALL WHEN I SUSPECT--
WITH THE ADVANCED TECHNOLOGY OF THAT ENGINE TO HELP ME, I'M SURE I CAN CREATE THE WARP-DRIVE ENGINE NECESSARY TO SAVE OUR PEOPLE--

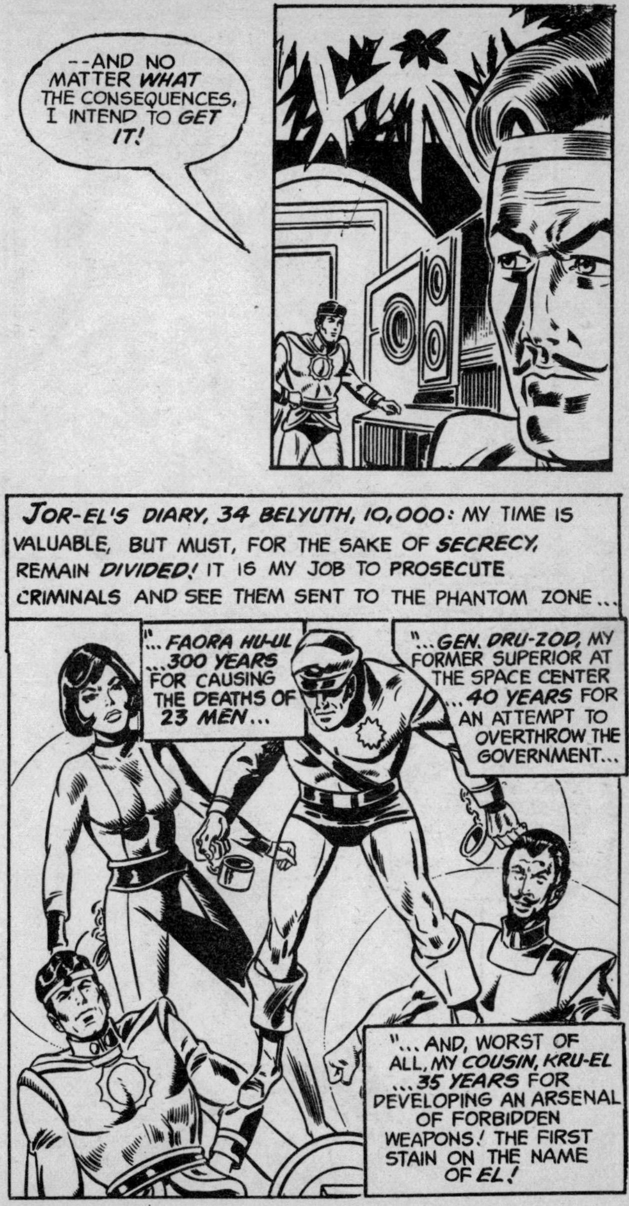
--AND NO MATTER WHAT THE CONSEQUENCES, I INTEND TO GET IT!
JOR-EL'S DIARY, 34 BELYUTH, 10,000: MY TIME IS VALUABLE, BUT MUST, FOR THE SAKE OF SECRECY, REMAIN DIVIDED! IT IS MY JOB TO PROSECUTE CRIMINALS AND SEE THEM SENT TO THE PHANTOM ZONE...
"...FAORA HU-UL ...300 YEARS FOR CAUSING THE DEATHS OF 23 MEN...
"...GEN. DRU-ZOD, MY FORMER SUPERIOR AT THE SPACE CENTER ...40 YEARS FOR AN ATTEMPT TO OVERTHROW THE GOVERNMENT...
"...AND, WORST OF ALL, MY COUSIN, KRU-EL ...35 YEARS FOR DEVELOPING AN ARSENAL OF FORBIDDEN WEAPONS! THE FIRST STAIN ON THE NAME OF EL!

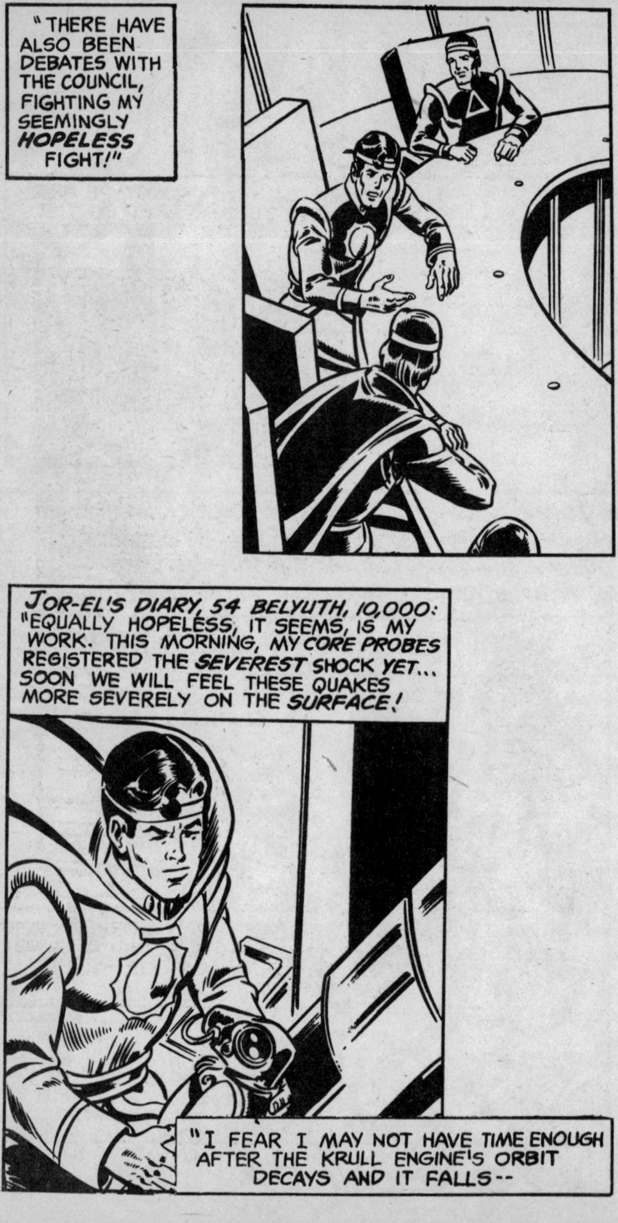
"THERE HAVE ALSO BEEN DEBATES WITH THE COUNCIL, FIGHTING MY SEEMINGLY HOPELESS FIGHT!"
JOR-EL'S DIARY, 54 BELYUTH, 10,000: "EQUALLY HOPELESS, IT SEEMS, IS MY WORK. THIS MORNING, MY CORE PROBES REGISTERED THE SEVEREST SHOCK YET... SOON WE WILL FEEL THESE QUAKES MORE SEVERELY ON THE SURFACE!
"I FEAR I MAY NOT HAVE TIME ENOUGH AFTER THE KRULL ENGINE'S ORBIT DECAYS AND IT FALLS--

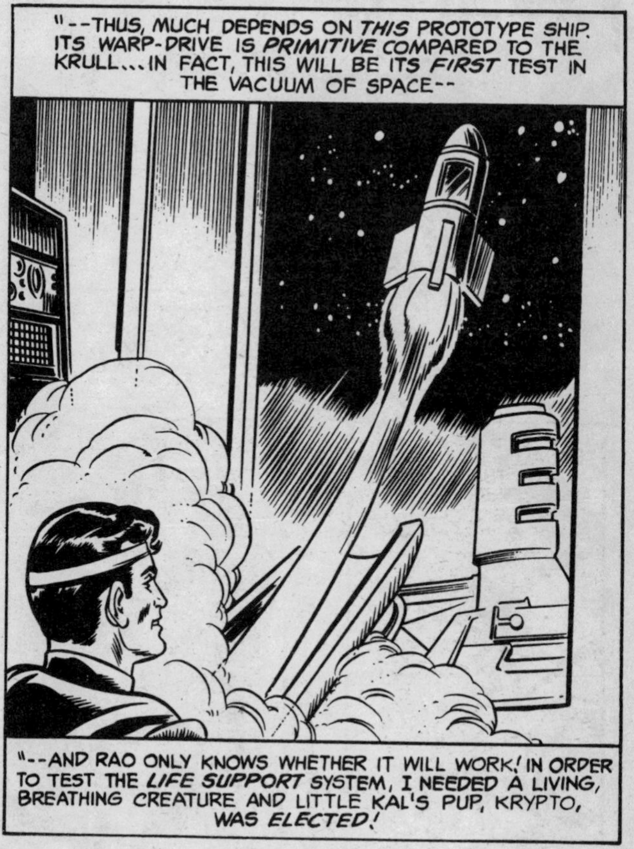
"--THUS, MUCH DEPENDS ON THIS PROTOTYPE SHIP. ITS WARP-DRIVE IS PRIMITIVE COMPARED TO THE KRULL... IN FACT, THIS WILL BE ITS FIRST TEST IN THE VACUUM OF SPACE--
"--AND RAO ONLY KNOWS WHETHER IT WILL WORK! IN ORDER TO TEST THE LIFE SUPPORT SYSTEM, I NEEDED A LIVING, BREATHING CREATURE AND LITTLE KAL'S PUP, KRYPTO, WAS ELECTED!

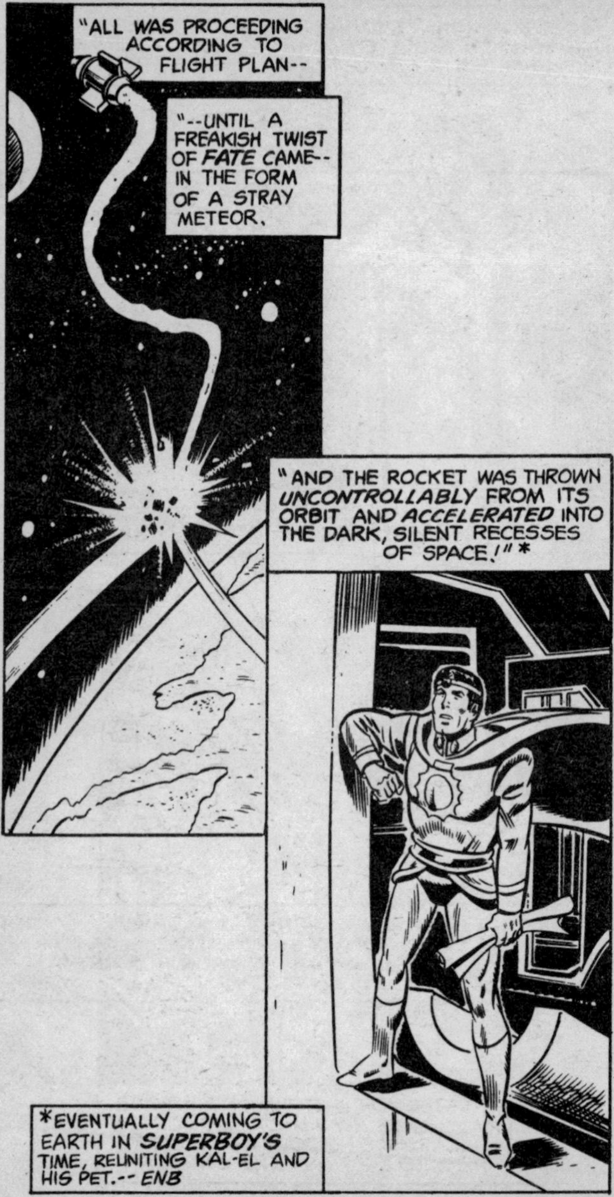
"ALL WAS PROCEEDING ACCORDING TO FLIGHT PLAN--
"--UNTIL A FREAKISH TWIST OF FATE CAME--IN THE FORM OF A STRAY METEOR.
"AND THE ROCKET WAS THROWN UNCONTROLLABLY FROM ITS ORBIT AND ACCELERATED INTO THE DARK, SILENT RECESSES OF SPACE!" *
*EVENTUALLY COMING TO EARTH IN SUPERBOY'S TIME, REUNITING KAL-EL AND HIS PET.-- ENB

JOR-EL'S DIARY, 12 OGTAL, 10,000: "ON TARGET! THE KRULL ENGINE COMPLETED *RE-ENTRY* JUST HOURS AGO, LANDING WITHIN A *HALF MILE* OF WHERE I PREDICTED!

"ONE PROBLEM, THOUGH. I CAN GET THE ENGINE, BUT I DON'T THINK I'LL BE GOING TO THE SCARLET JUNGLE--

"--ALONE!

" MY DETECTION INSTRUMENTS INDICATE *SURVEILLANCE* BY AN OFFICER OF THE COUNCIL POLICE, UNDOUBTEDLY SENT BY THEM TO KEEP AN *EYE* ON ME.

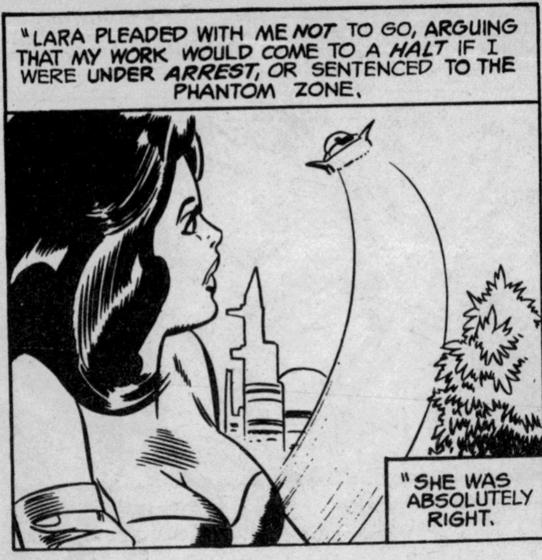
"LARA PLEADED WITH ME NOT TO GO, ARGUING THAT MY WORK WOULD COME TO A HALT IF I WERE UNDER ARREST, OR SENTENCED TO THE PHANTOM ZONE.
"SHE WAS ABSOLUTELY RIGHT.

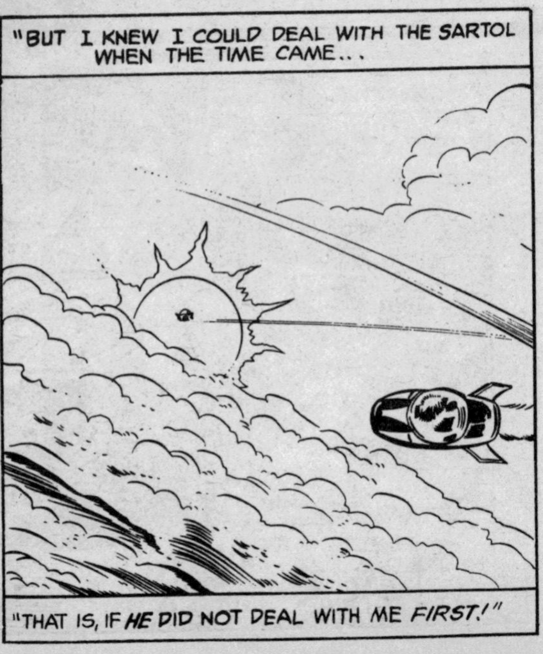
"BUT I KNEW I COULD DEAL WITH THE SARTOL WHEN THE TIME CAME...
"THAT IS, IF HE DID NOT DEAL WITH ME FIRST!"

"I HAD PAR-ES'S FLYER ON MY *SCANNER* AS I TOUCHED DOWN IN THE SCARLET JUNGLE. HE, HOWEVER, WASN'T TRUSTING TO *INSTRUMENTS* KEEPING MY SHIP IN HIS LINE OF SIGHT.

THIS MAN IS A *DEDICATED* OFFICER... HE WON'T BE EASY TO ELUDE!

CAN'T TAKE MY FLYER THROUGH THE JUNGLE, BUT, SINCE ALL THE *OTHER* EQUIPMENT CHECKS OUT--

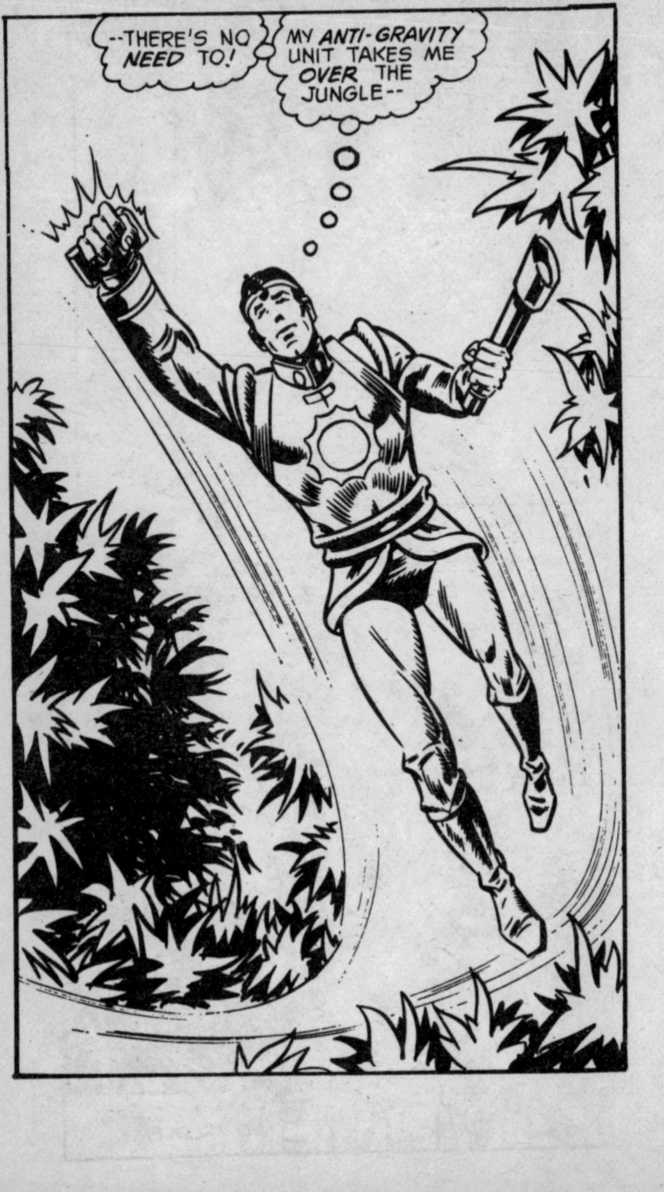
--THERE'S NO NEED TO!
MY ANTI-GRAVITY UNIT TAKES ME OVER THE JUNGLE--

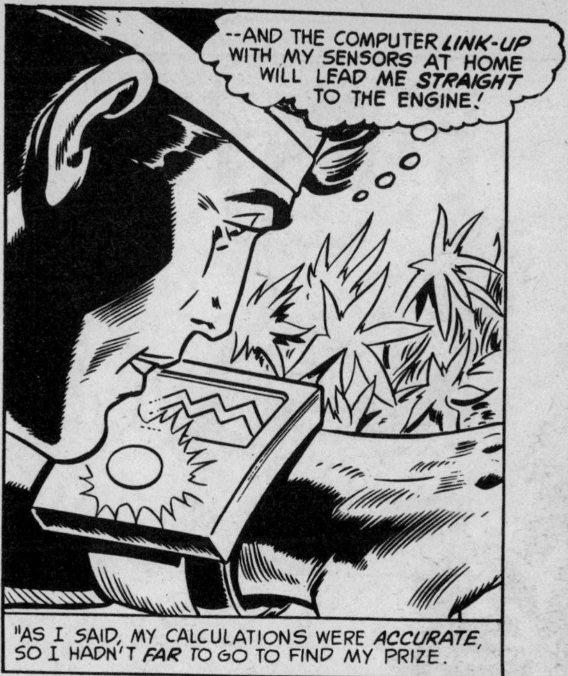
--AND THE COMPUTER LINK-UP WITH MY SENSORS AT HOME WILL LEAD ME STRAIGHT TO THE ENGINE!
"AS I SAID, MY CALCULATIONS WERE ACCURATE, SO I HADN'T FAR TO GO TO FIND MY PRIZE.

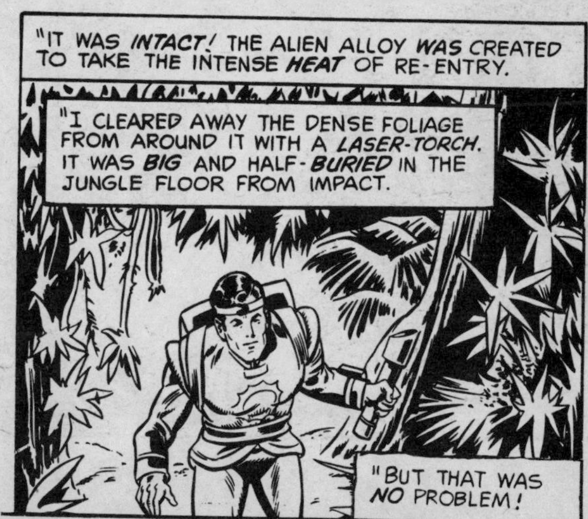
"IT WAS INTACT! THE ALIEN ALLOY WAS CREATED TO TAKE THE INTENSE HEAT OF RE-ENTRY.
"I CLEARED AWAY THE DENSE FOLIAGE FROM AROUND IT WITH A LASER-TORCH. IT WAS BIG AND HALF-BURIED IN THE JUNGLE FLOOR FROM IMPACT.
"BUT THAT WAS NO PROBLEM!

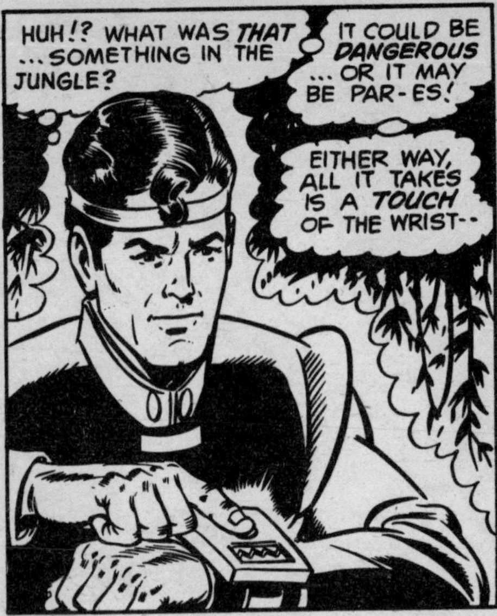
HUH!? WHAT WAS THAT ...SOMETHING IN THE JUNGLE?
IT COULD BE DANGEROUS ...OR IT MAY BE PAR-ES!
EITHER WAY, ALL IT TAKES IS A TOUCH OF THE WRIST--

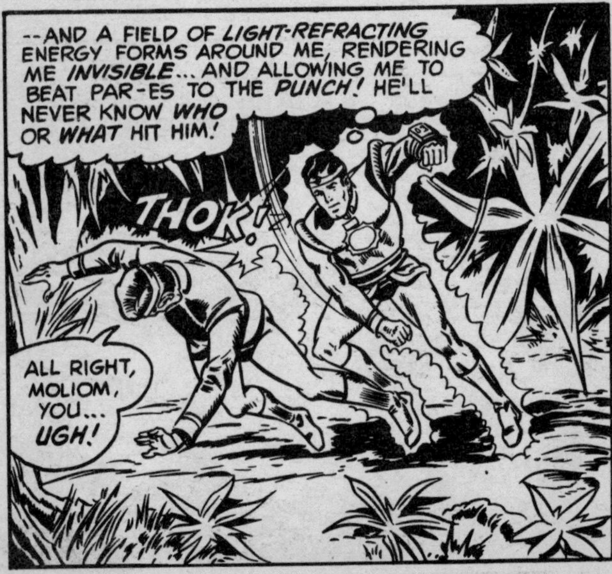
--AND A FIELD OF LIGHT-REFRACTING ENERGY FORMS AROUND ME, RENDERING ME INVISIBLE... AND ALLOWING ME TO BEAT PAR-ES TO THE PUNCH! HE'LL NEVER KNOW WHO OR WHAT HIT HIM!
THOK!
ALL RIGHT, MOLIOM, YOU... UGH!

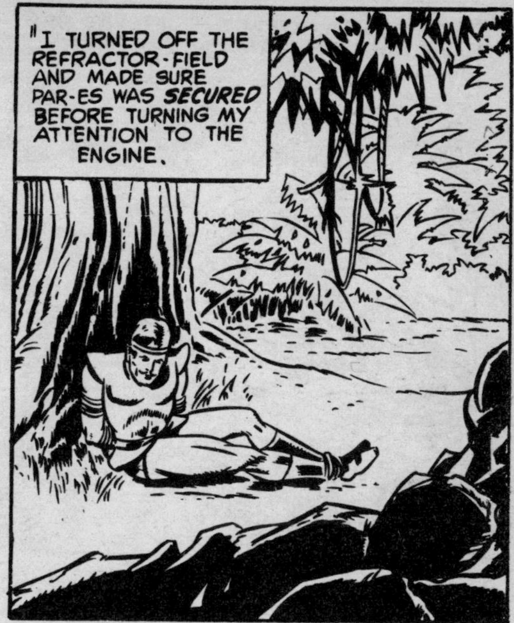
"I TURNED OFF THE REFRACTOR-FIELD AND MADE SURE PAR-ES WAS SECURED BEFORE TURNING MY ATTENTION TO THE ENGINE.

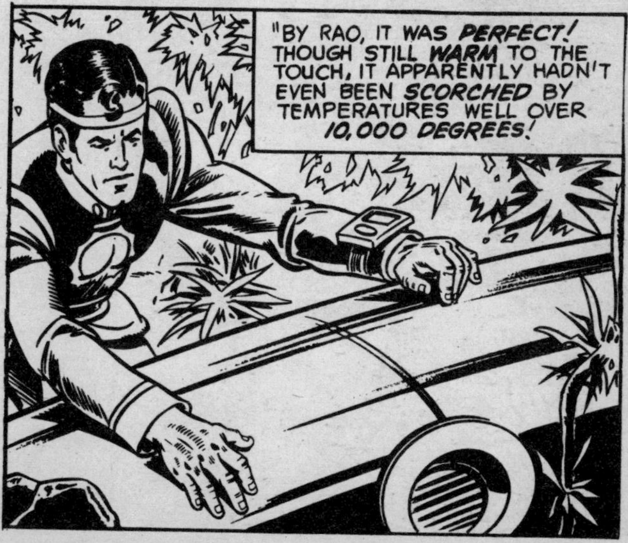
"BY RAO, IT WAS PERFECT! THOUGH STILL WARM TO THE TOUCH, IT APPARENTLY HADN'T EVEN BEEN SCORCHED BY TEMPERATURES WELL OVER 10,000 DEGREES!

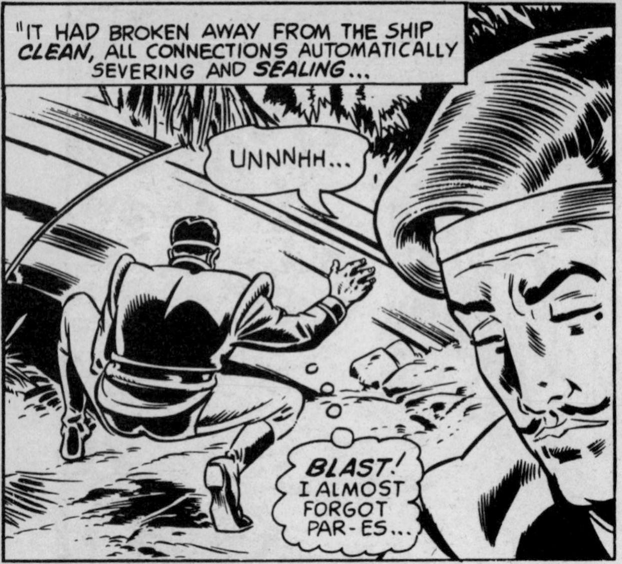
"IT HAD BROKEN AWAY FROM THE SHIP *CLEAN*, ALL CONNECTIONS AUTOMATICALLY SEVERING AND *SEALING*...
UNNNHH...
BLAST! I ALMOST FORGOT PAR-ES...

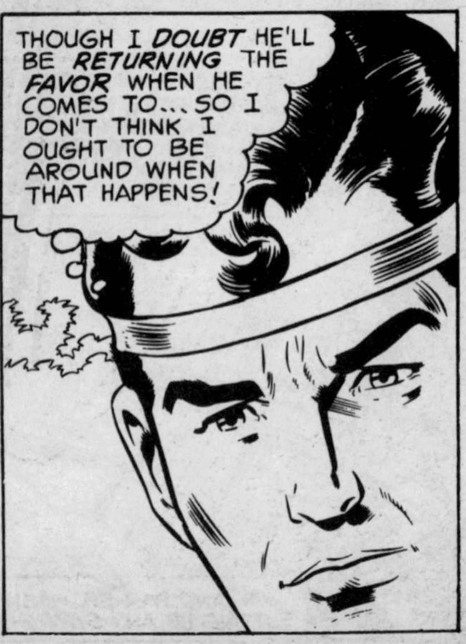
THOUGH I *DOUBT* HE'LL BE *RETURNING* THE *FAVOR* WHEN HE COMES TO... SO I DON'T THINK I OUGHT TO BE AROUND WHEN THAT HAPPENS!

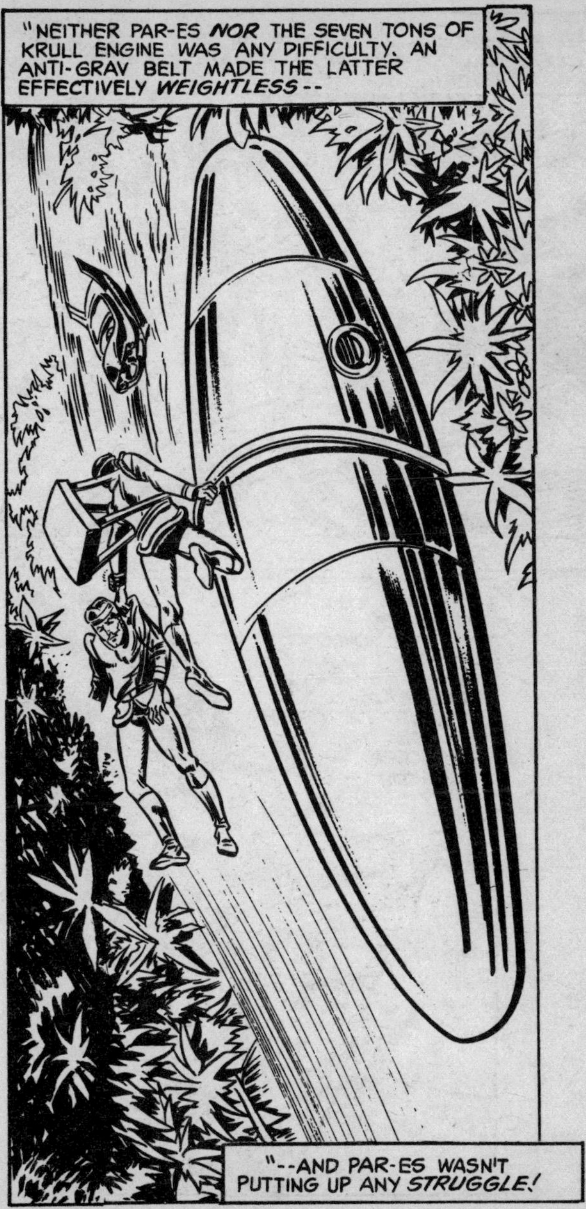
"NEITHER PAR-ES NOR THE SEVEN TONS OF KRULL ENGINE WAS ANY DIFFICULTY. AN ANTI-GRAV BELT MADE THE LATTER EFFECTIVELY WEIGHTLESS--
"--AND PAR-ES WASN'T PUTTING UP ANY STRUGGLE!

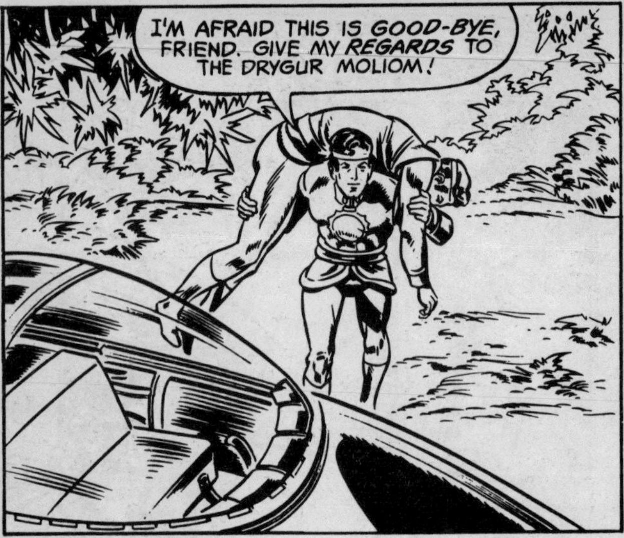
I'M AFRAID THIS IS GOOD-BYE, FRIEND. GIVE MY REGARDS TO THE DRYGUR MOLIOM!

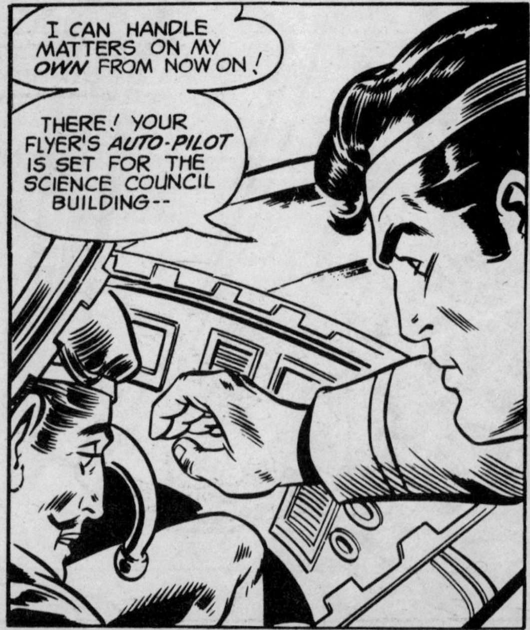
I CAN HANDLE MATTERS ON MY OWN FROM NOW ON!
THERE! YOUR FLYER'S AUTO-PILOT IS SET FOR THE SCIENCE COUNCIL BUILDING--

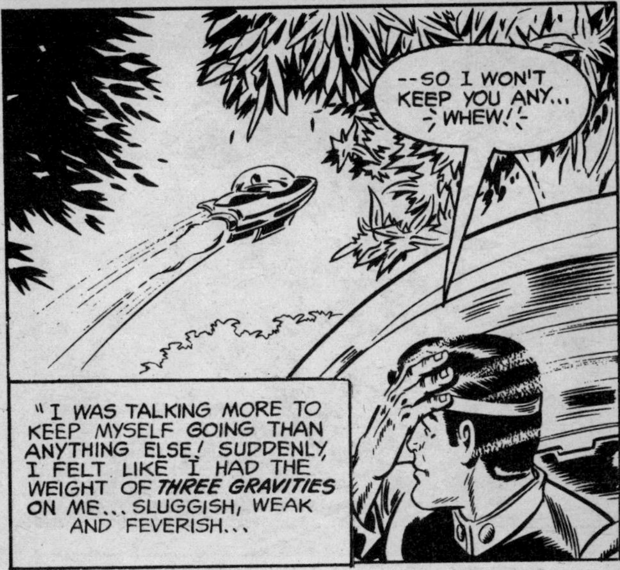
--SO I WON'T KEEP YOU ANY... WHEW!
"I WAS TALKING MORE TO KEEP MYSELF GOING THAN ANYTHING ELSE! SUDDENLY, I FELT LIKE I HAD THE WEIGHT OF THREE GRAVITIES ON ME... SLUGGISH, WEAK AND FEVERISH...

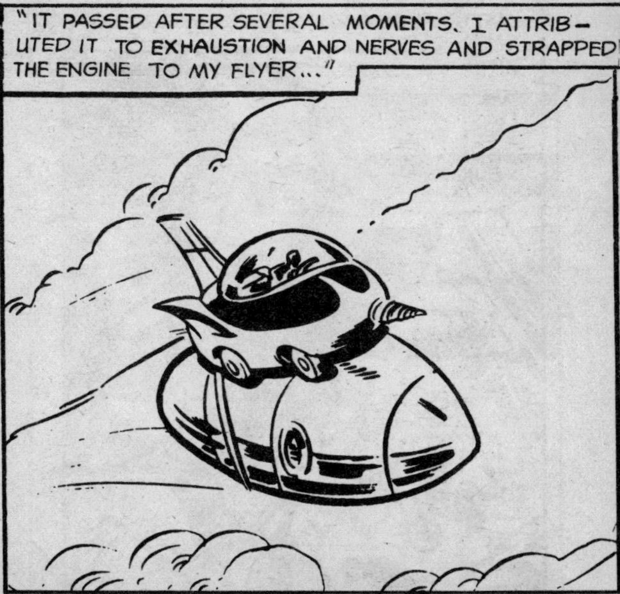
"IT PASSED AFTER SEVERAL MOMENTS. I ATTRIB-UTED IT TO EXHAUSTION AND NERVES AND STRAPPED THE ENGINE TO MY FLYER..."

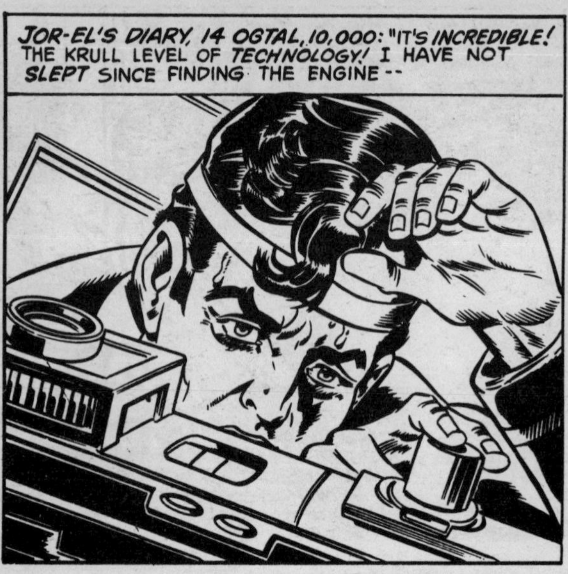
JOR-EL'S DIARY, 14 OGTAL, 10,000: "IT'S INCREDIBLE! THE KRULL LEVEL OF TECHNOLOGY! I HAVE NOT SLEPT SINCE FINDING THE ENGINE--

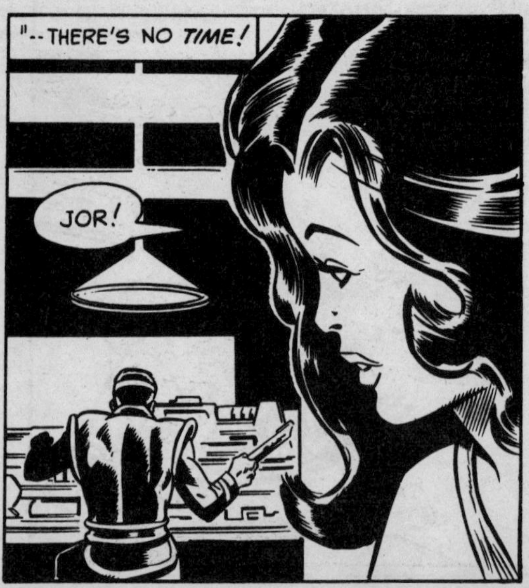
"--THERE'S NO TIME!
JOR!

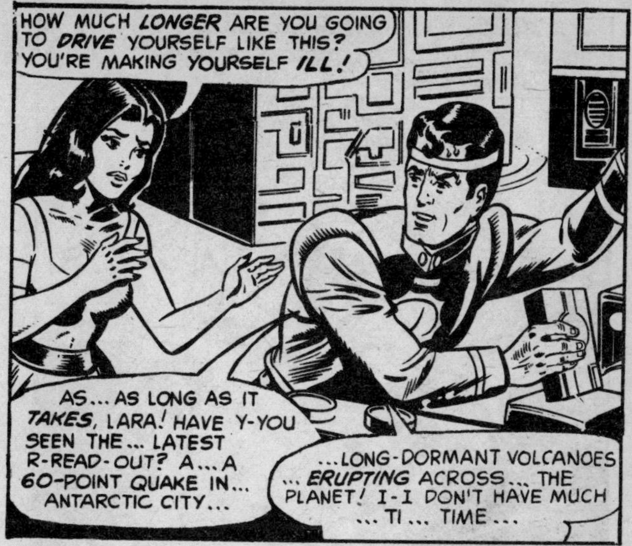
HOW MUCH LONGER ARE YOU GOING TO DRIVE YOURSELF LIKE THIS? YOU'RE MAKING YOURSELF ILL!
AS... AS LONG AS IT TAKES, LARA! HAVE Y-YOU SEEN THE... LATEST R-READ-OUT? A... A 60-POINT QUAKE IN... ANTARCTIC CITY...
...LONG-DORMANT VOLCANOES ... ERUPTING ACROSS... THE PLANET! I-I DON'T HAVE MUCH ... TI ... TIME ...

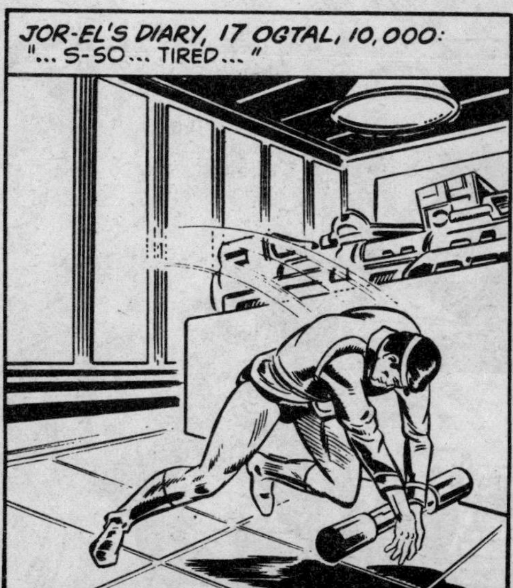
JOR-EL'S DIARY, 17 OGTAL, 10,000: "... S-SO... TIRED..."

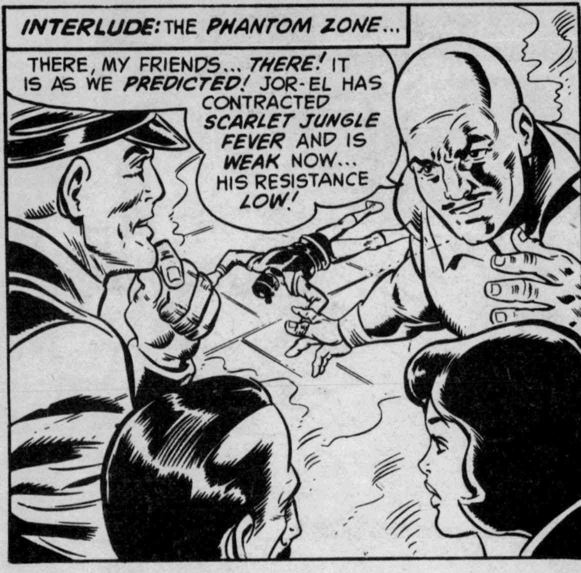
INTERLUDE: THE PHANTOM ZONE...
THERE, MY FRIENDS... THERE! IT IS AS WE PREDICTED! JOR-EL HAS CONTRACTED SCARLET JUNGLE FEVER AND IS WEAK NOW... HIS RESISTANCE LOW!

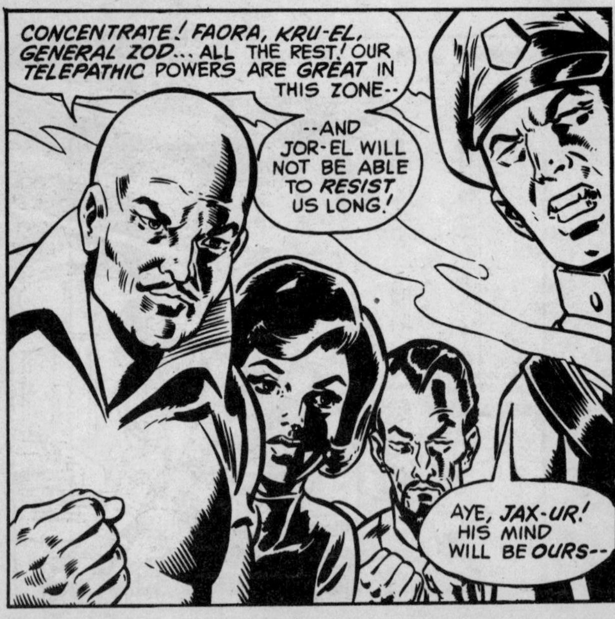
CONCENTRATE! FAORA, KRU-EL, GENERAL ZOD... ALL THE REST! OUR TELEPATHIC POWERS ARE GREAT IN THIS ZONE--
--AND JOR-EL WILL NOT BE ABLE TO RESIST US LONG!
AYE, JAX-UR! HIS MIND WILL BE OURS--

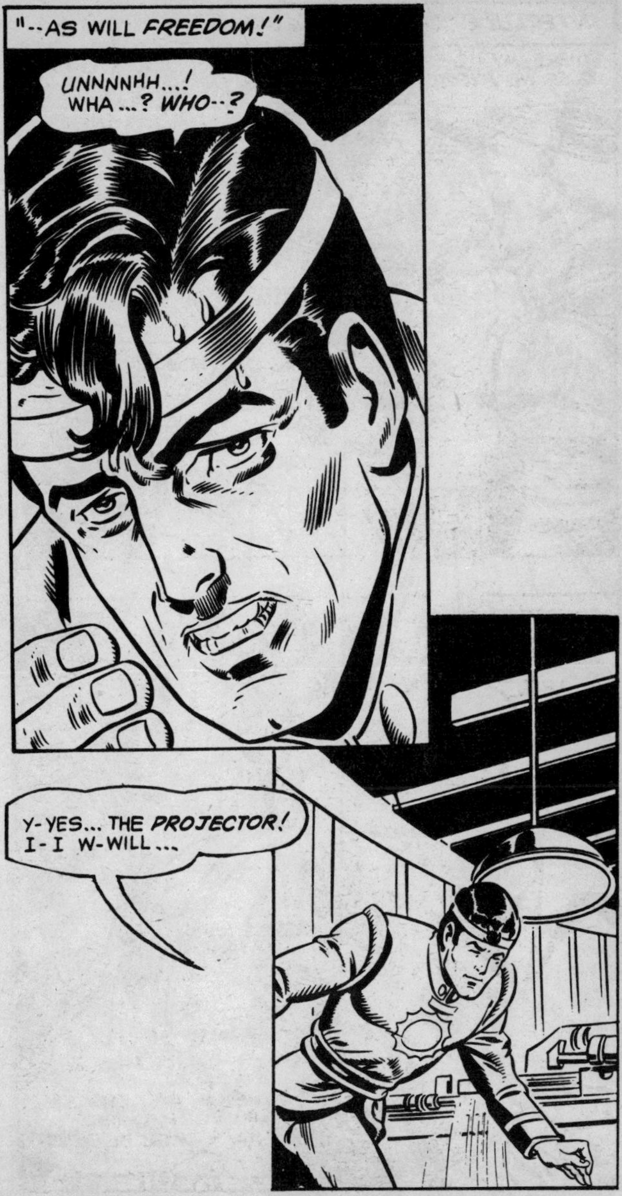
"--AS WILL FREEDOM!"
UNNNNHH...! WHA...? WHO--?
Y-YES... THE PROJECTOR! I-I W-WILL...

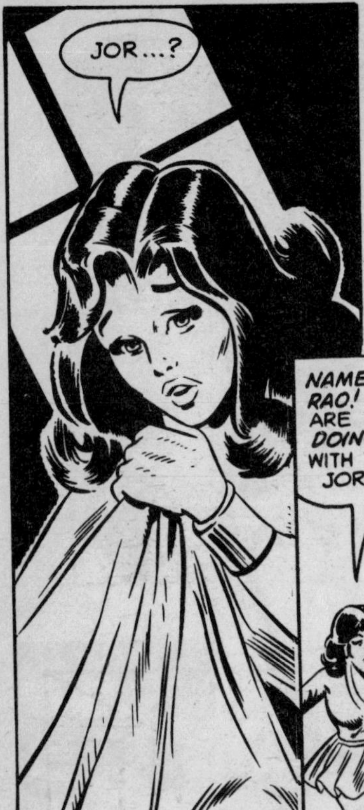
JOR...?

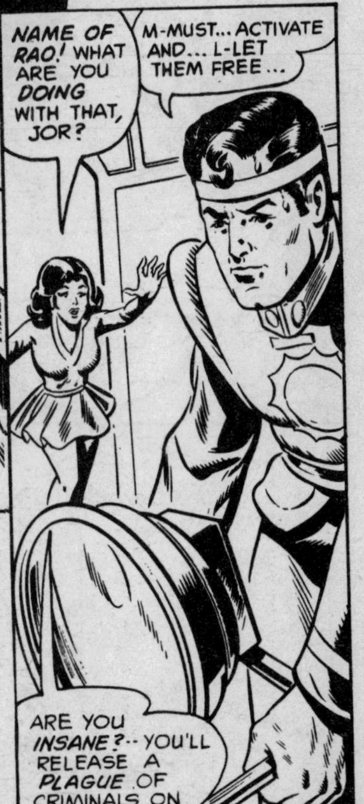
NAME OF RAO! WHAT ARE YOU DOING WITH THAT, JOR?
M-MUST... ACTIVATE AND... L-LET THEM FREE...
ARE YOU INSANE?-- YOU'LL RELEASE A PLAGUE OF CRIMINALS ON KRYPTON!

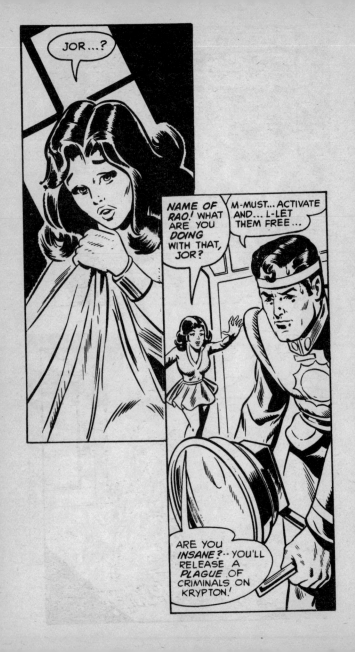

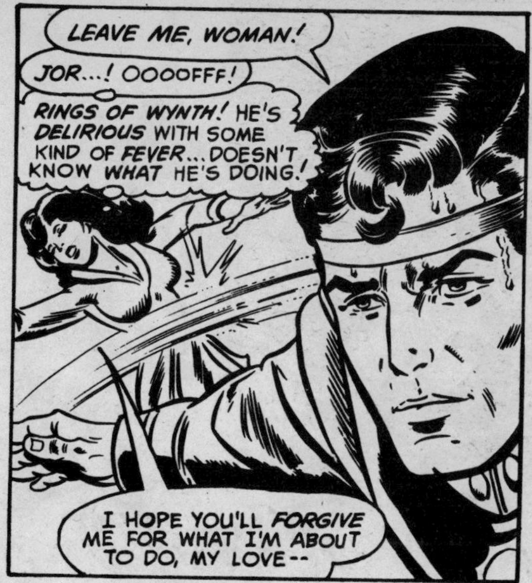
LEAVE ME, WOMAN!
JOR...! OOOOFFF!
RINGS OF WYNTH! HE'S DELIRIOUS WITH SOME KIND OF FEVER... DOESN'T KNOW WHAT HE'S DOING!
I HOPE YOU'LL FORGIVE ME FOR WHAT I'M ABOUT TO DO, MY LOVE--

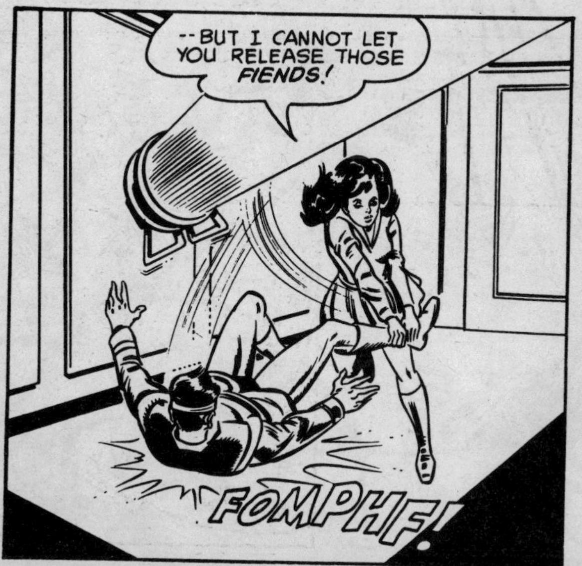
--BUT I CANNOT LET YOU RELEASE THOSE FIENDS!
FOMPHF!

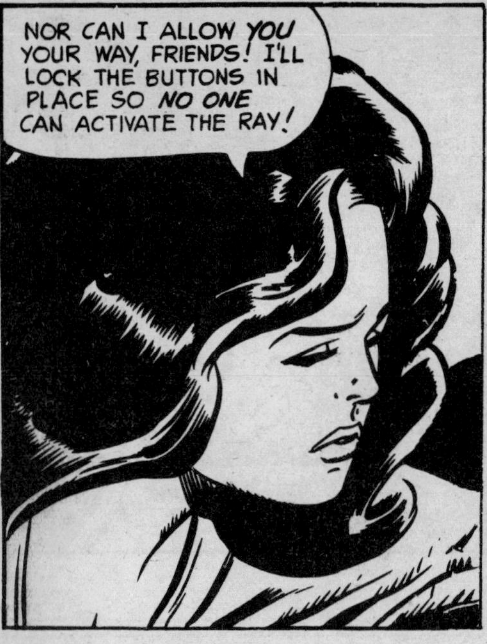
NOR CAN I ALLOW YOU YOUR WAY, FRIENDS! I'LL LOCK THE BUTTONS IN PLACE SO NO ONE CAN ACTIVATE THE RAY!

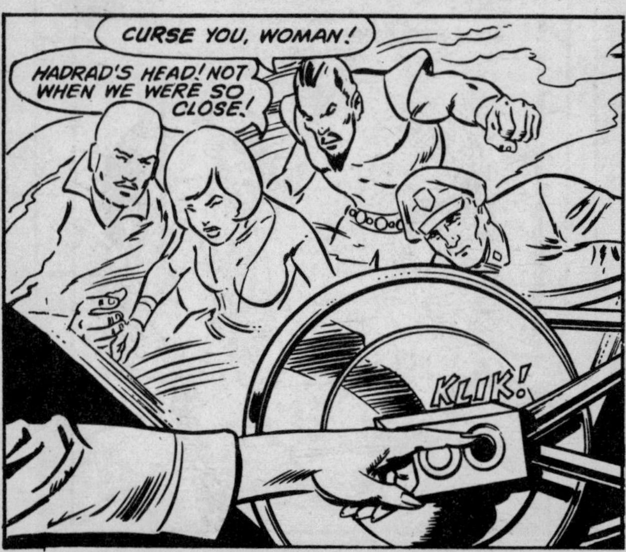
CURSE YOU, WOMAN!
HADRAD'S HEAD! NOT WHEN WE WERE SO CLOSE!
KLIK!

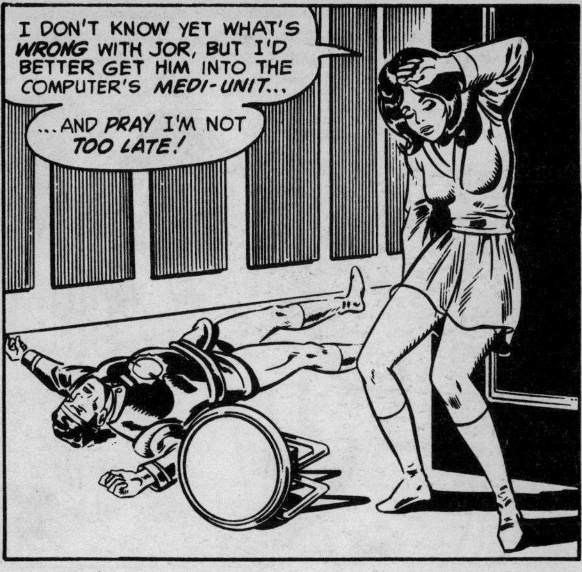
I DON'T KNOW YET WHAT'S WRONG WITH JOR, BUT I'D BETTER GET HIM INTO THE COMPUTER'S MEDI-UNIT...
...AND PRAY I'M NOT TOO LATE!

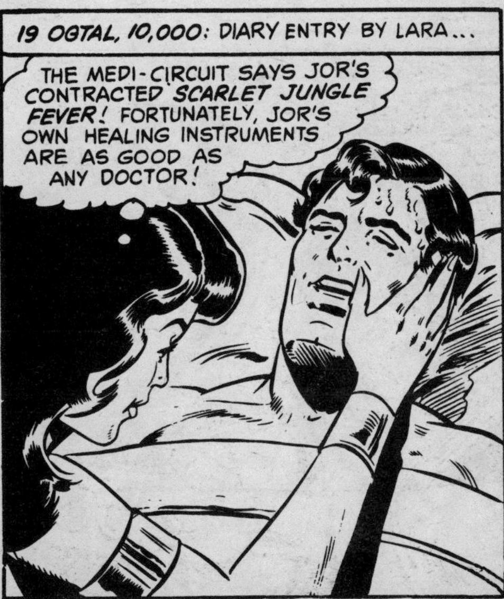
19 OGTAL, 10,000: DIARY ENTRY BY LARA...
THE MEDI-CIRCUIT SAYS JOR'S CONTRACTED SCARLET JUNGLE FEVER! FORTUNATELY, JOR'S OWN HEALING INSTRUMENTS ARE AS GOOD AS ANY DOCTOR!

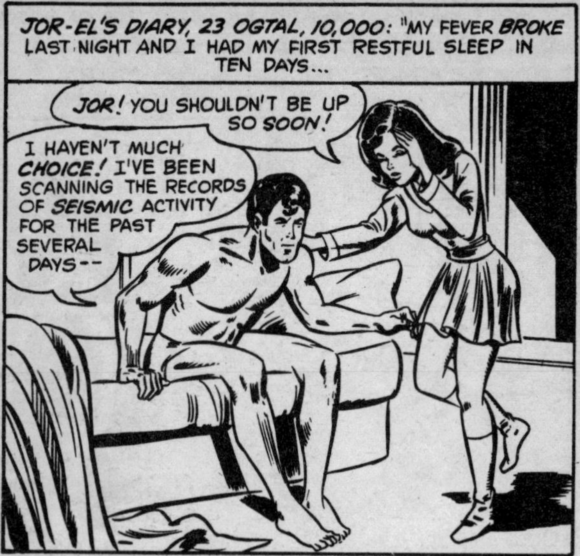
JOR-EL'S DIARY, 23 OGTAL, 10,000: "MY FEVER BROKE LAST NIGHT AND I HAD MY FIRST RESTFUL SLEEP IN TEN DAYS...
JOR! YOU SHOULDN'T BE UP SO SOON!
I HAVEN'T MUCH CHOICE! I'VE BEEN SCANNING THE RECORDS OF SEISMIC ACTIVITY FOR THE PAST SEVERAL DAYS--

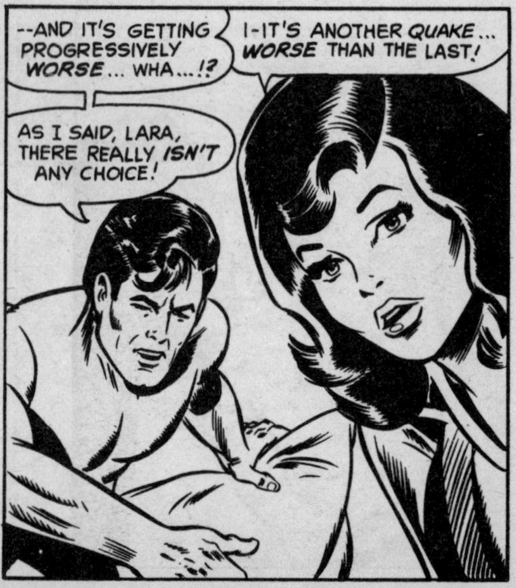
--AND IT'S GETTING PROGRESSIVELY WORSE... WHA...!?
I-IT'S ANOTHER QUAKE... WORSE THAN THE LAST!
AS I SAID, LARA, THERE REALLY ISN'T ANY CHOICE!

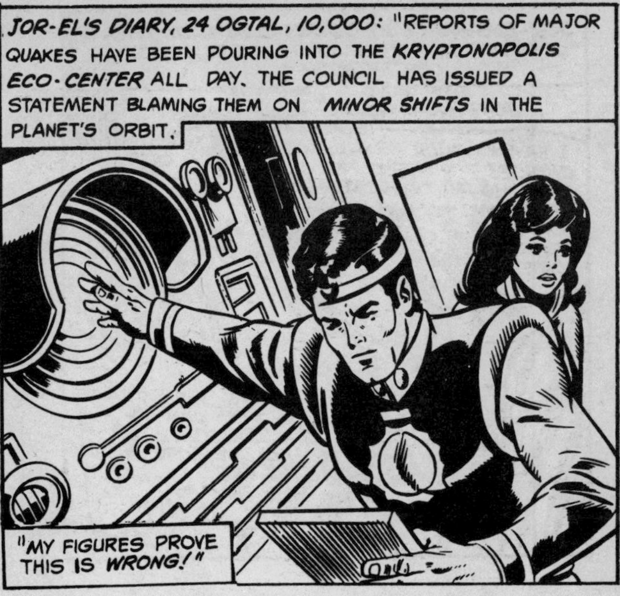
JOR-EL'S DIARY, 24 OGTAL, 10,000: "REPORTS OF MAJOR QUAKES HAVE BEEN POURING INTO THE KRYPTONOPOLIS ECO-CENTER ALL DAY. THE COUNCIL HAS ISSUED A STATEMENT BLAMING THEM ON MINOR SHIFTS IN THE PLANET'S ORBIT.
"MY FIGURES PROVE THIS IS WRONG!"

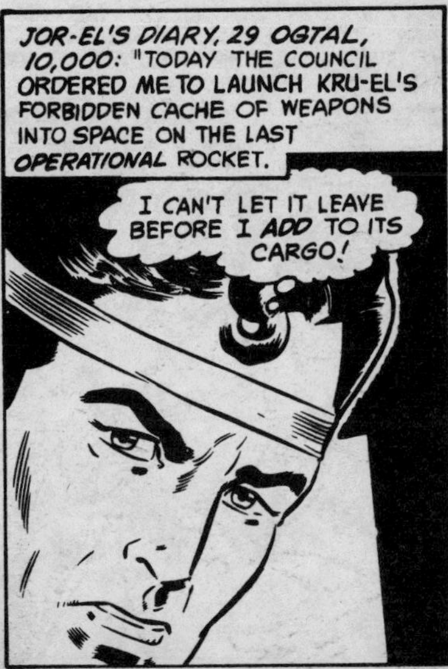
JOR-EL'S DIARY, 29 OGTAL, 10,000: "TODAY THE COUNCIL ORDERED ME TO LAUNCH KRU-EL'S FORBIDDEN CACHE OF WEAPONS INTO SPACE ON THE LAST OPERATIONAL ROCKET.
I CAN'T LET IT LEAVE BEFORE I ADD TO ITS CARGO!

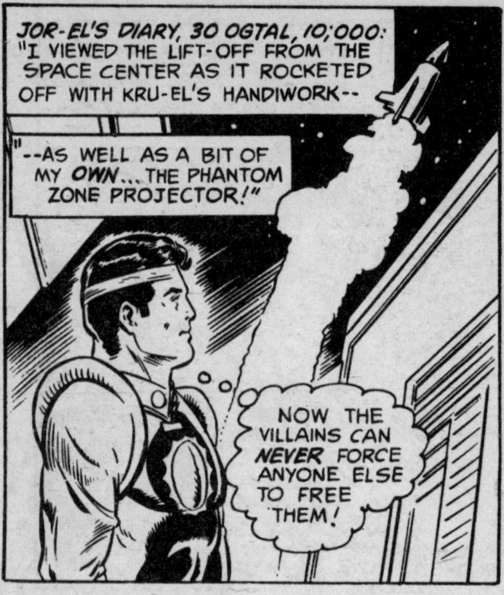
JOR-EL'S DIARY, 30 OGTAL, 10,000: "I VIEWED THE LIFT-OFF FROM THE SPACE CENTER AS IT ROCKETED OFF WITH KRU-EL'S HANDIWORK--
"--AS WELL AS A BIT OF MY OWN... THE PHANTOM ZONE PROJECTOR!"
NOW THE VILLAINS CAN NEVER FORCE ANYONE ELSE TO FREE THEM!

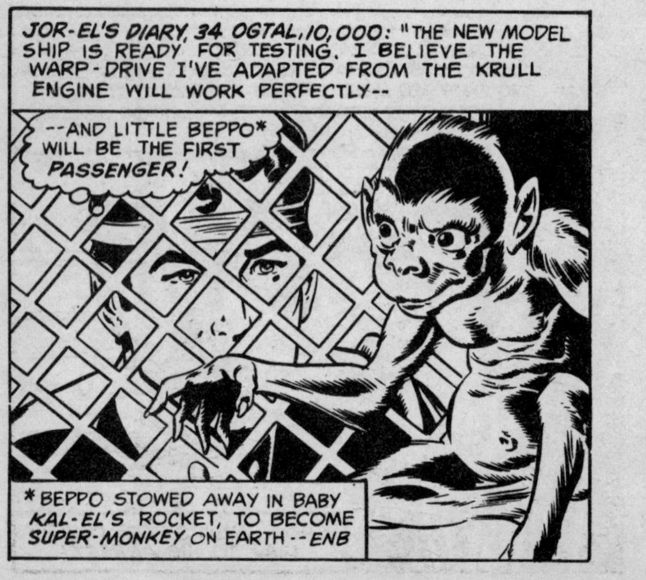
JOR-EL'S DIARY, 34 OGTAL, 10,000: "THE NEW MODEL SHIP IS READY FOR TESTING. I BELIEVE THE WARP-DRIVE I'VE ADAPTED FROM THE KRULL ENGINE WILL WORK PERFECTLY--
--AND LITTLE BEPPO* WILL BE THE FIRST PASSENGER!
* BEPPO STOWED AWAY IN BABY KAL-EL'S ROCKET, TO BECOME SUPER-MONKEY ON EARTH -- ENB

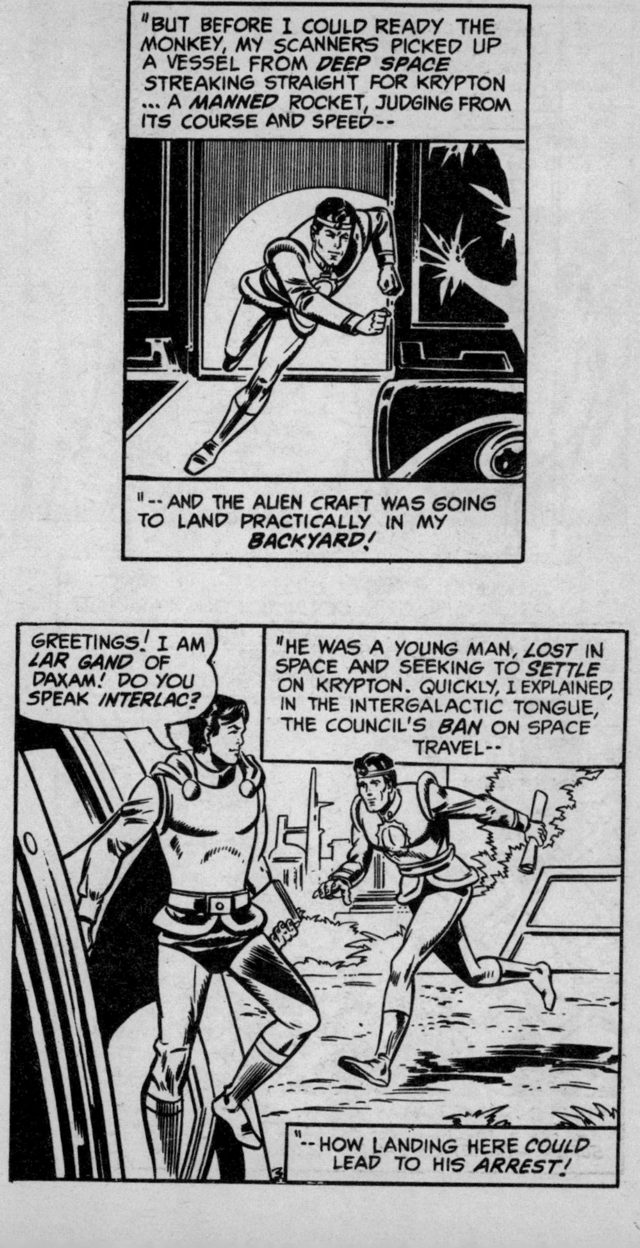
"BUT BEFORE I COULD READY THE MONKEY, MY SCANNERS PICKED UP A VESSEL FROM DEEP SPACE STREAKING STRAIGHT FOR KRYPTON ... A MANNED ROCKET, JUDGING FROM ITS COURSE AND SPEED--
"--AND THE ALIEN CRAFT WAS GOING TO LAND PRACTICALLY IN MY BACKYARD!
GREETINGS! I AM LAR GAND OF DAXAM! DO YOU SPEAK INTERLAC?
"HE WAS A YOUNG MAN, LOST IN SPACE AND SEEKING TO SETTLE ON KRYPTON. QUICKLY, I EXPLAINED, IN THE INTERGALACTIC TONGUE, THE COUNCIL'S BAN ON SPACE TRAVEL--
"--HOW LANDING HERE COULD LEAD TO HIS ARREST!

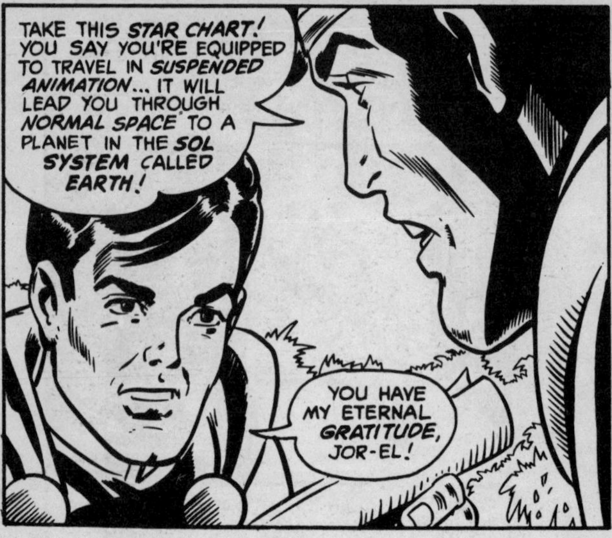
TAKE THIS STAR CHART! YOU SAY YOU'RE EQUIPPED TO TRAVEL IN SUSPENDED ANIMATION... IT WILL LEAD YOU THROUGH NORMAL SPACE TO A PLANET IN THE SOL SYSTEM CALLED EARTH!
YOU HAVE MY ETERNAL GRATITUDE, JOR-EL!

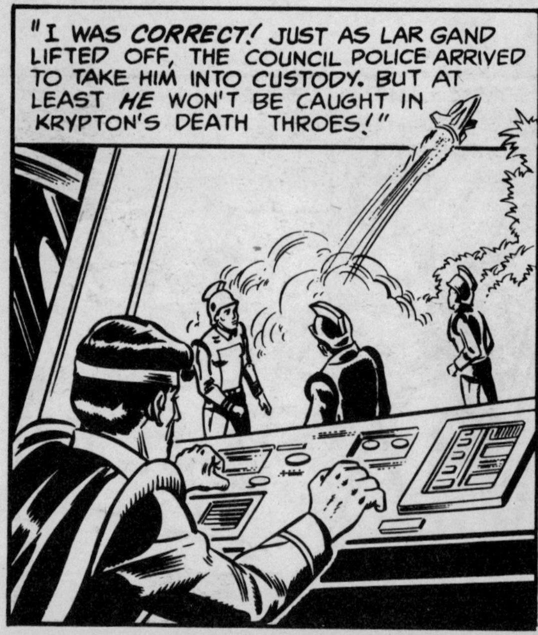
"I WAS CORRECT! JUST AS LAR GAND LIFTED OFF, THE COUNCIL POLICE ARRIVED TO TAKE HIM INTO CUSTODY. BUT AT LEAST HE WON'T BE CAUGHT IN KRYPTON'S DEATH THROES!"

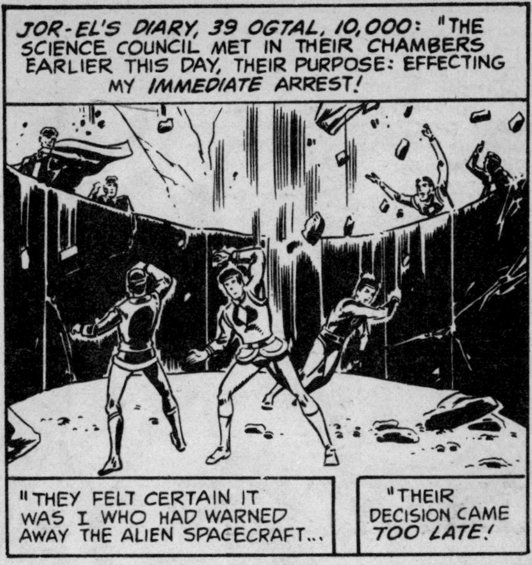
JOR-EL'S DIARY, 39 OGTAL, 10,000: "THE SCIENCE COUNCIL MET IN THEIR CHAMBERS EARLIER THIS DAY, THEIR PURPOSE: EFFECTING MY IMMEDIATE ARREST!
"THEY FELT CERTAIN IT WAS I WHO HAD WARNED AWAY THE ALIEN SPACECRAFT...
"THEIR DECISION CAME TOO LATE!

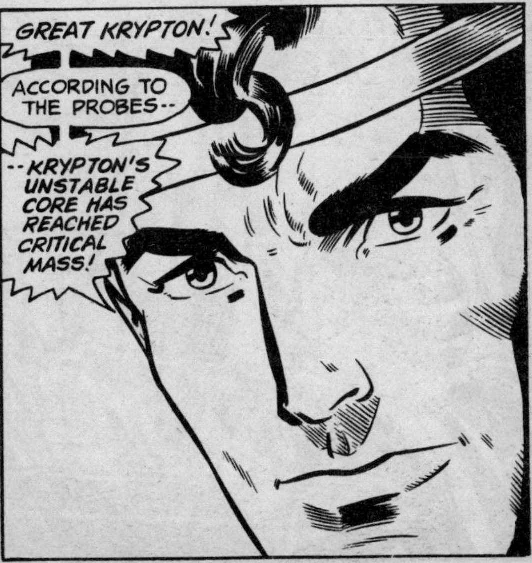
GREAT KRYPTON!
ACCORDING TO THE PROBES--
--KRYPTON'S UNSTABLE CORE HAS REACHED CRITICAL MASS!

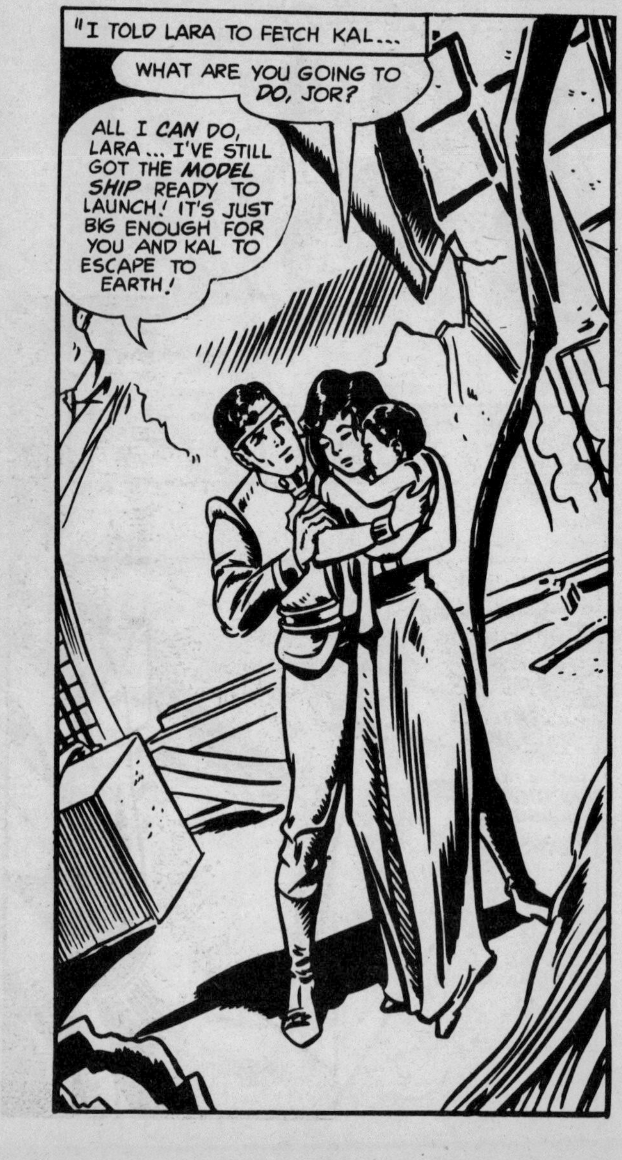
"I TOLD LARA TO FETCH KAL...
WHAT ARE YOU GOING TO DO, JOR?
ALL I CAN DO, LARA... I'VE STILL GOT THE MODEL SHIP READY TO LAUNCH! IT'S JUST BIG ENOUGH FOR YOU AND KAL TO ESCAPE TO EARTH!

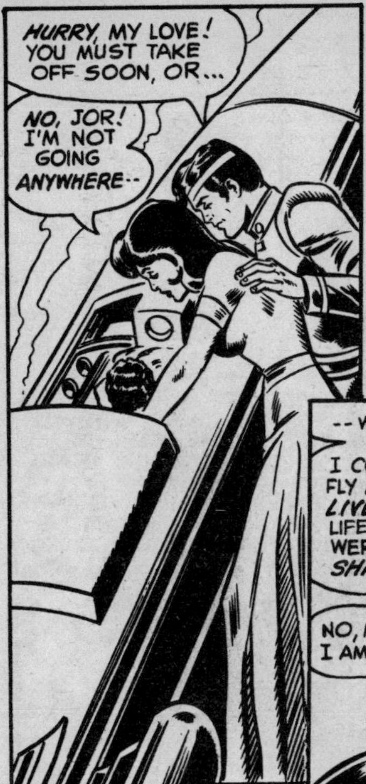
HURRY, MY LOVE! YOU MUST TAKE OFF SOON, OR...
NO, JOR! I'M NOT GOING ANYWHERE--

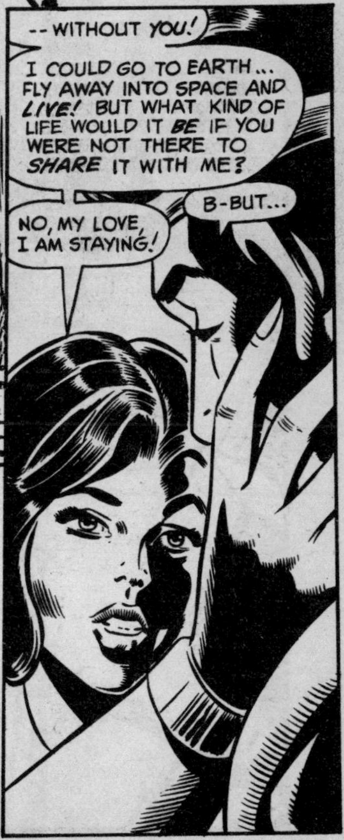
--WITHOUT YOU!
I COULD GO TO EARTH... FLY AWAY INTO SPACE AND LIVE! BUT WHAT KIND OF LIFE WOULD IT BE IF YOU WERE NOT THERE TO SHARE IT WITH ME?
B-BUT...
NO, MY LOVE, I AM STAYING!

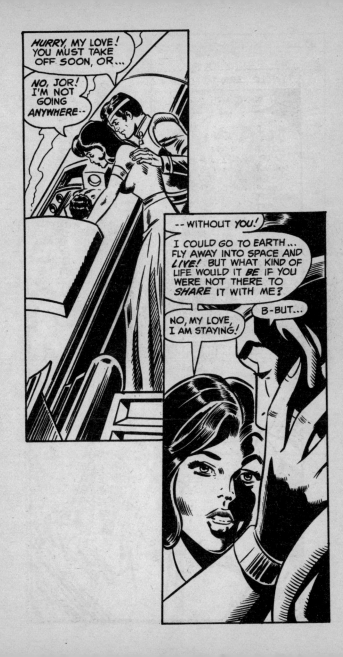

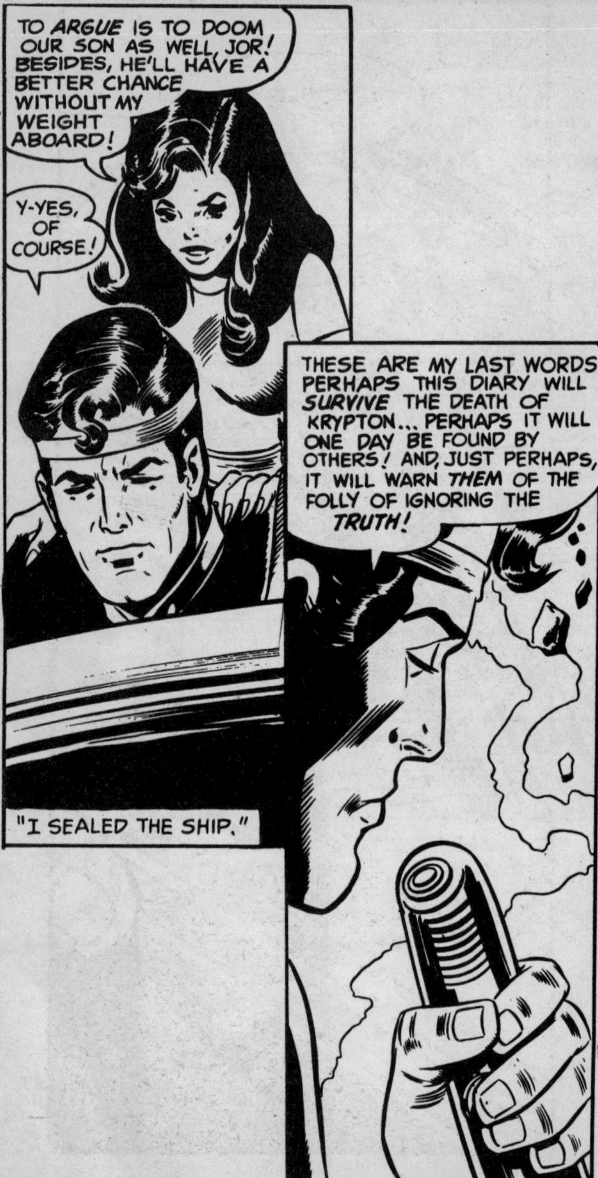
TO *ARGUE* IS TO DOOM OUR SON AS WELL, JOR! BESIDES, HE'LL HAVE A BETTER CHANCE WITHOUT MY WEIGHT ABOARD!
Y-YES, OF COURSE!
"I SEALED THE SHIP."
THESE ARE MY LAST WORDS. PERHAPS THIS DIARY WILL *SURVIVE* THE DEATH OF KRYPTON... PERHAPS IT WILL ONE DAY BE FOUND BY OTHERS! AND, JUST PERHAPS, IT WILL WARN *THEM* OF THE FOLLY OF IGNORING THE *TRUTH*!

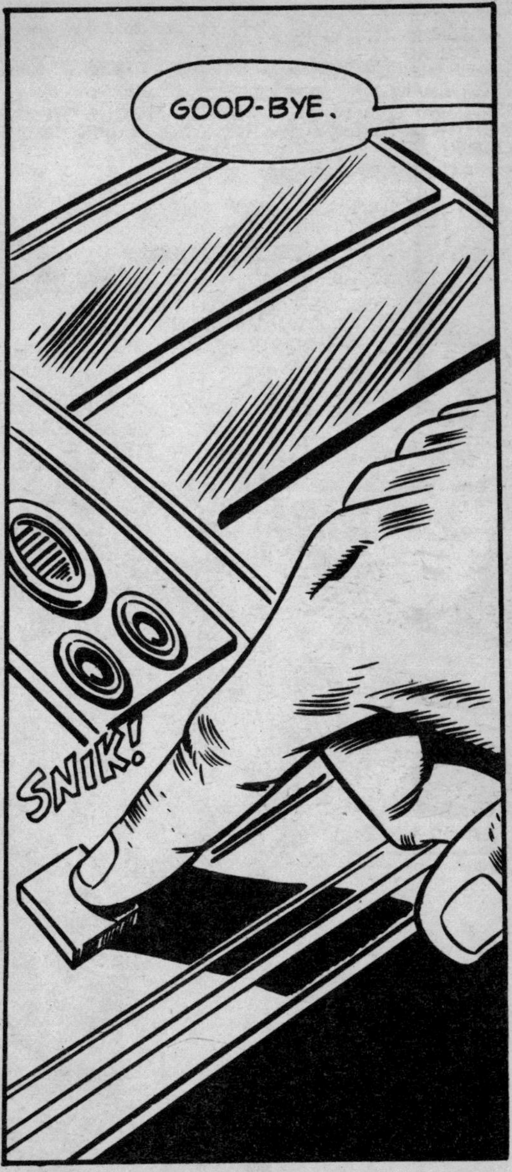
GOOD-BYE.
SNIK!

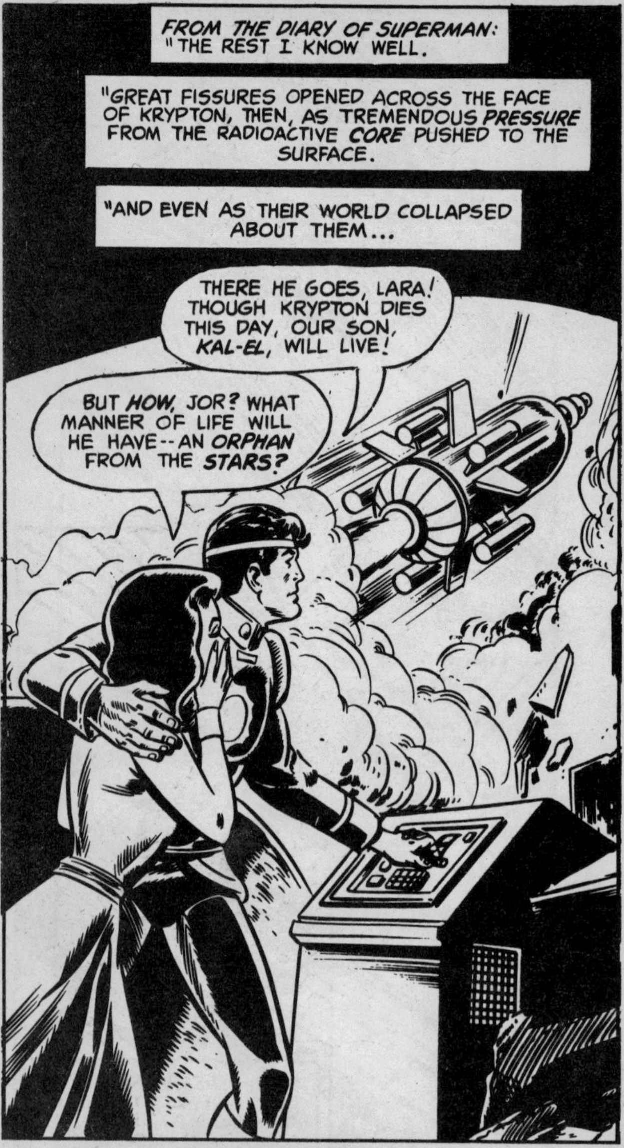
FROM THE DIARY OF SUPERMAN: "THE REST I KNOW WELL.
"GREAT FISSURES OPENED ACROSS THE FACE OF KRYPTON, THEN, AS TREMENDOUS PRESSURE FROM THE RADIOACTIVE CORE PUSHED TO THE SURFACE.
"AND EVEN AS THEIR WORLD COLLAPSED ABOUT THEM...
THERE HE GOES, LARA! THOUGH KRYPTON DIES THIS DAY, OUR SON, KAL-EL, WILL LIVE!
BUT HOW, JOR? WHAT MANNER OF LIFE WILL HE HAVE--AN ORPHAN FROM THE STARS?

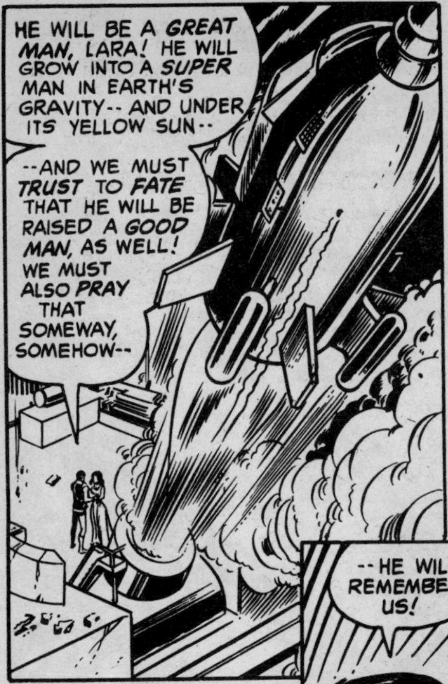
HE WILL BE A GREAT MAN, LARA! HE WILL GROW INTO A SUPER MAN IN EARTH'S GRAVITY-- AND UNDER ITS YELLOW SUN--
--AND WE MUST TRUST TO FATE THAT HE WILL BE RAISED A GOOD MAN, AS WELL! WE MUST ALSO PRAY THAT SOMEWAY, SOMEHOW--

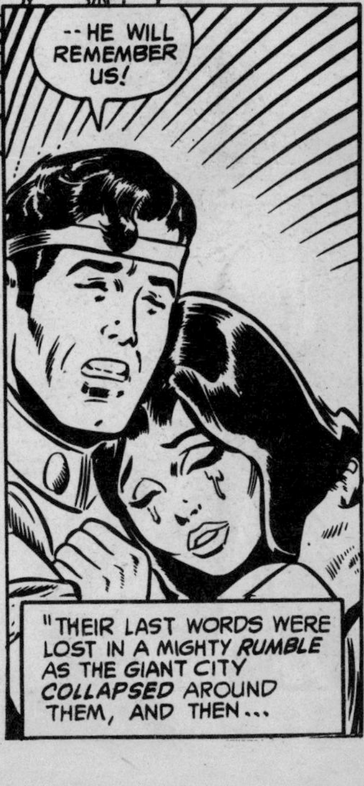
--HE WILL REMEMBER US!
"THEIR LAST WORDS WERE LOST IN A MIGHTY RUMBLE AS THE GIANT CITY COLLAPSED AROUND THEM, AND THEN...

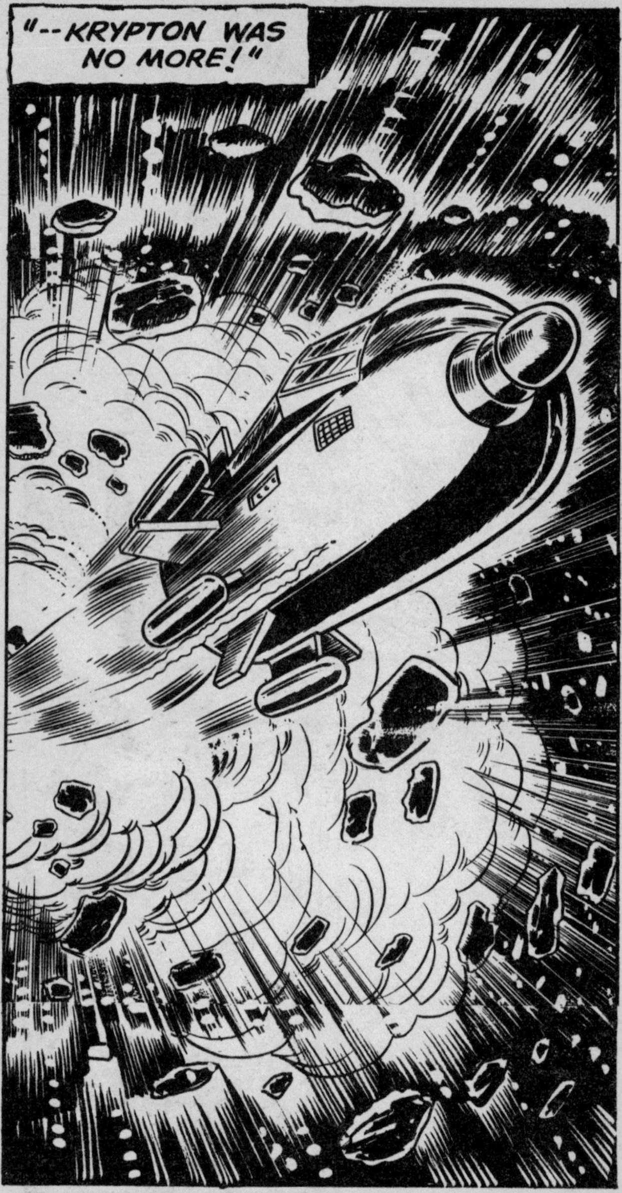
"--KRYPTON WAS NO MORE!"

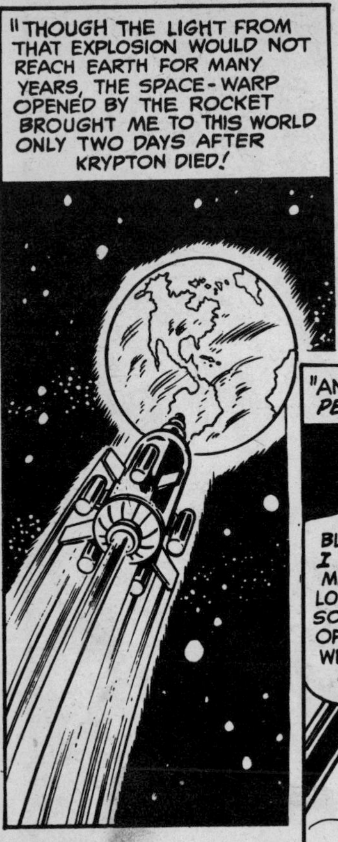
"THOUGH THE LIGHT FROM THAT EXPLOSION WOULD NOT REACH EARTH FOR MANY YEARS, THE SPACE-WARP OPENED BY THE ROCKET BROUGHT ME TO THIS WORLD ONLY TWO DAYS AFTER KRYPTON DIED!

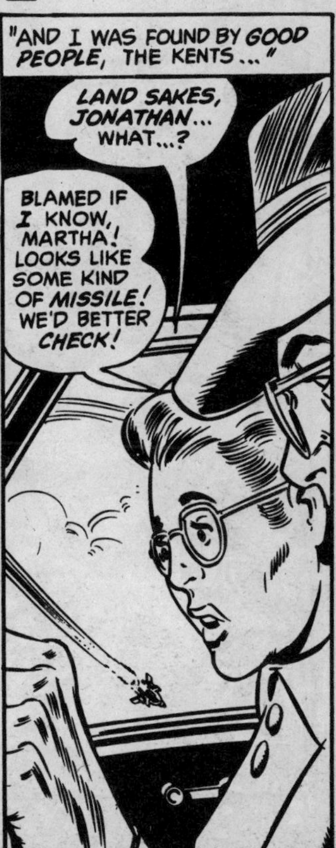
"AND I WAS FOUND BY GOOD PEOPLE, THE KENTS..."
LAND SAKES, JONATHAN... WHAT...?
BLAMED IF I KNOW, MARTHA! LOOKS LIKE SOME KIND OF MISSILE! WE'D BETTER CHECK!

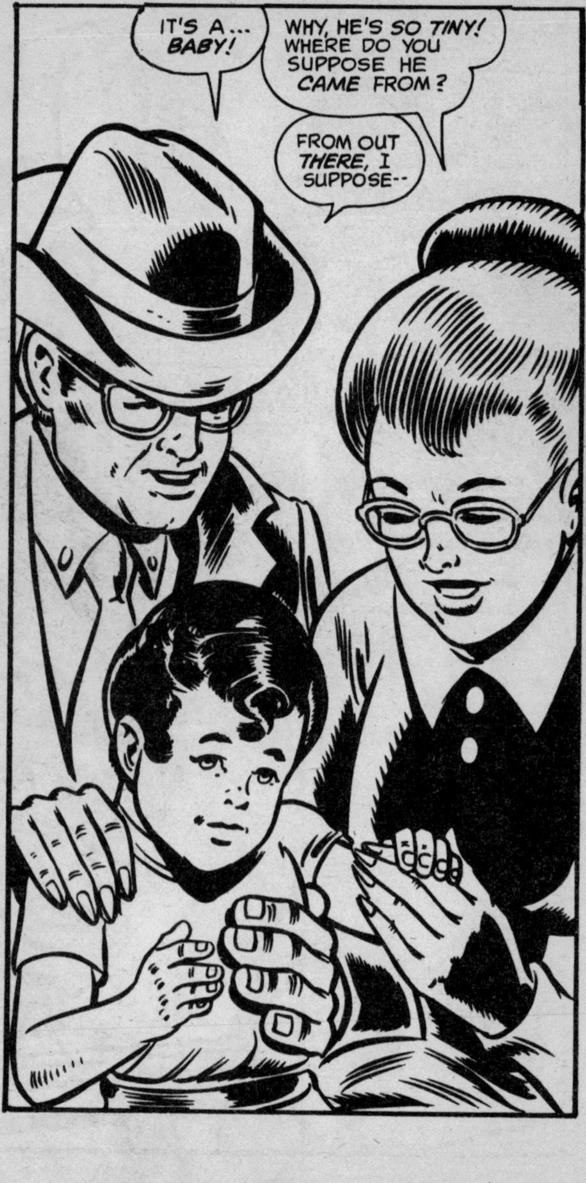
IT'S A... BABY!
WHY, HE'S SO TINY! WHERE DO YOU SUPPOSE HE CAME FROM?
FROM OUT THERE, I SUPPOSE--

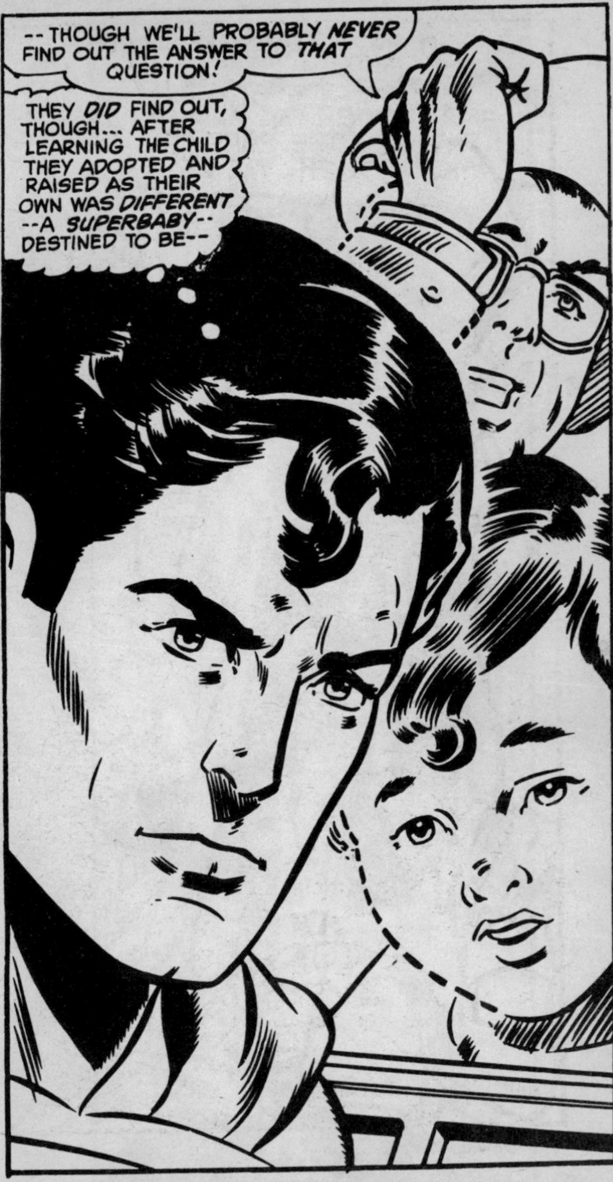
--THOUGH WE'LL PROBABLY NEVER FIND OUT THE ANSWER TO THAT QUESTION!
THEY DID FIND OUT, THOUGH... AFTER LEARNING THE CHILD THEY ADOPTED AND RAISED AS THEIR OWN WAS DIFFERENT --A SUPERBABY-- DESTINED TO BE--

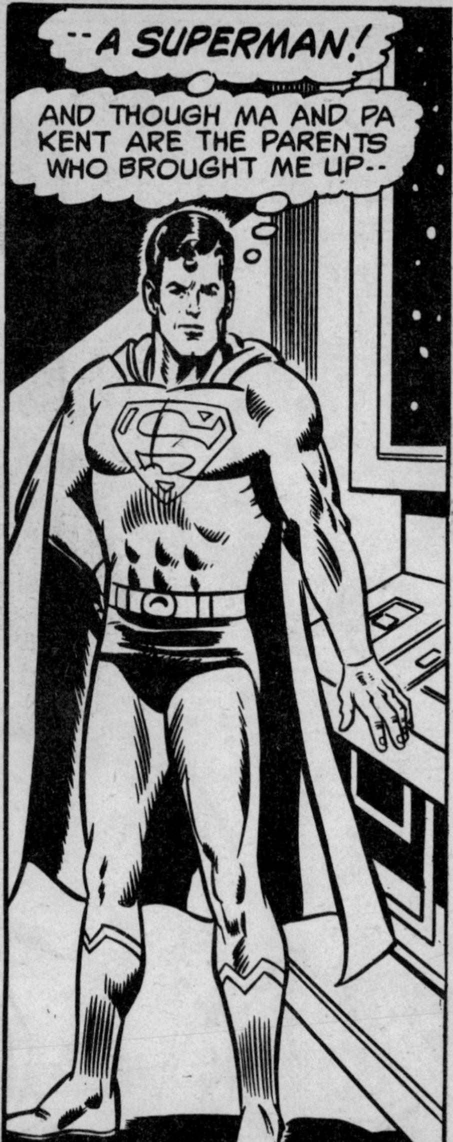
--A SUPERMAN!
AND THOUGH MA AND PA KENT ARE THE PARENTS WHO BROUGHT ME UP--

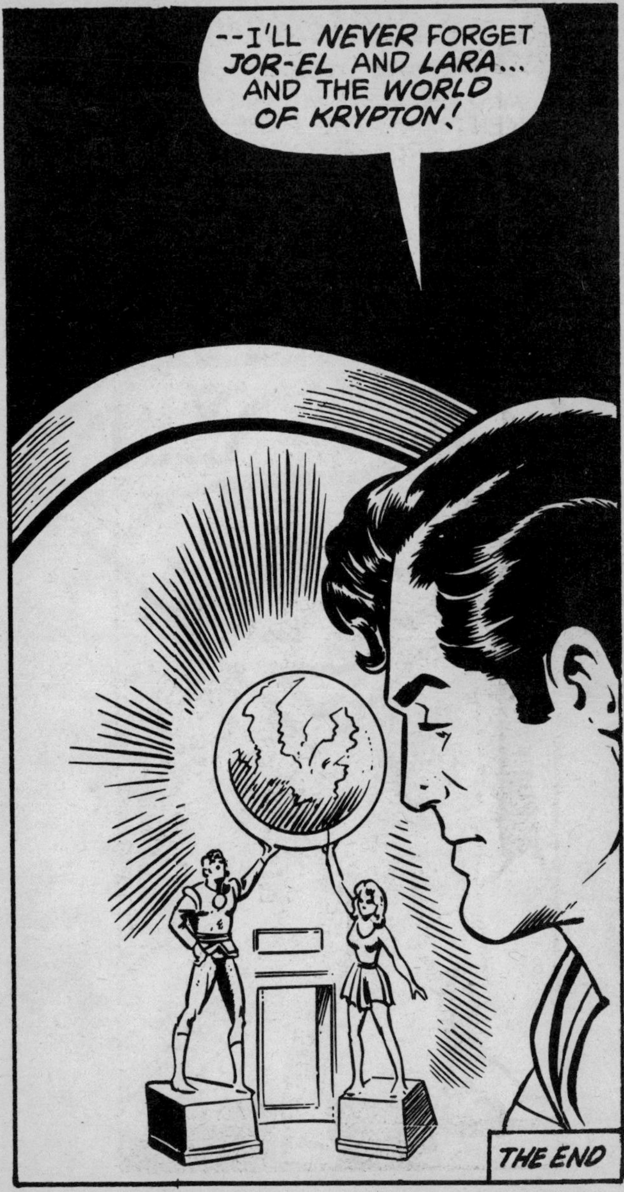
--I'LL NEVER FORGET JOR-EL AND LARA... AND THE WORLD OF KRYPTON!
THE END